Maya Blake's hopes o̶f̶ ... when she picked up her first ... did she know her dream would come true? ... still pinch herself every now and then to make sure it's not a dream? Yes, she does! Feel free to pinch her, too, via Twitter, Facebook or Goodreads! Happy reading!

Louise Fuller was once a tomboy who hated pink and always wanted to be the Prince—not the Princess! Now she enjoys creating heroines who aren't pretty push-overs but strong, believable women. Before writing for Mills & Boon she studied literature and philosophy at university, and then worked as a reporter on her local newspaper. She lives in Tunbridge Wells with her impossibly handsome husband Patrick and their six children.

BOUND BY HER RIVAL'S BABY

MAYA BLAKE

THE ITALIAN'S RUNAWAY CINDERELLA

LOUISE FULLER

MILLS & BOON

First Published in Great Britain 2022
by Mills & Boon, an imprint of HarperCollins*Publishers* Ltd,
1 London Bridge Street, London, SE1 9GF

www.harpercollins.co.uk

HarperCollins*Publishers*
1st Floor, Watermarque Building,
Ringsend Road, Dublin 4, Ireland

Bound by Her Rival's Baby © 2022 Maya Blake

The Italian's Runaway Cinderella © 2022 Louise Fuller

ISBN: 978-0-263-30071-0

02/22

MIX
Paper from
responsible sources
FSC
www.fsc.org
FSC® C007454

This book is produced from independently certified FSC™ paper
to ensure responsible forest management.
For more information visit www.harpercollins.co.uk/green.

Printed and Bound in Spain using 100% Renewable Electricity
at CPI Black Print, Barcelona

BOUND BY HER RIVAL'S BABY

MAYA BLAKE

MILLS & BOON

To Naana, my darling big sister.
This one, too, is for you, because over forty books later,
without those first Mills & Boon books
you let me borrow,
I wouldn't be living this dream.

CHAPTER ONE

'EXCUSE ME, SIR. Your eleven o'clock appointment is here.'

Atu Quayson looked up from the blueprint he'd been scrutinising, his eyes narrowing on the personal assistant quivering in his office doorway.

He was going to have to replace her. She was far too timid, too skittish to withstand the brutally demanding work environment he excelled in.

He was a driven man and a taxing boss.

Some called him impossible. Others labelled him an arrogant brute to work for. Maybe there was truth to it. Atu simply saw himself as the direct product of his upbringing and made no excuses for it.

Why, then, had he allowed his mother to talk him into hiring her? His lips twisted. Yes...a friend of a friend of a friend's daughter, whose many professional qualities had been lauded, only for him to discover differently within a day of her installation in his office.

He stopped himself from gritting his teeth.

Perhaps, as his mother had archly suggested, the problem was him. And, while he would never admit it to her, he was beginning to entertain the possibility that she was right. That his bitter and austere view on life was bleeding onto his hapless subordinates.

But that was a problem to be tackled later.

'I don't have an eleven o'clock appointment.'

His tone didn't invite testing or defiance. He'd learned

early in his professional life to memorise his daily schedule in case he needed to be flexible when new opportunities—or extraneous instances like his mother's interference—arose. He'd specifically cleared his diary until midday, when he met with his team of architects as he did every other Wednesday. A quick glance at his wristwatch confirmed that meeting was still an hour away.

Julie's—or was it Janet's?—eyes widened. 'Oh…um… I'm sorry, sir, but she's very adamant that you see her.'

His hackles rose higher. 'She?' Suspicion of his mother's hand in this too swirled acid through his gut. On top of everything else, he didn't need the once-a-month, stay-out-of-my-business verbal skirmish with his mother, a battle he usually fooled himself into thinking he'd won, only to discover she'd merely retreated to plot her next move.

'Did this person give you a name or a reason why she feels entitled to see me?' He made no effort to hide his disgruntlement.

Her fingers twitched a few times, then went into full-on hand-wringing. 'She said you would know what it was about. And her name is…' She stopped and cleared her throat, patently terrified to utter the name. 'Her name is Amelie Hayford, sir.'

Atu jerked upright, the unpleasant sensation in his gut thickening until his whole being was immersed in a soup of acid. Immersed in memories he didn't like to recall today or ever.

His heart slammed against his ribs, each beat echoing the surname no one in his family willingly spoke aloud. Not unless it was absolutely necessary. Unless it was a reminder to stay the course.

For the sake of vengeance.

For the sake of stoking the fires of retribution that kept his father alive even now, on what doctors whispered was his deathbed.

'What did you say?' His voice was an unsheathed blade and real apprehension shifted in the PA's eyes.

She cast a furtive glance over her shoulder, then whispered, 'A-Amelie… Hayford, sir,' as if lowering the decibels of her response would minimise its impact.

It didn't. Her confirmation merely increased the roiling inside him, shaking loose several pertinent questions.

Would she really dare?

Why hadn't she been stopped by Security at the entrance to his building?

How had she made it all the way to his penthouse office?

He operated from the top floor of his flagship Quayson Group hotel, located in the centre of Accra, for a reason— so casual acquaintances, unwanted guests and sycophants couldn't drop in at will. It was also why his security was top-notch.

His fingers started to clench but he wilfully stopped himself from tensing. Displaying the sort of emotion that bubbled underneath his skin was no longer useful.

Emotion had torn his family apart. Twisted obsession and forbidden love had ripped through it, the disease infesting everything he treasured, leaving devastation in its wake and him with the searing belief that control, emotional austerity and dedication to professional goals were the only things that would sustain him.

So he inhaled deeply and returned his gaze to the blueprints spread out on his table. 'Inform her that an appointment with me or anyone in my company needs to be assessed and agreed upon. Without exception. I'm not some fast-food drive-through she can swing past when the urge takes her.'

'Perhaps you'd like to say that to my face?' came a husky voice, making his PA jump.

Atu's head snapped to the doorway a second before the owner of the voice came into view.

With a confidence he would have admired, had he not been caught in the vortex of memory, bitterness and, yes, *shame*, the tall, voluptuous woman swept past the distraught PA and entered his domain.

As if she had every right.

As if she was intent on proving she wasn't still the timid child he'd grown up with, who'd lurked on the fringes of his close-knit friends and family group back when their families had been the closest of friends, instead of the vicious enemies they were now.

But hadn't he had a taste of the confident, defiant woman even back then? Hadn't she effortlessly punched through the brittle shell of anger and bitterness he'd built around himself that night eight years ago when, fresh from yet *another* row with his father, he'd crossed paths with her? Even then she'd sent him reeling hard, triggering an awareness that underneath her wide-eyed innocence a vibrant, passionate and confident woman lurked. One who'd burrowed beneath his guard…tempted him into a torrid episode that plagued him in imprudent moments.

Like now.

She moved towards him as if she owned the very air he breathed. And perhaps, on some level, she did. Because he was suddenly finding it difficult to take a breath, the captivating effect of her presence capsizing the smooth mechanics of his respiratory system.

He saw his PA reaching for the door to shut it, hurriedly making herself scarce, but his attention was wholly locked on the woman before him.

He ignored her question, attempting to catalogue the components of her that made up this curiously intriguing, highly unwanted package.

Faint gold and orange eyeshadow highlighted her big, beautiful eyes and flawless face. A face framed by the yellow and green patchwork making up her high kente headdress and the tasteful gold hoop earrings dangling from her lobes. Her chunky colourful necklace invited the gaze to the regal grace of her slim neck, sloping onto elegant shoulders, currently bare save for the thin straps holding up the knee-length bright yellow dress moulded to her body.

Long, shapely legs tapered down to feet adorned with stylish gold heels.

She was a woman who knew which colours did her justice, and she'd chosen well today.

Advancing further, she extended one graceful arm, set down her handbag before bracing her hands on her hips. She cocked one eyebrow in challenge.

She'd come prepared for battle. Her suit of armour was her confidence. Her unflinching pride. The intelligence shining in her eyes. Perhaps even her stunning beauty. Although the first three would have cowed a less formidable man, the fourth was the thing that clinched a victory.

He wasn't cowed. Because he couldn't forget for one second what this woman and the blood that ran through her veins embodied.

The destruction of his family.

He folded his arms, resisting the urge to rake his gaze over her once more. To linger on those plump lips he'd tasted once eight years ago, in a moment of madness that still haunted him.

He might have abandoned the pursuit of the opposite sex for a while, to concentrate on his current project, and to save himself the trouble of his mother's rabid matchmaking every time he so much as glanced at a woman. But he didn't welcome his suddenly raging libido reminding him of that fact now. Especially not with this woman.

'You're brave. I'll give you that. Arguably, foolish too. Either way, I recommend you turn around and use that door behind you while you have the chance.'

Her chin angled up higher, her stare growing bolder. 'Or what?'

He cocked his brow in return. 'Surely you can't be that dense? We may not have seen each other in eight years, but surely you haven't forgotten the circumstances of our last meeting?'

That harrowing day when two beloved people had been laid to rest, ironically and unfortunately in side-by-side burial crypts neither family had wanted to relinquish even in the face of their searing grief and loss.

Atu darkly mused what would be etched on their tombstones several lifetimes from now—the Quaysons and the Hayfords, two families who had vowed never to back down in destroying each other, even in death.

Shades of distress moved in her eyes, then disappeared in the next second. Atu wasn't sure whether to admire her strength of will or add it to the grievance list carved into his family's soul.

'I'm not here to rehash the past with you. Your actions left me with no choice but to come here. Or are you going to claim equal denseness?'

He shifted as her voice washed over him. She spoke in the accented Ghanaian English he would be able to pick out in a sea of a thousand voices anywhere in the world. Throughout his long absences from his motherland, hearing the distinct accent had triggered a sense of home and comfort he experienced whenever he heard it.

But added to Amelie's accent were British overtones— the result of having spent half her life studying and living in London.

His own speech was laced with the influences of a childhood spent in the States and then around the world, living the carefree life of the 'spare' while his much-beloved older brother revelled in being the heir.

Until it had all crashed to a bleak and devastating halt.

The reminder dragged him from his musings. 'What do you want, Miss Hayford?'

She tensed, most likely in reaction to his formal address.

Their last interaction that fateful weekend eight years ago had started off as a terse conversation, riddled with mild threats and spiked accusations, mostly fuelled by one too many cocktails.

And then it had turned into something else. Something he preferred to forget. But not even then had he been this formal.

Again, she got her emotions under control rapidly.

Reaching into her bag, she retrieved a sheaf of papers. 'My lawyers have informed you of my refusal to sell my resort to you on numerous occasions, *Mr Hayford*. And yet *this* arrived this morning.'

He allowed mockery to seep into his features and his voice. 'I'm aware of what my lawyers are doing on my behalf. What's your point?'

She slapped the documents on his desk. 'Since I can only conclude that there's been a break in communication, I've decided to tell you face to face. *I'm not interested.*'

'Don't the phones work in your backward resort? A shame you had to leave your little hamlet. Or have you moved back to the city?'

He knew the answer to that.

She lived near Saltpond, a thriving coastal city two hours west of Accra, while he resided in the capital. Accra was a rich and vibrantly diverse city, but it was also a relatively small city, made even smaller when one existed within the elite social circles he and his family inhabited. The same circles her family used to enjoy.

And when those two families were inextricably linked by personal tragedy, it was impossible not to be aware of one another. If she hadn't come straight here, he would've known by lunchtime that she was in town. Unfailingly, his mother would have made it her business to inform him and every member of the family that a Hayford was back in her beloved city.

'I'm not going to dignify your pathetic insults with a response,' she said, shoving the documents at him before pivoting away from him, her hands clenched into fists.

Her movement highlighted her proud breasts and curvy hips, contrasted by her tiny waist, currently cinched in by a wide tanned leather belt bearing the hallmarks of the talents of the Northern Region of their homeland. Heat punched into him as he watched her, unable to drag his gaze from a body that was a siren song he was sure must draw most men.

Most men.

Not him.

He mentally doused the flames invading his groin, summoning the iron-forged willpower that had helped him withstand his father's merciless censure for his part in their family tragedy and its ongoing dysfunction. The same dogged control that kept the vault of his guilt and regret intact.

To him, Amelie could only be an ornament that caught the corner of his eye. Intriguing for a vague little second, but forgotten about once he'd achieved his latest goal—acquiring the comparatively small Hayford Beach Resort and absorbing it into the latest Quayson Group project.

He refused to allow himself to dwell on those moments when he'd lost himself in the feel and taste of her, blindly and desperately seeking to forget the forceful demands of his father, the stark reminder that he would always be second-best. That he existed solely to be the wind beneath his more deserving brother's wings.

Just as he refused to accommodate the twinge of regret about giving in to his weakness with Amelie that night.

Because she'd been using him too...

All that mattered was the present. Pursuing his goal without the distraction she represented was why he kept his dealings strictly between their lawyers.

Her pacing brought her close once more, and he saw the moment she spotted the draft blueprints he'd been reviewing. Faint apprehension flickered over her face before being eradicated by utter derision.

'You've had blueprints done on *my* resort? You're getting a little bit ahead of yourself, aren't you?' she taunted.

'Not at all. In fact, my team is running a little bit behind schedule.'

Chocolate-brown eyes rose to his, anger sparking in the depths. Against the brown, the stark white of her eyes stood out sharply, highlighting her glorious mocha skin. It was several shades lighter than his own dark mahogany hue, and whatever make-up she'd applied made it gleam in the sunlight slanting through his windows.

Hell, she glowed with a vitality that made his fingers itch to explore her. He was sure this kind of radiance was reserved for some goddess. The kind that caused men to lose their minds. The kind of power her own sister had wielded against his brother. And look how that had ended.

Tragedy, devastation and the rabid quest for vengeance.

'Oh, and you can call off your spy,' she added with a snap. 'I know you conned my deputy manager into spilling company secrets. His employment has been terminated. And, just so we're clear, my resort isn't for sale now or in the foreseeable future.'

'Then why did you meet with investors from Dubai last month?'

Stunned surprise flickered in her eyes but her chin rose higher. 'That's no one's business—especially not yours or your deplorable family's.'

Fury sparked in his gut. While he had his own issues with his family, an inexplicable vein of loyalty had kept him anchored to them even as he'd enjoyed his hard-won freedom on the other side of the globe. That loyalty remained alive and well.

'Watch your tone,' he growled, all mockery wiped from his voice.

She didn't back down. 'What are you going to do? Have your security throw me out? I'll remind you that you're not the only one with connections. You currently have several deals in delicate stages. Think how it'll look if you're embroiled in a scandal. And, trust me, anything but a seemingly cordial meeting between us will make it onto social media within the hour. Are you willing to risk adverse publicity and displease your business partners?'

Her threats ignited a different fire inside him. He'd always relished a challenge, and even this brief skirmish— and he intended it to be brief, because every second in her presence reminded him of those forbidden minutes when they'd tangled together—roused the spirit of the Fante warriors who'd sired his bloodline and hers.

'I won't need my security to help me throw you out. I'll urge you to recall our family history. Remember how the Hayfords have fared against the Quaysons so far and consider the likelihood of you coming out on top of whatever scheme you're proposing.'

Her throat moved in a delicate swallow, but her gaze remained defiant. 'And that's a source of pride for you, is it?' she jeered, her nose very much in the air.

He recalled then that, while his family could boast an impressive pedigree, Amelie Hayford's progenitors were actual royalty. And with every flash of her eyes and haughty proclamation, the echoes of her regal forebears shone through.

Not that it mattered one iota in this time and place, he assured himself sternly. Her sister's emotional manipulation of his brother was partly the reason Fiifi was no longer alive. The reason his father was steeped in bitterness and his family irreversibly set on vengeance. Because someone had to pay, didn't they?

It was why he'd returned to the family fold after years of being labelled the black sheep—a title he'd nonchalantly shrugged on, another layer to add to the many denigrating layers his father had seen fit to saddle him with.

As for Amelie herself—perhaps if he hadn't let his base instincts take over that night, he would've been able to stop...

Enough!

This meeting had run long enough. As had the unsettling memory-dredging. 'It's time for you to leave. And I'd advise against talking to the press or making any precipitate moves against me or my company.'

Her eyes flashed. 'Tell me you'll stop sniffing around my business and you won't need to see or hear from me for the remainder of your despicable life.'

For some absurd reason, the thought of never seeing her again chafed—as if he'd brushed up against sandpaper in the dark. 'I'll have to disappoint you. Your little resort falls into my expansion objectives. Whether you make my acquisition of it hostile or civil is entirely up to you.'

'*Civil?*' She spat the word as if it was poison. 'You don't know the meaning of the word.'

He bit his tongue against reminding her that things between them hadn't always been hostile. That for a handful of minutes one memorable night she'd melted in his arms. She'd moaned his name and pressed her alluring body against his.

He clenched his gut against the unwelcome reminder. 'Really? What do you call showing up unannounced in my office, throwing down ultimatums?'

'You left me no choice. Stop coming after what's mine and I won't make any unannounced visits. Your actions are drawing unwanted attention and I won't have that.'

His eyes narrowed. 'What kind of attention?' he breathed.

He'd seen off the Dubai delegations, easily interesting them in his much more lucrative projects in Cape Town and Malaysia. Just as he'd seen off the Lebanese conglomerate and the US one before that.

Even without his father's zealous interest in acquiring the small resort on the beautiful southern coast of Ghana—simply because it was a Hayford property and, after a decade-long endeavour, the last meaningful Hayford holding and therefore the final thing standing in the way of the Quaysons accomplishing their revenge—Atu's own assessment of the resort and, more importantly, its potential had sparked an interest he'd been unable to ignore.

If he could achieve both his aims in one go, all the better.

'That's none of your concern,' she snapped, reclaiming his attention.

Her breathing had grown shallower with her agitation, dragging his focus to the pulse racing at her throat. To the impressive swell of her breasts and the rich, enthralling scent of her perfume. That maddeningly intoxicating mixture of shea butter and coconut that pulsed from her skin.

An image lit up in his head, of him burying his face in the curve of her neck, inhaling her scent while stifling a groan. Then gliding his tongue over that speeding pulse, being rewarded with her hitched breathing. Just like he'd done that night.

Awuradzi Yesu.

Thankful the curse hadn't slipped free of his control the way his thoughts were running rampant, he turned away from her, pinching the bridge of his nose when she continued speaking.

'There are literally miles of beachfront properties along the south coast. Why are you obsessed with mine?'

He faced her again, attempting not to fixate on the plumpness of the mouth that had spoken the words. 'You're in a prime location, with rich tourism within shouting distance. It's also an easy trek from Accra. I'd be a fool to overlook it.'

Her nostrils flared in anger. 'So you'll take it by force?'

For the briefest second, he experienced a pang of something eerily close to guilt. Then he shook himself free of it. 'Hardly. My lawyers have made you several very generous offers.'

'All of which I've turned down. Doesn't that tell you something?'

'It tells me you're stubborn. It also tells me you're in danger of finding yourself out of your depth if you cling to that stubbornness.'

'What's that supposed to mean?'

He allowed himself a small smile. 'You really think I'm going to lay all my cards on the table?'

Again, she easily smothered any trepidation she might feel. 'I have the blessing of the chief. Saltpond runs in my blood. Local support alone will ensure you lose any takeover bid.'

'You might have his ear, but what I offer will be far greater than any advantage born out of clansmanship.'

'And what's that?'

Atu decided it wouldn't hurt to demonstrate a fraction of the clout he wielded. 'Your resort employs how many? Sixty? Eighty?'

Her eyes narrowed. 'Ninety-five,' she bit out.

He stopped himself from smirking in triumph. Deep down, he hadn't wanted this task. Hadn't wanted to be here in Accra at all. He'd been perfectly happy in Malaysia, far away from the bitterness and the zealous family vendetta and politics. He had been fine leaving the running of the questionable family empire to his father.

In his resort on the Desaru Coast, he didn't have to see the cruelty-tinted grief etched into his father's face, the not-so-secret light in his parent's eyes that told him he wished things had turned out differently that night.

That perhaps even the wrong son had been taken...

Better still, there he wasn't reminded daily of his own disagreement with his father that day which had blinded him to everything else. Of the fact that if he'd focused his attention outwardly, instead of dwelling on the dejection churning in his chest, he would have noticed Fiifi was drinking too much. That the woman his older brother had purported to desire above all else had an agenda of her own...

He shook himself free of the grappling hooks of the past and laid down the bare facts for the woman standing before him.

'When I take over your resort and implement my expansion plans, I'll generate over three hundred jobs. I'll elevate the whole area and create healthy competition with the resorts in Cape Coast and Takoradi. Do you truly believe your chief will pass up such an opportunity?'

Doubt crept into her eyes and lingered for several seconds before she dismissed his words. 'He'll see through all that to the truth—that you're just in it for the profit.'

His eyebrows spiked. 'And you're not? Are you running a charity?'

'I provide a personalised experience, tailor-made for every guest. I'm not a faceless corporate giant that simply offers a place to lay your head for the night and charges a fortune for it.'

'You haven't done your homework properly if you believe the Quayson Group is just another run-of-the-mill chain hotelier.'

Her lips pursed. 'Stuff your corporate spiel. And stop trying to paint yourself as some altruistic businessman with the best interests of the ordinary man at heart. I've first-hand knowledge of the kind of man you are, remember?'

The force of their history ploughed through the space between them. For a single raw moment their combined grief and loss thickened in the air.

Then she pivoted and sashayed to where she'd dropped her bag.

He would have had to be dead from the neck down to stop his gaze from sliding down to her round, firm buttocks and her supple hips.

His mouth dried and he bit back a curse. He had a weakness for voluptuous women, and while, at twenty, Amelie Hayford had retained some aspects of girlishness, at twenty-eight she was all woman, with an hourglass figure that reminded him he was profoundly male and at risk of announcing that he was aroused by the very epitome of the goddess now taking command of his office.

'I thought you weren't here to dredge up history?' he replied, with more bite than he'd intended. 'But if you're in the mood for that, I can remind you of another time you played out of your league.'

She tensed, then sent him a searing glance over her shoulder. 'I have no idea what you're talking about,' she said a little too hurriedly. Too breathlessly.

Again, her chest rose and fell with her breathing, stirring his blood a little too fast.

She riled him.

Every Hayford riled him and his family in some way. But since that night when he'd let his emotions get the better of him, Amelie had been able to burrow deep under his skin, as if she had special dispensation from the gods to add an extra layer of hell, fashioned just for him.

He wasn't desperate to examine that particular layer—wasn't sure he wanted to discover what the unwanted ingredient was.

He especially wasn't interested in discovering if it was anything like what his brother had suffered from. Some had labelled it weakness. Others had called it obsession. Whatever it had been, it had driven Fiifi over the edge.

He, Atu, was above that. Had striven to keep himself from that kind of unnecessary entanglement. He wasn't about to start now.

'Count yourself lucky I don't have the time or inclination to refresh your memory.'

For a handful of seconds her eyes widened, her lips parting in a single breath. Then she faced him fully, spearing him with a fierce look from far too enchanting eyes. 'Luck has nothing to do with it. I'll just keep reminding myself that *okoto nwo anoma*. Isn't that how the saying goes?'

He tossed the proverb in his head, striving to maintain his cool. *A crab doesn't birth a bird.* Meaning he was culpable in whatever sins she laid at his family's feet.

'Again, while I'd love to compare notes on which one of us bears the most blame in our little family drama, I'm afraid I'll have to pass. I have a meeting in five minutes.'

Her eyes narrowed. 'Don't try me, Atu. I'm warning you.'

His name on her lips caused a deep rumbling inside him, like a shift of the tectonic plates that formed his existence. It pooled in latent heat in his groin and slowly intensified as they faced off.

In that moment, he realised that, no, he didn't resent this project thrust upon him as much as he should. Perhaps, subconsciously, he even relished it. Because, for good or ill, he wasn't going to let this go.

Hell, maybe this would be the purge that drove the dark shadows from his life.

The final slice of retribution for his family.

Especially for the brother he'd let down.

Maybe then he'd be free of the guilt and shame. Maybe then his father would even look at him without rancour from the cold embrace of his deathbed.

Whatever the reason behind it, the spark had ignited in him, and now grew to a burning flame of purpose.

He was going to conquer this thorn in his family's side once and for all.

And by coming here, Amelie Hayford had put herself in the centre of his war of redemption.

CHAPTER TWO

AMELIE WANTED TO scream in frustration—and, yes, also release the knot of trepidation in her gut—when the courier delivered the now familiar richly embossed white envelope with the well-known law firm's logo etched into the top right-hand corner.

For five days she'd fooled herself into thinking her actions had reaped the desired result.

She'd braved the lion's den and barely escaped with her emotions intact. So what if she'd been unable to stop the angry frustration and never-ending grief she carried from filtering through in unguarded moments?

Altogether, it had gone better than she'd hoped. She'd delivered her message. The big, bad corporate giant intending to invade her sanctuary would heed her warning and back off.

The old enemies her family had deliberately distanced themselves from by moving a few hundred miles would stay in their place and in the past.

How foolishly hopeful had she been?

'Don't try me, Atu. I'm warning you.'

That last volley, scrambled together after his pointed declaration that he couldn't even be bothered to dredge up those scorching, illicit moments they'd shared, had merely earned her stare and then a humourless, teeth-baring smile resembling a predator indulging in a weak prey's antics.

She'd known it was time to beat a hasty retreat.

Nevertheless, she'd been proud of not backing down.

Now she knew it had all been for nothing.

In typical Quayson fashion, he'd blithely ignored her, intent on taking what he wanted, regardless of who stood in his way. Regardless of the pain he caused.

With the delivery of yet another offer—sweetened with a further several hundred thousand dollars, as if money would sway her—it was clear Atu Quayson was still set on acquiring her resort.

She chewed worriedly on her bottom lip.

Her options were rapidly dwindling. Despite her bravado in Atu's office, the resort was struggling.

September was fast approaching, and with it the end of the peak and most lucrative season. In a little over a month she would be down to less than half-capacity, with even fewer guests until the Christmas period brought a seasonal end-of-year injection of cash. Cash she very much needed to make vital repairs, maintain general upkeep, and to fight whatever hostile takeover Atu Quayson planned.

But that injection would only be a few weeks' worth. She'd kept repairs and plans to hire new staff on ice, but sooner or later she'd need to undertake both if she was to keep up with the level of excellence she'd boasted about.

There was also the small matter of the refurbishment loan she hadn't known existed until after her father had passed away and she'd seen the true state of the resort's books. A loan she was still paying off and would continue to be saddled with for another five years. That was why she couldn't afford to let a single standard slip. Why she had to keep the serene swanlike glide for appearances' sake while pedalling furiously to keep afloat.

The cycle of just keeping her head above water wasn't going to hold for much longer. Especially when she was surrounded by sharks—the largest of which being her far too disturbing nemesis.

She'd tried to block out Atu's effect on her during their

meeting. Tried to smother the memories of the night her sister and his brother had died.

But all it had taken was one look for her to remember her years-long stupid crush, the sultry nights she'd spent fighting off the fevered arousal he sparked inside her with a simple glance, the days she'd spent back then cursing her family for not settling their differences, for robbing her of what she'd so deeply craved—the attention of the most dynamic man she'd ever known.

The Quaysons and the Hayfords hadn't always been enemies.

On the contrary, the first twelve years of her childhood had been a blissful adventure of joint family holidays, weekends and birthdays spent in each other's adjoining homes, small and large milestone celebrations filled with joy and laughter, the promise of endless possibilities.

Naana Quayson, the matriarch of the Quayson clan, was her godmother, for heaven's sake. They couldn't have been closer, except by being related by blood, if they'd tried.

It had started to go wrong over a simple business disagreement the summer she'd turned thirteen. Even then the two families had tolerated each other for a few more years. But like a rolling stone gathering momentum, petty rivalries had grown, and their inability to settle their differences had eaten its way like acid through their families.

Throw in Joseph Quayson's growing power, arrogance, and a series of risky but fruitful business ventures that had seen him gain financial leverage over her own equally proud, equally arrogant father, and the bonfire that would rip their families apart for ever had been lit.

That had been before personal tragedy had completely decimated them.

Joseph Quayson had lost his firstborn son and heir.

Amelie had lost her beloved sister.

She shook herself free from the memories. From the effect of what being in the same room as Atu after eight years had done to her equilibrium.

With one simple quirk of his eyebrow and a sweep of his arrogant gaze, he'd reminded her of their capricious history—especially the searing encounter that had catapulted her from girl to woman within a handful of heartbeats.

He'd reminded her that she was a woman with needs gone far too long unheeded and lately completely abandoned.

Her last two relationships had lacked the elusive spice and pit-of-the-stomach excitement she'd discovered she needed—missing ingredients that being in Atu's presence had effortlessly, annoyingly sparked.

Far too many times in his office she'd forgotten herself and made the mistake of entertaining the lustful need he'd evoked at their last encounter.

But she only needed to glance at her mother, see the far-away look in her eyes that said her thoughts were with Esi, her first child, to be brought back to earth. To remember that the memory of the sister she'd lost in the same crash that had killed Fiifi Quayson in that cruel and harrowing week of loss and tragedy eight years ago forbade her from ever thinking about their kiss.

That look arrived in her mother's eyes much too frequently these days and lingered for too long. It was a look Amelie had grappled with for a long time before accepting the hard truth—that for her mother she would never be as good as her sister's memory. Would never come close to filling the hole Esi had left in her mother's heart.

The fact that that, in turn, had left a hole in Amelie's heart wasn't a truth she liked to dwell on. Grief and wishful thoughts for a better relationship with her mother wouldn't keep a roof over their heads for long. Not if Atu remained hell-bent on acquiring her resort.

She set down the documents and clicked on her emails, rubbing her temples as she read the other buyout offers.

Now her treacherous deputy manager had been fired, she could keep this latest offer under her hat for a while, but inevitably Atu Quayson would get wind of it. He probably already knew that, as of today, his was the most lucrative offer. Just as *she* knew that even if he increased it by a thousand per cent she still wouldn't accept it.

Not without becoming a traitor to her family.

Not without breaking her mother's heart.

Amelie grimaced as memory broke the chain of her restraint again. Then she closed her eyes as she was propelled back to that night.

Fiifi, the Quayson heir, turning twenty-five had meant he'd been handed the much-anticipated keys to the kingdom.

The occasion had been marked by the party to end all parties. A party she and her family had been invited to, despite the mounting tensions crackling in the background like live wires. At the time, Amelie had been relieved when her parents had declined, and quietly ecstatic when Esi had insisted Amelie accompany her.

Fiifi had set his sights on her sister, and for all her strong-willed independence, Esi had fallen for him.

Amelie had kept her opinion that Fiifi was unsuitable for her older sister to herself—like the rest of the Quayson sons, he possessed far too many of his father's traits—purely because she'd wanted to go to the party for her own selfish reasons.

She'd wanted to be close to Atu.

So she'd dismissed the reason behind Esi's erratic behaviour, had turned a blind eye to the fact that beneath the wild gaiety her sister had looked desperately unhappy. That Fiifi had been equally worked up about…*something*.

Instead, she'd fixed all her attention on the second son brooding in the corner, glaring icily at anyone who ventured near.

It had taken two cocktails to bolster her confidence enough to approach him. To strike up an inane conversation that had turned those piercing dark eyes her way, then trapped her like hapless prey.

And when he'd silenced her with one long finger over her runaway mouth before leading her to an even quieter corner, she'd gone willingly, feverish anticipation firing up every cell in her body.

She'd happily ignored everything going on under her nose. By the time she'd come crashing back to earth, it had been too late.

The heart of her family had been torn out, shredded with pain and grief.

The family feud that had taken her sister had stolen her father too, four years later—although his demise had been slow and tortuous, coming by way of drinking himself into liver failure and eventual death.

This resort, despite its challenges, was the only substantial thing the family had been left with in the wake of years of feuding. Atu would get his hands on it over her dead body.

She looked up in relief as her manager, Maria, knocked and entered. 'You wanted to know when today's guests arrived? I've checked in a handful, but a few more have just turned up, including an…interesting one.'

Amelie nodded, gratefully putting her troubles aside for a while.

Greeting guests was technically Maria and her team's job, but Amelie loved knowing who was staying in her beautiful, quirky thatched chalets, and took delight in matching characters to the individually stylised suites and hearing positive feedback.

That attention to detail had earned her 'signature resort' status and glowing reviews—although not a boost in guest numbers. Nevertheless, she treasured those reviews as much as she treasured seeing her family name etched on the soaring wooden welcome arch at the resort's entrance.

The last thing she intended was to hand it over to the sterile, profit-orientated Quayson Group.

Her conscience stung with a flicker of shame as she rose from her desk. The Quayson Group resorts were spectacular. Luxurious to the point of decadence, with an eye-watering price tag to go with it, from what she'd seen online.

And, yes, it seemed they had the same ferocious attention to detail she admired.

Still, this resort was hers and—

Her thoughts screeched to a halt, along with her feet, when she stepped out of her office and saw the man standing at the far side of the reception area.

It was as if she'd conjured him up by thought alone.

Atu Quayson was facing away from her, his gaze on the jaw-dropping sea view that made hers the hilltop promontory location everyone within a fifty-mile radius craved. And yet she recognised those broad shoulders and tapering torso, that strong masculine neck and chiselled jawline. He didn't need to turn for her to recall the impressive blade of his nose and wide, sensual mouth. The sheen of his vibrant dark mahogany skin overlaying his sleek, well-toned male perfection.

His hair was close-cropped, the edges of his tight inky black curls neatly outlined by an expensive barber's clippers, perfectly delineating his face and compelling more than his fair share of gazes from the females who'd found reason to be in the reception area.

Amelie curbed a dart of jealous annoyance.

'How…when did he arrive?' she asked in a hushed tone, belatedly recalling Maria's allusion to their 'interesting' guest.

Amelie wished she'd paid more attention. Wished she'd had time to gird her loins, calm the erratic beat of her heart.

'About ten minutes ago,' Maria whispered back, wariness in her tone. 'He wasn't in a hurry to check in, which is why I came to get you.'

No, of course not. He was too busy eyeing up her business, seeking out its weak spots.

Like most of her employees, Maria knew the Quayson-Hayford history. It was right up there with local folklore, after all, she thought dryly.

'I don't remember seeing his name on the guest bookings.' She was one hundred per cent sure she'd have noticed.

Maria's lips pursed. 'Neither do I. But there's a corporate booking which is probably his. The name didn't ring any bells. I'm sorry, Amelie.'

She touched the older woman's arm reassuringly. 'Don't be. You weren't to know.'

About to stalk over to him, she paused. 'Is my mother here?' she asked, panic flaring inside her. The last thing she needed was a confrontation between her mother and the black sheep of the Quayson family. Or any member of that family, for that matter.

Maria shook her head. 'She asked for lunch to be delivered to her at the residence.'

Amelie breathed a sigh of relief, although this was yet another sign of the changes in her mother, who'd taken to spending the majority of her time at the home they shared at the edge of the resort instead of coming for the daily lunches she'd used to take in the restaurant, just to keep an eye on things.

'Are you going to allow him to stay?'

Maria asked the question Amelie herself had tossed feverishly in her mind moments ago. To all intents and purposes Atu Quayson was a guest. Manufacturing a reason to reject his confirmed booking went against her principles.

She gritted her teeth. 'I don't think I have a choice.'

Maria nodded with a touch of sympathy and then, beckoned by the concierge, she excused herself.

Amelie stepped behind the reception desk, took her time to greet the new guests, while keeping a surreptitious eye on Atu.

She knew the moment he turned from the view because her skin heated up and the hairs on her nape tingled with deep awareness as he strode towards the desk, his gaze pinned on her.

The air thinned out, making breathing difficult. When she managed to snatch in a quietly desperate breath, it was to have her senses infused with the dark, earthy spice of his aftershave, coupled with a layer of male pheromones that caused her belly muscles to tremble.

'Good afternoon, Amelie.'

She wanted to demand that he not use her given name in that far too evocative way. That he stop leaning on her oak-hewn countertop, exposing his brawny forearms and powerful wrists, those capable hands and far too elegant fingers that made her want to relive his touch. *Again.*

No, she most definitely wasn't going to think about that.

Instead, she pinned a cool, professional smile on her face, forced the traitorous swarm of butterflies down. 'Mr Quayson, I'm sure there must be some mistake. If you took a wrong turn, I'd be happy to point you in the direction of where you wish to go…'

That slow, predatory smile reappeared, and his incisive gaze combed leisurely over her body before meeting hers. 'No need. I'm exactly where I need to be.'

She tilted her head contemplatively, allowing a musing smile to play at her lips, and immediately regretted it when his gaze zeroed in on her mouth. 'Really?' she asked. 'Because I don't see your name anywhere on today's reservations list.'

'I've already given your receptionist the name the booking was made under. I'd be happy to repeat myself if necessary?' he offered, mockery thick in his voice.

She quietly bristled at the faint insult, but managed to keep her smile in place. 'Any reason why you felt the need to hide behind a corporate name?'

He shrugged, drawing her attention to the insanely broad expanse of his shoulders. His were the type of shoulders a woman fantasised about clinging to in the depths of passion. Gripping desperately to as she was swept away by bliss.

Objectively speaking, of course, she cautioned herself. Because this particular exhibit of male perfection was strictly out of bounds.

'If I'd wished to infiltrate your little resort, I would've found a way to do it without your knowledge. I booked under a corporate name because my team knows I value my privacy. Speaking of which—perhaps we should get on with things, before my infamy gets the better of the situation?'

His droll voice made her glance around.

Sure enough, a smattering of onlookers were lurking, either anticipating fireworks or just keen to be in the revered orbit of a Quayson.

Beyond the fact that Atu Quayson's well-publicised rebellion against his father had earned him the 'black sheep' label long before he'd succeeded at building his own individual hotel empire, before returning to the family fold two years ago, the Quaysons' wealth and stature had already gained them revered status in Ghanaian society.

Acknowledgement from a Quayson was almost literally worth its weight in gold. Joseph Quayson was known to occasionally lavish gold nuggets from his private goldmine upon friends and loved ones in a show of extravagant generosity.

A goldmine which should've partly belonged to my father.

That searing reminder helped dissipate a few layers of Atu's effect on her, helping her focus as she straightened her spine. 'Of course,' she said crisply. 'A paying guest is a paying guest.'

With swift efficiency, she booked him in, choosing the most exclusive of her ten VIP chalets. Besides being one of the best chalets, it was also at the furthest end of the grounds, on a high cliff overlooking the sea. With any luck, he wouldn't need to encounter her mother any time soon.

Or at all, if she convinced him to leave…

She activated his key card, but he stopped her before she could summon a bellhop.

'That won't be necessary.' He lifted a sleek weekend bag, and she spotted the super-exclusive designer logo etched into the rich brown leather. 'This is all I have with me.'

Perhaps she should've been relieved he wasn't planning on a long stay, but all she felt was a greater wariness that he believed whatever he'd come here for would be achieved within a day or two.

His fingers brushed hers as he took the key card. She snatched her hand back, unwilling to endure another second of the fever that rushed through her system at his touch.

'What I would like is an escort to my room, though,' he drawled, in that deep, far too sexy baritone that sang along her nerves before burrowing into her secret places. 'Just in case I wander into places I'm not supposed to be.'

Knowing he'd read her thoughts made her skin tingle with even more awareness. 'You're here, in my resort, in the first place. Did you think about whether I'd want you here before you arrived?' She couldn't stem the bitterness in her voice.

He shrugged, a lazy stretch of muscles that said he didn't give a damn about her thoughts. That he wouldn't be moved by word or deed to do anything other than what he wanted. 'I'm hoping that by the time I leave here we'll both have something we want.'

She gritted her teeth, kicking herself for immediately attributing a personal, *sensual* connotation to those words. She was far from desperate sexually, but perhaps she should've gone on a date or two in the past year. Maybe then she wouldn't be so...*aware* of him.

She sucked in a stealthy breath. 'I wouldn't hold your breath, if I were you. I would say, though, that the view from your chalet is exceptional and best enjoyed before the sun goes down. I'll show you the way.'

'Ah, the personal touch. I'm honoured.'

The droll look he sent her told her he knew the game she was playing. That he was willing to play along. For now.

With every cell in her body Amelie wanted to stay behind the reception desk, with the solid, hand-carved polished wenge wood as a sturdy buffer. But that would be as unconscionable as baring her throat to him and inviting him to take a maiming bite.

And why that savage imagery should drag a boatload

of heat low in her belly, Amelie refused to ponder, as she briskly rounded the desk and approached him.

'This way.' She indicated the wide arched hallway to their right and watched his gaze fall on the colourful bangles adorning her wrist. Heat flared higher in her belly and she hastened her steps. The quicker this was over, the quicker she could retreat and re-strategize.

She took him down winding paved paths bordered by a profusion of the bold, exotic flowers that were her head gardener's pride and joy. On a normal day she would have literally stopped to smell the roses, but Atu Quayson's solid, unyielding presence behind her overshadowed everything else.

'This is where you make polite chit-chat, isn't it? Or does that courtesy not extend to me?' he drawled.

She stopped in her tracks, then pivoted to face him, all pretence at being unaffected evaporating at his domineering tone and imposing presence. 'Why are you really here?' she snapped, before she could stop herself.

'You turned up uninvited at my office to state your case—'

'So, what? This is payback?'

He shrugged again, his eyes conducting a slow, searing scrutiny of her face that made her want to squirm. To slick her tongue over suddenly tingling lips.

'Perhaps yearning from afar doesn't work for me any longer. I needed to see what I desire up close.'

He was talking about *business*. She knew that. And yet heat funnelled up from her toes, rendering her weak and needy and speechless, making her jaw slacken and her mouth drop open as she stared up at him.

His infuriating male perfection seemed to have multiplied a thousandfold since she'd visited his office.

For a long spell they regarded each other, the atmosphere snapping with electric currents she feared would zap her if she so much as moved.

'Shall we?' he urged, his gaze sweeping over her lips

again before meeting her eyes. 'Unless you wish to invite more gossip by standing here glaring at me?'

Amelie roused herself with self-loathing effort, shuddering to think how much time had passed as she'd stood there, gaping at him.

She whirled and continued down the path, but she couldn't help flinging over her shoulder, 'Don't act like you care about gossip. You knew the commotion you'd create by coming here and you did it anyway.'

'Why, thank you. I wasn't aware I held that sort of power,' he stated drolly.

A sharp pang darted through her chest, his offhand attitude and arrogance making her voice shake as she snapped, 'Is this all a game to you?'

All traces of humour left his face, replaced by a flinty, narrow-eyed gleam in his eyes that sent different tingles down her spine.

'I don't have time for games, Amelie. I wouldn't need to be here at all if you'd listen to reason. You want me out of your life this badly? Give my proposal the proper consideration it deserves and we won't need to see each other again,' he bit out.

Something about hearing that he'd rather be anywhere else than there stung deeply. Made her twist around and continue down the path leading to his chalet.

She told herself it was no use arguing with him—that his inability to take no for an answer wasn't her problem. If he wanted to pay to stay at her resort, and then leave with the same *no* she'd been saying for months, then on his head be it.

And yet her vision blurred slightly as the chalet came into sight...

The horrifying knowledge that his words had burrowed deep enough to draw tears snapped her spine straight. She hadn't weathered storms of grief, loss and watching her mother sink deeper into the pain of her sister's death to the exclusion of all else just to get emotional over the callous words of a ruthless businessman with only his bottom line in mind.

But he's not just that, is he?

Jaw clenched, she pushed away the fiery reminder as they arrived at the allocated building.

Each chalet had a unique name and symbol carved into its front door. Her breath caught in her throat when Atu reached out and traced his fingers over the *sankofa* symbol that his chalet was named after, depicting a bird retrieving its precious egg. He was admiring the rich wood and intricate workmanship. So why did it feel as if he was stroking her skin?

Probably because that same symbol was also a love symbol...

As if she'd spoken that unacceptable thought out loud, his gaze flicked to her. It held hers for several seconds before, with a smooth swipe of the card, he let the door spring open.

She should leave. She'd done her hospitable duty, after all.

But he waved her in and Amelie found herself entering the room, the charged atmosphere intensifying as he followed close behind.

The panels of the shutters were made of thin strips of woven bamboo, and opened out to let the sea breeze in. The mid-afternoon sun's rays streamed in from the picturesque windows and wide balcony doors. The theme extended to the lamps dotted around the room, and the swinging half-doors that led to the bathroom.

'Ninety per cent of the furnishings in this room are locally sourced,' she said proudly.

His lips twitched. 'As opposed to the mass-market-produced ones you think adorn my hotels?'

'I don't think it. I know it for a fact,' she said, and then almost kicked herself. Now he knew she'd taken an interest in his hotels.

The twitch turned into the ghost of a smile. 'Local is

good and admirable. But I run a global business. Which is why I insist on both local and international sustainability.'

Her eyes widened before she could stop herself.

'You didn't know that?' he mused sardonically. 'And I thought you knew everything about me.'

'I know enough to know what I want. And what I don't.'

His nostrils flared—a sign that he wasn't as amused as he appeared. That some of the capricious atmosphere they'd been unable to escape was finally seeping beneath his guard.

Good. She hoped it sent him packing as quickly as he'd arrived.

The thundering in her chest suggested she might not get her wish as he sauntered over to the cherrywood wardrobe, dropped his weekender into it, then faced her, hands braced on his lean hips.

'This is adequate enough, I suppose,' he said, after a cursory look around.

Knowing he was attempting to rile her only made her fight harder to rise above it. She smiled through a quick tour of the chalet, pointing out the various unique items she'd gone to great lengths over to ensure her guests' comfort.

Done, she faced him once more. 'It's far above "adequate", Mr Quayson. Or are you simply not man enough to admit it?'

The heated gleam in his eyes made her regret her taunt for a mere second before a traitorous sliver of excitement made her wonder how he would react.

His gaze narrowed momentarily, before flicking behind her. Heat ramped through her when she followed his gaze to the sumptuous bed behind her.

'Don't throw down gauntlets that might get you into trouble, Amelie. After all, we don't want to scandalise your precious guests or your beloved townsfolk, do we?'

She cleared her throat, shoved her hands into her pockets so he couldn't see her nails biting into her palms to counter the effect of his words. 'We have a turndown service, if you'd like that. There's a list of every service in the brochure on the dresser—'

'I think I'm content with the finer offerings of your chalet.'

She pinned a professional smile on her face and headed for the door. 'In that case, I'll leave you to it.'

'Amelie.'

The low rumbled command of her name made her freeze.

'You're sitting on a goldmine here. But from what I've seen, you're nowhere near reaping the full rewards of such a place. I hear you're barely breaking even.'

The dart of pain was unexpected, spiking her agitation all over again. 'You hear wrong,' she countered bravely, hoping he wouldn't spot the lie. 'And you should be careful about using the word *goldmine* around these parts. You don't want to be thrown off the premises before you've had time to sample premium Hayford hospitality.'

Something indecipherable flickered across his features. Then one arrogant eyebrow cocked. 'I can't change the fact that my family owns a goldmine. Or that it's one of the many subjects you and your family find objectionable. It doesn't change the truth. You're hurtling towards the red at breakneck speed, and being stubborn won't get you out of your troubles,' he stated, without an ounce of regret.

She forced herself not to react, despite the constricting of her heart. Despite wanting to rail at fate for all the sorrow and terrifying challenges she'd had to endure because of what he and his family had done to hers.

And, yes, the Fante pride that burned through her blood wouldn't let her back down. He was on her turf. And she didn't intend to give him a single excuse to wrong-foot her.

With that thought in mind, she opened the door, breathed in the sweet ocean air and forced calm into her roiling mind. 'This conversation is over. Now, would you like your complimentary bottle of champagne delivered to you now or later?'

He slipped one hand into his pocket and sauntered towards her, as if he had all the time in the world and had zero qualms about making her wait. 'I'll have it later. With my dinner. Which I'd like you to join me for.'

Amelie tightened her fingers momentarily on the door, then shook her head. 'I'm sorry, but I'll have to decline.'

His lips twitched. 'Do me a favour and drop the niceties. You're not sorry at all. Tell me why,' he ordered, with a bite in his tone.

'I can list a dozen reasons. But the only one pertinent here is that I don't fraternise with guests. Unless you're ready to admit you're not here as a guest but have come to harass me?'

He shrugged broad shoulders that immediately commanded her attention. She allowed herself a mere flicker of a glance before dragging her gaze away. The great thing about her resort was that there was always something spectacular to look at. And in that moment, the sun's rays bouncing off the brilliant red and blue hull of a fisherman's canoe was the perfect tableau to distract herself with.

Definitely *not* the breathtaking tower of a man who was watching her with silent speculation from a few feet away.

Slowly, the humour vanished. 'We both know why I'm here. My advice to you is this—don't make it harder than it needs to be.'

'Here's my answer—your family has done enough damage to mine. So as long as there's breath in my body I'll fight you. And I'll win.'

CHAPTER THREE

THROUGH A COMBINATION of sheer luck and dexterous scheming, Amelie managed to avoid running into Atu at all the next day. But that didn't mean she hadn't caught far too many glimpses of him—starting from the moment she'd woken up.

The one-hundred-and-eighty-degree sea view from her bedroom granted her one of the best views of the sunrise. It was where she enjoyed her morning coffee while running through her day's itinerary.

It was also where she'd choked on her coffee as she'd watched Atu saunter out of the sea at six a.m., his glorious body gleaming under the rising sun's adoring rays like a mythological god.

Even from behind the safety of her whitewashed shutters, the sight of his long, sleek limbs and tempered muscles had made her belly clench and her sex heat in shameless need.

As if he'd sensed her ogling, he'd turned his head towards her window, those probing eyes searching her out, mocking her held breath and the deep awareness charging through her body.

She'd stood her ground and refused to retreat when he'd prowled to the edge of the picket fence boundary between the resort and her home. He hadn't looked up at her window again, seemingly content to enjoy the spectacular sunrise. But she'd suspected he knew she was there.

As aware of her as she was of him.

She'd taken her time to finish her coffee before showering. And if she'd lingered under the cool water in the hopes of dousing the treacherous flames that seemed to take hold of her every time Atu glanced her way, that was her business and no one else's.

She'd been guiltily thankful that her mother wasn't up; that her pain-dulled eyes wouldn't probe hers and somehow discover that Amelie was tolerating their enemy under her resort's roof.

But her secret hopes that her unwanted guest would depart were repeatedly dashed as he made his presence felt continually throughout the day.

She ate her lunch in her office, after seeing him seated in the dining room, casually scrolling through his tablet as he sampled her chef's best dishes.

Mid-afternoon, Maria gleefully informed her that Mr Quayson was enjoying a cocktail at the seafront bar and had signed up for one of the much-loved informal beachfront dinners she threw twice a week for guests.

Amelie had discovered the joy of combining helping the locals offload their day's catch, fresh from the sea, with a seafood-themed dinner, cooked over an open firepit right on the beach, accompanied by music and dancing from a local dance troupe.

As much as she was reluctant to admit it, hosting the dinners had alleviated a little of her loneliness and the stark absence of a relationship—especially as she knew many of her ex-friends from her former prosperous life were in serious relationships, or married with children.

The thought of Atu ruining her organised life made her grind her teeth. And yet, as evening approached, she found herself double-checking her hair and make-up, spritzing on her favourite perfume, while attempting to corral the swarm of butterflies fluttering in her belly before making her way towards the beach.

At the top of the gentle slope leading down to where her staff had set up in preparation for the evening's activities, she stopped and took a deep breath. The air was clean and fresh, the dark caramel-coloured sand inviting her to kick off her shoes and experience its warmth barefoot.

Low, wooden-slatted chairs had been grouped in a wide circle around a large firepit, and on either side of the circle two food stations were manned by professional chefs.

One of the waitstaff spotted her and headed over with a drinks tray. Amelie bypassed the chilled glasses of *nsaafuo*, the locally produced palm wine, in favour of her preferred drink—a mango and guava cocktail laced with ginger and rum. Palm wine had a tendency to go down too easily and sneak up on the unsuspecting with its alcoholic punch.

She needed her wits about her while Atu was around.

Her face burned as she recalled the last time she'd been tipsy around him. She'd not only made a fool of herself, she'd ignored the warning signs that her sister needed her. The ball of sorrow in her stomach made Amelie fear she would live with that regret for the rest of her life.

She mingled with her guests, ignoring the dart of hollow disquiet when she didn't spot Atu. Was she seriously disappointed that he wasn't here? What was wrong with her?

Shaking the feeling off, she threw herself into hostess mode, and soon the mouth-watering smells of grilled seafood and roasting meat were easing the tension that had taken hold of her all day.

Maybe her prayers had been answered and he'd left the resort—

'There you are.'

She started, twisting her head to meet the sardonic dark chocolate gaze of the very man she'd been thinking about. Suddenly the air seemed crisper, the tang of ginger on her tongue sharper. The cool air drifting in from the ocean making her aware of every inch of her skin.

She hated to admit that he made everything so much more vibrant. Made her feel insanely...*alive*.

What did it say about her that her enemy did this to her? *But he hadn't always been her enemy, had he?*

Before that fateful weekend she'd harboured a crush that had bloomed into something stronger, more potent. But everything that had come after had shown her those emotions were a mistake, that she should be thankful it hadn't gone beyond a torrid embrace. Like her parents, she'd learned to her cost that the Quaysons, and especially their black sheep, weren't people she wanted to tangle with.

So why couldn't she free herself of those electrifying minutes? Why, even now, did her face trace his chiselled features, lingering far too long on those sensual lips, remembering what it had been like to be devoured by them?

Wishing she could experience it again?

'Cat got your tongue?' he drawled, before his gaze fell to her drink. 'Or is it something else? If I recall, two drinks were your limit.'

And just like that, sparks flew under her skin. She glanced around, thankful that the local troupe's beating of the *kpanlogo* drums was loud enough to drown out his words. 'Not that it's any of your business, but I wasn't drunk that night, and I wouldn't be so distasteful as to fall about drunk in front of my guests now.'

A smile flicked at one corner of his mouth, as if he was enjoying riling her. 'Good to hear.' He sipped his own drink, his gaze conducting a head-to-toe scrutiny. 'Being relaxed looks good on you.'

'Then it's a shame you're here to ruin my vibe.'

His amusement turned into a full-blown smile, making her toes curl deep into the sand and her belly tighten at the transformation of his face.

Dear God, he had no right to look that breathtaking.

When she managed to drag her gaze away, she noticed the avid female looks slanting his way. Which only made her belly tighten harder, this time in…jealousy?

She shook her head, desperately dissipating that absurd notion.

'I've spent the day interacting with a few of your guests.

They speak admirably of your efforts here. You should be proud.'

'I am,' she replied, unable to stem the warmth flooding her at his words. But then she caught herself and forced a glare his way. 'If you feel that way, why are you trying to take it away?'

Frustration and that ever-present hint of ruthlessness flickered over his chiselled face. 'Because I've also seen that beneath the shine and gloss things are beginning to fray at the edges. You need an injection of serious capital, and fast. Are you going to deny it?'

She pressed her lips together, refusing to answer.

Impatience flitted over his face. 'This place can be world-class, Amelie. With every advantage and success at your fingertips. The Quayson Group can make that happen.'

'Sure, while stamping your name all over it.'

The hardness in his eyes intensified, and that foolish shred of hope attempting to flare to life died a quick death.

'It's the only way. A partnership between us would never work,' he said.

Why did that sting so much? For a single moment she hated the feud which had dogged their families. Then she reminded herself who was behind it and hardened her emotions.

'I see the shutters coming down,' he bit out derisively.

'No, what you see is me reminding you again that this conversation is inappropriate—now or at any time in the future.'

That earned her a narrow-eyed look of mockery. 'I'm beginning to think you enjoy butting heads with me.'

The intuitive remark about something she'd been denying since their heated exchange in his office startled her. But before she could summon an adequately cutting response, she heard her name being called out.

Even before she turned, she was dreading confirmation of the owner of that voice.

Sure enough, Joyce Blankson, a wealthy socialite and

one-time close friend of her parents, was making her way gingerly through the sand.

Amelie groaned under her breath.

'Something wrong?' Atu asked.

She shook her head, refusing to lose even more of her composure. 'I think my vibe is about to be ruined even further.'

'Amelie, there you are. I was hoping I'd run into you this weekend,' Joyce said, brazen curiosity in the gaze darting between her and Atu.

'Good evening, Auntie.' Although the woman was no blood relation, Amelie used the respectful term afforded older folk. 'I hope my staff are looking after you?'

The woman, who had delicate, birdlike features, gestured with bejewelled fingers. 'Of course they are. Your exemplary service is the reason I keep returning.'

That and gathering as much gossip as she could to relate to her friends in the city. The wealthy socialite thrived on ferreting out people's deepest, darkest secrets and sharing them with whoever would listen.

Amelie's mother had once stated that Joyce would befriend a shiver of sharks if it got her the latest gossip.

'Thank you, Auntie,' she replied politely.

Joyce eyed Atu in open speculation. 'You're the last person I expected to see here.'

She sensed Atu stiffen, but his faintly forbidding expression didn't alter. 'Am I?' he answered coolly.

Joyce waved her hand again, making the expensive bangles on her wrist tinkle. 'Every person in this country knows your two families don't mix. Which makes me wonder why you're at this resort at all—never mind socialising with a Hayford.'

For a moment Amelie wished she'd stayed in her office, instead of coming out here to show Atu that she wouldn't be intimidated into avoiding him in her own resort.

It was too late now. The proverbial cat was out of the bag.

Atu sent Joyce a thin, humourless smile which made the

older woman blink warily. 'I believe that's my business, Auntie. Can we help you with anything else?' he asked, not bothering to thaw the layer of ice in his tone.

Joyce's lips pursed. Sending him an approving glance, she spun on her heel and walked away.

'Do you know what you've done?' Amelie sniped, while attempting to keep her smile in place.

'Refused to lower myself to idle gossip?'

'You've ensured that news of your presence here will be all over the country by morning.'

His eyes narrowed. 'I thought I'd already done that by turning up in the first place?'

As if drawn by a magnet, her gaze swung towards her home, her teeth worrying her lower lip.

'Your mother still doesn't know I'm here, does she?' he intuited accurately.

Amelie sucked in a breath. 'I haven't seen the need to inform her of your visit, no.'

'So you'd rather she heard it from Accra's biggest gossip?' he demanded, eyeing the older woman, who even now was sending them surreptitious glances from a distance.

It was a miracle her mother hadn't already discovered the ever-increasing pressure being put on her by the Quayson Group.

Pain rippled through her as she acknowledged why. While her father had been alive her mother had had something to live for, despite the demise of her much-beloved eldest daughter. With him gone, her once-vibrant mother had withdrawn deeper into herself, and the presence of her youngest remaining child had done nothing to pierce her veil of grief.

'I'll tell her in my own time,' she responded, her vehemence from before curiously absent. If her mother found out about Atu's visit, and his family's unrelenting efforts to acquire their resort, it would break her—perhaps irreparably.

She looked up, and found him watching her with a pensiveness that made the breath snag in her throat. She was struck with a wild urge to plead with him to leave her and her family alone.

An intense look entered his eyes just then, as if he'd read her thoughts. As if he *wanted* to hear her beg.

Aware of eyes watching them—especially Joyce's—she took a step back from him. 'I need to attend to my guests. Enjoy the rest of your evening, Mr Quayson.'

His jaw gritted for a moment. Then his fierce expression eased.

She didn't fool herself into thinking she'd escaped scot-free.

For the rest of the evening she ensured she remained outside his immediate orbit, and despite sending her a few levelling glances, he didn't venture any closer.

But even as she left her guests with endorsements of another successful evening ringing in her ears, she knew she was only prolonging the inevitable—both with her mother and with Atu.

When she found herself still awake after midnight, tossing and turning, she was frustrated but not surprised. She was also a little ashamed at the relief she'd felt when the housekeeper reported that her mother hadn't left her room all day, or taken any calls.

Before retiring to bed, Amelie had stood outside her mother's room, gnawing on her lip as she contemplated telling her about Atu. The thought of bringing further pain had made her shy away, even as she'd berated herself for ignoring a looming problem.

Wouldn't her mother be proud of her if she succeeded in sending Atu packing?

And then what?

Those three words eventually dragged her out of bed and onto the quiet stretch of beach.

The moon hung low, creating a wide beam of light over the still ocean. Just like the beauty of sunset, experiencing the serenity under moonlight reminded her of how much she loved her little corner of the earth. How hard she was willing to fight to hang on to it.

But how?

Half-formed solutions darted through her brain, each one less feasible than the last.

Lost in thought, she didn't notice she'd approached the border between her home and the resort until she looked up.

Into the eyes of Atu Quayson.

She had a fleeting urge to turn around, to rush back to the safety of her bedroom. But her feet refused to obey that thought. Then her stubbornness kicked in.

'What are you doing here?' she asked.

He shoved his hands into the pockets of his linen trousers, stretching the material across his taut thighs.

Not that she was looking.

'I couldn't sleep. From the looks of it, neither could you.'

He approached as he spoke, and this close, his presence overwhelmed her. Reminded her of the thinness of the sleeveless thigh-skimming tunic she'd thrown on to come out. And the fact that she was only wearing a flimsy thong underneath.

She folded her arms across her chest as a cool breeze blew over her.

Ruthless impatience flitted over his face. 'There's one simple way to end this.'

Days of frustration threatened to boil over. 'Have you stopped for a moment to think what this might do to my mother?'

His jaw tightened for a moment and she thought she spotted a hint of regret in his eyes before she admitted she was deluding herself. Because when his gaze fixed on her, it was the harsh regard of an apex predator unwilling to consider the frivolous emotions of its prey.

'I don't deal in sentiment, Amelie. This is business—pure and simple.'

'Silly me. Of course you don't. And I don't remember inviting you to use my name.'

'Don't you?' he enquired silkily. 'Maybe not recently, but I recall you wishing I would on another occasion.'

Her next breath evaporated from her lungs. 'Your memory might be faulty.'

A sardonic gleam lit through his eyes. 'Don't shame us both by pretending you don't know what I'm talking about.'

Her heart hammered against her ribs. Did he remember their encounter as intensely as she did?

'Yes, I remember,' he said, as if she'd asked the question aloud.

She wrapped her arms around her middle and raised her chin. 'Whatever you think you remember, we both know it meant nothing. Let's leave it buried in the past where it belongs.'

For a moment he looked furious. Offended. He took a single step towards her, determination in his stance.

'But is it, though?' Before she could answer, he continued. 'Because it feels like it's right here between us. Getting in our way.'

'This may just mean business to you, but don't you get it? It's all *personal* to me. Every grain of sand on this beach, every leaf on every palm tree means something to me. But then that's your way, isn't it? First your brother—now you've come to finish the job.'

His eyes narrowed into dangerous slits. 'What exactly do you believe my brother did?' His voice was a sheet of thin ice over a frozen lake. Ominous and dangerous.

She refused to back down. 'What you're doing now! You see something you want and you do everything in your power to take it, regardless of the distress you cause.'

'Attaching sentiment to professional dealings is a bad business model.'

'While your problem is attaching none! Even if I wanted to, why would I allow an emotionless automaton to take charge of what I hold most dear?'

'Did you believe I was so unfeeling when you threw

yourself at me eight years ago? When you were busy getting what you wanted from me?'

'Excuse me?'

'No, you're not excused,' he condemned harshly. 'You were good at blinding me—I must give you that. But if you're throwing blame around, have the decency to take your fair share. You saw something you wanted—me—and you went for it, didn't you?'

She gasped. 'How dare you?'

'Amelie—'

'No!' She batted away his warning, years of pain, grief and anger congealing into a tight ball inside her. 'Haven't you taken enough? Why this resort? Why not one of the thousands anywhere else in the world?'

She hated that her voice emerged shakily. That even now she couldn't dismiss him as callously as she wanted to. That a part of her still wished all the acrimony between them didn't exist.

So that what? So she could throw herself in his arms the way she couldn't seem to stop imagining doing every time he was within touching distance?

'Because I'm the devil you know,' he rasped chillingly.

She froze in place. 'What's that supposed to mean?'

He shook his head. 'Tell me what you meant about Fiifi,' he gritted out, completely ignoring her question and her other indictments.

For a moment she regretted bringing up his dead brother. For dredging up memories they'd both rather forget. 'I hate to speak ill of the dead, but do you deny that had he been alive he wouldn't be doing the same thing you're doing now?'

An emotion closely resembling anguish lanced across his face, then was swiftly extinguished. 'You seemed determined to tar every member of my family with the same villain's brush. Have you considered that, were he alive, all this animosity might have been resolved by now?'

In her lowest times she fooled herself into considering

that. Then she was reminded that their families had been well set on enmity long before they'd lost their respective siblings. And, hell, the Quaysons had even revelled in their superiority.

'I don't believe that. Not when—'

'When what?' he snapped.

The knot in her stomach grew. 'The apple doesn't fall far from the tree, so of course Fiifi was acting the typical Quayson, but you were there that night. You knew something was seriously wrong. And he'd upset my sister before the party...'

He stiffened. 'What are you trying to say, Amelie?'

'That maybe you...we...could've done something. Instead of...'

'Instead of allowing ourselves to be distracted? Or is the blame one-sided?'

She shrugged. 'If you hadn't dragged me away—'

His harsh laugh froze her accusation. 'You can rewrite history all you want, sweet Amelie, but you came willingly. You were as eager to taste me as I was to satisfy that wide-eyed hunger you did such a poor job of hiding.'

His eyes narrowed, but she caught the flash of smugness within.

'Tell me, was I your first kiss?'

She turned, blindly stalking towards the gate.

Firm hands cupped her shoulders, stalling her flight. 'The truth is difficult to swallow, isn't it?'

'Stop it!'

The words were as much for her as for him. Because while she'd kissed a few boys previously, the kiss they'd shared had shown her a far superior realm of passion she'd never forgotten or duplicated. And, yes, she hated him a little for that.

'Let me go,' she rasped, doing her utmost to ignore the heat of his touch branding her, making her feel things she didn't want to but couldn't stop yearning for.

'Why? So you can run away? So you can slide between your sheets, smug with your righteous indignation?'

She tore herself free of his hold and whirled to confront him. 'No, so I can pretend you don't exist for a few blessed hours.'

For a moment a bleak look scraped across his face. Then he gathered himself with a formidable willpower she secretly envied.

'As regrettable as that incident was, burying our heads in the sand this time won't make any of this go away.'

A cold shiver washed over her, and it had nothing to do with the breeze coming off the ocean. 'You regret it?' she blurted, before she could stop herself.

One eyebrow rose mockingly. 'Don't you? Isn't that what all this extra animosity aimed at me in particular is all about?'

He was giving her the perfect out. She drew in a shaky breath and took it, ignoring the hollow in her gut. Ignoring the vice tightening curiously around her chest.

'You're right. It was a mistake.'

He stared at her for a charged moment, then turned his profile towards the ocean, leaving her to collect her tattered composure.

Another breeze washed over her and she shivered.

His gaze swung to her and she knew he hadn't missed her reaction. Within one moment and the next he was shrugging off his shirt.

'Wh-what are you doing?' she blurted as he came towards her.

Another mirthless twist of his lips. 'You may believe I'm your enemy, but I don't want you catching cold and falling ill. Or worse.'

She aimed a glare his way. 'Not until I've signed on whatever dotted line you're determined to foist upon me, you mean?'

That look of fury returned. This time accompanied by a

flash of disappointment. As if he had a right to such a lofty emotion where she was concerned.

She tried to summon her own outrage, grinding her teeth when she failed miserably because all she could feel was the warmth from his shirt as he draped it over her shoulders. All she could smell when she took a breath was the scent of his aftershave and that unique brand of masculinity that had drawn her like the proverbial moth to a flame ever since she hit puberty and crossed that forbidden line from family friend to something...*more.*

She wanted—no, *needed* to refuse this small offer of comfort.

Hand him back his shirt. Leave the beach.

Return to her room and come up with a definite plan that removed him from her life for good.

So why was she drawing the flaps of his shirt closer? Why were her fingers clinging to the warm cotton as if she'd never let it go?

Why were her eyes drawn to the torso moulded by the pristine white T-shirt he wore underneath the shirt?

Her gaze lingered on the outline of the chiselled six-pack, dropping lower to the faint bulge at the front of his linen trousers, her breath catching all over again at the memory of his arousal against her belly that weekend, when they'd given in to temptation, oh, so briefly...

She must have made a sound at the back of her throat, because his head swung towards her, his eyes holding hers for an age before he exhaled harshly.

His lips firmed and for a long stretch he didn't speak. Then, 'You need to accept that I'm the best bet you have right now. I'm going to win eventually. How soon depends entirely on you.'

His implacable conclusion sent icy shivers coursing through her. In that moment, she regretted every moment of weakness. Regretted feeling bad for evoking that hint of disappointment in his eyes.

She had nothing to be ashamed of. Not when vanquishing her and her family was his true purpose.

She snatched his shirt from her shoulders, crushing her body's instant insistence on its warmth as she tossed it back to him. 'You should know by now that threats don't faze me. We're still here, still standing, after all you and your family have done. So go ahead—do your worst.'

Head held high, she whirled away.

She only made it three steps before he captured her wrist. She spun around, intent on pushing him away. But that ruthlessness was coupled with something else. Something hot and blazing and all-consuming in his eyes.

She belatedly read it as lust just before he tugged her closer, wrapping one hand around her waist and the other in her hair.

'This stubborn determination is admirable. Hell, I'd go so far as to say it's a turn-on, because God knows I admire strong, wilful women,' he muttered, his lips a hair's breadth from hers. 'But fiery passion will only get you so far.'

'And what are you going to do about it?' she taunted, a little too breathlessly. Every cell in her body traitorously strained towards him, yearning for things she knew she shouldn't want, but desperately needed anyway.

He froze, and then, with a strangled sound leaving his throat, he slammed his lips on hers.

Just like those charged pockets of time that had trapped them sporadically since his arrival, time seemed suspended in static electricity as his lips devoured hers.

There was nothing apologetic or hesitant about Atu's kiss.

He kissed her as if he was starved for it. *For her.*

And, heaven help her, after fighting and craving this insane chemistry in equal measure for days…*years*…the battle went out of her.

She surrendered with a broken moan which he immediately pounced on, parting her lips with his and brazenly stroking her tongue with his.

Static electricity turned to dangerous, thrilling lightning, sending decadent shivers coursing through her body. Her senses blazed as he pulled her deeper into his arms, wrapping his heat around her while he tasted her over and over.

And then, as swiftly as it had arrived, the spell was broken by the crest of a wave washing over their feet.

She gasped, then shuddered as reality harshly intruded.

Even then she was reluctant to pull away from his warmth, from the hypnotic kiss. A kiss that was a world away from the one they'd shared all those years ago. But it turned out *that* kiss had been a precursor…a delightful appetiser before a decadent main course which she'd merely sampled.

And as she stared up into his face, at the far too chiselled perfection of her enemy, she wanted to throw caution and every last sane thought away and experience it again.

The potency of that need made her wrench herself free from him, her body shaking as she stumbled a few necessary steps back.

Self-preservation insisted she salvage the moment. She opened her mouth. 'You… You…' Then she cringed as words failed her.

Eyes hot and alive with lust only moments ago cooled, the faintest grimace darting over his face before his features settled into a haughty mask. 'I'm sorry. That shouldn't have happened.'

Dear God. He regretted this kiss too…

The hazy, heady emotion receded, leaving her nonplussed. But then a shot of feminine power restored her equilibrium. Because while he might be regretting it, his body supplied ample evidence of what their kiss had done to him—mostly below his belt and in the unevenness of his breathing.

Still, she wasn't about to show her bewilderment. 'You're right. It was a mistake,' she said, even as she inhaled his scent from the shirt that had somehow found its way back onto her shoulders, keeping her warm in the cool air.

That increasingly riveting twist of his lips appeared again. 'I said it shouldn't have happened. I didn't say it was a mistake.'

A dull throb at her temples told her she needed to retreat. Attempt to regroup. But then how many times had she done that in recent days? And how well had it worked?

'Meet with me tomorrow, Amelie.'

She opened her mouth, automatic refusal surging. But over his shoulder a light flicked on in the top left corner of her house. Her mother's bedroom light.

She swallowed, the thought of being discovered on the beach with Atu sending trepidation dancing in her belly.

He followed her gaze. Then his eyes narrowed on her face. 'One hour. Let's discuss this properly once and for all.'

Amelie knew better than to insist he leave her resort after that hour. She suspected he was about to unleash the big guns. Wasn't she better off meeting him and arming herself instead of being taken by surprise by his next move?

His gaze remained locked on hers, his body solid and immovable in front of her, as if he had all the time in the world. And in this instance, didn't he? Wasn't she the one facing another fiscal quarter of intense challenges unless she came up with a miracle?

'Fine. Eight o'clock tomorrow morning. My office,' she offered briskly.

He shook his head. 'I have other business in the morning, and I'd prefer somewhere we're not interrupted. I've booked your private chef service for tomorrow. I'll have him prepare us a meal in my chalet.'

His faintly raised eyebrow dared her to object. The thought of being alone with him sent frissons of foolish excitement coursing through her body. But she'd wasted enough time on this beach, beating her head against the brick wall of his resistance. Not to mention that completely inappropriate, earth-shaking kiss…

'Amelie.'

Steel edged his voice. As if, like her, he was reaching the end of his endurance.

Another light came on—this time in the living room downstairs. Her mother was looking for her.

'Fine. Dinner. I'll be there.'

She ignored the flare of triumph in his eyes.

'Sleep well, Amelie.'

She didn't respond because she knew she wouldn't.

Instead, she attempted to shove her roiling emotions away as she re-entered her home.

Her mother was wearing a long nightgown with a robe thrown over it. Amelie's heart lurched as she took in her stooped, grief-shrouded form as she stood staring at her sister's portrait.

'Maa?'

She turned, her eyes momentarily blank before settling on her. 'Where were you?'

'I went for a walk on the beach.'

A frown creased her mother's forehead. 'At this time of night?'

Amelie started to shrug, then froze when the faint aftershave of the man she'd been kissing filled her nostrils.

Her heart banging against her ribs, she bit the inside of her lip when her mother's gaze shifted to the shirt, her frown intensifying.

Her mother opened her mouth, most likely to demand why she was wearing a man's shirt, but Amelie spoke hastily. 'We need to talk, Maa.'

'About what?'

'About the resort.'

Weariness and grief settled more heavily on her mother's shoulders. 'You're in charge of it now, Amelie. Whatever it is...handle it.'

As much as she wanted to grasp that lifeline, she knew her mother wouldn't forgive her once she discovered her involvement—albeit reluctant—with the enemy.

'You need to know what's going on.'

Her mother half-heartedly waved a hand at her, her gaze drifting back to the portrait on the wall. 'It can wait till tomorrow,' she said, with surprisingly firm dismissal.

Amelie stared at her for a moment longer, wishing her heart didn't ache with the pain of being completely ignored by a mother who grieved for her child as if she was the parent to one and not two children. As if she, Amelie, had died too the night her older sister had perished in that car crash.

CHAPTER FOUR

'WE HAVE A PROBLEM.'

Amelie stopped herself from groaning as Maria entered her office. Every instinct said that whatever the problem was involved Atu Quayson. She knew he was a problem for her. She hadn't been able to stop thinking about him all day. He'd invaded her thoughts during her meetings, with those sizzling minutes in his arms, his mouth on hers, re-playing in her brain on an endless loop.

Oh, yes, she laid the blame for her complete lack of con-centration firmly at his feet.

'We do?' she answered, forcing the memories from her mind. And failing.

Maria's face contorted in a grimace. 'We're short-staffed in the spa. Dzifa has a family emergency. I've had to send her home.'

Amelie nodded, almost welcoming the chance to *not* think about Atu Quayson for a fraction of a second. Not to think of their charged conversation on the beach and the kiss afterwards.

She also didn't want to recall that her mother had left instructions with the housekeeper this morning that she wasn't to be disturbed, even by her daughter, thus ensur-ing their talk wouldn't happen today.

What did it say about her that she'd rather face a staff shortage problem than deal with the hard knot of pain and desolation that came with her mother's rejection?

'Okay. So let's move some other staff around. We have two more masseurs, don't we?'

Maria shook her head. 'They're fully booked for the next four hours. And we have a VIP appointment that can't be moved.'

Something in her manager's tone captured her attention. 'Who's the VIP?'

Maria stared steadily at her. 'Who do you think?'

For the smallest, most shameful instant, Amelie was pleased her head masseur was unavailable. Because the thought of someone else's hands on Atu's body triggered an emotion that absurdly resembled jealousy.

You're losing it...

'Mr Quayson's appointment is in...' Maria glanced at her watch and sighed. 'Nineteen minutes.'

Amelie massaged the bridge of her nose, the sensation of being caught in the fabled spiderweb of Ananse the Trickster of native Akan folklore closing over her.

'Amelie? You don't want me to cancel, do you?' Maria pressed with quiet urgency.

She firmed her lips to stop the *yes* she yearned to say from spilling free. 'No, I don't.'

Maria gave a brisk nod, but continued to stare at her.

After several seconds, Amelie raised her eyebrow. 'Was there something else?'

'No, that's it. But, just to be clear, *you're* taking the appointment, right?' Maria asked. 'Or will you swap with one of the other girls?'

Heat swept through her—which she quickly banished before it took hold. A situation like this was why she'd taken a massage course three years ago. This wouldn't be the first time she'd stepped into a different role besides the one marked *Resort Director* on her office door.

Putting her degree in hospitality to good use had taught her to be versatile to daily demands, especially the challenges of juggling tight finances.

'I'll take the appointment.'

Even if that means touching him? Again?

'You sure?'

'I'll be there in ten minutes,' she said firmly.

After a probing look, Maria left, leaving Amelie with a belly quivering with trepidation and...*anticipation*.

No, not anticipation.

What had happened on the beach last night couldn't happen again.

So why, after retreating to her bed last night, only to spend hours tossing and turning and replaying their conversation about the family feud, those charged accusations, and that kiss, had she grabbed her laptop to try and discover more about Atu Quayson?

Because his reaction to her words had been...unexpected. His disappointment. That bleakness. And, yes, even that flash of anguish had thrown her. Enough for her to contemplate—for the briefest minute—the possibility of accepting his offer.

But how could she?

As much as he mocked her emotional attachment to her business decisions, she couldn't separate herself from it. Considering his offer would decimate her mother. Besides, at no point last night had he denied feeling the same unease about the night of that party.

She'd known her sister was upset, that her and Fiifi's gaiety had felt...*forced*. It had been hiding an underlying unhappiness which they'd covered up with excessive drinking before the fiery crash that had killed them.

Had Atu known that when he'd led her away from the party and into that sizzling embrace that had wiped her mind of everything else?

While she knew she couldn't absolve herself from culpability, had he used her to cover his own demons that night?

The breath shuddered out of her as the possibility settled into her bones, reaffirming the impossibility of considering his proposal. Because in doing so, wouldn't she be betraying her sister once again?

Ignoring the cold bleakness trawling through her, she yanked open a drawer, took out his laundered shirt.

She made her way to the spa, ignoring the inquisitive looks from guests and staff. *Just a few days longer*, she repeated under her breath, as she set out the sensual aromatic oils. Atu Quayson couldn't stay here for ever.

But he *could* fill a room with his presence, she accepted resentfully, when he walked into the spa minutes later. All female eyes tracked him with an avidity that rekindled her irritation.

His dark green short-sleeved shirt showed off brawny arms, the buttons undone drawing attention to his strong throat and smooth chest. His linen trousers gave the impression he was fully embracing the casual resort life, but she wasn't fooled.

He took his time to survey the room, his incisive gaze missing nothing. Seeing his lack of surprise at her presence, Amelie wondered if he'd known about her absent staff. He seemed to know everything else that happened around here, after all.

When he made a beeline for her, his gaze fixing on hers with laser-like intensity, she was almost convinced of it.

'I'm your three o'clock, I believe?' he drawled, his eyes lowering to rest on her mouth for two heartbeats.

She fought to maintain her composure. 'Yes, you are. If you'd like to come with me?'

She dragged her gaze from his heated one that said he was reliving their kiss. That her attempt at stiff formality merely amused him.

'Did you sleep well?' he asked as they entered the VIP spa room furthest from Reception.

She cast what she hoped was a carefree glance over her shoulder. 'Like a baby, thanks.'

His derisory look challenged her answer.

She brazened it out and headed for the preparation table. 'Make yourself comfortable. I won't be a minute.'

Setting out the oils and choosing soothing music to accompany the session put her nerves on edge. Lowering the lights to create the right ambience suddenly made it all feel much too intimate.

Get yourself together!

Finishing quickly, she turned, fixing her gaze just past his left shoulder. 'I'll just step out and let you get ready.'

'No need. I haven't had the misfortune of being labelled a prude yet. Besides, you've seen me in less before. Or was that not you, watching me from your bedroom window yesterday?'

She chose silence, and tried to ignore her tingling senses when he started undoing his shirt.

'Not to stereotype, but I wouldn't have taken you for the massage-loving type,' she blurted, mostly in a wild bid to dissipate the thickening atmosphere.

He shrugged. 'I've learned that a well-skilled massage isn't without its benefits. Besides, my mother tells me I should relax more.'

She opened her mouth to ask after his mother, and then pressed her lips shut. That near-slip made her heart thud in her chest. Sweet heaven, her mother would call her a traitor. Or worse.

'You *can* ask after her, you know. It's not a cardinal sin.'

She flicked her gaze to him, expecting another sardonic look. Instead, he regarded her steadily, with an almost encouraging look in his eyes.

She shook her head. 'What's the point?'

His eyes hardened a touch. 'The point is you were her favourite godchild.'

Her heart lurched in remembrance of the affection his mother had showered on her as a child. Before everything had turned to sorrow and ash.

'It didn't feel like it when our parents were declaring war on each other after…after the accident. And following through on it, I might add.'

Joseph Quayson had ruthlessly wielded his power within days of the double funeral, decimating what had remained of the Hayford businesses until her father had had no choice but to sell all his smaller interests and relocate his family to Saltpond.

Again, she expected a cutting response, but all Atu did was nod. 'Heavy and unexpected loss has a way of bringing out the worst in all of us,' he said cryptically.

She frowned, trying to read his expression, but it remained veiled, and his usually sensual lips were set in a thin line. She yearned to ask him what he'd meant last night about going with the devil she knew. Whether all those years ago he'd deliberately aided the distraction that had taken their attention from their siblings.

But all of a sudden she feared his answer. Feared that she couldn't endure another layer of the guilt she already felt. So she remained silent.

'As much as it makes you feel better to put a barrier between us, we will always have a connection, Amelie,' he said into a silence broken only by the tinkling Tahitian music playing in the background. 'And I, for one, won't pretend it doesn't exist.'

The rasped warning made her go cold, then hot, her heart striking a runaway rhythm again. Because she'd experienced that visceral connection last night. Had been unable to think of little else since...

'Are you ready? I'd like to get on with it, if you don't mind?'

Without answering, he shrugged off his shirt.

Her mouth went dry as heat flooded her.

Yes, she'd seen him stride godlike out of the ocean yesterday, wearing only brief swim-shorts. But that had been from a safe distance.

And, yes, she'd also spent time lazing around the pool at his lavish family home when her sister and his brother had been alive.

But that had been a time of foolish crushes and girlish dreams.

A time before tragedy struck.

This… *This* was something else.

And then he casually stepped out of his trousers, leaving him clad only in black cotton boxers, and she forgot how to breathe properly.

Not even her wild girlish dreams had done an adequate job of preparing her for the up-close perfection of Atu's body. There wasn't a spare ounce of flesh anywhere on his sleek, well-muscled frame. His six-pack made her fingers burn to touch him. His thighs and calves were thick without looking as if they were out of a bodybuilder's catalogue. Hell, even his feet were a work of art, and she wasn't a huge fan of feet.

When he walked past her towards the massage table, she couldn't help but ogle his tight buttocks. She didn't realise she was locked in place next to the prep station until he glanced over at her, one eyebrow quirked in mild amusement.

The bastard knew exactly what he did to her.

'Amelie.'

'Y-yes?' She cringed at her husky stuttering.

'Relax.'

She blew out a half-irritated, half-control-seeking breath, hating him for his conceited confidence in his perfection.

Before she could direct him, he lay face-down on the table.

Somehow she summoned enough professionalism to do the job.

To her eternal gratitude, he didn't indulge in chit-chat as she worked on his back, thighs and calves. But when he flipped over, Amelie couldn't hide from his steady, unabashed scrutiny. She ignored her hammering heart, the blood rushing too fast through her veins, and hastily moved away when she was done, telling herself that she didn't miss the feel of his smooth muscles beneath her fingertips, the warmth of his flesh or the satisfaction of easing his tense muscles.

She hadn't compromised her professionalism by jumping his bones.

She clung to that as she turned around—only to lose the smile she'd pinned on her face. He'd pulled on his trousers but his shirt remained draped over the chair. And he was watching her with that insane intensity.

'Stop looking at me like that.' Her attempted snap came out more like a breathless plea.

'Like what? Like you're the woman I kissed last night who kissed me back? The woman who's dying to deny the chemistry between us at all costs? Are you going to continue to bury your head in the sand?'

His words stung. 'It's called being a professional.'

She was surprised when he nodded in agreement. 'And I commend you for it. But our history goes beyond professionalism. This thing's been following us for eight years. Perhaps we need to put it to bed once and for all?'

A charged sound escaped her before she could stop it. And when she opened her mouth he beat her to it.

'If you're about to deny it, save your breath.'

She balled her hands until her fingers bit into her palms. 'I was about to say it doesn't matter. One of us needs to keep a level head.'

His mouth twitched, but humour was missing from his eyes. 'I've never kept a level head around you, Amelie.'

She gasped, her gaze locking on his of its own volition. His eyes smouldered with heat she knew would singe if she ventured closer. And yet she couldn't resist testing its warmth.

He reached out and snagged her wrist, firmly but gently tugging her close until she was trapped between those thighs she'd ogled only a short time ago. She could break his hold and march out the door…but, again, she didn't want to.

One small step, then another, pressed her up against him. The scent of the massage oils combined with his unique scent pulsed all around them, creating a sensual, aromatic cocoon she didn't want to rupture.

A shamefully needy and helpless sound broke from her throat when his gaze dropped to her mouth, his hunger a blatant statement.

'Kiss me,' he commanded, in a low, hypnotic voice.

'Atu…'

Again, his lips twisted… Again, they were absent of humour. 'You whispered my name just like that that night. Do you remember?'

Automatic denial rose to her throat, but it felt like sacrilege to deny that moment. It had changed everything for every one of them. Two families had been shattered, the destinies of two dynasties altered for ever.

His gaze flicked between her mouth and her eyes, burning with a fever she wanted to consume her.

'Don't deny it,' he commanded again.

'Is this your idea of putting this thing to bed?'

Shadows of the haunted look she'd seen that night eight years ago lurked. 'No. I should've specified that pun was very much intended,' he delivered thickly.

'Why…?' Amelie wasn't sure what she was asking.

For several moments he didn't reply. Then, 'Because there are some ghosts we can never lay to rest. But this needn't be one of them.'

'What are you saying? That a kiss will work this out of our systems?'

She couldn't disguise the need in her voice.

He heard it.

Far too arrogant satisfaction eased over his face as he nudged her closer. 'It's a start. Let's find out, shall we?'

With undeniable compulsion, she draped her free hand over his shoulder, then gasped when he brushed his lips over the sensitive skin in the crook of her elbow.

Untamed wildfire blazed through her veins. When she shuddered, he repeated the action, then settled back to watch her, his smugness intensifying when she remained still, silently yearning for more.

Slowly, his other hand curved around her waist, holding her in place, then caressed lower to grip her hip.

'I'm waiting, Amelie,' he drawled, and the vein of authority in his voice made her shiver. 'You're not evoking fire and brimstone on my head…your breathing is short, sweet and sexy…and you haven't stopped licking your lower lip in anticipation since I asked to taste you. So I'm guessing you want this too,' he stated.

It was the kind of confidence that usually irritated her. Instead, her core clenched with desire, the peaks of her tingling breasts tightening painfully against her dress.

Since he'd swaggered back into her life, she'd striven to resist him at all costs. But Atu Quayson was an unstoppable force of nature. He made her want to scream in frustration and moan with a need she hadn't felt in a very long time. And, yes, even while she despised herself, in the knowledge that perhaps when her sister had needed her most she'd been spellbound by him, she couldn't deny this insanity she'd only ever experienced with him.

He was also the last person she should be craving—for a million reasons. Yet none of those reasons mattered now. Not when he was so close, so…*vital*. Not when every cell in her body yearned for one small taste.

And what if he was right? What if she could rid herself of this desperation once and for all?

'For the love of God, do it before one of us expires from the suspense,' he growled, his lips a hair's breadth from hers.

With a strangled moan ripped from her soul, she surged up and sealed her mouth to his.

He gave a gruff sound of satisfaction, his hand tightening on her hip while the other captured her nape. He allowed her to explore him, savouring the smooth yet firm texture of his full lips, the power in the arms that held her, for all of a minute. Then he took control, parting his lips to invade hers with his tongue.

Atu explored her with unabashed hunger, devouring her

as he pulled her closer, until they were half splayed over the massage table. He gave another groan of approval as her breasts connected with his naked torso. Not even the fleeting thought that she'd leave this room with oil stains all over her dress was enough to pull her away from the sensational magic of his thrilling kiss. Her moans mixed with the tinkling of soothing music and his occasional groan as they found new ways of pleasuring each other, of stoking a hunger that always hovered far too close for comfort.

But then she'd never associated comfort with this man.

He was dangerous to her in every way. Private. Professional. *Emotional.*

That final reminder made her jerk away from him, taking several self-preserving steps back. She shut her eyes, her chest heaving as dismay filled her, opening them when she heard him move.

Sweet heaven. What was wrong with her?

His eyes narrowed as he breached the gap between them. 'If you're thinking about coming up with some spurious excuse to cancel dinner with me tonight because of what just happened, forget it,' he warned her tightly.

She pushed against his chest. He resisted for a fraction of a second before he stepped back, but his eyes remained on her. Demanding. Domineering.

'If that's what it takes to get you out of my hair, I'll keep our dinner appointment.'

Satisfaction flashed through his eyes before he walked over to snag his shirt, slipping it back on with an animalistic grace that had her biting back another moan.

She needed to get out of here before she compounded her questionable behaviour by jumping him again. Since the usual professional courtesies seemed inane, in light of what they'd done, she headed for the door without a word.

'Amelie?'

She pivoted to face him, her racing heart speeding up even further.

'You give a good massage.'

Her face burned. 'I hope if you leave a review you won't make any comments about what happened *after* your massage.'

Any semblance of civility left his face as it tightened. 'One of these days your need to cast me as the villain might get you into more trouble than you can handle.'

Why the hell did that threat only light up a fire in her pelvis? Maybe because somewhere deep in her psyche she knew the kind of trouble he meant would never be unwelcome? Even now, as displeasure tautened his face, the live wire of their chemistry continued to sizzle and twist its way between them, demanding attention.

'You created your own notoriety by labelling yourself the black sheep of the family. Don't blame me for believing the evidence you present,' she replied.

But as she walked away she couldn't ignore the flash of shame she experienced. Because he was right. She was clinging to every bad impression she'd formed about him to put a barrier between them, while her own decisions kept weakening it.

But wasn't the alternative an even scarier prospect?

Because didn't she suspect that the crush she'd always harboured for Atu Quayson might have morphed into something more dangerous, more life-altering?

Just...*more*?

Seven o'clock arrived far too quickly. And as she approached Atu's chalet, she asked herself for the millionth time if she was doing the right thing.

Even Maria had looked sceptical when Amelie had informed her where she was headed, her gaze taking in the jade-green knee-length wraparound dress made of soft cotton that emphasised Amelie's small waist and moulded her curves, the edges trimmed with the same *sankofa* kente design that labelled Atu's chalet.

She'd given her word, however. And, like with everything connected to the maddening man, doing anything other than proving she was a strong, independent woman severely chafed.

At her knock, he opened the door, and despite his being fully dressed, not shirtless as when she'd last seen him, that perfidious lust-filled sensation sped up her heartbeat again.

Every stitch of clothing, from the pristine white shirt with its sleeves folded halfway up his strong forearms, the dark trousers, to his polished handmade shoes, shrieked bespoke sophistication.

His earthy aftershave seemed to reach out to her, intent on reminding her what it had felt like to be pressed against that prime, ruggedly male body.

He returned her gaze with a blatant scrutiny of his own that did nothing to calm her nerves. 'Come in.'

She pasted on a cool smile, her wedge heels clicking on the wooden floor as she entered, acutely aware that he followed close behind.

'Would you like a drink?'

Alcohol probably wasn't a great idea, but she needed something to calm her nerves. 'A white wine spritzer, thanks.'

As he went to the small bar at the opposite end of the chalet, the heavenly scent of sizzling prawns hit her nostrils. Moving towards the double doors, she spotted her chef, tucked away in one corner of the balcony, preparing their dinner.

Then her gaze took in the whole scene.

Wooden candelabra she'd designed herself, lit with scented candles, were positioned on a pristine white-clothed table with a kente runner, complemented by tasteful silverware.

The intimate setting made her heart lurch. Made her dwell for several dangerous moments on the secret wishes she usually refused to acknowledge in the light of day.

On the loneliness that had become a cloak she couldn't seem to shed.

'I thought we'd eat first, then get down to business,' Atu said as he returned, holding out her drink.

Her stomach gave an insistent growl just then, reminding her that she hadn't eaten since breakfast. She felt her face warm up, but all Atu did was give an almost indulgent smile as he waved her outside.

'Come. Let's not keep your chef waiting.'

Mensah, the chef, smiled when he saw her. 'Good evening, Amelie. I hope you're hungry.'

Her smile was easier. 'I'm in for a treat, I'm sure.'

She'd subsidised the skilled young chef's culinary education, and been thrilled when he'd accepted a position on her staff. He was an invaluable asset who kept their loyal guests returning time after time.

But for how long? What if by this time next year she was forced to lay off some or all of her staff, including Mensah?

'Do all your staff call you by your first name?'

She started at Atu's low, disgruntled demand. He stood next to the table, his hands gripping the chair he'd pulled out for her.

Her pulse kicked again, this time with shameless glee. 'What's it to you? Surely you're not jealous?'

Shadow and lightning moved through his eyes, reminding her that theirs was a history made of secretive highs and grief-stricken lows. That the illicit connection they couldn't seem to escape had come with a steep prize.

'Let's not invite indigestion as an unwanted third guest, shall we?'

Perhaps it was because she'd felt that same bite of jealousy that she let him off the hook. She took her seat, sipped her spritzer and enjoyed the glorious sunset that arrived minutes before their dinner was served.

The prawn and pawpaw salad drizzled with a lemon dressing was superb, and she found herself responding to the easy conversation Atu initiated, his desire to stay away from business or personal subjects making the food go down with ease.

He declined coffee, and she refused dessert, opting for a second glass of spritzer.

She spotted the blueprints laid out on the dining table that was tucked in one corner of the living room as she followed him inside after the chef had departed, a wide smile on his face after accepting a giant tip from Atu.

Curbing a fierce urge to look closer, she dragged her attention away. Only to spot the packed weekender standing near the bedroom doorway.

'You're leaving?' she blurted, actively despising the chasm that yawned wide somewhere in her midriff.

His gaze flicked from the bag to her face. 'Is that disappointment I hear, Amelie?'

'Of course not,' she retorted briskly, despite her belly dipping alarmingly at the way he'd said her name.

His features hardened with sharp intent. 'However this meeting ends, I'm leaving at the end of it.'

She hated the way her chest clenched at those words. He was leaving. She should be celebrating. And yet not even the idea that she wouldn't need to explain his presence to her mother alleviated the curiously bereft hollow inside her.

Because her instinct warned her that while he might walk away if she persisted with her *no* at the end of this meeting, the future of her resort would still hang in the balance.

Unbidden, her gaze darted back to the blueprints.

He waved her towards them. 'Shall we…?'

She remained rooted to the spot, almost afraid to venture closer. Not because she feared she wouldn't like whatever he laid out for her, but because she was worried that she *would*.

He spotted her reluctance, his jaw tightening. 'Can you keep an open mind, just for tonight?'

'What's the point?'

A twitch rippled through his jaw. 'Nothing worth achieving in life comes without a measure of risk.'

Amelie felt herself wavering, but firmed her resolve as a memory flickered at the back of her mind. 'Yesterday you said I should accept the devil I know. What did you mean?'

That familiar shadow drifted over his face. When his jaw clenched tighter, she thought he wouldn't answer. But then, 'I'm not the only one in the Quayson Group who wants this to happen. You probably know that by now.'

Ice danced down her spine. 'You mean your father?'

His gaze didn't waver from hers. 'Yes,' he stated unequivocally.

'So what you're saying is that, no matter what I do, you and your family are coming for me?'

Impatience dragged away the shadows. 'You barely broke even at your last quarter. You need to make changes or you'll sink. Sometimes you have to make tough decisions for the greater good.'

'And you believe "the greater good" is giving you what you want and watching you walk away with the only thing that keeps my mother from falling apart?'

His nostrils thinned on a sharp inhalation. And, yes, it pleased her to see his frustration had intensified too.

Join the club.

Without answering, he strolled to the blueprints, placing his after-dinner glass of whisky next to the large sheets. For an age, he simply stared at them, and with each moment that passed, her resolve crumbled a little.

She *yearned* to see those blueprints.

'I'm willing to make a concession,' he said.

Why the hell did her heart jump at that? He was acting as if she owed him the right to make concessions, not the other way around.

'You forget that you're the one in need, not me.'

He raised his head and speared her with incisive eyes. 'I'll keep your name in whatever contract we agree between us.'

Amelie was glad she'd held her ground. 'Insult me some more, why don't you?'

His eyes narrowed. 'Is a hostile takeover really what you want? I could buy all the land around you, build another resort and overwhelm you within the year. Then buy you out for pennies on the dollar.'

The heart that had jumped a minute ago plummeted to her feet. It took everything in her not to show how alarmed she was at his threat.

'At least I'd go down fighting. History would show I didn't give in to the almighty Quaysons.'

'Maybe you would—but would it keep you warm at night?' he taunted coolly.

'Maybe not. But neither will handing everything I've worked for over to you. I'd say we're at an impasse. But I never wanted to deal with you in the first place, so...' She let her words trail off, staring him down in open challenge.

He stalked to the window, frustration in his every step. Despite the volatile atmosphere between them, she couldn't keep her eyes from following that hypnotic, leonine swagger, from watching the wide expanse of his shoulders, the gladiator-like line of his torso, tapering down to the tight clench of his buttocks, and the powerful legs that had trapped her so firmly this afternoon.

Her mouth dried and her nipples puckered in recollection of being up close against all that masculine power. All that thrilling heat and sensual promise.

With equal grace, he pivoted. Caught her unguarded gaze and stopped in his tracks.

For an age, they stared at each other, one turbulent subject momentarily abandoned in favour of another rife with equally heightened, equally disturbing power.

She held her breath as he stalked his way back to her to stand a foot from her, staring down into her upturned face as she fought to remember to breathe.

'Tell me what you want.'

The low-voiced demand was half growled, sending frissons of heat dancing over her skin.

Several requests rushed to the tip of her tongue, each one hotly discarded as inappropriate, traitorous and far too demeaning. Because, first and foremost, she wanted to feel those sensual lips on hers, those arms and hands branding her body. Then she wanted the hostilities between their families done away with. After that she wanted a thriving resort that equalled the Quayson Group.

And she could have none of them.

Because the man who could grant her all those things was the same man seeking to take away her most precious possession.

'It's just you and me here right now, Amelie. No one else.'

Her lips twisted, but he held up a hand before she could speak.

'And you have my word that I won't use whatever you say against you.'

She searched his face, wondering why her instincts weren't shrieking at her. And she realised why... She believed him.

But just in time she reminded herself that it didn't matter. Nothing mattered besides doing the right thing by her family. Which meant rejecting everything Atu stood for.

So she gave the only answer she could. 'I want nothing from you.'

CHAPTER FIVE

ATU BIT BACK a growl of frustration. His father's constant calls demanding progress were the reason he was cutting his trip short. Because unless Atu warned the old man off face to face, his father might try a different tactic altogether. One that would definitely achieve an adverse effect with Amelie. Possibly distress her even further.

He tried not to examine the flash of protectiveness that lit through him at the thought. Just as he'd tried to dismiss her heated accusations last night. And failed.

He'd walked for a solid hour after their encounter on the beach, the demons of the past dogging his footsteps and his thoughts. He'd seen no merit in admitting to Amelie that, yes, he'd known something was wrong with his brother that night. That, fresh from his latest vicious confrontation with his father, fresh from being chillingly reminded that he was second-best and was only needed as the support act for his older brother, he hadn't been in the mood to heed his instinct.

Furious with his inability to crush that knot of pain in his gut at his father's words, Atu hadn't stopped to examine whether the throwaway comments Fiifi had been making in the weeks before his twenty-fifth birthday held any weight. Hadn't wondered why his brother was drinking more than usual—why his interaction with Amelie's sister seemed a little more fraught than usual. Besides, hadn't theirs always been a hot-blooded relationship, full of angst and overblown displays of emotion? A textbook *Romeo and Juliet* relationship fuelled by the increasing tensions between their families?

He'd ignored his instinct and just about everything else the moment Amelie Hayford had sashayed up to him, her beautiful eyes wide and hungry, with that body that seemed to have accelerated from girl to woman overnight, stoking lustful flames he'd been trying to ignore for months.

He hadn't needed that particular temptation. Not on top of everything else. Not when he'd been silently condemning his own brother for obsessing over a woman who'd merely added to the frictions within the family.

Yet all it had taken was a look from her alluring eyes, the sound of her sultry voice as she'd asked if he was okay, to turn the blaze into an inferno.

And even after all this time—after tasting her on the beach last night and this afternoon in the spa room—Atu couldn't even say definitively that he wouldn't succumb to temptation again if he could go back…

Teeth gritted, he focused on their conversation. 'When was the last time you took a vacation?' he asked, his frustration mounting higher.

Confusion wrinkled her smooth brow. 'What?'

'It's not a trick question, Amelie.'

God, why did simply uttering her name make the blood surge faster through his veins? She twisted her lips to the side, a tic he recognised meant she was measuring her words. Probably debating whether to give him a straight answer or make him work harder for it.

Why the hell did that turn him on? He inwardly shook his head. It was a good thing he was leaving. This woman came with far too much baggage, on top of the family issues already writhing between them.

'I don't remember.'

'I have a proposal for you,' he said.

Her eyes widened, then dropped to his mouth before darting away hastily.

Satisfaction eased through him. He wasn't ashamed to admit that seeing her sexual interest, no matter how quickly suppressed, pleased him.

'Not that type of proposal. But we can tackle that later if you want.'

Her eyes immediately flashed, singeing him even from across the room. 'In your dreams.'

He suppressed a smile.

The animosity she'd shown him thus far had almost convinced him he was fighting a losing battle. But her responses told a different story.

Not that he was going to use their chemistry in that way.

First he would win her business professionally. Then he would slay this particular sexual beast that had been reawakened since she'd walked into his office last week.

No. Not since last week.

Since a timid young woman—now a confident, take-charge temptress who drove him insane—had attempted a flirtation without realising the fire she was stoking. She'd been far too beguiling even back then. In the intervening years Amelie's allure had simply grown.

Remember what this woman means to your family.

He gritted his teeth and pushed that thought away. He might be undertaking this project at his father's command, but that didn't mean he wouldn't do things his own way. After all, he'd done it multiple times before—made a few billion while cloaked by his black sheep label.

But you want to earn his regard. His respect. Isn't that why you returned? To earn a crumb of the easy affection your father gave Fiifi?

The reminder chafed but, try as he might, he couldn't dismiss it. Couldn't cauterise the open wound of rejection and disregard he seemed to reap from his father simply by breathing.

'Malaysia or Malta. Take your pick,' he said, his tone harsher than he'd intended.

She started, her beautiful eyes widening. She'd edged

towards the table while he'd been lost in his bitter thoughts, casting furtive glances at the blueprints.

'What are you talking about?'

He nodded to the blueprints. 'We'll visit one. Or both. You can assess the finished project for yourself. See my vision of what this place could be.'

Interest sparked in her eyes. Then frustration bit through him when he saw her eyes dim.

'No. That's out of the question.'

'Because you're afraid?'

Her plump lips pursed and heat shot through his groin. 'Excuse me?'

'I didn't stutter, Amelie. In business, you either move forward or you die.' He shrugged. 'Some would say that applies to life too.'

A look shrouded her face. He wanted to ask what or whom she was thinking about, but he forced his mind to remain on business. For now.

It occurred to him then that he didn't know if she was involved with anyone. And that thought chafed too.

'Is it just your mother you're concerned about? Or is it someone else? A lover, perhaps?'

His breath locked in his chest as he waited for her to cycle through her outrage and give him an answer.

'Not that it's any of your business, but, no, there's no lover.' She tilted her head, eyeing him with mockery and a trace of something else he couldn't quite decipher. 'Since you think I'm capable of duplicity, I take it *you* go around kissing other women when you're involved with someone else?'

The fire in her eyes intensified the heat in his groin. Dear God, he wanted to be consumed in it. 'Is that your way of asking if *I'm* seeing anyone?'

'It's my way of warning you not to tar me with the same brush as you.'

With a start of surprise, Atu realised he was enjoying

this. Her spark had ignited something within him, burning away the ennui he'd dwelt with for the last few years.

He strolled around the table, drawing closer until only a few feet separated them. He inhaled, unable to stop himself from drawing the sensual, sexy scent of her perfume into his lungs.

This was complicated, dangerous territory. But he couldn't resist. Just as he'd been unable to resist her eight years ago.

She's not offering now...

He curbed another smile. Perhaps not. But he'd always enjoyed a challenge.

'Something funny?' she snapped, her fingers tightening around her glass.

'Anyone told you you're simply alluring when you adopt that affronted minx routine?'

Her delicate jaw clenched. 'It's not a routine.'

'It is jealousy, then?' He'd experienced an unwanted taste of it, watching her smile at the chef earlier this evening. Payback was a satisfying bitch.

She blinked. Then her gaze swept away from his. He wanted to cup her chin, redirect those stunning eyes back to his.

'Can we get back to business, please?' she asked.

'I'm not seeing anyone, by the way, so you can put your claws away.'

Her lips worked, no doubt formulating a cutting response.

He turned to the blueprints, simply to avoid bending low and fusing his mouth to her far too enticing lips.

'So...which one?'

Her gaze dropped to the table and a wave of longing swept over her features, quickly extinguished as she folded her arms. 'I can't.'

He'd learned as a child, faced with the severe imbalance of affection from parents who had clearly favoured their firstborn son, that to be taken seriously he had to be assertive, to make his demands heard or be lost in chilling indifference. He'd been forced to suppress softer feelings that would only earn him ridicule from his father and pity from his mother.

Excising that trait had served him well into adulthood. More and more he reaped the benefits of it. He went after what he wanted with little regard for the consequences.

So he waited as Amelie battled with herself. She swallowed, her arms relaxing as her gaze dropped down to the table once more. 'Malaysia,' she murmured.

He nodded, curbing a wild, almost possessed need to march her to her residence, make her pack right away so they could leave.

'How long has Maria worked for you?' he asked.

Her gaze continued to linger on the blueprints as she answered, 'Almost as long as I've been in charge.'

'So she knows the workings of this place inside out?'

She started to nod, then stopped herself, frowning as his meaning sank in. 'If you're suggesting—?'

'That you take a bold step towards salvaging a sinking ship? Yes, I am.'

He expected another cutting retort, but another expression crossed her face, this one containing a haunted yearning he wanted to deny but knew only too well. It resembled the same yearning he managed to keep locked down tight. Most of the time…

'I don't know how my mother will take it.'

The faint vulnerability in her voice threatened to soften something inside him. He knew only too well what it was like to go against a parent's wishes. But wasn't the reverse why he was here?

While he was proud of the wild success he'd achieved outside of his family's sphere of influence, he still bore the Quayson name. And, while he didn't feel the need to atone for his black sheep status, didn't he feel…something close?

His own father had threatened everything from cutting him off financially to totally disowning him eight years ago. He'd gone through with the first but, being down one heir, he'd had to rethink alienating his remaining two sons.

Amelie and her mother would see things differently a year or two from now, when he'd turned the fortunes of this resort around. Granted, it would have his family's name plastered all over it, but he had never claimed to be a saint.

His gaze fell on the plump lower lip she was worrying with her white, even teeth. His shaft swelled as memories of kissing those lips reignited, reeling out like the sharpest 3D movie, until he had to suppress a groan and lock his knees to keep from reaching for her, repeating the heady episode that had fevered his blood and interrupted his thoughts these last few hours.

No, he was far from sainthood. But he also knew now wasn't the time to give in to rampant temptation. Not when his father was making threats.

'I can have my people meet with her, if you want.'

Fierce protectiveness washed over her face. 'No. Absolutely not.'

Her reaction made him wonder whether the rumours he'd heard about Priscilla Hayford's reclusiveness were true. Whether the loss of her eldest daughter and husband had permanently broken the strong and compassionate woman she'd been before all the acrimony had set in.

And how much his own father was culpable.

He swallowed the distaste filling his mouth.

'I'll leave you to deal with your mother on your own.'

The vulnerability remained, even as that stubborn chin lifted. 'You're assuming I'm agreeing to this...'

'I haven't heard a *no* yet.' Again, he infused implacable challenge into his tone. Then he glanced pointedly at his watch. 'I have a meeting in Accra in a few hours. What's your answer, Amelie?'

Now that he'd sensed her acquiescence, the need to bind her to him rippled through him like a fever. As did the need to be free, even if for a short period, from his father's vengeful directives.

'I'll come on one condition.'

He neutralised his features, dead set on not showing an ounce of the emotion roiling through him. Emotion he deciphered as thick, unrelenting *anticipation*.

'I'm listening.'

'If I'm not convinced by what you show me in Malaysia, you'll leave me alone.'

The thought of walking away from her—for any reason—triggered a negative reaction in him. While he was convinced visiting his resort would change her mind, her condition wasn't one he was going to accept.

He refused to ask himself why he felt so strongly about it, and knew his rejection of it stemmed from a place he didn't want to examine.

'No, I don't need to grant that condition. You'll come. You'll like what you see. And you'll accept my terms.'

Her jaw slackened for a moment before she caught herself. 'Your arrogance truly knows no bounds, does it?'

He allowed himself a small smile of satisfaction, which swiftly turned to clawing hunger when she gave a small gasp and her gaze dropped to his mouth.

'No, it doesn't. And you'll be glad for it when you reap the rewards from giving me what I want.'

Amelie sipped the perfectly chilled vintage champagne just served to her by an impeccably dressed flight attendant, fervently willing her hand to stop shaking and her head to stop reeling.

The drink went down smoothly, but it did nothing to calm her nerves.

She wasn't sure what surprised and disturbed her most— the fact that she'd gathered the courage to pack her suitcase, climb into the back of the sleek and shiny town car Atu had sent to Saltpond this morning to bring her to Accra, or the fact that she'd done it despite the distressing row with her mother last night, once she'd made up her mind to go ahead with this.

Her soul shrivelled in recollection of her parent's reaction to the news that she was accompanying Atu Quayson to Malaysia and considering his offer to subsume their resort.

Her mother's look of utter devastation had passed quickly, to be replaced by disappointment, then fury at what she'd stated was Amelie's failure to keep 'that evil family' away from her beloved legacy.

'They're threatening to take over with or without our co-operation, Maa,' she'd pleaded. 'I need time to find a way out.'

'And your way of finding time is to fly off with the Quayson boy?' she'd replied scathingly, her grief-filled eyes darkening with disappointed fury. 'You are a Hayford. I expect you to tell them we will never co-operate. But, no. You have been seen accommodating him in our resort instead,' she'd accused hoarsely.

Amelie gasped. 'You knew?'

'Of course I knew. Just because I'm not involved in the day-to-day running of the place, it doesn't mean I don't take an interest in what's happening here. It's all we have left after those people took everything away from us!'

'But you never talk to me about it. You don't even…' She'd bitten her tongue, reluctant to admit how she truly felt about her mother cloistering herself in the master suite day after day, only emerging occasionally, cloaked in grief and with a faraway look that said she didn't care about the present or her remaining daughter, only the past and the husband and child she'd lost in quick succession.

'I don't even what? Hold your hand and tell you every day what a good job you're doing?'

Every cell in her body had yearned to scream *Yes!*—to regress to being a needy child seeking acceptance and affection from a parent. She'd wanted to demand why that was too much to ask. But she'd feared the answer. Feared her mother might tell her she didn't merit the same love her sister had so easily been granted. That the endless stream of devotion she'd showered upon her older sister and her husband was long depleted. Or, worse, that any remaining reserves she could dredge up would only go to sustain the memory of her firstborn and never be extended to her remaining living child.

Amelie hadn't wanted to be reminded that, despite her parents adoring their firstborn daughter, they'd fervently wished their second child to be a son. They'd never got over their disappointment when their wish hadn't been granted.

She'd pushed the stark reminder to the back of her mind as her mother had condemned her for her decisions.

'How do you know he's not simply getting you out of the way so his father or brother can take over anyway?'

For some reason her insides had tightened at this indictment against Atu. She'd found herself defending him. The man she'd kissed not once but twice, when she should be staying far away from him.

'Because if he really wanted that he could've done it from the comfort of his office back in Accra. He didn't have to come here and talk to me.'

And then she'd realised she believed it. Perhaps it was foolish, but she didn't hate Atu's stance in coming to the resort to face her, instead of leaving it to his team of cutthroat lawyers and business executives.

Her mother's eyes had narrowed then. 'Sweet heaven, you sound as if you're defending him.'

She'd ignored the traitorous heat climbing into her face. 'I'm not. But if you've been keeping an eye on things, then you know we're barely hanging on. Would you prefer to do nothing at all? I don't have any other choice, Maa.'

'Your father would've found a way,' she'd muttered then, her face clouding over before she'd turned away from Amelie, shutting her out with the same finality with which she'd been shutting her out for years.

Amelie had been alternately grateful that her mother hadn't seen the pain coursing through her and angry with herself for the immediate instinct to suppress that pain, to bear it in silence so her mother wouldn't suffer further.

Perhaps because she'd been worn down, she'd found herself beginning to look forward to leaving the resort behind for a while—even if it was with Atu.

And then a different sort of emotion had struck.

One she was still trying to suppress.

It was the quiet fizz of excitement, bubbling just beneath her skin. It had grown audaciously when she'd met with Maria, to temporarily hand over the reins of her beloved resort.

When Maria's scepticism had given way to supportive understanding, Amelie had had to blink back tears. If nothing else, she knew her resort would remain in competent hands while she was away.

So now here she was, after being whisked through VIP Customs at Accra's Kotoka International Airport, then driven across the baking tarmac to a gleaming cream private jet with gold trimmings and the 'Q' logo exhibited boldly on its tail fin. Minutes later, she'd been ensconced on the Quaysons' jaw-dropping, extremely luxurious private jet, waiting for the man himself before they took off for Kuala Lumpur, via a quick refuelling stop in Dubai.

A small crew consisting of two pilots and four attendants had greeted her, then informed her that Mr Quayson would be arriving shortly.

She took another sip of champagne, enjoying the taste in spite of giving up on the drink doing anything to calm her nerves. She doubted anything would, but perhaps during this time away she would find a solution to her problem that didn't involve extending her mother's pain and misery.

She was still busy ignoring the sceptical voice taunting her that pigs might fly before that happened when she looked up to see Atu striding down the aisle towards her.

Dear God, he had no right to look this good. Had no right to interfere with her heart's rhythm the way he so effortlessly did just by existing. She tried not to ogle the sight he made in a torso-moulding polo shirt and cargo pants... how each movement of his body reeked of utter confidence.

When he stopped beside her, fixing his far too vivid gaze on her, she wanted to rail at the fates for the breathless fever raging in her pelvis.

'Your journey from Saltpond was fine, I hope?' he enquired, his voice low, deep, and devastating to her equilibrium.

She cleared her throat and attempted a light, casual tone. 'Yes, thanks.'

'What's wrong? And don't tell me it's nothing.'

She knew he was seeing the same shadows and weariness she'd spotted in her bathroom mirror this morning.

'My mother didn't take the news well.'

He remained silent for a moment before his nostrils flared. 'And yet you still came.'

There was speculation in his voice, along with a note she couldn't quite decipher, and it sent tingles down her spine.

She shook her head. 'I don't want to talk about my mother. Or our families.'

He studied her for several more seconds. Then he summoned an attendant. When she hurried over, an eager smile on her face, Atu nodded towards Amelie's glass. 'I'll have the same, thanks,' he said, without taking his gaze off Amelie's face.

She wasn't sure why her breath snagged in her throat as they waited for all of ten seconds before his drink was delivered.

Around them, the crew were readying for take-off. The doors were sealed; the pilots had disappeared into the cockpit. But all she could focus on was Atu leaning forward, his broad shoulders filling her vision and his fresh citrusy aftershave playing havoc with her senses.

'I have two proposals for you,' he told her.

Her mirthless laughter seared her throat. 'I'm still on the fence about the wisdom of the last one I agreed to.'

He shrugged, drawing her attention to the latent power in his broad shoulders, to the reality that he only needed to be within touching distance to make her feel shamefully breathless.

'This one might cause a little less stress. Perhaps even alleviate it.'

The plane gave a small jolt as it left the hangar. A drop of champagne spilled from her glass onto her fingers. She raised her hand and licked the droplet, then inhaled sharply when he gave a low growl.

The resulting punch of feminine power made her smile confidently. 'Let's hear it, then...'

He seemed to be having trouble focusing on their conversation, and Amelie couldn't help the flash of excitement that lit up in her belly.

'I want to call a truce. No dredging up our history unless we both want to discuss it.'

Which left business—and the remaining subject that had occupied her mind for far too long. The one seeming to loom even larger than the elephant in the room that was their family feud.

Even other peripheral subjects, like how exactly he'd earned the 'black sheep' label, felt secondary to the live wire of the chemistry writhing between them.

It was a charged subject that he wasn't going to place on the back burner of his 'truce' proposal, judging by the fierce intensity in his eyes, the way his gaze kept raking her face, lingering at the pulse beating in her throat...

'You said two. What's the other?' she asked as the plane rumbled onto the runway.

It gathered speed, as did the urgency of Atu's regard. She dragged her gaze from his, glanced out of the small porthole at the buildings flashing by. Soon they would be airborne, winging away from the responsibility and heartache she'd been consumed with since her sister, and then her father, had passed away.

Since continuing the family legacy had become her only focus.

Her shoulders lost a touch of their tenseness, and the

tightness at her temples she'd learned to live with eased as the plane gained speed.

Then his fingers brushed over the back of her hand, willing her focus back to him. The stark need in his face made her breath feel strangled in her throat.

'I want you in my bed. I want you underneath me. I want… I *need* to know what it feels like to possess you,' he rasped.

'This isn't going away…'

His words from the beach resonated within her.

'If I take you up on your…proposal…it'll be on my terms. You may have got me here by taking away most of my choices, but this won't be one of them.'

She saw his untrammelled need to dominate her in this too. A need she suspected had been branded into his DNA. He was the alpha male, intent on having his way in all things.

But she boldly held his gaze, the urge not to let her own need defeat her into submitting surging furiously inside her.

The ripple in his jaw told her he was displeased, but then a flash of admiration gleamed in his eyes.

Still, she held her breath, until he lifted his glass, not quite touching it to hers, but not acquiescing either.

'I reserve the right *not* to make it easy for you to prolong it. That's my best and final offer.'

Maybe it was her sense of freedom, the relief that accompanied leaving her troubles behind if only for a short time, that made her lean forward.

'Challenge accepted,' she said, and touched her glass to his just as the wheels of the plane left *terra firma*.

She took another sip of her drink and together they watched the city fall away beneath them. She only turned her attention back to him when the jet broke through the clouds. And only as she watched his own shoulders drop did it register that he'd been tense too.

As if he too had needed the escape.

But surely not?

He and his family ruled the city beneath them. Between the goldmines and the luxury hotels and the numerous banking interests, they'd been elevated to an eye-wateringly wealthy status decades ago.

Amelie secretly suspected that, while the two men had once been friends, it had been her father's obsession with keeping up with the Quaysons and ultimately failing that had contributed to the initial rift. The tragedy of losing their eldest children in the same accident had been the straw that had finally broken the camel's back.

She glanced at Atu now from beneath her eyelashes, watching him sprawl in his seat, effortlessly drawing her attention to his body.

He locked his eyes on her before she could look away.

She opened her mouth, then realised she didn't want to talk business—and talking about sex was way too risky, considering how she was feeling.

Which left her with nothing to say and an ever- increasing desire to give in to his *sooner rather than later* time frame.

Clearly deciphering her dilemma, he let loose a conceited smile as he watched her. 'Don't tell me your little condition is already causing you problems?' he drawled with wry amusement.

'Not at all. I was wondering why you came back to Ghana, considering you've set the hotel world alight in Asia and Europe,' she blurted, plucking the subject out of the air.

Humour evaporated from his face. 'I believe that falls under one of our no-go areas.'

She swallowed at the hard bite to his words. Then she felt a weird little sense of kinship with him, because she suspected his reasons were familial and as strained as hers were.

'Why aren't you seeing anyone?' he parried.

It was her turn to be unnerved. 'Excuse me?'

'After going to great lengths to state your stance on fidelity, I'm wondering why a beautiful woman like you is single. It can't be for lack of male attention.'

'No, it's not. It's by choice.'

There was no need to tell him she hadn't felt like dating recently. That the spark he evoked so effortlessly in her was totally missing with every other man she'd met in the last few years.

Something flickered in his eyes—a flare of possession and intent that made her body prickle alternately with heat and cold. But she didn't have to dwell on it because he'd reached into his briefcase and taken out a thick brochure. Although the heading stated it was a guest activity list for the Q Cove Resort, there were no pictures, just glossy text.

'I know you've seen the blueprints, but I want you to see the finished product first-hand. Make a list of what you'd like to experience while we're there.' He slid it across to her, then rose. 'I have a few calls to make. I'll see you in a few hours.'

Amelie watched him leave with a sense of loss—a feeling she was starting to associate with watching Atu walk away from her.

It struck here then that now he'd got his way, and she'd agreed to hear him out, she'd expected him to press his advantage at the first opportunity. But she should've known that he'd do the opposite. After all, she'd handed herself over to him for the next two weeks.

Had he grown bored? Like a predator with its prey finally within its grasp?

She grimaced, irritated by using that unfavourable description.

She was no one's prey!

So why was she feeling at odds because he'd left her so soon? Bereft, even?

Exasperated with herself, she flicked through the brochure, her eyes widening at the extensive range of sustainable services Atu's resort provided. A man-made, rain-fed lake delivered water and electricity to the whole resort, making it completely self-reliant. A high percentage of the resort's food was grown on-site or sourced through local merchants. It had achieved an industrial level of recycling that made her own previously held belief that her resort was sustainable a laughable joke.

Every stitch of fabric used at his resort was sustainable—including the staff's clothing. Guests were encouraged to use the on-site couturier for the duration of their stay and donate their clothes to charity before departure, and the subtle encouragement to travel light and reduce their carbon footprint had worked wonders.

She read through it twice, fighting twinges of jealousy. Grabbing a pen, she ticked several random boxes, assuring herself that it wouldn't live up to her expectations.

Atu returned just before they landed to refuel in Dubai. Expecting more of that sexual intensity from him, she was again nonplussed when he went into flawless host mode.

'The attendants will be along with some refreshments. Lunch will be in fifteen minutes.'

They ate in companionable silence, and then he sat back after their meal was done and they'd taken off again. 'I have a few more items to take care of. There's a bedroom in the back if you want to rest.'

She followed his gaze to the door at the rear of the plane, then immediately felt light-headed as sensual images bombarded her. All she needed to do was say the word and she would experience the full, mind-melting magic he'd already given her a taste of.

She squirmed as heat spiked through her.

Was she really built for casual sex?

Or was she overthinking everything?

Theirs would be a mutually agreed-upon casual fling. Not like the melodramatic one Esi had had with Atu's brother. There would be no emotions and therefore no heartache—

'Amelie?'

'Hmm?' She glanced up at him.

His gaze was filled with amusement and heat as he waved a hand at the brochure. 'I asked if you'd chosen.'

'I...um... Yes.'

He picked up the brochure. 'Spear fishing, wind-sailing *and* abseiling? Very brave for the girl I remember, who was afraid to even venture near the swimming pool until I coaxed you into it. Are you sure you don't want to add bungee jumping to your list, just to make it a total adrenaline junkie's experience?'

Her eyes widened in mild shock—both at the activities she'd so carelessly picked and at the fact that he remembered those long-forgotten times. She had indeed had an initial fear of swimming in the big children's pool. All it had taken was one of Atu's rare smiles and his cocky teasing to make her take the plunge.

But those idyllic days were far behind her.

'I'm sure. And, in case you haven't noticed, I'm not that girl any more.'

Something dark and thrilling flashed in his eyes. 'I've noticed,' he replied, with an intensity that sat heavily between them.

When she ventured a look at him, she caught a shaft of pain in his eyes, quickly disguised as he picked up his glass of wine. Again, questions brimmed on the tip of her tongue, but, reminded of their agreement, she bit them back. Or at least she tried to.

The words that spilled from her lips were the last she'd expected. 'What's your reason for being unattached?'

His eyebrows rose.

'What?' she demanded, even as her inner voice asked her what she was doing. 'You can ask me, but I can't ask you?'

His lips twisted and his lashes veiled the look in his eyes. When they rose again, she gasped at the unabashed hunger in his eyes. 'Because I like a challenge, and they've become thin on the ground recently...'

The unspoken *until now* trumpeted loudly between them. She wanted to snap that she wasn't a recreational diversion for him to pass the time with. But wasn't that essentially what they'd agreed? A tryst while they were away from the condemning eyes of their families to dissipate this chemistry between them?

And, deep down, didn't going toe to toe with him make her senses sing?

Beware of the dangerous road you're taking...

'Be careful you don't go from boredom to being completely out of your depth,' she told him.

He threw back his head and laughed, and Amelie was struck dumb by the transformation of his face.

In an instant she was transported back to being a wide-eyed teenager, watching Atu Quayson charm every female within a square mile with his insanely gorgeous smile, feeling her heart crash about in her chest before swan-diving into her belly.

It made her literally hold her breath, and she felt almost mournful when it disappeared, like a spectacular mirage, always destined to be a wonderful but fleeting thing.

True enough, he sobered up quickly. 'I'd consider myself well-warned, but I doubt the caution is necessary.'

'Why not?'

The eyes that met hers were cool and jaded. 'Because I'm yet to meet a woman who under-promises and over-delivers. One who doesn't have a hidden agenda buried beneath false charm, superficial beauty or overblown emotions.'

For some reason his answer twisted something inside her, making her clutch her glass tighter. 'How utterly appalling for you,' she said, gleeful when her words emerged as dryly as she'd intended them. 'So you've given up the search for your one true love?'

Instead of the sardonicism she'd expected, his face assumed a granite harshness that made her belly flip over.

'True love?' he echoed with searing bitterness. 'So-called true love killed my brother and your sister, Amelie. I'd be careful how you throw about those meaningless words. People pay for them not just with their own lives but with the scarred lives they leave behind.'

Her mouth gaped in shock as he surged to his feet and strode away from her without a backward glance.

CHAPTER SIX

ATU SLAMMED THE meeting compartment door with more force than necessary, seething more at himself than at the woman he'd marched away from.

Granted, he'd had a stronger reaction to Amelie's words than he'd expected. It had been years, after all, since anyone had dared to utter those two words in his presence.

Hell, before this week he'd resisted every effort to be drawn into conversation about the brother he'd held in such high regard and lost. Just as he'd resisted discussing the reasons behind Fiifi's erratic behaviour just before his death until Amelie had brought it up on the beach.

True love... Romeo and Juliet...

He wasn't sure when he'd grown to despise those words with such vehement force.

Perhaps it had been when his older brother had announced to him—in confidence—that he intended to walk away from the family. To give it all up in the name of love.

Atu had pleaded with him to reconsider. Because even then he'd known that he wouldn't be considered an adequate replacement. That, should his brother leave, purportedly to pursue an acrimony-free life with Esi Hayford, the stark indifference he'd inspired in his father would be made more acute.

Or perhaps it was when he'd watched Fiifi make a fool over himself over a woman who, despite her clear feelings for his brother, had wanted him to jump through a thou-

sand hoops, playing games that had driven his brother insane with jealousy and rage, triggering the recklessness that
had eventually taken his life.

All in the name of *true love*…

Even before the weekend his brother and Amelie's sister had perished, he'd known that emotions were inconve-
niences to be placed at arm's length…further even, if one
could help it.

Worse still, they were a sharp tool wielded by the cruel.

Like his father.

Joseph Quayson was fond of publicly proclaiming to
love all his sons equally, but Atu had known it was a lie
long before he'd grown out of short trousers. Behind closed
doors, Atu and his younger brother, Ekow, had always been
made unequivocally aware that they were the second and
third acts to their brother's illustrious existence. Fiifi was
the chosen son and they were the spares, created to prop
up his pedestal.

As much as it had grated, even then Atu had chosen to
believe that if he toed the line some crumbs of affection
might drop his way. That his father would acknowledge and
perhaps even respect him as a rule-follower…someone he
could trust to be a solid second.

But the dearth of his father's regard and his own mounting disinclination to be anyone's second had gradually created fractures, scarring his relationship with his father long
before that fateful weekend and its aftermath, which had
started the pressure for him to step into his dead brother's
shoes.

And all that had been besides his father's indiscretions,
the clear evidence that his parents' union had been built on
lies and convenience for the sake of appearances.

His lips twisted.

True love didn't exist except in the minds of those who
wanted to make excuses for their outrageous behaviour.

It was why he'd vowed long before he'd reached adulthood not to encumber himself with relationships. Mutually

beneficial liaisons were enough for him. Or at least they'd been enough until they'd grown stale and left him jaded.

Wasn't it, therefore, the height of irony that he'd allowed himself to be talked into returning home because of...*emotions*?

His mother's tearful pleas for him to return. His father's stern demands from what doctors had cautioned was most likely his deathbed that he did not disgrace the family further by refusing to do the right thing. Even Ekow had weighed in, and the strain in his younger brother's voice had told him he was at breaking point.

Atu hadn't had the heart to correct his father when he'd played the emotional blackmail card and insisted that it was what his dead brother would've wanted. So he'd returned... despite the twisting in his gut as he questioned whether he'd done the right thing.

Pacing his plane's meeting area now, he let out a low, frustrated growl as the release of tension he'd experienced when the plane took off came crowding back. He strolled to one window, braced his hand above it and stared unseeing at a cluster of cumulus clouds before casting a glance at the door.

Of all the women in the world, Amelie Hayford had to be the one to burrow this deep beneath his skin, frustrating him, dredging up memories he didn't want to unearth and, yes, a passion the likes of which he'd never experienced.

He'd left the ball in her court.

But now he was glad he'd stated upfront that he would not be making it easy.

Because he needed to free himself of this *insanity*.

He needed to be free of every last Hayford, once and for all.

Slapping his hand on the polished surface above the window, he straightened, ignoring the acidic churning in his stomach that mocked his last thought.

One way or another he would conquer this fever. Perhaps

even dislodge this cloud of guilt hanging over him for not being there for Fiifi in his last hours.

And in so doing he would break this bewildering hold Amelie had on him.

The Q Cove Hotel was a dream.

It was almost as if Atu had reached inside her most treasured fantasy of the perfect resort and recreated it, brick by brick, in real life. It was a vision in white set on a flat quarter-mile pristine expanse along the Desaru Coast in the eastern corner of Malaysia.

The whole resort backed on to a verdant tropical jungle.

It was breathtaking—especially seen from the comfort of the sleek helicopter that had transported them from the airport in Kuala Lumpur. Compared to her resort, Q Cove was miles away in size and luxury.

'Everything you see here will work just as well back at your resort. And with the ocean on your doorstep, it'll thrive just as well, if not more,' he said.

But Amelie was only half listening, her thoughts occupied with the changes in him.

He'd emerged from the meeting area twenty minutes before they'd landed as if their terse exchange before he'd stormed off hadn't even happened.

Instead, he'd turned on the charm offensive.

She wasn't entirely sure how to take it. On the one hand, she felt a stark need to know what he'd meant by his statement. More importantly, *who* he'd meant. Because someone had sown the seeds of those beliefs in him. And somehow he'd indicted her sister in whatever was behind his storm of words.

She'd fought the urge to go after him on the plane, to demand an explanation. Instinct had warned her to stay away. Because wasn't there a grain of truth in what he'd said? As a child, she'd believed her mother loved her enough to sustain whatever pain or strife life threw at them. But what should've been undying love had withered away under the strain of grief.

Was that true familial love? Or had she lived with an illusion before the scales were pulled from her eyes? Was it love if it could fade so quickly?

In contrast, though, she knew Esi had loved Atu's brother. Granted, it had been a melodramatic kind of love, involving copious tears interspersed with bouts of delirium, making Amelie's heart swell in awe and alarm at the grandeur of her sister's love for the firstborn Quayson.

She'd suspected saying that to Atu wouldn't go down well, so she'd retreated to the bedroom suite and attempted to rest, only to be confronted with a whole set of niggles that had meant sleep was out of the question.

The bedroom had been just as tastefully and luxuriously appointed as the rest of the jet, but it had been impossible for her to relax knowing that at some point Atu had slept on this same bed, probably with a woman...

She'd jackknifed up in bed then, unsure whether to be disappointed or afraid at the direction of her thoughts as she'd hastily returned to her seat, her thoughts in even deeper turmoil.

She glanced at him now as the helicopter settled down on the designated helipad, reminding herself that the end goal for him in all of this was to get his hands on her family's property.

The rotor blades were still spinning when he stepped down and held out his hand.

Because the resort was on the coast, the rich salty tang of the ocean blended perfectly with the dense lushness of the jungle, evoking the sensation that she was breathing in nature itself.

'Welcome to Q Cove.'

She slid her hand into his, fully expecting—and receiving—a sizzle of electric heat at the point of contact. Alongside that, she already felt mounting trepidation. That moment on the jet might have passed for him, but now she knew where he stood on emotional entanglements, she couldn't dismiss the peculiar bubble of dismay inside her.

She pressed her lips together as a trio of staff approached them.

'Welcome back, Mr Quayson.' A man in his late thirties greeted them.

Atu nodded and introduced him with a brisk smile. 'My resort director, Irfan, and his assistants, Nur and Michelle. This is Amelie. She'll be staying with me at the villa while we're here.'

She exchanged greetings with them, even as her senses flared to full alert at Atu's words. When Irfan and his team waved them towards the battery-operated buggies that waited nearby, she glanced at Atu.

'I thought I'd be staying at the resort in a hotel room?'

He caught her wrist in a loose hold and directed her towards the first buggy. 'We didn't discuss your sleeping arrangements, but I should've mentioned that this resort is fully booked all year round. There's a seven-month waiting list.'

Her eyes widened. 'Seriously?'

One corner of his mouth lifted. 'Feel free to double-check with Irfan if you don't believe me.'

'So why is this villa unoccupied?'

'Because it's my personal property. No one stays there but me. And if you're worried that you'll find yourself in a clichéd one-bed situation, just so I can have my way with you, don't be.'

Why did that both irritate and disappoint her?

She shook her head. 'What's that supposed to mean?'

His head tilted arrogantly. 'You'll see.'

With an audience within earshot, she had no choice but to curb all her questions and take a seat in the buggy. Irfan joined them, while Michelle and Nur stayed to supervise the unloading of their luggage.

'Would you like a tour now or after you've rested, Miss Hayford?' Irfan asked.

As much as she was dying to explore everything she'd seen from the air up close, she was aware her eyes felt gritty and her skin a touch grimy. Travelling for almost eighteen hours, even in jaw-dropping luxury, didn't necessarily equate to restfulness—as she'd discovered first-hand.

Plus, she didn't think she could concentrate until she knew what Atu meant by her 'sleeping arrangements'.

She saw him slide her a glance just as she opened her mouth, and he answered before she could. 'The tour can wait until later, Irfan. I'm sure Miss Hayford would like to rest after we've had some refreshments.'

Irfan nodded deferentially. 'Of course, sir. I've arranged for a light meal to be delivered shortly. I've also put the staff on notice for any activities you would like to partake in.'

They were approaching a flat-roofed building with greenery peeking out from the top. Smartly dressed smiling staff moved with brisk efficiency, serving the few guests who milled about what appeared to be a sun-dappled reception area.

'Will there be anything else?' Irfan asked as he stepped out.

'That will be all for now, thank you.'

Amelie gazed about her with mounting interest. 'It's green everywhere,' she murmured, then realised she'd spoken aloud.

Atu nodded. 'Every guest suite was constructed either beneath a tree or with a living garden on its roof to encourage interaction with wildlife.'

Looking closer, she realised that the wood she'd thought was white from the helicopter was really a pale gold, almost matching the grains of golden sand on the beach.

She noticed that the suites grew larger and were set further apart the further they went. Then her breath caught as she spotted the structure Atu was heading towards.

The villa was magnificent.

Constructed between two large arching acacia trees, with half of its frontage wrapped in lush laburnum climbers, it blended into the forest effortlessly, and yet it owned its jaw-dropping presence.

Wide glass windows reflected the greenery and the pale wood cladding, and a wide stone-paved path connected straight down to the beach in one stunning flawless sequence of forest and beach that was simply breathtaking.

He stopped in front of a wide carved teak door, with a discreet gold plaque beside it that labelled it *Q Rainforest Suite*.

'My God, it's beautiful...' She didn't realise the soft, awed words had slipped out until he slanted her a steady glance.

'Yes. It is,' he responded simply.

He parked the buggy, stepped out and held out his hand to her.

Inside, the cool interior soothed her senses. Large, expensive tiles echoed with her footsteps, and tasteful local art provided punches of colour throughout.

Atu led her through to the living room and she stopped in awe. The walls were made entirely of glass, providing perfect staging for the rainforest that gave the villa its name.

He pressed a button and one section of the glass slid smoothly away.

The burst of birdsong was magical, accompanied occasionally by another sound she didn't immediately recognise.

'What's that?'

'We have a few families of silvered langur monkeys in the forest. If you're lucky, you might spot them while we're here.'

Slightly overcome by the sheer beauty of her surroundings, Amelie closed her eyes, lifting her face to bask in the dappled sunlight streaming in through the branches and leaves overhead.

She sensed his scrutiny and, almost compelled, opened her eyes to find his gaze fixed firmly on her.

Each room was as entrancing as the last, but it was the location of the bedroom he led her to that floored her. The glass-windowed theme had continued throughout, and the sight of the jade-tiled hot tub and adjoining small pool steps from the bedroom suite made her jaw drop. And in the middle of the pool was a smaller bed, complete with white fluffy pillows and white sheets.

It was a heavenly invitation to sleep under the stars serenaded by the sounds of nature.

The idea that she might recreate something equally enchanting at Saltpond made her yearn to blurt out that, *yes*, she would partner with him.

But then it wouldn't be a true partnership. He would be her boss. The one she answered to on a daily basis. He would be in her life for the foreseeable future... unless she chose to walk away.

Unless she let her family down...

But then hadn't she already done that in her mother's eyes?

'What's wrong?' he demanded, with an edge in his voice.

Again, a need to keep the peace made her shake her head. 'Nothing that won't work itself out eventually,' she stated archly.

He eyed her silently, then nodded.

The rest of their tour took in a state-of-the-art kitchen, a rooftop garden, another, larger swimming pool, and countless seats positioned perfectly around the villa from which to enjoy the bounteous nature all around.

The arrival of their refreshments was timed perfectly with the end of the tour. Amelie sank into an overstuffed seat in the living room and accepted a glass of fruit punch from the smiling staff member, who then turned to Atu.

'Sir, Irfan wants me to let you know that he can arrange for Assan to come by, if you want?'

For some reason his face tightened. 'No, that won't be necessary.'

She nodded and left, and Amelie glanced at him. 'Who's Assan?'

The frown didn't totally leave his face as he answered.

'He's a top masseur I poached from another resort eighteen months ago. He's in high demand in the resort…normally booked weeks in advance. But he makes time for me when I'm here.'

'And you don't want him to come because…?'

His gaze swept down for a few beats before lifting and spearing hers. 'If anyone's going to charm you with the wonders this place provides, it's going to be me.' He smiled drolly at her shocked expression. 'Does that make me sound primitive?'

'I… Yes,' she responded honestly.

He shrugged away the indictment. 'So be it.'

And that was the end of it.

Simply because she was unnerved and secretly thrilled by that raw statement, Amelie also chose to leave it alone.

They enjoyed their refreshments for a few minutes before she chanced another glance at him. His gaze was on the pool, and there was a curiously relaxed expression on his face. She'd sensed the tension leave his body as they took off from Accra, but this was something more. Something deeper.

It resembled the same sensation she felt when she'd had a particularly great day at her resort.

'This place means something to you,' she said.

His face remained serious, but he shrugged. 'It was the very first thing I built from the ground up on my own. I'm not ashamed to admit it's a source of pride.'

She stemmed the twinge of envy and took another sip of her drink. 'How long did all this take?'

'Two years of hard work.'

There was a tight tone in his voice that jangled her nerves. 'Just hard work?'

A bitter smile twitched at his lips. 'The challenge of striking out on my own while fighting my father's influence gave it an extra edge.'

Amelie tensed. It wasn't the first time he'd hinted at being at variance with his father. And certainly going against the domineering Joseph Quayson's wishes had partly contributed to his 'black sheep' label. But when it came right down to it, she'd always believed family and legacy came first for him. Was she wrong?

'He wasn't on board with you doing this?'

A tic throbbed at his temple, but he continued to gaze at a dragonfly flitting over the gently undulating water of the pool. 'If his not being "on board" with me relocating to the other side of the world meant throwing as many obstacles in my way as he could, then no. He wasn't.'

'But you did it anyway?'

Amelie realised she was leaning towards him, something inside her straining for his answer. She wasn't looking for validation so she could take the same route with her mother. Was she?

For the briefest moment Amelie caught the hint of bleakness in his eyes. An instant later it was gone.

'I'm the black sheep, remember?' His wry tone held a hint of bitterness.

'Yes, I remember. But some would say you took the negative connotations of that and made it into something better.'

She knew that not once in the midst of all his disagreements with his father had he brought his family name into disrepute.

Despite the shadows circling in his eyes, he lifted one brow sardonically. 'Is that admiration I hear in your voice?'

She shrugged, unwilling to admit that, yes, it was. And perhaps a little bit of envy. Because he'd done what she'd been unable to do—stepped out from beneath a sibling's imposingly large shadow to succeed in the face of formidable odds.

'Maybe your father felt it too. Maybe that's why he was against you leaving?' she said.

'Or maybe he just wanted me to be something I'm not,' he rasped.

'That sounds familiar,' she muttered, and then her stomach dropped when she realised she'd spoken out loud.

Circumspect eyes locked on hers. 'Your sister?'

This time her shrug was leaden, the earlier conversation with her mother echoing in her head. The urge to clam up, protect the vulnerable heart that still wanted her parent's affection and regard, burned fiercely. And yet she still found herself responding.

'Losing her was devastating for my parents. For me. But I never thought—' The lump in her throat stopped her.

Atu leaned forward. 'Never thought what?'

The demand was low-voiced...gentle, even.

She curled her fingers tighter around her glass. 'That it would devastate them so much they'd close themselves off to...everything else.'

'Not to everything else. To you. They acted like they didn't have another child. One who was living and breathing and required care and acknowledgement.'

The certainty in his voice said he knew what she meant. Perhaps even *felt* it. Had *lived* it.

For a charged span of time, neither of them spoke. Their powerful connection of empathy felt almost seismic. He was her enemy. They should have nothing in common. She shouldn't feel this swell of emotion for what he'd suffered. What they'd both suffered.

And yet...

'Have we actually discovered common ground on something?' she asked, with a laugh meant to alleviate the gravity of the realisation.

He tensed at her words, and a flash of bewilderment darted over his face before Amelie sensed his withdrawal.

'Maybe not entirely. My "black sheep" label has served me well, while you've done the opposite—attempting to fit into a mould for the sake of pleasing your mother.'

Fresh from empathising, she felt hurt prickle in her chest. Suspecting he was saying this just to distance himself from their shared experience didn't alleviate the feeling.

'So you want me to become a rebel?' she asked.

'The strongest steel is forged in the hottest flame,' he

replied cryptically, with a few more shadows darkening his eyes.

When he knocked back the rest of his drink and stood, she knew the subject was closed.

The late-afternoon sun lingered on his face, making her breath catch at the sheer perfection of his dark skin and the sensual lines of those lips she secretly yearned to savour again. The punch of hunger low in her belly made her avert her gaze before she gave herself away.

'Did you get much rest on the plane?' he asked.

The change of subject further threw her. 'Not as much as I'd have liked.'

'I'll leave you to rest, then. You'll find the senior staff's numbers next to the phone in your bedroom. If you need anything, call one of them.'

She looked up in surprise. 'You're leaving?'

'I have an engagement in Kuala Lumpur. I'm not sure how long it'll go on for. If I don't see you tonight, I'll see you at some point tomorrow.'

Her heart lurched with something cuttingly close to disappointment. What kind of appointment did he have? Was it with a woman? Despite declaring that he wanted her in his bed, he'd never assured her of exclusivity. He was an extremely eligible bachelor with a selection of drop-dead gorgeous women at his beck and call.

Mood dimmed, she set her cocktail down. 'Have a safe trip. I'm sure I'll be perfectly fine,' she replied crisply, despite the squeezing in her chest.

He frowned, as if that wasn't the answer he'd wanted to hear. Then, with a curt nod, he turned and walked away.

She stayed outside, wondering if the sun had dipped or if her plummeting mood was responsible for the sudden chill she felt.

CHAPTER SEVEN

ATU DIDN'T RETURN to the villa.

Amelie knew because she'd crashed just before sunset, with jet lag hitting her hard enough so she'd barely got through dinner and a shower before sliding gratefully between the sheets. Only to wake up just after one a.m.

She'd known she should attempt to regulate her sleep patterns, but she'd risen anyway, with a biting need driving her into walking through the villa.

She'd pulled herself up short when she'd stood on the threshold of what was evidently the master bedroom, where the impeccably made, patently un-slept-in bed had made that unsettling feeling in her midriff return full-force.

What the hell was wrong with her? Wandering around Atu Quayson's villa unnerved by the fact that she missed him?

The thought had sent her scurrying to bed, where she'd suffered restless sleep until the early hours.

Now she'd risen with a determination to do what she'd come here to do. Explore every facet of what had made the Q Cove Hotel elevate itself above being a mere resort. She might not have a rainforest to tempt guests to Saltpond, but she had the ocean, the culture and the personal touch.

Whether Atu intended to get involved or not shouldn't matter. In fact, he could stay in Kuala Lumpur for as long as he pleased.

After a dip in her pool, and a rinse-off under the rainforest shower in her suite, she placed a call to Irfan. The manager was there in minutes to escort her to breakfast before commencing an extensive tour of the grounds. He didn't volunteer Atu's whereabouts and she praised herself for not asking.

Still, she kicked herself when, a few minutes after she'd returned to the villa after a day spent exploring, her heart jumped when the phone on her bedside table rang.

'Hello. Did you miss me?'

His voice was a dark rasp that sent delicious unwanted shivers over her skin.

The sensation made her strike an offhand reply. 'Not at all. In fact, it's been a relief not to have you breathing down my neck.'

'And in amongst that relief did you enjoy yourself?'

She bit her lip. Answering *yes* would play into his hands. Answering *no* would be a lie. 'I need more than a day to make up my mind one way or another.'

'Of course you do. A word of caution, though. The careful approach doesn't win you any accolades.'

'What's that supposed to mean?'

'It means that every once in a while you need to be bold. Take what you want and to hell with everyone else.'

'Is that the way you operate?'

'Of course. Why else would I be so wildly successful?' he queried, with a devilish mockery which should have horrified her and yet aroused something in her that had gone dormant since his short absence.

The unnerving feeling escalated, making her shift in her chair. 'Was there a particular reason you called?'

He waited a beat, as if to let her pulse race faster for no other reason than waiting for him to speak. 'I called to let you know I'll be held up for another night.'

Amelie found herself biting her lip hard, with an unpleasant feeling dragging in her belly. Sternly reminding herself that what he did was none of her business didn't soothe her one iota.

'Amelie? Did you—?'

'I heard you. Like I said, you don't need to rush back on my account. Stay away as long as you like. Goodbye.'

She hung up before her voice got huskier. Before the sensation roiling in her stomach bled through into her voice.

There were three restaurants on the resort, one of them run by a Michelin-starred chef. There were numerous evening entertainments around the resort. She didn't have to stay in the villa on her own.

And yet she couldn't summon the interest to dress up and explore any of them.

Instead, she drummed up another weak jet-lag excuse, feeling a little guilty when Irfan commiserated and promised to send along her dinner.

Luckily, the feeling of unsettlement didn't follow her into sleep. She woke up rested and determined to put Atu out of her mind completely.

She donned her red-and-white-striped bikini, thought for a moment about taking a dip in her own pool, then decided a few laps in the bigger pool would set her up properly for the day ahead.

Her bare feet hardly made a sound as she walked through the villa, refusing even to glance towards Atu's as yet unslept-in suite.

At the edge of the pool, she paused to dip her toes in the water. The cool temperature was perfect, and she found herself smiling before catching herself. She wasn't supposed to enjoy herself like this. Was she?

Sure, at some point yesterday she'd accepted that if this partnership was with anyone else but a Quayson she would've been sorely tempted. But it was impossible. It would never work. Would it?

How would you know unless you try?

Her heart squeezed in recollection of her mother's accusation. But hadn't her late sister rebelled repeatedly and yet still been loved by her parents?

The mother she'd known as a child had been loving and

considerate. A powerhouse socialite renowned for her host-ess skills. Watching her mother effortlessly navigate char-ity galas and parties, expertly gliding through small talk, had shaped Amelie's own decision to become a hotelier. She'd dreamed of working alongside her sister and par-ents, expanding their small empire into something equal-ling the Quaysons'.

Losing her sister, then her father, had fractured that dream. But was it unthinkable that she and her mother could make it work if only her mother would come around?

She executed a perfect dive into the pool, hoping to si-lence the voice that urged her down a possibly rocky path.

Twenty minutes later she crawled lazily to the far side, resting her arms on the infinity edge and gazing at the waves leisurely lapping the shore thirty feet away.

When the tingling between her shoulder blades started, she assumed her muscles were simply reacting to the work-out. But then that unique awareness arrived, making her belly clench for an entirely different reason.

She whipped her head around, the air locking in her lungs at the sight of Atu, standing on the edge of the pool, wearing a pair of navy swimming trunks that nearly made her swallow her tongue.

He was like a virile male god, moulded from the rich clay of their shared motherland. From the tips of his dense black closely cropped hair to the soles of his bare feet, he was…beautiful. Flawless in a way that made every cell in her body rush to painful life. It was as if he'd taken the ox-ygen with him when he left and was arrogantly gifting her the vital joy of breathing again now he was back.

For the life of her, Amelie couldn't find the strength to be outraged. Because that emotion fizzing beneath her skin… It was pure delight.

'I… You're back,' she stated, then cringed at the breathy, inane statement.

Luckily, he didn't mock her for it. Instead, his gaze latched on her with vivid focus, making her aware of every bead of moisture clinging to her skin, the way her nipples pebbled beneath the water, the rush of heat between her thighs.

'I arrived late last night. You were already in bed.'

Was there a mild rebuke in there somewhere? She shook her head. Too many emotions were clashing against one another for her to decipher them properly.

'I was tired—and still a little jet-lagged,' she tagged on, in case he'd spoken to Irfan and knew of her excuse for staying indoors when she should have been socialising, making useful contacts for her resort.

He nodded, then turned to the lounge table a few feet away, drawing her attention to a wide, shallow tray piled high with breakfast delicacies. He picked it up and walked down the steps into the pool. When he was half submerged, he set the tray on the water and gently nudged it towards her.

Amelie barely glanced at the floating tray, her attention wholly absorbed in watching his smooth powerful strokes as he swam closer.

He arrived beside her, and his presence blocked out everything else but him.

'Do you feel better rested now?' he asked, and that low voice vibrated through her.

She swallowed. Her body's increasing tingling was mildly terrifying. 'Um…yes. Thanks.'

'I brought breakfast. Eat. You need your strength after that mammoth workout.'

Her gaze flitted to the glass walls of his bedroom. They were still opaque, not cleared by the remote control as she'd done hers, so she could enjoy her view of the rainforest. 'You were watching me?'

'It was difficult not to. You're a mesmerising swimmer.'

She shrugged, fighting off the treacherous thrill his compliment caused as he poured orange juice into two stout crystal glasses and held one out to her. She took a sip, welcoming the coolness, even though it did nothing to soothe her emotions.

Accepting a small plate of buttered toast from him, she ate a few mouthfuls. 'It was a matter of learning how to swim properly or be cowed into not learning at all.'

A frown appeared between his eyes. 'Who discouraged you?' he growled.

'No one in particular. But I was the youngest amongst our…the group, and sometimes my reluctance to get involved made your brothers and my male cousins impatient. I got my head dunked under the water a few too many times for my liking.'

Amelie noticed with mild surprise that the memory wasn't as bad as she'd imagined it would be. That, while the boys had been boisterous and even alarming back then, in hindsight it hadn't been so terrible. That a part of her wished she'd taken the time to enjoy those moments.

'So you took a bad situation and made it better?' he said, eyeing her with that unsettling intensity.

'There's no profound life lesson in there. I got fed up with swallowing chlorinated water and problem-solved by learning to be a strong swimmer. That's all.'

'I'm not sure what it says about me that I didn't notice.'

The words were murmured, almost as if he was questioning himself rather than her. But before she could read more into it, he slanted another glance at her.

'You never answered my question yesterday.'

She took her time to pour coffee, adding cream to hers and passing a black one to him. 'What question?'

He arched a brow at the coffee, and she realised she'd poured it the way he liked it. Her skin was just heating up with that bewildering faux pas when he replied, 'Did you miss me?'

The tight edge to the question should have irritated her. Instead, the fizzle beneath her skin intensified.

What the hell was wrong with her?

'I hardly think you need me to feed your male ego. Weren't your activities in Kuala Lumpur enough to scratch whatever itch you had?'

'Do I take it that waspish tone you took with me yesterday before hanging up was because you believe I was conducting more than just business in KL?'

'What you do and where you do it is none of my business, I'm sure.'

'Somehow I doubt that.'

'Excuse me?'

He took his time to pick up a tiny fork, spear a cube of melon and hold it to her lips. There was something almost decadent about being fed by him. Something she found irresistible.

Something she couldn't seem to keep fighting.

As she accepted and chewed the fruit, he replied, 'You're riled up...ready to cut me down with that beautiful tongue. Why? Because you believe I've been burning up another woman's sheets?'

'Have you?' she blurted out before she could stop herself. Then she held her breath, a large part of her terrified of his answer.

When had he drawn so close...so she needed to tilt her head to meet his gaze? How had she not noticed that his arms were now braced on either side of her waist in the pool, caging her in? That his gaze had grown all-consuming, sparking with a voracious hunger that echoed and pulsated low in her belly?

'As much as it disturbs me to admit it, I haven't been able to think about another woman besides you since you stormed back into my life.'

Her jaw sagged, and then her heart lurched, before banging so hard against her ribs she feared she would bruise. 'You... I...'

'It's almost gratifying to see you at a loss for words,' he said, lowering his head until they almost breathed the same air.

Every argument she'd had with herself thus far unspooled in her head, growing weaker as it was dashed against the force of her desires.

She'd wanted this man since she was a teenager. Since he'd given her a painfully insufficient taste of him and she'd been introduced to true unquenchable hunger. And while she was admitting truths to herself, she begrudgingly accepted that the high bar he'd set in her fevered dreams all those years ago had set a standard the handful of men she'd dated since had fallen short of.

He was the reason her relationships had been lacklustre.

And, yes, she was breaking sacred rules by colluding with the enemy. But right in this moment, with heat blazing from his eyes, he didn't feel like the enemy. He felt like a euphoric drug she simply had to consume.

So take it! Take it now or you'll regret it...

Her heart quaked but she boldly met his gaze. 'Don't be so pleased about me being at a loss for words. In fact, you should pray for the opposite.'

A tremor moved through him. Then he stilled. 'Why?'

'Because then I can tell you what I want.'

The inferno built in his eyes, threatening to consume her. But his iron control held him rigid, even as his nostrils flared.

'Tell me,' he growled.

'I want you.' The words emerged in a hushed burst, laying her needs bare.

The arms braced on the pool tiles bunched hard, but still he held himself at bay, as if he didn't trust himself to draw any closer. From his haggard demeanour, he was hanging on by a thread.

'Be explicit, Amelie. Just so we're both clear,' he grated.

The wave of need and feminine power sweeping through her made her want to list every act she wanted him to perform on her. But in the end expediency won out. Because, dear God, she'd waited long enough.

Eight years.

'Take me to bed. Make love to me.'

The moment the words were out of her mouth he captured her waist and swung her out of the pool. With lithe, jaw-dropping strength, he vaulted out and swept her up into his arms, marching with single-minded purpose into the villa and down the wide hallway that led to the master suite.

Amelie couldn't tear her gaze away from the square jaw and stark hunger on his face. He was breathtaking.

Beautiful.

And when he kicked his bedroom door shut and set her down beside his bed, with his fingers trailing down to link with her own for a few moments, she felt beautiful too. Truly wanted for the first time in a very long while.

Here, now, with his gaze raking over her face with such blatant need that an exhilarating thrill coursed through her body, she wasn't an afterthought or a reliable combatant to hold the line against an enemy.

She was Amelie Hayford—a woman with long-buried needs about to be fulfilled.

He reached behind her and slowly untied the strings of her bikini top, letting it drop without a care where it landed.

With ease that testified to his strength, he plucked her up again and placed her in the middle of the bed. Then he stood back.

Eyes squarely pinned on her, he trailed a finger over her cheek, along her jaw, then down her neck. She trembled when he lingered on the pulse beating there, then continued the sizzling path down between her breasts.

Her nipples furled into tight points, and it felt all the more maddening when he ignored them and caressed his way further south to her belly button before reversing direction.

This time when he reached her breasts he palmed one mound, then swallowed hard as she moaned.

'God. You're beautiful.'

'Atu...'

Lean, strong fingers hooked into her bikini bottoms, yanking them off in one smooth move.

Completely naked, Amelie felt like a decadent offering, lying there under the heat of his gaze. Heart slamming hard against her ribs, she started to reach for him, but he caught and pinned her arms above her head, leaning down to take her mouth in a consuming kiss.

Her moan was uninhibited. The thrill of his hands on her body was sending her straight into that sublime place where pleasure lingered, beckoning her into deeper bliss.

Her cry of protest when he pulled away a minute later made him smile. His gaze travelled over her, as if he was committing the curves and valleys of her body to memory.

Planting a knee on the bed, he lowered his face back to hers and took her mouth in another deep kiss. This time he didn't restrain her, and Amelie curled one hand over his nape, holding him to her as she parted her lips for him, savoured him hungrily.

Again, he ended the kiss far too soon, his tongue travelling down her neck, licking over her pulse before going lower.

She gasped as his hand palmed her breast again, toying with her nipple until her back arched off the bed. Until fevered sensation rippled like a restless tide over her.

And when his mouth dropped to capture one peak in his mouth, Amelie gave a tortured moan. Her fingers bit into his shoulder and she revelled in the answering shudder through his body. He tormented her for several minutes, then journeyed south, peppering kisses over her flesh.

'Let me see you,' he demanded gutturally. 'Show me what I crave.'

She gave a helpless moan as her thighs fell wide open. For a charged spell, he simply stared down at her core, his eyes burning flames of need. Then he passed the pads of his fingers over her damp flesh.

Pleasure rippled through, intensified when he seemed absorbed with watching her every reaction to his touch. 'So soft… So responsive…'

'Please…'

His nostrils flared as he shamelessly basked in his masculine prowess and the knowledge that she was putty in his hands.

The need to reciprocate, to tug him under her mercy as he was doing to her, made her surge upright. His eyes flashed at her, but she ignored the imperious command she was sure hovered on his lips and grasped him through his trunks.

He hissed, his body jerking against her hold. 'Amelie...' he warned hoarsely.

'Do you want me to stop?' she asked, more than a little awed by the power and thickness of him.

A muscle ticked in his jaw for a second or two. Then he firmly removed her hand from his rigid shaft. 'You'll get your chance later.'

With that, he pushed her firmly back onto the bed and dragged her thighs wider apart.

Casting one last searing look at her face, he lowered his head to her. His carnal kiss was bold, arrogant and sublime. There was no hesitancy in his sampling of her. His tongue owned her in broad strokes that had her head rolling back on the pillow.

'Oh...oh, God!'

Firm hands held her still as she trembled, sensation piling high with every lick, every kiss. She curled her fingers into his thick hair, torn between pushing him away so she wasn't wholly consumed by this insane fever and holding him closer to speed up the rush of ecstasy.

But Atu danced to his own tune, dragging her right to the brink, then retreating until she was sure she would go out of her mind.

Fierce brown eyes rose to lock with hers, eagerly absorbing every gasp, every breathless plea, while his tongue continued to wreck her.

'Oh, God...please!'

Redirecting his lips to that bundle of nerves, he thrust two fingers inside her.

Amelie's groan of pleasure bounced off the walls as she careened once more to the edge of bliss. But he'd driven her there countless times, and she was suddenly terrified he would leave her there. Her abdomen clenched and she held her breath, her gaze still locked with his.

'So strong. So stubborn. Give it up,' he growled hotly. 'Come for me.'

Her scream of release drowned out his grunt of satisfaction as she let go, her body contorting with searing bliss that ravaged every nerve ending, altering her from the inside out.

She felt his lips leave her core, trail up her body as she continued to shiver and burn. He dropped a branding kiss on her mouth before she felt him move away.

Through lust-drenched eyes she watched him shuck off his trunks. Then she shivered once more at the sight of his impressive shaft.

He reached into the bedside drawer and withdrew a foil packet. Donning the protection, he prowled back onto the bed.

'Do you know how long I've thought about this?' he rasped against her lips.

She squeezed her eyes shut, desperate to savour every moment. 'No, I don't.'

He gave a low, almost self-deprecating laugh. 'Yes, you do. We've both wanted this for far too long.'

He arranged her so that her back was flush against his heated front, then hooked an arm beneath one thigh. With his other hand, he caressed her nape in a sensual hold. Then, with his eyes on hers, Atu thrust hard inside her, burying himself to the hilt.

Amelie cried out at the tumult of sensation, at the fullness of him, the power and potency of his possession making her eyes roll. His answering groan as he withdrew and penetrated her once more started a chain reaction inside her she couldn't have held back if she'd tried.

She didn't even attempt it.

For so long she'd craved this. Now it was hers.

He was hers…for now.

She reached back and curled her hand over his nape,

holding on for dear life as sensation built and built, then tossed her over the edge into sheer bliss.

Atu held her, his fingers digging into her hip, as she shuddered through her climax. Then, just as she was catching her breath, he flipped her over, dragged her hips up until she was on all fours, then stroked back inside her.

Amelie suspected that he was branding her in a way that would remain with her for ever.

She clutched the sheets and held on for dear life as he sent her soaring once more. Words, time and space ceased to have meaning. Her body was a mere instrument which he used to show her how he could master her every sense.

And when her next release claimed her, he permitted her only a short respite before he flipped her over again, his sweat-slicked body bracing against hers as he kissed her long and deep, then drew back.

'Again, Amelie,' he ordered hoarsely.

And, sweet heaven help her, she was helpless to resist.

He'd stayed away as long as he could. At first he'd been righteously adamant that business justified his being away. But when the meetings were over and he still stayed away, Atu knew he was actively avoiding Amelie. Avoiding rekindling that moment of almost *intimate* common ground he'd felt discussing their shared experiences with their parents. The feeling that she *understood* him. Perhaps wouldn't judge him for the choices he'd made.

But the longer he'd stayed away, the more resentful he'd been for allowing *emotion* to keep him away. Especially when he'd promised himself emotion would never be the basis of his actions.

Finding himself outside her door late last night after a mad dash flight from Kuala Lumpur that his pilot was probably still disgruntled about, his urge to knock, to see her, had confirmed that something had shifted irreparably.

He couldn't stop thinking about Amelie Hayford. She was wedged firmly under his skin. And not even the phone calls he was avoiding from his brother and father—calls he knew he'd have to answer soon—were enough to dissuade him from taking what he wanted.

Taking her...

Last night he'd forced himself to retreat to his own room and buried himself in even more work until sleep had claimed him.

The sound of her diving into the pool this morning had roused him from sleep. He'd stood at his window, hypnotised by her smooth glide through the water. A nugget of a memory had sharpened, and he'd recalled that she'd been part of her swim team at her boarding school, winning more than a few awards.

He'd shaken his head when he'd realised he hadn't moved in twenty minutes. Something about this woman commanded his attention to the exclusion of all else.

With another bracing twist of memory, he'd accepted that perhaps he needed to cut his late brother some slack—because if this was even a sliver of what Fiifi had felt for the other Hayford sister...

He'd clenched his jaw.

No, he'd told himself. He was confusing lust with the overblown emotions triggered by his brother's melodramatic relationship with the older Hayford sister.

And when he'd changed into his swimming gear and ordered breakfast for them both, he'd told himself it was simply to progress the reason they were at this resort in the first place.

Now, as he thrust inside her, with the most sublime sensations buffeting him, even as a stark hunger clawed through him, making him wonder if he'd ever get enough of her, he knew that every reason except *this* had been a secondary pretext.

The feel of her...vibrant, passionate...her sultry voice moaning his name as bliss swept her away... It smashed the ennui he'd been living in to smithereens. But what was more disturbing—what he needed to get a handle on as quickly as possible—was this out-of-control feeling.

And what better way than by doing this? Drowning himself in her tight, supple body?

With a roar that seemed dragged from his very soul, he claimed his release, and felt another wave of bewilderment sweeping over him at the depth of his need. At the faint voice that whispered its doubt that his need of her might ever wane.

It will, he stressed to himself as he collapsed next to her, their bodies slick and their breath panting. As he pulled her close and revelled in the sexual aftershocks that shivered through her body. *It had to.*

Because he wanted her resort—perhaps now more than ever. For one thing, he abhorred the idea of Amelie falling into the clutches of some greedy corporate shark—and, yes, he intended to ignore *that* irony. And also, while he knew he'd meet resistance from his father, Amelie's passion about her resort would come in handy when he took over.

Is that all?

He ignored the taunting query and pulled her closer, unable to resist caressing her firm flesh. Then he tensed as her brown eyes darkened with a touch of wariness.

'What is it?' he asked.

She slicked her tongue over plump lips swollen from his kisses. 'This has happened so quickly...'

'On the contrary. I believe this was long overdue.'

She bit the corner of her lip, her wariness intensifying. 'I know we agreed to sex for the sake of...of getting a handle on this thing between us...'

He didn't feel the need to state that, while theirs was a chemistry unlike any other, he was disillusioned enough to know that despite what he'd felt a few minutes ago this too would pass. In a month from now, perhaps even in less time, he would be back in that jaded place, ennui once again his companion.

But for now he intended to enjoy the thrill of the chase.

Are you sure that's all it is?

He brushed away the irritating question that whispered at the back of his mind, scoffing at what else it might be.

She worried her lip again and his stomach tightened further.

'If you're about to pump the brakes, it's too late. That particular horse has bolted, Amelie.'

Her eyes sparked, and he wanted to smile through the unsettled sensations spiking through him. *Awuraze*, her spirit was intoxicating. One thing he was certain of was that, whatever time they had together, boredom wouldn't be their problem.

'I wasn't going to… I don't regret it,' she murmured.

Atu despised the magnitude of his relief, which threatened to evaporate almost immediately. 'But…?'

'But…for however long this lasts… I don't want anyone to know.'

It took a few moments for him to grasp her meaning. Then rebellion clenched hard in his gut. 'What?'

Her sweet chin lifted, her beautiful features gaining a resolute look that further hardened his insides. 'You heard me. I want strict discretion.'

He pushed back from her, a ragged disgruntlement building inside him as he realised she meant every word.

'I'm not some sleazy secret to be kept under wraps,' he growled.

He was Atu Quayson.

Powerful. Influential.

He'd been born with the proverbial silver spoon in his mouth, but he'd carved his own stratospheric path, thereby gaining choices few men were privileged to have. With a simple phone call he could have a dozen women ready to jump to do his bidding. Not the other way around.

But, perversely, knowing he had the power to grant her wish made him withhold it. Shedding his control now would only make him weak.

'I detest secrets,' he bit out, memories of keeping Fiifi's

intention to walk away from his family and the tragedy that had led to churning through him. Perhaps if he'd forced his brother to state his intentions openly, and if he hadn't been so wrapped up in his own dejection, Fiifi would still be alive. 'Especially unnecessary ones. If you're with me, we own our affair.'

The flash of understanding in her eyes came and went far too quickly, but he felt it to his core. Just as he felt the flicker of misgiving that replaced it.

He tilted her face to his, registering her smooth, supple skin. 'Tell me you want me,' he commanded, a need to hear her confirmation swelling inside him.

She licked her lower lip, making him stifle a groan as he waited impatiently.

'I want you,' she confirmed huskily.

'Then have me. Without reservations.'

'Wouldn't that make me a blind fool?'

'It would make you a woman who sees what she wants and takes it.' His hand slid down her neck to the pulse racing at her throat, then lower, over one breast to her pounding heart. 'The woman underneath this, who is straining to loosen the reins of obligation holding her back.'

She made a small keening sound filled with need and he couldn't help himself. He pressed his advantage. Because that was the sort of man he was. Wasn't that one of the many accusations his father had levelled at him? As if the same single-mindedness his parent now demanded he use to cement the Quayson legacy was a flaw.

He moulded her breast, flicking his thumb over her erect nipple. She gasped against his lips and, devil take him, he needed her to come apart. Needed to make her feel the same fever that hadn't abated one iota from his blood.

Rising from the bed, he disposed of the condom, then swept her up once more. A few steps and they were at his plunge pool. He walked them through the warm water, then deposited her on the wide divan bed set on the pedestal in the middle of the pool.

Dappled sunlight bathed them as her fevered eyes met his, her lips slightly parted as she panted softly. 'Atu... What...?'

'I haven't come anywhere close to having my fill of you. Don't deny me.'

Hearing the hint of a plea in his own words further perplexed him. Where the hell was his famed control?

For a suspended heartbeat, she held her breath. Then it whooshed out softly as she shook her head. And when he positioned himself lower on the bed, her eyes widened into shocked orbs.

'Again?'

He laughed under his breath. 'Oh, yes, sweet Amelie,' he rasped, firmly pushing her back until she was propped up on her elbows as he boldly parted her thighs.

Atu couldn't take his eyes off her. She glowed under the Malaysian sun, with fat drops of water he wanted to lick off clinging to her smooth skin. But her intoxicating scent was calling to him, and he was helpless to resist.

His breath threatened to strangle him as he trailed kisses over her inner thighs and over the perfectly groomed trail of curls framing her feminine core. With a low, hungry growl, he slicked his tongue over her.

Her sweet cry was music to his ears. Yes, he wanted her as driven and helpless as he felt—wanted her to be mindless with only thoughts of him.

So he parted her wider, savoured and feasted until her head rolled back on her shoulders. Until her breaths panted from her and his name punctuated her husky moans.

Only then did he centre his attention on her clitoris, swirling his tongue expertly over the swollen bundle of nerves until she cried out sharply.

Atu held her until her breathing quieted. When he tugged her into his arms, he sensed her confusion.

'Don't you...? Aren't you...?'

Her gaze darted from his in a surprisingly coy way that gave a hint of her relative innocence. And why the hell did *that* reignite a primitive blaze inside him?

Before temptation overtook him, he rose from the bed. He'd wanted to remind her of how combustible they were together, and he'd done that. Now he needed to wrestle back some control before his foundations were breached irreparably.

'I need to return a few calls before the business day ends in Ghana.'

The blatant desire in her eyes as her gaze drifted over him threw a thin balm over the sensations roiling inside him. But as he walked away, he suspected that little victory might mean nothing unless he succeeded in keeping his fast-dwindling control...

Amelie watched Atu walk away with her heart lodged firmly in her throat. She wasn't sure which stunned her more—the sublime sex Atu had just gifted her or the fact that it had left her needing him more... Even now, as her body throbbed in the aftermath, her senses still awash with her release, she craved him again.

She dragged the sheet over her chest, pleased he hadn't stuck around to witness how totally swept away she'd been by the act, how completely she'd immersed herself in the experience of being possessed by him. The man she'd secretly crushed on since her teenage years.

That dismaying feeling was why she'd blurted out the need for discretion. It had stemmed entirely from the compelling need to do the opposite. To throw caution to the wind and claim him, if only temporarily.

To desire, regardless of the consequences, the way her sister had.

As she sank back onto the bed, another thought struck her. Atu had only asked how she was enjoying his resort since his return. He hadn't applied the intense pressure she'd expected. It was almost as if he was content to step back and let the magic of Q Cove work itself into her consciousness.

Was she wrong about him? Or was it a calculated exercise in patience meant to lower her defences?

Her mind drifted back to what had happened minutes ago. He'd gifted her sublime pleasure and, despite his blatant need, he'd walked away.

Against her will, something softened inside her, which then opened the door to possibilities she'd convinced herself were forbidden to her.

An association with a Quayson.

Perhaps even a chance that this thing between them didn't have to end so soon.

Her heart shuddered as she rose from the bed, quickly washed off in the pool, and then, wrapped in a bathrobe, returned to her suite.

Was it even possible? Or was she letting herself be swayed by his words…letting the freedom of being away from responsibility prompt her into dreams that had no hope of becoming reality?

Dressed in capri trousers and a flowery top, she emerged half an hour later to find Atu in the living room, looking out at the pool. Suddenly self-conscious, Amelie averted her gaze. She would probably never look at another swimming pool without recalling the intensely sexual moments she'd experienced today.

But it wasn't as easy to avert her gaze from *him*.

As if sensing her scrutiny, his head whipped towards her, his gaze charting her body the way she'd done with his. 'Good, you're dressed.'

She nodded. 'Where are we going?'

His lips twitched. 'No need to look so wary, Amelie. It will be enjoyable.'

She pressed her lips together, fighting the urge to blurt out the confusing questions she was grappling with. To seek some sort of assurance that all this wouldn't end up in more heartache for her.

But how could she without sounding the opposite of the strong, capable woman she'd insisted she was? Hadn't Atu himself declared how disillusioned he was with women who displayed overblown emotions? Seeking emotional assurances from him a mere hour after they'd made love was as good as inviting him to pigeonhole her.

His eyes narrowed, tension zipping the space between them. 'Amelie?'

She suppressed the ripples of agitation and smiled. 'I'm ready.'

For a long moment he stared at her, then nodded. 'Let's go, then.'

A gleaming top-of-the-range four-by-four waited for them at Reception. They drove into the rainforest, where he produced two pairs of binoculars and introduced her to the thrills of wildlife spotting. Dusky leaf monkeys, oriental pied hornbills and even a rare eagle dazzled her senses. Time passed in a colourful blur of heady experiences, and before she knew it, they stood beneath the canopy of soaring trees.

Amelie glanced nervously at the long ropes dangling from them and the geared-up attendants nearby. 'I know I picked abseiling as one of the activities, but it may have been a mistake.'

A sober look settled over his face. 'Maybe it was. But are you going to pass up the chance to view reality from a different perspective?'

Something clenched inside her. He wasn't referring to just abseiling. But suddenly, when she would have challenged him before, trepidation held her back. Because the gathering certainty that she *did* want to look at life from a different lens wouldn't leave her.

It was a relief to throw herself into the exhilarating but mildly terrifying abseil from the top of the meranti trees, leaving her muddled thoughts far below. But when they reached the bottom, and Atu put his arm around her waist and drew her close, every apprehensive sensation came rushing back.

They still lingered as she dressed for dinner several hours later.

Her rich purple and green *dashiki* dress moulded her

body from chest to hip, before lightly flaring to her ankles, and the spaghetti straps ensured she kept cool in the humid temperature. She'd rolled up a matching scarf into a headdress, before securing jade-green chandelier earrings.

A spritz of her favourite perfume, a quick glide of dark plum lip gloss before stepping into thin-strapped heels, and she was done.

Atu was stepping out of his own suite as she left hers.

He froze at the sight of her, his fierce scrutiny making her aware of every inch of exposed flesh.

'Ahwofe dua,' he announced huskily. 'You look intoxicating.'

Ahwofe dua—loosely translated as beauty tree. She felt her face heat in a blush. Then her whole body followed suit as he smiled and every cell in her body reacted to the drop-dead effect of his handsomeness.

'Thank you,' she murmured around a suddenly clogged throat.

His heated gaze stayed on her for a few more beats. 'Come,' he instructed, holding out his arm to her. 'Our culinary adventure awaits.'

They took a buggy, leisurely winding through paved stone paths bordered with miniature palms and wide-leafed plants that she brushed her fingers through as they passed. The air was perfumed with the scent of exotic flowers, reminding her of her own lovingly tended shrubbery back at her own resort.

They pulled up at the base of a large acacia tree, and Amelie's jaw dropped as she lifted her gaze.

The restaurant was laid out across three large trees, intricately linked with platforms and walkways and illuminated with miniature lanterns strung together and woven through the trees.

He led her up a spiral staircase built into the trunk of the tree. Across the wooden gangway, their table was set on the middle platform, pristine flatware gleaming on a white tablecloth and a view of the setting sun on the ocean creating yet another magnificent scene.

Once the waiter had uncorked and poured vintage white wine, and the master chef had personally delivered their freshly prepared tempura and sushi, Atu eyed her over the rim of his glass.

'Are you going to finally admit that you like my resort?'

She bit her lip, then nodded. 'Yes. It's beautiful.'

The expected smugness didn't arrive. Instead, he nodded solemnly, his gaze lingering over his creation.

'Why Malaysia?' she prodded, after they'd eaten a few bites.

A touch of cynicism twisted his lips, but his gaze stayed on the beach a moment longer before he replied. 'It was nothing profound. I packed a bag, boarded my jet and instructed my pilot to take me wherever he chose. He's half-Malaysian. He brought me to his home. I hired a jeep, drove all over for a month and ended up here. The possibility of what this place could be took hold. Delivered the purpose I needed.'

She swallowed the question that attempted to spill free, but it rose again in the next breath. 'What made you pack a bag? Why did you leave Ghana?'

The clenched fingers on his glass and the downward sweep of his gaze said he wasn't in the mood to answer. But she curbed the urge to switch to safer subjects. She'd shared her body with this man. Perhaps she was foolish to allow a sliver of emotion to sneak into every intoxicating sensation he evoked in her, but she couldn't halt the need sweeping through her. The urge to delve beneath his surface.

After an age staring into the light golden contents of his glass, he raised his head. 'I found that I didn't want to step into the still-warm shoes of my recently deceased brother.'

She winced, her heart squeezing for him, her own fingers tightening around her wine glass.

'Not after being assured over and over again that I was second-best,' he added.

Had things really been that bad?

'It wasn't a secret that you butted heads with your father from time to time, but he was always boasting about your accomplishments. You and Ekow's—not just Fiifi's.'

A chilled look swept over his face. 'He was very skilled in projecting the exact image he wanted. It didn't suit him to announce that he favoured one son over the others. My mother, of course, went along with whatever he decreed. Including insisting that I assume every role that had been laid out for the heir apparent after they lost their precious son.'

'You're not their firstborn, but was taking on the mantle so bad?' she dared, then watched his eyes freeze over completely.

'You mean like you did?' he queried in a cool voice. A voice unlike that of the lover who'd lavished her with sublime passion this morning.

Despite his coolness, she didn't shy away from answering. Because it was what she'd done. And, despite her mother's censure, she believed she'd done a good job. 'Yes.'

But it wasn't enough. It might never be...

She suppressed a dart of desolation as he answered.

'Yes. It turned out I wasn't very adept at playing the diplomat, you see. I had strong opinions, which I expressed freely and frequently.'

Amelie took a bolstering gulp of wine, memory flitting through her brain. 'Fiifi was strong-willed too, but he was also the type to—'

'Pretend to bend to accommodate his heritage and destiny. It was his talent. While I was deemed rigid. *Unaccommodating.*'

She peered closer at him, the urge to know him digging deeper, despite the beginnings of tension arrowing across the table at her. 'Pretend? What does that mean?'

'It means he was better at playing the heir than I could ever have been. Until he decided to abandon the game altogether.'

Despite the chilling bitterness in his voice, she felt his pain. Wanted to wrap her arms around him. She resisted.

'I can't tell whether you liked him or loathed him for not being alive.'

An almost haunted look wove through the chill. 'He allowed himself to be led astray by lofty ideas and emotions. Saying I would give anything to have him back won't change anything, but I regret not acting sooner to convince him that his so-called love was nothing but wishful thinking. I regret not having the chance to talk him out of it.'

Goosebumps prickled her arms, a chill sweeping over her at his words. 'You wanted the chance to talk him out of...falling in love?'

'You sound horrified,' he observed with stony accuracy. 'Why? It's the truth. You opened this can of worms, Amelie. I believe it's on you if you don't like its contents.'

CHAPTER EIGHT

AMELIE WASN'T SURE how the atmosphere had shifted so suddenly. But now the subject had exploded between them, there was no going back.

'What you said to me on the plane… Do you think Fiifi moulded himself into what my sister wanted? Is that why you said their relationship was a lie?'

He stiffened. Then the thunderous look in his eyes turned into resentment. 'It's my turn to regret this subject being brought up.'

'Why? I thought I was the one who was too timid to confront reality.'

His lips twisted, but no sign of humour lightened his face. 'Touché.'

She pressed her lips together and waited. And waited. 'So…?'

'I didn't say their relationship was a lie. But they believed themselves to be in love. And love is a lie.'

His utter conviction reached across the table and wrapped its merciless talons around her chest, crushing her with each breath. 'What?'

Eyes bleak with the certainty of his belief met hers. 'They had a chemical reaction to each other, which they falsely believed to be a grand cosmic event they were prepared to risk everything for. And to what end?'

'Because it was worth nurturing? Worth building a life on?'

'What life? One where they eventually tired of each other

and realised they were trapped? Or one where they brought children into the world only to play favourites because there wasn't enough *love* to go around?'

She set her glass down before she spilled her wine. 'You really think all relationships have a short shelf life?'

He shrugged. 'I've yet to be proved wrong so far.'

'What about your parents?'

His face tightened. 'Obligation. Duty. I don't have a problem with agreed unions that have mutually beneficial goals, provided both parties enter into it with their eyes wide open. What I have a problem with is basing a relationship on false promises and failing to nurture the children you bring into the world.'

With each pronouncement, she felt something wither inside her. 'How long have you felt like this?'

'What does it matter?'

She gave up any pretence of finishing her meal, her appetite gone. 'I simply want to know if this cynicism is reversible or whether you're a lost cause.'

The formidable and ruthless Atu Quayson was roused into life then, his narrow-eyed gaze piercing her where she sat. 'I'd advise you against any virtuous notions of changing my mind. You won't succeed.'

Somehow she managed to summon a small, self-assured smile, even as her insides churned. 'Are you sure? You've labelled me stubborn on countless occasions, if I recall.'

For a moment he seemed almost perturbed. Then his lips flattened. 'You're not the first to try. What makes you think you'll succeed where others have failed?'

The notion that other women had tried to change him sent acid flooding through her system. She pushed the sensation away, refusing to accommodate it when she was fighting for something that felt...vital.

'Because I'm me. The woman you want—perhaps only in this moment, according to you. But I'm also a Hayford. We have a connection. Perhaps a similar connection to the one your brother had with my sister. You have confessed that I drive you insane, after all.'

He shifted in his seat, as if her words had stirred his frozen soul. 'But, unlike her, you will not die. I forbid it.'

The utterly cavalier way in which he decreed it drew a bark of laughter from her. 'You do, do you?'

'Yes. I would prefer you stick around for a while.'

'Why?'

His eyes positively smouldered, branding and possessing her from across the table. 'Because now I've had you, I regret not doing so long before now. I don't intend to let you go until I've had my fill of you. And you're not allowed to take yourself out of my immediate sphere until I do.'

Electricity and need, affront and that roller-coaster sensation all became live wires within her, snaking and twisting and snapping until she didn't know whether she wanted to jump up and run away, or reach across the table and drag his arrogant head to her and kiss the living daylights out of him.

The effort it took to contain it had her bunching her fists in her lap, the remains of her meal forgotten as she stared at him. 'This…this is why you're called the black sheep, isn't it? You're not a rebel or a playboy or even a disruptor. You're simply utterly ruthless in what you want and to hell with everyone else. And your father didn't like that about you, did he? At least, not at first? He wanted you to be a team player. On a team he fully controlled. And you refused, didn't you?'

A grim smile snagged the corners of his lips for a nanosecond. 'Yes, I did. He lost his firstborn and decided his second would be the perfect replica. Only he didn't ask my permission, nor care that I wanted to be my own person. I didn't change for him. I don't intend to change for anyone else.'

He knocked back the last of his drink and set the glass firmly on the table. He was back to his true diabolical self.

But for a single moment in time she wondered if it was all true. Whether there wasn't a part of him…the part she'd

caught a glimpse of in bed this morning…that wasn't lay-
ering on this mantle of brutishness to protect himself from
the indifference shown him by his father?

One eyebrow slowly lifted, as if daring her to voice that
tiny misgiving.

*When someone shows you who they are, believe them
the first time.*

That memorable quote whispered through her head.

'Tell me something, Atu. When all of this is done…when
this chemistry wears itself out…will you go away and never
think of me again?'

Again, he started, fisting his hands on the table before he
consciously relaxed them. 'When all of this is done, unless
you change your mind about selling outright to me, you'll
retain a vested interest in your resort. That means our paths
will likely cross from time to time.'

She wanted to reply that she didn't mean professionally. But she already felt so raw and vulnerable. The parts
of her that continued to wish for *personal*, not business,
for *affection* instead of blueprints, were leaving her more
and more exposed.

A waiter approached and asked if they would like dessert. With her vanished appetite showing no signs of returning, Amelie shook her head.

Atu rose and helped her out of her chair. Casting her another piercing look, he held out his arm.

Still caught in this curious dance they seemed to be
doing, she stood and slipped her hand into the crook of
his elbow.

Their trip back to the villa was conducted in silence.

Her heels clicked as she walked into the hall. Then her
feet seemed to slow of their own accord. She heard him
come up behind her, pause a foot away. Heard him inhale
long and deep. Then his hands were cupping her shoulders.

'Join me for a nightcap?' It was part request, mostly
command.

Logic prompted her to say no, but she found herself nodding instead. He rubbed his hands up and down her bare arms once, then moved away.

She followed him into the living room, watching as he crossed over to the extensive liquor cabinet before her attention was drawn to the window.

Outside, the rainforest was settling for the night, trees swaying gently and the muted sounds of animals calling to each other providing soft background music.

She accepted the mystery drink he handed her. She tasted it, her eyes widening in surprise at the rich tartness and fizz that exploded on her tongue.

'Good?'

'Very. Thank you.'

He inclined his head, then crossed over to settle on the sofa. 'I met with my architects while I was in KL.'

'If you're going to push me about the resort—'

'I don't need to. Irfan has kept me informed about your in-depth tour of the place. You wouldn't be so interested if you weren't already invested. I also know you'll work your way through to saying yes to me when you're ready. But the new blueprints for your resort are almost completed.'

She tensed, several darts of hurt spiking through her. 'If you've already started the process without me, why are you bothering to tell me?'

His shoulder twitched in a shrug. There was not one iota of remorse for his actions on his face. 'I saw no point in wasting time.'

'I haven't said yes.'

Yet.

The word hovered between them. With every passing second, she was more convinced this was the only right way forward.

'We're not leaving just yet. Whatever changes you wish to make to the blueprints can be made. In the meantime, feel free to take your time about capitulating to me. I'll do my best to hold back my impatience.'

Her breath caught. 'Can you actually breathe up on that mountain of arrogance where you insist on dwelling?'

He sat back…no, *sprawled* back in his seat, his arms spreading out to rest on the top of the sofa, a fatuous smile on his face. She wanted to wipe it off.

'The air is perfectly fine up here. And so is the view. You should join me.'

A part of her hated that he was right.

Everything she'd discovered about Q Cove had made her fall in love with the place. She knew now why it was booked solid months in advance.

Another part of her hated that his complete and utter self-assurance was so sexy. So…*arousing*.

'I'm perfectly fine where I am, thank you,' she said, cringing when her voice emerged a tad too primly.

'Are you?' he invited, his body still relaxed, on display, effortlessly disrupting her breathing and her ability to form coherent thoughts. 'Then why do you stare at me with longing in your eyes?'

She gasped. 'I wasn't—'

With an impatient growl, he leaned forward and pressed his thumb to her lips, silencing her. Her heart leapt in her chest, and her outrage was nowhere to be found as he proceeded to explore the outline of her lips in a heated, leisurely fashion.

'There's nothing wrong with wanting, Amelie.'

She felt herself sway forward, then quickly caught herself. 'Good. Then you won't mind that I've taken Irfan's advice and booked Assan for tomorrow morning. So whatever plans you have will have to wait until I've experienced his sublime massage that everyone's recommending.'

He stiffened and his eyes flashed, right before he withdrew his touch.

She immediately wished it back.

'Is that so?'

'You don't sound very pleased about that…' She was poking a sleeping tiger. And yet she couldn't stop.

He shrugged, but she suspected he wasn't as carefree as he pretended.

Abruptly, his hand returned to her face, whispering a caress down her cheek. 'If that is what you wish for, then that's what you'll have.'

Her breath shuddered out of her when his caress continued down her neck to the juncture of her shoulder, down her arm to circle her wrist.

Slowly, keeping his eyes on hers, he lifted it to his mouth. The kiss he deposited on the inside of her wrist was slow, exploratory, as her pulse beat against his lips.

'If you're done with your nightcap, I'd very much like to pick up where I left off this morning,' he said thickly.

And because she now knew what making love with Atu entailed, knew that the purest strain of pleasure awaited her, she let herself melt into his arms, quietly reassuring herself that now she knew his true stance on entanglements she was well-armed against hurt.

Atu felt her ripple around him in her third release and knew he was about to be driven clean out of his mind. Yet he couldn't get enough of her.

Perhaps that should have been his first inkling that this thing with Amelie was different from any other liaison. Even while he was inside her he already dreaded when it would be over.

A novelty in itself, he mused darkly to himself several hours later, that he was suffering from separation anxiety, when he was usually the first to leave a woman's bed.

Beside him, the woman he'd taken repeatedly throughout the night slept soundly, one hand curled on his chest. Her sweet cries had filled his ears and topped up his satisfaction. Now daylight filtered through the trees of the rainforest, and he was caught in the rare position of being...*unsettled*.

Perhaps it had something to do with that question she'd asked him at dinner last night.

'When all of this is done, will you go away and never think of me again?'

She shifted beside him and he looked down into her beautiful face. Her lips were slightly parted, her breathing steady.

Would he miss her?

Why did he need to contemplate that question now? They had time. At the very least, time to indulge in more of this. And time to complete the project he was almost certain she would come on board with.

So why delve deeper into the emotions he'd sworn never to explore now?

He shifted, still a little dismayed that he'd let his guard down so spectacularly last night. Broached questions he should've left alone, reopening old wounds that should have healed by now but still festered just below the surface.

Perhaps he'd been raw from the phone call with his father when he'd left Amelie in bed that morning.

The old man's health might be failing at an alarming rate, with the heart disease he'd ignored for far too long putting him out of reach of effective medical intervention, but his bark still packed a punch.

While he knew that there was no way he could manipulate his second son into doing his bidding, his father still found a way to make his voice heard—as he had done repeatedly during their phone call.

His father's displeasure as to why progress had not yet been made on the Saltpond project had been evident. Atu's response that things would get done at his own pace had triggered the usual torrent of disagreement.

And, as usual, his mother had stepped in to make the peace, pretending not to take sides, but inevitably falling in with her husband's wishes.

He'd been more than relieved to end the call. Even more thankful that he was halfway around the world. Why had he delved back into the subject of his dysfunctional relationships when Amelie had asked last night? Especially when he rarely spoke of his relationship with his father?

Hell, he hadn't just answered her questions—he'd volunteered a torrent of personal, private details.

What the hell was wrong with him?

The question pinged around in his brain with no resolution. And when the answer was taken out of his hands by the movement of her body against his, he eagerly allowed the distraction.

His body roared into life, eager to explore this new and mind-melting avenue so he wouldn't have to think about his family with its tragic flaws and bitterness and indifference. An avenue where the only thing that existed was the surprisingly passionate generosity of a unique woman.

She opened her eyes and for a moment he saw sweet confusion flit over her face. Primitive pleasure fizzed through him at the coyness that washed over her face, and then a sweet smile curved her sensual lips.

'I could hear you thinking in my sleep. I wish you hadn't done it so loudly.'

He felt his lips curve in a smile, and for the first time he didn't mind the morning-after awkwardness that lingered only briefly before he put a stop to it all by bending down and taking her lips in a kiss that started off lightly but gathered strength, unravelling him as it heated up.

Half an hour later his senses were still reeling, and the state of confusion he was getting mired in had only worsened.

He glanced towards the bedroom she'd disappeared into after their shower together, fighting the urge to go to her when he was finished dressing.

Whatever this unsettling feeling was, it would dissipate with time.

They had history. A charged history that had always

meant this association wouldn't be as smooth as all his others. Nothing more.

And as for that voice that mocked him for his reluctance to dig deeper? He ignored it.

CHAPTER NINE

AMELIE'S HAND TIGHTENED on the phone, her mother's sorrow and fury rolling over her in waves that made her stomach clench in despair.

Perhaps she should have waited until her roller-coaster emotions had quieted. But they'd shown no signs of doing so after ten days spent in Atu's bed.

Sweet heaven, the feelings he'd dragged from her... Elation. Wonder. Yearning. Passion she wouldn't have believed she was capable of before that first night.

So what if threaded through those feelings was a quiet despair that Atu Quayson didn't believe in love? Hadn't she concurred with him that theirs was only a strong chemistry which would dissipate once they'd explored it? What did love have to do with it?

She shied away from the way her heart lurched at the seemingly innocuous question and continued to lurch with growing alarm every time she screamed in his arms. Every time his fingers lingered on her face, a look of faint bewilderment in his eyes as he watched her, then tumbled her into another mind-bending climax.

'I'd hoped you'd be done with this foolishness and be back home by now. Instead, you call with this news?' her mother demanded now, bringing Amelie tumbling back to earth and the reality that with morning always came the reminder that she still existed within the cyclone of a family feud.

'What I said before hasn't changed. We need to face reality.'

'But why does our reality have to involve *them*? Of all possible business partners, Amelie! You had to choose them?'

She didn't have the heart to say she hadn't *chosen* Atu's attention—that it had been the other way around. Then her mind flew back to last night and the hours that had followed. The sublime pleasure. The revelations of her own passion.

The things they'd done to each other!

It was a good thing she'd decided which way she was leaning with Atu's resort proposal while he was away in Kuala Lumpur, even though she hadn't yet informed him of her decision. Otherwise she would have had a hard time believing the transcendental sex hadn't swayed her.

She squeezed her eyes shut, blocking out the stunning view as she tried to refocus, tried to stem the pain as she reasoned with her mother. 'Isn't it better to deal with the devil you know?' she asked, echoing Atu's words.

'No, it's not,' her mother replied sharply. 'You're all I have left, Amelie. And I'm sad that you would break my heart this way.'

'Maa—' She flinched as the line went dead.

She told herself her mother needed time to come to terms with what was happening. That in this case the end would justify the means.

But Amelie couldn't stop the deep wave of despair that washed over her. Because even if she was making this decision with her head, and not her heart, she couldn't completely rule out the possibility that her heart was caught somewhere in the growing turmoil.

Atu stopped in her doorway, that feeling of protectiveness rising in him again when he caught the flash of pain in her eyes as she hung up.

'What's wrong?'

Her gaze veered from his and she tossed her phone onto the bed. He fought the urge to cross the room, pull her into his arms. One of many compulsive reactions that took him by constant surprise. It was almost as if his willpower had taken a permanent leave of absence around Amelie.

'I called home to check in with Maria. And to talk to my mother,' she replied, her voice subdued.

He didn't need a play-by-play to know who'd caused the anguish etched on her face. *He* still felt echoes of a similar emotion after his latest call with his father.

They hadn't discussed their family since the night he'd thrown the vault wide open. A part of him wanted to keep the vault shut on his own feelings, spurred him on to keep that condition in place. And yet he couldn't stop himself from speaking.

'Change isn't always comfortable. If this is a family legacy she truly wants to nurture and build, then she needs to think about your wishes—not just what she wants. And not what your father and sister would have wanted.'

She flinched and he felt a flash of guilt. But he stood resolute. For some reason getting her onside had now become *vital*. Her passion, her dedication—hell, even her stubbornness—were traits he found admirable.

And not just in the boardroom.

Discovering Amelie was passionate in every area of her life only fed the ravening hunger inside him.

'You want me to go to war with my own mother?' she asked.

He wasn't aware he'd moved until the scent of her perfume teased his nostrils. Until the sweet bow of her lips was only a few tempting inches away.

'I want you to fight for what you want.'

'And if I lose?'

Her voice trembled and he experienced that flash of guilt again. But this time a stronger wave of protectiveness rushed in along with it.

He clenched his gut against letting that sensation linger. Those were dangerous, life-altering emotions, similar to those his brother had felt before everything had turned to ash. He needed to leave emotion out of it.

And yet weren't the emotions Amelie expressed so fervently the very thing that drew him like a moth to a flame?

And how did that work out for the moth?

He suppressed a grim smile at the dark reminder.

'If you lose, then you'll know one way or the other, instead of merely existing in a half-life.'

She inhaled sharply, the shards of pain she tried so valiantly to hide darting all over her beautiful face. 'You think I've been living a half-life?'

'I think you have reserves of potential you're holding yourself back from exploring,' he answered.

'So you're the black sheep and I'm the forgotten daughter who can't get anything right?'

Fury rumbled through him. 'Did she say that to you?'

'Until today she's tolerated my running of the resort. Losing my father so soon after my sister… She hasn't coped very well.'

'You mean she expects you to be the perfect daughter but has abandoned any pretence of being a parent?' His indictment came out harsher than he'd meant it, but he didn't take back the words.

Again, she gave a pitiful shrug. 'Just now…she said I'd broken her heart.'

He clenched his teeth. Then, unable to resist, he tilted her face up to his. 'Put that out of your mind, Amelie. Live your life. If the path you choose causes her heartache, then you'll just have to reconcile yourself with it. We all have to live with our choices. Don't bury yourself in her needs.'

It struck him hard then that the resort was the last thing on his mind. He wanted her to thrive, full stop. The thought of Amelie being diminished in any way troubled him.

Her eyes grew suspiciously wet and Atu wanted to kick himself. But the tears never came. She worried at her bottom lip with her teeth, making him groan inwardly. Then she squared her shoulders and nodded.

He wasn't exactly sure why her bravery sent a dart of pleasure through him, nor was he certain why ensuring she wasn't sad felt so important. Perhaps he was simply weary of the heavy cloak of retribution he'd felt bound to bear.

Whatever…

'What about you?' she asked.

'What?'

'You just told me to live my life. What about you? Are you going to keep butting heads with your father for the rest of your life?'

He tensed, conflicted over whether or not to tell her that his father didn't have much time left, so that wouldn't be a problem for much longer. He was unprepared for the wave of despair that swept over him. Was he going to let another opportunity pass without clearing the air? Despite their volatile relationship, would he be able to live with himself?

'Atu?'

'He's sick,' he confessed gruffly. 'He likes to pretend he's invincible, but the doctors don't hold out much hope.'

She gasped, sympathy filling her eyes. 'What? How…? When?'

'A while. He ignored the doctors' advice about his heart. Now it's too late.'

Her throat moved in a swallow. 'I… For what it's worth, I'm sorry.'

It was worth a lot. Much more than he wanted to admit. At every turn she surprised him. Now with her generosity towards the man who was intent on decimating her family as a last act from his deathbed.

It was almost enough to provoke *emotions* in Atu. If he believed in them.

To alleviate the unnerving emptiness triggered by thoughts of his dying father, he stepped closer, tugged her into his arms and sealed his mouth to hers the way he'd been dying to do since he entered the room.

When he lifted his head, he was smugly pleased to see her desire-glazed eyes. He should have taken the win, but apparently the dam he'd breached wasn't enough, and he found himself wading further into that emotion pool.

'Any particular reason she accused you of breaking her heart?'

Her fan-shaped lashes swept down as she gathered herself. When she lifted her gaze, the shadows of pain had receded, replaced by the passionate determination that had drawn him since he'd first become aware of the little sister of the woman his brother had lost his head over.

'I told her I was thinking of partnering with you on the resort project.'

His heart leapt even while his eyes narrowed. 'You're *thinking*?'

'I didn't see the need to tell her that I'd already decided to say yes to you,' she murmured.

He allowed himself a smile that probably reeked of triumph. 'Good to hear. You'll find that I'm a worthwhile ally.'

They were officially working partners. And sexual partners for the time being. Both his expectations had finally been realised.

So why did he feel as if time was already slipping through his fingers?

Amelie followed the path down to the private beach attached to Atu's villa four days later, smiling at the maid who set a tray of cold drinks down and promptly made herself scarce.

Once she'd greenlit the project, they'd flown to Kuala Lumpur to meet with Atu's team. Now new blueprints were being drawn up, with a heavier emphasis on eco-lodges and greater sustainability.

She'd been reviewing the contracts when a maid had informed her that Mr Quayson required her presence on the beach, giving her the perfect excuse not to think about the way her heart continued to squeeze every time she recalled the harrowing conversation with her mother.

Her mother might never come around. But Amelie had to keep reminding herself that what she was doing was perpetuating a bigger legacy—not just for the small family she had left, but for her community. Perhaps for the children she might have one day.

That constant reminder was what kept her from sliding into despair over her mother's cutting disapproval.

Sipping her drink now, she approached a curtained cabana set up on a wide platform between two palm trees. Stepping inside, she stopped at the sight of Atu, leaning against a massage bed.

'Um…what's happening?'

He smiled, and her stomach performed a breath-snagging flip-flop.

'You wanted a massage. I'm here to deliver.'

'Is this why my appointment with Assan keeps getting mysteriously rescheduled?'

He shrugged. 'I can top what he offers. If not, he'll be made available to you at the very next opportunity.'

Her smile turned into a laugh. 'Competitive, much?'

He winked at her. 'Always.'

She found herself smiling, then bursting into laughter. His eyes widened fractionally, making her self-conscious. 'I think I might try Assan anyway, so I can compare it to you.'

Humour vanished from his face. 'I despise the thought of another man touching you—even professionally. If that makes me a primitive bastard, then so be it,' he said, without a hint of apology.

She was an independent forward-thinking woman. A strong feminist. Yet the growly possessiveness in his voice made her knees weak and heat dampen her core in a way that would have shocked her only a little while ago.

But hadn't all her previous notions when it came to living her life fallen by the wayside where Atu was involved?

Was this how her sister had felt about Fiifi? Had she been driven into taking drastic decisions, triggering the tragic events that had shattered their families?

He frowned. 'What's wrong?'

She shook her head. 'Nothing.'

He took her chin in his large, firm hand. 'Tell me,' he insisted.

'All the no-go areas we agreed not to touch on seem to be rushing at us.'

His eyes narrowed. 'Family again?'

She nodded. 'My sister. Your brother.'

Tension rippled through his jaw and his hand dropped from her chin. 'What about them?'

'Did you have any idea that things were so...*charged* between them?'

His bark of laughter was laced with bitterness. 'Everyone knew that your sister was driving Fiifi to insanity, Amelie.'

A plaintive inner voice demanded to know why she'd brought this up now. But she glared through her distress. 'Excuse me?'

'Don't pretend you don't know what I'm talking about.'

She'd heard the accusations enough times to know their families blamed each other for the deaths of their first-borns. Somehow she hadn't considered that Atu shared that sentiment.

She jumped from the massage table, her throat tight with prickling tears.

'Where do you think you're going?' he demanded.

'I don't think I can bear you to touch me right now.'

'Because you don't like hearing the truth?'

'The truth according to you. I have a different version of events. One where it was *your* brother who played games with *my* sister and drove her to act out of character.'

He folded his arms, his jaw rippling. 'Whatever was pushing them, they escalated a dangerous situation by driving drunk and then crashing. Perhaps we should leave that particular episode where it belongs.'

'But how can we? Isn't the past that lies between us the reason you've dragged me across the world?'

Something gleamed at the back of his eyes—perhaps a dart of hurt at her indictment. Her heart twanged uncomfortably, but before she could speak, he let out a heavy sigh.

'Fiifi was used to getting what he wanted when he wanted. He'd never known true denial. Everything he wished for, he got.'

'Until he met my sister?' Amelie knew how long Fiifi had pursued Esi before she'd even agreed to go out with him.

Atu shrugged. 'She was a challenge, according to him.'

She bristled at the statement. 'One he had to conquer by any means?'

A shroud of pain drifted over his face. Then his features hardened. 'I'd like to think neither of them wanted that eventual outcome.'

'But he pushed and he pushed, until...'

Atu's eyes narrowed. 'If you're suggesting it's a Quayson trait, you're wrong.'

'Why? Because love isn't a characteristic of the Quaysons, as you claim?' She shook her head. 'Whether you want to admit it or not, *passion* and *love* drove them. Granted, it wasn't neat and clinical, like you think relationships should be.'

His jaw gritted. 'This isn't about how I feel—'

'For once, you're right. This is about *them*. I think it's time we admit that whether or not my sister was driving your brother to distraction, or whether or not she was giving him a hard time because she didn't have his attention when she demanded it, doesn't matter any more. They were adults—responsible for their actions. And, as tragic as those actions were, blaming them, or ourselves, won't change anything. We can't change the past.'

'Perhaps not—but we can use it to inform us.'

'Of what, exactly? That love doesn't exist?' Before he could respond, she pushed on. 'This from the man who returned to his father's bedside despite everything?'

He stiffened. 'What are you trying to say?'

'That you *feel*, Atu. You try to hide it, but you feel everything—perhaps even more than most.'

He stiffened even further. 'I wouldn't lay bets on that if I were you.'

'No? Then answer me this. Deep down, do you believe, had your brother lived, that you could've talked him out of the way he felt about my sister?'

His brows clamped together. Then his lips thinned. But in his eyes she saw a wavering—the first sign that Atu was uncertain about something.

She wasn't sure where she found the utter conviction to place her hand on his chest and lock eyes with him. 'You don't, do you? You can't prove to me that he didn't love her.'

'No, I can't. There was an intensity about what he felt for your sister…'

She fought a smile at the almost disgruntled admission, even while she felt a punch of sadness that he couldn't utter the word *love*. 'Okay. So we're going to let this go. Right here and now.'

Amelie could have sworn that swiftly behind the rebellion that blazed through his eyes came relief, but both emotions disappeared in seconds.

'Just like that?' he asked, but again, the heaviness from moments before had lightened. As if a burden had been lifted.

She shrugged, barely able to contain the punch of emotion reeling through her. She'd never stopped to think how her sister would have felt about this. Now she had, she knew Esi would never have wanted this enmity on her behalf. Not when she'd openly rebelled, choosing Fiifi despite their families' fierce disapproval.

'We have enough things to butt heads over. I'm choosing this not to be one of them.'

After an eternity, he nodded. 'Very well.'

Relief and a profound serenity swelled through her. But when she started to pull away, he held on. 'Where do you think you're going?'

'Oh… I thought…'

Her words trailed away as she saw heat slowly gathering in his eyes. 'The massage is still happening. Unless you want to butt heads about that?'

Answering heat collected low in her belly, and her fingers curled into his chest. 'No, I don't,' she said breathlessly.

'Take off your clothes,' he growled.

Amelie was thankful she didn't have to dwell on the enormous ghost they'd just laid to rest. Because if she did, then she might start to wonder whether there were other battles they could conquer. Other miracles they could create.

Sheer possibility made her hands tremble as she reached for the ties securing her sundress. It fell from her shoulders, leaving her in a white bikini.

Her breath caught when he turned to face her, subjecting her to a long, lingering scrutiny that ended with a tight look of hunger on his face.

After another age, his gaze dropped to her bikini top. 'That needs to come off too,' he said, his deep voice gravel-rough.

Unlike her session with him, this massage wasn't happening with any semblance of professionalism. Atu was touching her because he wanted to. And she was allowing it because the need to have his hands on her invalidated any common sense that should've dictated her actions.

She wanted this. Full stop.

'Now, Amelie...' he growled, implacable command in his eyes.

Her trembling hands rose to the back of her neck, pulled on the strings. She caught the cups before they fell free and then, heat suffusing her whole body, arranged herself on the table before discarding the top.

Behind her, he made a rough sound. She was too afraid to look. Too afraid to confront the depths of emotions rampaging through her.

Again unlike her, he didn't choose meditative stress-relief music. Instead, the strains of soulful jazz permeated the room, making her groan under her breath.

Was she surprised that he knew what that kind of music did to her? That some of her most memorable moments had involved dancing carefree to the music she loved?

She swallowed hard when the scent of hemp oil teased her nostrils. Unable to resist, she turned her head, watched him flick the top of a small bottle and dribble golden liquid into his palm. Still pinning her with his fierce gaze, he slowly rubbed his hands together, then slid them firmly over her shoulders.

She couldn't voice anything besides his name, because he intuited her every need. His firm hands paid exquisite attention to her fingers, palms and arms until she sighed with pleasure. Then he moved to her legs.

She hadn't wasted any time wondering if he would be a decent masseur. Atu was exceptional. And, just like everything else he did, its effect frightened her a little.

'Deep breaths, Amelie. No use fighting this. Let it go.'

She'd instinctively tensed at her thoughts, but somehow she doubted he was talking about the massage.

She was in this thing for the foreseeable future.

The most vital thing was not to hand over anything else that was precious to her.

Like her heart.

Even if she had a stomach-hollowing suspicion it might be too late…

Those moments in the cabana set the tone for their remaining days in Malaysia, and then continued into the next week when they flew to Malta.

Maria was holding the fort admirably back home, and until she signed on the dotted line, Amelie had decided to keep the news just to her. Her manager had been thrilled, and the offer from Atu of a bigger role in the new resort had brought even more enthusiasm.

Perhaps that was why Amelie had gone a little crazy and agreed to Atu's suggestion to extend their trip by another two weeks.

Staying away longer also meant she didn't have to face her mother just yet. Amelie hoped by the time she did she would also have the completed blueprints that she was sure would make the vision she'd chosen more palatable to her mother.

If Q Cove was a sublime sanctuary, nestled between the beach and the rainforest, Q Valletta was a perfect haven, poised above the culturally vibrant Mediterranean city. Atu's signature luxury was everywhere, and every guest's wish was a phone call or an attentive staff member away.

They'd spent an extra week in Malaysia because she hadn't been able to tear herself away from the resort. And although she was exhausted when they landed in Malta, on account of Atu's insatiable demands upon her body during the flight from Malaysia, she threw herself into exploring the hotel and the city the moment she was rested.

Their week passed in a blur of resort-planning, sightseeing and sublime sex—the kind she was sure skilled authors rhapsodised about.

Then, on their last day, her life began to unravel.

Although she didn't know it, it had started with an email from Maria the night before.

Call me when you have a minute, please?

She'd missed seeing it because they'd been at a VIP-only nightclub until the early hours, and then had fallen into bed after frenzied lovemaking against the wall on their return.

And this morning Amelie hadn't surfaced until gone ten a.m., only to rush to the bathroom with the kind of nausea that mocked her for overindulging in oysters the night before.

Now, leaving the bathroom, she let her mind idly tumble through dates and monthly cycles, only to freeze in the middle of the suite.

A whole week had passed since her period should have made an appearance!

She swayed as the connotations hit her—hard.

Luckily, Atu had risen earlier, to meet with his resort manager before they headed for the airport, so she was alone.

She stumbled back to bed, frantically grabbing her phone to double-check dates, dismissing the flashing email icon.

She felt a cold wave wash over her as her suspicions were confirmed.

Shocked, she couldn't stop every possible worst-case scenario from crashing through her head—the worst being her mother's voice, condemning her to eternity.

Then her spine stiffened, and her shaky hand drifted over her flat stomach.

These past few weeks had shown her how different things could be, hadn't they? *If* she was carrying the Quayson-Hayford heir, surely it wouldn't be the end of the world?

Sharp on the heels of that thought, she felt her spirits plummet.

Yes, it would be. Atu didn't believe in love. He believed in business arrangements, not arrangements of the heart. Whereas somewhere in the heady circus of the last month she'd lost her heart to her family's sworn enemy.

But he wasn't her enemy any longer.

He was the man she'd spun dreams around as a starry-eyed teenager, and he was the man she'd given her heart to as a self-aware woman.

But still... *A baby.*

The idea saturated her, and with it came a quiet awe which grew and grew and made her shattering heart swell with a different emotion. An emotion that affirmed to her that she would love this child with every fibre of her being. That she would not play favourites the way her parents and Atu's parents had done.

She'd forged a new beginning for herself in Malaysia. This would be another wonderful new beginning. A challenge she would rise to.

The urge to know for sure one way or the other grew too large to contain. They weren't due at the airport for another two hours. Rising, she threw on her clothes, grabbed her phone and headed for the door—abruptly stopping when the butler assigned to their suite appeared from the kitchen.

'May I help you with anything, madam?'

'Can you let Mr Quayson know I've stepped out for a few minutes? I'll be back shortly.'

He nodded, executing the courteous little bow she suspected was ingrained into every Quayson Group staff member.

The wild, foolish hope that this would be a new beginning for her family and Atu's family grew larger as she followed the concierge's directions to the pharmacy two streets away. Snatching a pregnancy test off the counter, she completed her purchase and was back in the suite within ten minutes.

In the bathroom, she stared at herself in the mirror, the notion that her life might be about to change yet again dousing her in chills.

You can do this.

Willing her fingers to stop shaking, she pulled out the test.

But no amount of reaffirming words could make her stay calm as the flashing word confirmed her new reality.

She was pregnant with Atu's child.

CHAPTER TEN

THE KNOCK ON the bathroom door made her jump.

'Amelie?'

She bit her lip, unsure whether her voice would hold if she tried to answer. Her heart ramming hard against her ribs, she stumbled to the door and turned the handle.

'Amelie, are you okay?' Atu's brow was knotted in concern, his gaze raking over her face. 'The butler says you haven't had breakfast yet. Is there something—?'

He froze, his gaze latching on the testing kit sitting on the counter before widening on her face.

She knew the exact moment the truth hit him. Heard his sharp inhalation as his gaze fixed on hers, searching wildly. And it was because she was staring directly at him, feverishly reading his expression the way he did to her when they were in bed, that she saw his rejection of the truth she'd just dropped into his lap.

When he compounded it by taking a stunned step backwards, everything inside her froze.

She wouldn't have thought it possible that her world could go from hopeful and awe-filled to desolate within three heartbeats. And yet she felt fiercely proud of herself as she straightened from wilting against the doorjamb and walked past him into the suite.

'You don't need to worry. I'm not about to hit you with a paternity suit. The child will be my responsibility alone.'

'Excuse me?' His voice was iceberg-cold.

'You heard me.' She glanced over her shoulder, even now attempting to see if she'd been mistaken, if a small part of him shared this quiet happiness moving inside her.

But no.

If anything, his features had grown more granite-like. He was an imposing pillar, his arms folded across his chest and rejection stamped into every inch of his being.

'I imagine men in your position are hit with demands like that every other week?' she said, attempting to infuse a casualness she didn't feel into her voice. It fell far short. 'I'm just saying you don't need to worry about anything like that with me.'

His eyes narrowed. 'Don't need to worry about…?' He shook his head as if he couldn't quite believe what was happening. 'Are you serious?'

She wanted to laugh, but suspected it would come out as a totally different, unwanted sound, so she clamped her mouth shut.

'You tell me you're pregnant… No, wait… I won't make the mistake of assuming. *Are* you pregnant with my child, Amelie?'

She whirled around then and felt something wither inside her. All along, part of her had known her stupid dreams were based on wishful thinking. Dear God, he couldn't have spelt it out any more plainly for her, and yet she'd still lost her heart to this man.

Clearly tired of waiting for her answer, he stalked into the bathroom and stood frozen, staring down at the stick proclaiming that he was about to become a father.

Was that a shudder going through him?

She couldn't look any more, so she turned, entered the dressing room and started packing her case.

Minutes passed in scalding silence. Then she heard him approach.

'When did you know?' he breathed, his voice barely a rumble.

'Does it matter?' That compulsion struck again, dragging her gaze to him. 'I promise I didn't trick you.'

His face darkened and a tic pulsed in his jaw. 'Don't put words in my mouth. I have a right to know when my child was conceived, do I not?'

This time she couldn't stop the laughter that seared her throat. 'I can't give you a time and date, Atu.'

He exhaled noisily, one hand dragging over his nape as he paced to where she stood. 'How do you feel?' he asked gruffly.

Something inside her—a hard knot she realised she had formed to protect her from her shattered dreams—threatened to dissolve, but she held tightly on to it. Asking after her health didn't mean he was ready to embrace fatherhood. He'd do the same for the butler, or any of his thousands of employees.

'I feel fine. I thought I was having a reaction to the oysters from last night, but it turns out…'

He held her gaze for a moment, his lips pursed, and then he nodded.

For a full minute they regarded each other in stony silence, the *joie de vivre* they'd basked in for the past month gone for ever.

Unable to stand it any longer, she turned and continued her packing.

'Leave that. Let the butler take care of it,' he instructed.

She shook her head. 'No. I'm done.'

A vice tightened around her heart as the words echoed in her head.

She wasn't the one who was done. The tension gripping his shoulders announced that *he* was done.

And over the next hour, as they were chauffeured to the airport, Amelie's worst fears came true. He'd barely said a word to her, his tablet his sole focus as they transferred from car to jet.

The moment they took off, he rose. 'If you're still feeling unwell, I suggest you go and lie down in the bedroom.'

Bitterness soured her mouth. 'So we're not going to talk about this?'

He shook his head. 'You're pregnant with my child. That's a definitive situation if ever there was one, isn't it?'

Desolation threatened to sweep over her again, but she summoned fury instead. 'You make me sound like a hopeless, inevitable cause.'

He slanted her a grim smile. 'No, Amelie. What you are is pregnant, and the consequences of that can only go one way.'

She gasped. 'If you think I'm going to get rid—'

'Let me stop you right there. You're carrying my heir. While the news may have come as a shock, know that I intend to claim my flesh and blood in the fullest possible sense.'

He was saying the words she yearned to hear. But every drawn line on his face, every ragged breath he took, the distance he'd placed between them, told her this was far from a happy outcome for him.

So she let his words drift over her, accepting that this was a moment for retreat and regrouping.

Because a Quayson was threatening to claim what was hers. *Again.*

She'd handed over her resort, her soul and, most foolishly, her heart.

Her baby was hers to keep. Because not for one moment would she subject it to the same brutal rejection she'd suffered.

She stood, not looking back as she made her way down the length of the plane to the bedroom suite. It was only after she'd shut and locked the door behind her that she collapsed into a heap on the bed.

For the next hour she let her emotions free, sobbing into the pillows until she was drained. Then, against her will, she fell asleep.

Once again Atu paced the confines of his plane's conference room—only this time, neither anger nor frustration dogged his steps.

There was shock—although, in hindsight, the passionate frenzy with which he and Amelie had explored each other these past few weeks should have given him a heads-up—and dread. Because he knew next to nothing about babies except that they were completely helpless and sponges for whatever emotion was focused on them.

And that drew the worst sentiment—a debilitating sense of *fear*. Yes, he, the all-powerful Quayson who hadn't hesitated to risk being disowned, despite his father's threats, who'd borne the shame and guilt of knowing he'd let his brother down without buckling, was terrified of this new challenge.

Because it was a sacred challenge.

What would his brother advise if he were alive?

Seize the moment?

Live your life?

Wasn't that what his brother had been trying to do? Hell, hadn't he shrugged and recommended Atu do the same if that was what he wanted, and to hell with the consequences? What was life worth if the only thing he'd let matter to him was striking the next deal?

Hadn't this past month shown him a stark difference from the life he'd led before Amelie? Those feelings of protectiveness and possessiveness…that need to be close to Amelie when logic dictated he pull back… They'd stubbornly lingered, right alongside their insane chemistry, which had grown and morphed until it seemed to have attained a life of its own.

A life that bore no signs of diminishing.

A life full of…*feelings*.

He passed a hand over his rough stubble and wasn't surprised to feel it trembling.

A baby. *His child*.

He'd meant it when he'd stated his intention to claim it. But then what? He was great at instructing a team of talented architects to draft blueprints for his masterpieces.

But the stark realisation that he had no one to rely on as a father but himself made his insides congeal.

Because what tools did he have to fashion the most important blueprint of all?

How could he claim his child when he had no idea how to be a good father?

Amelie awoke at a knock from one of the attendants, telling her they were about to land in Accra. Realising she'd slept through the whole flight stunned her. Straightening her clothes, she secured herself in the armchair next to the bed and fought the fresh tears that rose.

She'd left here over a month ago, confused and desolate at the turn of events in her life. Then, for a few exhilarating weeks, she'd believed her life could be turned around. Yet now here she was, even more devastated and desolate than before.

She'd dared to love. And she was about to lose.

When the plane drew to a halt, she rose from the armchair, freezing when Atu appeared in the doorway.

'Did you sleep?' His voice was still cool.

She nodded. Then her throat dried as his gaze drifted over her, lingering on her belly for several charged moments.

'Come. The car's waiting.'

She went to retrieve her handbag from the bedside table, then jolted as several pings sounded in the quiet cabin.

Grabbing her phone, she stared down at the screen.

Thirteen messages from Maria.

Aware of Atu waiting impatiently by the door, she shoved the phone back into her bag and slung it over her shoulder.

She would check them in the car.

The same sleek town car that had driven her from Saltpond waited on the tarmac. She barely registered the short drive from the airport to Atu's home in Quayson Hills. She tried not to be awed by the sense of her insignificance in the face of the power and might of a man who even had an exclusive city enclave named after him.

'I intend to claim my child in the fullest possible sense...'

Amelie straightened her spine. She'd vowed not to let herself be cowed by him. She wasn't about to start now.

'Why are we going to your house?'

'Because we need to talk.'

'Haven't we done that already?'

Piercing eyes met hers. 'Hardly. You announced you were pregnant with my child and then proceeded to shut me out. I, in turn, made a claim on it. Unless you've had a profound change of mind, I think we need to arrive at some compromise.'

Compromise.

Not exactly business-speak, but not warm and fuzzy either.

'Atu...'

'I called my private doctor from the plane. He can see us tomorrow, if that's acceptable to you?' he said gruffly.

That traitorous place inside her softened some more. Because she already loved this baby more than anything, she couldn't fault Atu for taking time out of his busy life to ensure its well-being. But as the driver pulled up the long driveway and stopped in front of a jaw-dropping mansion, the full impact of his words registered.

'Tomorrow morning? Does that mean you expect me to sleep here? With you?' She ignored the harsh tautening of his face, panic flaring inside her. 'Because—'

'I have a dozen guest rooms, Amelie. You can take your pick if the thought of sharing a bed with me appals you now,' he returned tightly.

He flung the door open before she could respond, then held out a hand to help her out.

Aware of the driver, and of the two members of his staff unloading their luggage, Amelie pursed her lips.

The interior of Atu's house was as stunning as the outside, but besides a vague perception of soaring ceilings, exquisite art and plush carpeting, she barely registered it. Her sole focus was the broad-shouldered man leading her into a vast living room.

Going to a well-appointed bar, he poured her a glass of mineral water, then a shot of whisky for himself.

She sat and he remained standing, his crystal glass clutched in one hand.

'I will be in this child's life. Full-time. I want that to be a given before we go any further.'

This child. Not her. The vice squeezed so tight around her heart she was stunned it could still beat.

'It's your turn to tell me what you want,' he said.

Despair shuddered through her, and the thudding of her heart was almost a dirge for every shattered hope.

'I want...' She shook her head. 'What I want is impossible for you. I know that now.'

His lips parted, as if he wanted to refute that, but his phone rang just then. He ignored it, his eyes fixed on her.

'Aren't you going to get that?' she asked.

He reached for his phone at the same time as his doorbell pealed, followed seconds later by urgent footsteps.

Amelie looked up in surprise as Ekow, Atu's younger brother, strode into the living room. The brothers were of equal height, and he bore the same unmistakable Quayson swagger, the same chiselled good looks. And right now the same tight-jawed expression Atu was wearing.

His gaze rested on her for a moment, his lack of surprise making her wonder if Atu had mentioned their affair. But then she recalled the dozens of guests who'd seen them together at her resort. By now everyone in the country knew they'd been together for the last few weeks.

'It's good to see you, Amelie.'

Since she wasn't sure if she believed him, she merely nodded.

He turned to his brother. 'I need to talk to you.'

Atu frowned. 'It'll have to wait. We're in the middle of...' His words trailed off as his brother shook his head.

'It can't. Dad's in hospital. His doctors think he's got pneumonia.'

The slash of pain and worry on Atu's face made her heart lurch. Those were real human emotions. So why didn't he feel any for her? Was she truly as lacking to everyone as her mother found her?

She wrapped her hands around the handbag in her lap to disguise their trembling and felt her phone vibrate again.

The brothers were speaking in low, urgent voices, so she rose, walked a few feet away and pressed the phone to her ear.

For several moments she couldn't quite make out what Maria was saying. When she did, every atom in her body froze.

'Amelie? What is it?'

She stared in horror at Atu, the enormity of her gullibility threatening to drown her. 'My God… This was all an elaborate plan, wasn't it?'

'What are you talking about?' he bit out.

'You tricked me into leaving the country so…so you could do this!'

His already thunderous brow darkened even further. 'I've no idea what you're talking about.'

'Pull the other one, Atu.'

A tic appeared at his temple. 'Please do me the courtesy of telling me what I've done before lobbing accusations at me.'

'You *know* what you've done, you bastard. You made sure I was on the other side of the world and then got your bank to buy up my business loan. You couldn't even be bothered to give me the partnership we agreed on, could you?' Her prickling eyes swung to his brother. 'I'm guessing you were in on this too? You don't seem surprised to see me here.'

Atu's jaw worked furiously. 'Amelie, don't…'

'Don't what? Call you the slimy bastard you truly are?'

'Watch your tongue,' he warned silkily.

She didn't care what audience they had. Hell, she wanted to scream at him from the top of her lungs. But she had a new life growing inside her—one that absolutely required she keep a level head.

'I'll fight you. Mark my words. I will fight you until I have no breath left.'

His face twisted.

Only yesterday she might have fooled herself into thinking that was a display of anguish. She knew better now. He had no feelings for her. And as she watched, he dragged himself back under furious control.

'Whatever you think I've done, you're wrong.'

'Save it, Atu. Your bank bought up my business loan two weeks ago. This morning your lawyers are calling it in. They've given me forty-eight hours to pay up or they'll take my resort. You were always going to go ahead with or without my agreement, weren't you?'

For a fraction of a second his face slackened with shock. Then he turned to his brother. Ekow's subtle shake of the head stopped whatever question he'd been about to ask.

He turned back to her. 'I need to go. But we're not done talking. I'll be back in a few hours. We can finish then.'

Amelie stepped forward, anger threatening to take over. 'Perhaps you didn't hear me? I want nothing to do with you. And I'm most definitely not staying here.' Her grip tightened on her phone. 'And, just so we're clear, our agreement is off. If you set foot in my resort, I'll call the authorities.'

His head went back as if he'd been struck. 'Are you sure you want to go down that road? After all, if what you're saying is true, then the resort will be mine in two days anyway.'

She wanted to cry. No doubt it was the pregnancy hormones at work. Instead, she clenched her jaw until the sensation receded. Then, to her eternal glee, she managed to summon a smile. 'It's mine until then. And you're not welcome there.'

Whirling around, she hurried out of the living room, just in time to see a maid rolling her suitcase towards the stairs.

'Wait!'

She hurried over to grab it just as Atu lunged forward, as if to stop her. At the last moment, he balled his fists.

'This isn't over, Amelie…' he breathed. 'Far from it.'

Her hand tightened around the handle of her suitcase and, desperately, she took a few more steps away from him.

He followed her outside, where the driver still stood beside the car. 'Take Miss Hayford wherever she wants to go.'

And because it was the quickest way to get away from the man who'd completely decimated her life, she slid back into the car, averting her gaze from him as he stood watching her being driven away.

The sight of his father, hooked up to half a dozen machines, reduced to a husk when just over a month ago, despite the fact he'd been ill, he had retained layers of his former power and vibrancy, shocked Atu to his core.

He remained frozen in the doorway of the private hospital suite until his mother looked up. 'Aren't you coming in?'

His father's thin lids flickered. Then he opened his eyes. 'Ah, the black sheep graces us with his presence…'

His mother rose, brushed a kiss on her husband's jaw before crossing over to do the same to Atu. 'I'll leave you two alone.'

'I sent you to do a job—not to succumb to the witchcraft of another Hayford temptress,' his father snarled the moment his mother shut the door behind her.

Fury spiked through him, but he kept it leashed. 'Do not call her that.'

'Why not? The other one led your brother astray!'

'She didn't. He loved her. And she loved him back.'

He was fairly sure he understood the emotion now. Because tonight he'd felt the same desperation Fiifi had displayed. That need to burn the world to the ground just for a chance to see Amelie smile at him again. To have her wrap her arms around his neck and stare up at him with those beautiful eyes.

But with another cruel Quayson act, he'd lost any chance with her. 'Why did you do it?' he asked.

His father didn't bother pretending ignorance. 'Because you'd gone soft. Because they need to pay for taking my son from me.'

'No, Dad. You did that all on your own.'

His father's lips twisted. 'So, what? You're going to give it all up for love too? Just like your brother?'

Astonishment froze his spine. 'You knew?'

'Of course I knew! Why do you think I wanted you around to talk some sense into him? But you couldn't even do that, could you?'

'Yes, I failed at that. But *you* failed us all. Don't worry— since you want me in charge so badly, I will take control of this family. But I'll do things differently. As of today, this campaign of retribution is over. Wherever he is, I know that's what Fiifi would want. I plan to earn his forgiveness by doing that, at least.'

Shock widened his father's eyes. Then fury replaced it. '*I* will never forgive you,' his father rasped, just as the machines started wailing.

It took a monumental effort for Atu to swallow the rock lodged in his throat. 'I know. And I can't change that. But, for what it's worth, I forgive *you*.'

CHAPTER ELEVEN

AMELIE LET HERSELF into her home two hours later, her eyes gritty with unshed tears and her insides numb. She'd hoped to feel a modicum of joy at being home, but even now every treacherous bone in her body wanted to be back with Atu—*before* she'd discovered the depth of his betrayal.

But she would wean herself of that, somehow. Just as she'd—

'You're home at last.'

She froze in the living room doorway, her gaze clashing with her mother's. Despite the lateness of the hour, her mother was fully dressed. And the gaze she fixed on Amelie was firm and direct.

Unable to stop herself, she let her hand fly to her flat belly. The belly she'd been caressing all through the journey from Accra. Despite the devastating unravelling of her hopes and dreams, she felt a fierce protectiveness and love for the child growing inside her. She had vowed that nothing and no one would stop her from being the best mother she could be. Not even her own mother.

'What are you doing up, Maa?' she asked, her heart firmly lodged in her throat. After what she'd been through with Atu, she couldn't take further censure or rejection. Couldn't even dredge up any hope for the acceptance her heart craved.

'You were supposed to be gone for only two weeks,' her mother said.

'I know.' She swallowed, and braced herself for what she needed to say. 'Maa, I need to tell you something...'

Priscilla Hayford nodded, a knowing light shifting away the traces of sorrow, replacing it with a glimpse of the mother Amelie had used to know. 'You love him, don't you? The Quayson boy?'

Amelie's chin quivered, seismic emotion shaking through her. 'Yes. Do...do you hate me?'

Shock filled her mother's eyes. '*Hate* you? Why would you think that?'

Her despondent shrug weighed a hundred tons. 'Because I'm a disappointment. Because I've betrayed our family. Because you said I was breaking your heart by going with him. You said—'

'Hush, child. No parent wants to be reminded of how they've failed their child. I'll have years to flay myself for that, believe me.'

Stunned, Amelie's mouth gaped. 'What?'

Her mother shook her head mournfully. 'When you didn't return two weeks ago, and Maria told me you'd extended your trip, I was terrified.'

'Maa—'

'No, it was the wake-up call I needed. The thought that I was losing you too... These past few weeks I've had nothing but time to think really hard about what I've done, Amelie. I've been forced to consider that maybe you didn't want to come back because there was nothing for you to come back for. Not even your mother—because I haven't been here for you, have I?'

Unable to lie, Amelie shook her head.

Her mother swallowed hard. 'Oh, my child. I'm so sorry.' Her voice broke as she held out her arms.

Amelie flew into them, greedily snatching at the affection she'd missed so terribly for most of her life. 'Oh, Maa.'

Her mother soothed her through her quiet sobs. 'I know I've been lost in grief. I know I've done a poor job of showing you how treasured you are. I promise I'll do better. Now, tell me what's happened.'

'Are you sure? It's not… I don't know if…'

Her mother drew back, her gaze drifting from the hand Amelie still splayed over her stomach to her face. 'Whatever it is, we'll get through it, child. You're home now, and I'm here for you. Now, tell me everything.'

With another sob spilling free, Amelie unburdened all the pain and devastation in her heart.

Atu walked along the beach, contemplating and discarding snippets of conversation as wave after wave of despair washed over him.

He'd checked into Amelie's resort last night, making sure his staff had booked him under a corporate name again. He'd taken her wishes seriously, even though technically his family bank owned the resort now.

Not that he planned on activating any of the repossession clauses.

He was the head of his family now, after all.

Another wave of despair passed over him, steeped in sorrow he doubted he would have felt only a few months ago.

Before her, he'd closed himself off, just so this level of pain wouldn't penetrate his armour. A few short weeks was all it had taken to crumble every brick of the foundations he'd erected around his heart.

Now he mourned his father, who'd passed away a week after their return, and he lived in a state of awed hope for the child he hoped to become a better father to than his own father had been to him.

But most important of all, his heart ached with longing for the woman he'd fallen hopelessly in love with.

The woman who had refused every contact from him until he'd been forced to retreat.

Misery shuddered through him, and he realised he'd stopped on the edge of the boundary separating Amelie's house from her resort.

A figure drifted towards him. His heart lurched, then somersaulted, before hammering hard.

The person drew closer and his spirits dropped.

It wasn't Amelie.

But the unmistakable figure of her mother was hard to miss. She came towards him, her eyes narrowing as recognition sparked in a face so similar to that of the woman he loved.

'Atu?'

Despite the dark emotions swirling inside him, he summoned a dry smile. 'Yes, Auntie.'

Her face softened for a fractional moment. 'What do you want?'

His gaze drifted past her and up to Amelie's window.

Before he could voice the longing burning in his soul, she spoke again. 'Perhaps I should ask what took you so long?'

His gaze flew back to her. 'Why? Is she...?'

'Alive? Barely. Eating?' She shrugged. 'Only for the sake of the child she carries. Is she wearing a look similar to the one on your face? Most definitely.'

The last was said with a bite of accusation that sent another shiver over him.

He hadn't seen or spoken to Amelie's mother in almost a decade, and yet beneath her shroud of grief he spotted in the older woman the formidable woman the daughter was turning out to be.

Several scenarios had unfolded in his brain of how he would conduct this meeting, but he hadn't factored in encountering the mother instead of the daughter.

Still, he thought grimly, he was fighting for his life. 'I want to see her,' he said.

'You can want all you like. My daughter does as she pleases.'

Was that a hint of pride in her voice? Before he could be certain, another figure drifted down the path leading to where they stood.

His heart started hammering wildly in his chest as he stared. This time it was Amelie.

He wasn't aware her mother had moved closer until she touched his arm. 'Tread carefully, son, but tread well. For the sake of my grandchild.'

His heart leapt at the words, but he barely sensed her leave. Every scrap of his attention was pinned on Amelie.

She'd lost a little weight. Her face was drawn. But she looked breathtaking. Every sleepless night he'd spent re-living each moment of their four weeks together had done little justice to the real living and breathing woman in front of him.

'What do you want?' she asked.

He didn't answer for several moments, simply content to be drenched in the sound of her voice.

'I couldn't stay away. I know you wanted me to, but I couldn't.'

She wrapped her arms around her waist and Atu saw her shiver. As much as he was dying to rip off his shirt and cover her with it, he forced himself to stay still. But his eyes couldn't stop devouring her. Cataloguing every square inch of the body he adored more than life itself.

She gave a harsh laugh. 'You've done very well for two months. Why not for the rest of your life?'

'Because I won't make it.'

She inhaled sharply, and her gaze dropped from his as if she couldn't bear to look at him. She started to turn away. 'I can't do this.'

'Please.' The word shot out of him. 'I deserve every accusation you throw at me, but hear me out. I beg you.'

She paused, still half turned from him. His eager gaze drew down her body, lingering on her belly. His heart caught at the sight of the slight swell where his child grew.

He dragged his gaze back to her face, then summoned the words he didn't really want to speak. 'You heard my father passed away?'

Her lips pressed together and then she nodded. 'Yes. I'm sorry.'

He forced a shrug, but the lance of pain arrived anyway. 'I thought I'd feel nothing when the moment came. But nothing ever prepares you for that. Just like with Fiifi. It takes the legs from underneath you.'

Her face softened and she turned fully to face him once more. 'Yes, I know. Emotions are like that. They catch you when you least expect it.'

He nodded, a half-smile tugging at his lips. 'It's the darnedest thing… For so long I hated him for not loving me as much as he loved his firstborn son. But I came running the moment he said he needed me.'

'It's because he was your father. No matter what happens, every child wants their parents' love.'

Again, his gaze dropped to her belly, every cell in his body yearning for the child she carried. 'Amelie…'

'I'm fine. The baby is fine.'

He wasn't aware he was holding his breath until it exploded out of him. The hand he lifted to grip his nape trembled wildly against his skin. He remembered to nod, his scattered mind attempting to form more words when all he wanted to do was reach across the gap between them, drag her into his arms and never let go.

'I resented Fiifi for being the sole recipient of our father's love and respect, for being the favoured son. Sometimes he was cruel about it. Other times he was smug. But it was the pity I hated most.' He saw her lower lip tremble and he shook his head. 'This isn't a sympathy petition. I just wanted to explain why I am…why I *was* the way I was.'

She gave a small enlightened smile. 'You don't need to explain it to me. You closed yourself off to protect yourself from being hurt.'

He gave a harsh laugh. 'There's closing yourself off and there's doing what I did. I left Ekow to take up the mantle that should've been mine—my responsibility. I did to him the same thing my father did to me, and I didn't see my family for years because I was angry and ashamed. Then, when I came back, it was only so I could help my father perpetuate a feud that should never have started in the first place. You were right. What happened to Fiifi and Esi was a tragedy—that's all. It wasn't worth breaking up our families into even smaller pieces.'

She gave another short soft gasp. 'What are you saying?'

'That at some point I should've tried to be a better version of the man who sired me. Instead, I walked in his footsteps, uncaring of who I hurt.'

She shook her head, her look fierce as she glared at him. 'Don't say that about yourself. I refuse to believe that the man I gave myself to is the man you describe. You could've taken this place from me months ago, but you didn't. Did you authorise your brother to call in the bank loan?'

Anger roared through him again at what his father had done. 'No. I'd never do that. Bankers who take advantage of people in situations like yours are the worst of the worst.'

Her anger receded and a resigned smile appeared. 'Your father did that, didn't he?'

He nodded. 'He had our lawyers draw up papers to buy out the loan and file the demand. He waited until we were out of the country to do it. Ekow tried to stop him when he found out, but it was too late.'

Her gaze flitted over his face, then veered away again. 'Is that why you're here? To discuss the resort?'

Another harsh laugh erupted from his tight throat. 'The resort is the last thing on my mind, Amelie.'

'Then why are you here?'

'I told you. I'm here for you.'

Her nostrils flared. 'But I'm not yours.'

'Believe me, I know. But I want you to be.'

Her eyes widened. 'What?'

'You heard me.'

Her face shuttered. 'But...you don't believe in love.'

He snorted. 'This is another revelation I'm grappling with. It turns out it doesn't matter how tightly you close yourself off. All it takes is a beautiful, compassionate woman with unstoppable determination and ferocious passion to sneak beneath your guard.'

'Atu...'

He jerked forward. 'I love you, Amelie. I may have loftily declared that love doesn't exist, but I have no other description for this feeling in my heart that I have for you and only you. I used my parents' marriage and what I saw of Fiifi and Esi's relationship as a yardstick to judge the world by. I never wanted anything like that, so I wrote off all relationships. But you made me want more, Amelie. You made me yearn for something more than landing the next deal. Waking up next to you made me realise what I was missing. The simple pleasure of holding your hand while you laughed brought me untold joy.'

Like magnets, his eyes were drawn to her belly again.

'I want to be a better father to our baby than mine was to me. And if we're blessed with more children, we will do even better...spread that love so none of them ever feel rejected.'

He wasn't aware he was drawing close until she tilted her face up to his, tears in her eyes. He brushed them away with his thumbs, his heart spilling over and burning through the desolation. The fact that she wasn't walking away made him hope that perhaps he had a chance.

'I'll do anything for a chance to show you that I can be different. Be a man you can be proud of.'

'You already are.'

His heart crashed into his ribs. 'Does that...? Are you...?'

Joy surged through his veins as she reached for his hand, lifted it and pressed it to her cheek. 'I've loved you since I was eighteen, Atu. I convinced myself it was just a teenage crush, that I wasn't worthy of you...'

He opened his mouth to quickly refute that, but she pressed a finger against his lips.

'Seeing you again made me recognise that it had been love all along...that I've been waiting for you all this time.

But when you told me in Malaysia that you didn't believe in love, I lost hope. I convinced myself that simply being with you until we had to part was okay. Then I found out I was pregnant.'

Shame clouded over his hope and joy, and he grimaced. 'I know the statistics surrounding safe sex. I also recall how desperate we were for each other. That kind of desperation doesn't always lend itself to practising safe sex. And yet the news still floored me. And I let every moment of doubt about my ability to sustain a relationship ruin that moment. Please know that I wasn't rejecting you, my love. I was rejecting even the slightest possibility that I could be a good father to our baby.'

'Do you still doubt yourself?'

'I know that with you by my side I can be different. I'll do everything in my power to ensure that our child has a safe and happy home. That he or she will never feel the rejection and indifference I felt.'

'I know you will.'

He looked deeper into her eyes, joy surging anew at the look on her face. 'Does that mean…? Will you…?'

She nodded, tears flowing freely down her face. 'I love you, Atu. My deepest wish from the moment we met was to be with you.'

With a gruff exhalation that he would deny for ever was actually a half-sob, he gathered her into his arms. Pure happiness washed over his senses, and the dark hopelessness that had dogged him for the last two months vanished as he sealed his mouth to hers, stealing the kiss he'd been yearning for since she'd appeared.

When they finally broke apart, he cupped her jaw, his thumbs drifting reverently over her swollen lips.

'I want to get our mothers together. I don't care if they can't bear to be in the same room with each other. This is too important. I want to put a ring on your finger at the earliest opportunity. I want you walking down the aisle blooming with our baby. I need to make you mine as soon as possible, and then I want us to live the rest of our lives in sublime happiness.'

Sweet laughter exploded from her, her hands going around his waist to hold him as tightly as he was holding her. They kissed again, and when he lifted his head, her smile was pure bliss, a wonderful precursor to everything he knew he would achieve if she became his.

'Can we make that happen as soon as possible?' he asked.

'Oh, yes, I'll make it happen.'

His smile felt as if it would crack wide open with the happiness in his heart. 'Thank you.'

'Prepare yourself, though. My mother has been waiting for you to turn up for the last two months. She may have cursed your name a few times for your tardiness in claiming me and your child.'

He gathered her closer still, unable to bear even an inch of space between them. 'I'll make it up to her. I'll make it up to everyone. Now that I'm the head of the Quayson clan, I declare this senseless feud over.'

She smiled. 'Just like that?'

'You've shown me that with love underpinning what matters, anything is possible. I intend that to be my life's motto.'

Her tears flowed again. But he wasn't worried because he knew they flowed with love. For him. For the two families they were about to reshape into one, and for the brand-new family they would create.

Love would take care of them all.

And he couldn't wait to get started with her by his side.

EPILOGUE

Two years later

'I THOUGHT WE agreed that you wouldn't ride these things on your own?'

Amelie curbed a smile as she brought the electric buggy to a stop next to her glowering husband. But beneath the glower she spotted a flash of concern, and immediately forgave him for being all alpha.

'No, Husband. *You* decreed that I shouldn't ride them without you.'

He passed a hand over his nape, his nostrils pinching as he inhaled long and slow, and she swallowed the laugh bubbling up her throat.

'Amelie, you're eight months pregnant. Be reasonable.'

'If you didn't want me riding them, you shouldn't have introduced them to the resort. I suggested bicycles, remember?'

If anything, he looked even more pained. 'I shudder to think of you riding a bicycle while heavily pregnant with my baby.'

He helped her out of the buggy and she wrapped her arms around his neck, sighing in happiness when his hand slid possessively over her swollen stomach before snaking down to rest on her hips. She revelled in his warmth, his closeness, in the devotion that blazed from his eyes.

Her resort...*their* resort...was now three times the size

of the original, even while they'd kept it exclusive and self-sustainable, and it made walking around it in her condition uncomfortable. Plus, she'd been testing out the snazzy new solar-powered buggies they were hoping to encourage their guests to use to explore the resort.

The project had taken a year to complete, and while their guests might not have a rainforest or sky-high trees to abseil down, they had the rich heritage of Fante history in nearby Cape Coast and Elmina, and her fishing tours and local sustainable jewellery workshops had been a hit.

Bookings had gone through the roof, and the announcement of her new role as Vice President of the Quayson Group had been met with sound approval.

But, while she was thrilled that the career she'd always dreamed of was now in full realisation, it was her personal life that fulfilled her the most.

'If you're done with attempting to give me a heart attack, can I tempt you with—?' He stopped as the sound of laughter pealed down the path, followed by a child's joyful squeal.

They turned to see her mother and his strolling towards them, each holding the chubby hand of their eighteen-month-old daughter, Amaya.

'Mama! Dada!'

Atu released Amelie and scooped up their daughter in his arms, making her squeal even louder. 'How's my gorgeous princess?'

Amaya beamed at her father, then immediately pointed at the buggy. 'Buggy! Ride!'

Atu groaned, a pained grimace crossing his face. 'See what you've done?' he asked from the corner of his mouth.

Amelie couldn't stop herself laughing.

His grimace melted away as he watched her, his eyes turning molten with love and the type of passionate heat that dismissed even the remotest idea that he found her ungainly form anything but intensely sexy.

'I can't help it if my daughter shares my adventurous spirit.'

The baby in her womb kicked, as if reminding them

not to forget him. She passed her hand over her swollen belly, the love she'd thought she'd never have overflowing in her heart.

Atu moved closer, sliding his hand over hers. The baby kicked again, and a wave of love moved over his face. 'I can't wait for our son to be here. He'll save me from being vanquished by feisty women.'

She snorted. 'Says the man who led the knocking ceremony instead of staying out of sight like tradition dictates. I didn't see you shying away from incurring the wrath of the elders.'

Usually only the leading members of both families conducted the knocking ceremony, the 'knocking' being a formal seeking of permission to take a woman's hand in marriage. But Atu had led his family, his impatience and the residual fear of rejection that hadn't quite died with his father pushing him to flout tradition.

He shrugged. 'I wasn't about to let anything stand in the way of my marrying you. I'd waited for you long enough,' he murmured, sliding one arm around her shoulders to draw her close.

She would have thought it impossible a moment ago, but she felt her heart grow even larger, happy tears threatening.

'We were just taking this one to lunch,' Naana Quayson said, her indulgent smile encompassing them both.

No longer under his father's overbearing influence, his mother had gained a second lease of life—which included utterly doting on her granddaughter. She'd thrown herself into planning their wedding, much to their secret frustration sometimes, and was now co-opting her own mother into organising an elaborate christening celebration for her second child, in between feverish attempts to find a bride for Ekow.

She saw a figure moving towards them from the beach and smiled. Ekow had driven to Saltpond for the weekend. He was a frequent visitor when she, Atu and his niece weren't travelling to their other resorts.

The resemblance between the brothers was striking.

They both had the same jaw-dropping presence and bone structure, although Ekow's eyes were a shade lighter than Atu's, and Amelie found his smile wasn't quite as breath-robbing as his brother's.

She caught the frown pleating his eyebrows as he got closer. 'Is everything okay?' she asked.

Ekow's jaw clenched before he neutralised his features as his niece peered up at him. He stroked a finger down her soft cheek, then tickled her under her chin. Once he'd earned himself a giggle, he answered. 'I've been dealing with an online security issue at the bank. Every time I think it's handled, it rears its head again.'

'It's not like you to be annoyed over a simple IT problem,' Atu said.

Ekow's nostrils flared in annoyance. 'It is when it's been going on for several weeks.'

Atu frowned. 'So it's not a simple tech issue?'

Ekow grunted. 'My cybersecurity team is handling it. Their preliminary report has pinpointed the source to South Africa. I might need to head down there and deal with who-ever's attempting to hack into my bank…'

Since getting reacquainted with her husband's family, Amelie had learned that the streak of ruthlessness his father had engendered in them ran deep. With Atu, it had been the cloak he'd used to hide the hurt of his father's indifference and rejection.

Seeing the look in Ekow's eyes now, she wondered how deep his wounds ran. He caught her gaze and the look mellowed, that trademark devastating Quayson smile sliding into place. 'For now, though, I'm going to immerse myself in the delights of this awesome place.'

He sauntered off with his niece and the two grandmothers.

'Your brother has that look in his eyes you used to get when you were in warrior mode,' she said.

Atu smiled. 'I won my queen. I no longer need that particular setting. Now I'm more about making love. Repeatedly…' he growled in her ear.

'Well, I pity whoever is messing with his beloved bank.'

'So do I. But enough about my brother…' He took her hand and helped her back into the buggy.

'Where are we going?'

'Somewhere we won't be disturbed for at least an hour. Unless anyone wants me back in warrior mode,' he promised darkly, making her laugh again.

A few minutes later Amelie gasped at the sight before her. A bountiful picnic had been laid out, complete with large throw pillows for her to rest on.

'You've brought me to my favourite place.'

It was the spot where he'd told her he loved her. The place where the miracle of love had come true for them.

'Of course. I had to get you alone somehow.'

'You get me to yourself every single night.'

He gave a smug smile, which slowly turned molten as he took her hand and helped her onto the blanket.

'Even if I could spend every second of every day with you, it wouldn't be enough. I intend to love and treasure you through this life and well into however many afterlives we get.'

Tears prickled her eyes. 'I promise to do the same,' she vowed.

* * * * *

THE ITALIAN'S
RUNAWAY
CINDERELLA

LOUISE FULLER

MILLS & BOON

CHAPTER ONE

'RIGHT, SO I'LL speak to you later. Unless, of course, you want to go through it one more time?'

Shifting the phone against her ear, Talitha St Croix Hamilton bit down hard onto the pen between her teeth. It was the only way she could stop herself from screaming at her boss.

She had been flattered and surprised that Philip had asked her and not her more experienced colleague Arielle to meet with their prospective new client.

'I'm throwing you in the deep end,' he'd said by way of explanation. 'Might as well find out early on if you're going to sink or swim. Or just need armbands,' he'd added drily.

He had seemed unperturbed by his decision at the time, but now that the meeting was less than an hour away she wondered if he was starting to have second thoughts.

'Absolutely not,' she said firmly, with a flick of her long blonde ponytail. 'Really, truly, Philip. I've got this.'

'Good,' Philip said, equally firmly. 'My apologies for the interrogation. I really do have complete faith in you, Talitha, but it's my name above the door so I need to be sure you're sure.'

A rush of gratitude moved through her veins. Philip Dubarry was a good boss. She liked him. He paid well.

He treated his staff with respect. He was patient and generous with his time and knowledge. But he was also a control freak. A micromanager who found it hard to let go of the reins even briefly.

Although she couldn't really blame him.

For starters, she had only been working for him for seven months. Plus, she had a sneaking suspicion that she had only got the job in the first place because Philip had bought and sold paintings for her grandfather, Edward.

Back in the day, thanks to the success of her great-great-grandfather's engineering firm, her family had grown very rich, and their estate, Ashburnham, had quickly became home to one of the most important private art collections in England.

She took the pen out of her mouth and tossed it onto the desk.

Not anymore.

The St Croix Hamilton name still packed a punch socially, but most of the good art had been discreetly sold, and the once beautiful Georgian mansion was now falling into disrepair. Whatever money there had been was now owed in triplicate to the bank.

But she wasn't going to think about that now. She needed to bring her A game to this meeting with the VIP. Her pulse danced nervously. Not easy when she didn't even know who she was meeting with.

She did know that they were intensely private and rich.

Very, very rich.

At least she was dressed for the part, in this season's Giles Deacon. Of course, it wasn't hers. The floor-length striped silk dress would have been heart-stoppingly expensive to buy outright, but she had found this place in Chelsea where they rented out designer dresses by the day for less than lunch at Kitty Fisher's.

And it was a good choice. Judging by the numerous

admiring sideways looks she'd received as she'd walked down Bond Street in the warm, late June sunshine she wasn't the only one to think so. But for her it was more than just a stunningly beautiful dress. It was her armour.

Beneath she might be quaking, but nobody would ever know. Nor would they guess that the once mighty St Croix Hamiltons were defaulting on their loans or that the glistening diamonds hanging from her ears were actually exquisite fakes.

'You'll do fine.' Philip's voice snapped into her thoughts. 'Speak clearly. Smile as if you mean it. And most importantly of all remember that the client—'

'Is always right.' She finished the sentence for him, paused, then said as casually as she could manage, 'So we really know nothing about them?'

'Nothing at all. But that's why they come to us, Talitha. If they wanted a circus they would go to Broussard's.'

Philip sniffed dismissively down the phone and she smiled. Broussard's ran with all the big-name celebrity art collectors—the rock stars and actors and film directors who liked the hype of the auction.

But for those ultra-high net worth clients who preferred anonymity in their buying habits, there was only one dealer of choice in the world of high-end art acquisition. Philip was valued as much for his discretion as his expertise. And his reputation had paid enormous dividends. While smaller than most of the other dealers, he now had a stable of secretive but enormously wealthy collectors ranging from self-made tech magnates to royalty.

After Philip had hung up, Talitha flipped open her laptop and flicked through her presentation one more time. She so badly wanted this to go well. It wasn't exactly a promotion, but it would mean she could go back to the bank with something more than just her name for collateral.

It would prove that she had got this job through merit—that it wasn't just for show. And that she was taking their 'advice'. Working hard and being taken seriously at work. Surely that counted for something?

It *had* to count for something because she was running out of options.

Don't go there, she told herself. *Don't worry about what might never happen.*

Except it would happen. If she couldn't persuade the bank to extend the loan, then all of it would be gone for ever. The estate would be sold to the highest bidder and her grandfather would lose his home.

She pushed back against the lump building in her throat, steadied her breathing. He deserved more than that. He alone had done the right thing. He was the only person she had ever really trusted.

Her pulse skipped a beat. Or rather he was the only person deserving of her trust.

He had never let her down, and she wasn't going to let him down now. Whatever it took, she was going to get the bank to back off.

'Talitha?'

She glanced up. Philip's faultlessly professional PA, Harriet James, was hovering in the doorway. 'They're here. I'm just going to go down to Reception to greet them.'

'Thanks, Harriet. I'll see you in the studio.'

She was suddenly acutely conscious that she was trembling. More than trembling. Her whole body was quivering—like her grandfather's favourite spaniel Bluebell at a shoot.

But it was okay to be nervous, she told herself as she made her way upstairs. And she wasn't trembling just from nerves—she was excited too.

The studio was on the top floor, and it was her absolute favourite room in the building.

Thirty years ago, Philip had bought the first of the four adjoining townhouses that would eventually become his gallery and offices. The cavernous studio stretched across the length of all four of the houses, and as well as being a meeting room it doubled as a light-filled ever-changing showcase for Dubarry's collection of art, including her current favourite Cy Twombly 'Blackboard' painting.

Even on London's greyest days it was an uplifting, inspiring space. Hopefully, it would inspire her mystery buyer to reach deep into their cavernous pockets.

Her pulse twitched. She could hear footsteps and Harriet talking—very high and very fast, as if she was nervous. Talitha frowned. That was a first! Even when one of the workmen had accidentally set fire to the building during the recent redecoration of the offices the PA had maintained her Sphinx-like aura of calm.

Suddenly Talitha's body was quivering again. For Harriet to be that one edge it must be royalty. An emir, maybe, or perhaps the ruler of some European principality.

Smoothing her hair, she took a breath, pinned a smile to her face and turned as Harriet walked into the room followed by a group of dark-suited men.

But she only saw one.

For a few mindless seconds she stared at the tall, dark figure at the front, and then her smile froze to her face and she stood welded to the spot by a pain she had never felt before…a pain she couldn't even give a name to.

It wasn't him. It couldn't be, she told herself. Everybody had a twin in the world, and this must be his.

Harriet was still talking but her words were muffled and distorted, as if they were coming from underwater. Around her the lines of the room seemed to blur and sway. Only the man at the front stayed solid and clean-edged.

For the last few years hardly a day had gone by when she hadn't thought about him, or a night when he hadn't trespassed into her dreams.

But nothing could compare with the man himself. And, of course, now that he was here it made perfect sense that he should be her secretive collector.

Dante King.

Even at the embryonic stages of his career he had been reserved about his life. She had known he was close to his parents. He'd spoken briefly but often to both of them, always in Italian, and she had assumed his reticence to discuss them was down to his having a traditional Mediterranean protectiveness of his family. At the time his quiet but steady devotion had reminded her of her grandfather.

Of course, she had assumed that once they got to know one another better he would open up to her.

Her chest tightened.

What a joke. Despite supposedly planning for a future together, Dante had excluded her from his life, keeping her at arm's length from everyone who mattered to him.

Her stomach clenched. Knowing how much he cared about his family, she had glossed over her own useless parents, but she needn't have worried. He was only interested in people who could help him become master of the universe.

And now here he was, standing in the studio.

The richest man no one had ever heard of.

Every devastating inch of him.

From the mussed-up dark hair to the soles of his hand-made leather shoes. Staggeringly handsome, unequivocally male.

Once upon a time he had been the man she'd adored

so much that it had hurt to be away from him even for a moment.

Her pulse trembled. He was also the man who had told her he loved her and then taken her heart and broken it into a thousand pieces.

A shiver ran through her body.

Three years ago, in a Milanese bar filled with boisterous, swaggering Italian men, he had turned heads with his quiet, serious beauty. And it wasn't just the flawless curves of his face. Back then there had been a hint of softness, a vulnerability beneath those sculpted cheekbones, that had made every woman in that bar—including her—glance over for a fraction longer than entirely necessary.

But she was a different person now.

Today she was under no illusions. She knew Dante King had no soft side, that he was a man on a mission. Single-minded, driven, relentless. Blinkered, by an empire-building ambition that had consumed his life, leaving no room for anything or anyone else. Including her.

Especially her.

Stomach lurching, she fixed her gaze on his coldly handsome face. And now he wasn't just a King in name. With his business empire straddling the globe, he ruled a metaphorical kingdom. Her breath caught in her throat. She had to admit, it suited him. He looked incredible. And utterly formidable.

Harriet cleared her throat. 'Mr King, I'd like to introduce you to our acquisitions associate, Talitha St Croix Hamilton.'

She gave a brisk nod in Talitha's direction.

'Talitha will be your guide, your counsel, your adviser. But here at Dubarry's we believe that the best advice we can give to collectors is to trust yourself and your taste. Your wishes are paramount. Whatever you want, we can get it for you.'

Dante lifted a smooth dark eyebrow. 'Anything I want?' he repeated.

Talitha swallowed hard as his grey eyes flickered in her direction. Now that the shock was fading she felt fragile, jumpy; her throat was dry and tight.

Harriet smiled. 'Even pieces that are not officially for sale. For example, last week Talitha had a client who wanted a black and white de Kooning. She found a collector in Japan who owned the painting. Then she found another, more important de Kooning in San Francisco. She sold that painting to the Japanese collector, and he sold his painting to our client.'

There was the tiniest of pauses, like a caught breath. A ghost of a smile played around his hard mouth. 'That's a rare talent,' he said coolly.

Talitha's chest squeezed tight. His face was impossible to read, but the achingly familiar sound of his voice, with the slight roll to his 'r's hinting at his Italian parentage, made her pulse accelerate so fast that she had to curl her toes inside her shoes to stop herself from turning and running for the door.

But then those piercing grey eyes intercepted her light brown gaze and suddenly breathing, much less running, was impossible as, inclining his head fractionally, he subjected her to an agonisingly slow, searching appraisal that sped up her already racing pulse.

'Ms Hamilton. How have you been?'

There was a beat of silence.

'You two know each other?' Harriet's curious gaze jumped back and forth between them like a metronome.

Known. Loved. Lost, she thought, fighting the wild beating of her heart as a curl of anger and misery tugged at the rapidly fraying threads of her self-control.

For perhaps a fraction of a second she thought she saw a flicker of something in his cool grey eyes…a primitive darkening that made it difficult to breathe. Then it was gone, and she was left wondering if, like everything else about their relationship, it had been a figment of her imagination.

'No, I wouldn't say that,' he said slowly. 'But our paths did cross briefly. Back in the day.'

She forced herself to meet the challenge in his eyes.

That was one way of putting it. Another might be that he had played her. He had seen the weakness in her, but not bothered exploring the reason behind it. Instead, like all successful predators, he had exploited it with the ruthless efficiency that had made him one of the youngest billionaires in history.

His business, KCX, was not the largest yet, but it was the fastest growing digital asset exchange in the world, and its stratospheric rise should have made its creator and CEO a household name. But Dante King avoided publicity and rarely gave interviews.

That didn't mean you should underestimate him, though, she thought, her senses primed for fight or flight as his eyes locked with hers. Not if her experience was anything to go by.

Had he ever cared for her? Or had it all been about her connections?

Her pulse trembled as he turned his head minutely in Harriet's direction.

'Ms James… Gentlemen… Could you give us the room, please? I'd like to talk to Ms Hamilton in private.'

He spoke quietly, and there was nothing in his face to give even the slightest clue to his thoughts, but there was unmistakable authority to every word and within seconds they were alone.

Suddenly the huge room seemed airless, small.

Talitha felt every muscle tense. Given how many times she'd played out this scene in her head, she should have used up all her anger and frustration. But as the door clicked softly shut she felt a wave of rage rise up inside her and, spinning towards him, she went straight on the attack.

'What are you doing here? It's been three years, Dante.'

Her throat tightened. Three years of hiding from the past. Hiding from her feelings. Three years of trying to put her shattered life back together. People said that time was a great healer, but their hearts hadn't been trampled on by Dante King.

He took a step forward, the overhead lights carving a shadow beneath his cheekbones. 'I know how long it's been, Talitha.'

Watching his mouth form the syllables of her name made her skin grow hot and tight. 'Well, you've wasted your time.' Her heart was hurling itself against her ribs so hard that she thought it might burst through her chest.

He had left her behind when he'd gone to visit his family and like a fool she had sat and waited for him.

And waited. And waited.

Three whole weeks without a word.

Given how her parents had acted, you would have thought she'd know better, but she had been in thrall to her fantasy of love. So in thrall she would probably still be sitting there waiting if she hadn't bumped into Nick and found out the truth. That Dante had used her for who she knew—not wanted her for who she was.

Afterwards, she had spent months trying to live without him. Months hating him.

Did he really think that he could just turn up out of the blue after all this time and ask to talk to her in private? Who *did* that?

Glancing over at his unforgivably handsome face, she

felt acid burn in her throat. Someone without a compassionate bone in his body, that was who.

She shook her head. 'We're not going there. Not now, not ever. If you wanted to talk then maybe you should have thought about it at the time. But you didn't.'

Didn't. Wouldn't. *Couldn't.*

She banked down her misery, remembering the tautness of his jaw. He literally couldn't say the words. And it wasn't as if he'd tried to fix things afterwards. She had thought he might, hoped he would. But he had not so much as texted her.

He stared at her in silence, considering her words, considering his response, and she felt her stomach lurch again. She knew his tricks, knew how he used silence as a weapon, watching, waiting for her to lose the thread of her argument.

Well, this time he could wait—just as she had waited in his apartment.

'There was nothing to talk about. You overreacted—as usual.'

Her fingers curled instinctively into fists. *Overreacted—as usual.* She gaped at him, stunned at his careless tone. She had been trying to save their relationship.

'I'd rather overreact than underwhelm,' she snapped.

Something flashed in his dark eyes, and when he spoke his voice was dangerously soft. 'I'm sorry to disappoint you again, but I didn't come here to talk to you, Talitha.' He moved past her, stopping in front of a striking geometric Frank Stella canvas. 'In fact, I wasn't aware that you were employed by Dubarry's.'

It took a moment for his words to sink in.

So it was just a coincidence?

Her breathing jerked and she felt her face grow warm. What had she been thinking? Three years ago Dante had proved unequivocally that he didn't care about her. She had known then that he was a heartless, self-serving bastard, so why had she thought he'd come looking for her?

She clenched her teeth. Because misjudging him was an art she'd perfected.

'You were never aware of me.'

He didn't turn around and she stared at his back, her heart hammering against her chest. He had been standing like that in the bar in Milan the first time they'd met, and she should have seen it as an omen—a sign of things to come: Dante looking the other way, his attention fixed on the horizon, on a future that didn't include her.

She should have had more sense than to get involved with him in the first place, but she had let her body override her brain, let her libido quash common sense and the evidence of her parents' miserable marriage and allowed her gaze to hover on the loose curl of dark hair grazing the collar of his T-shirt and on the definition of muscle beneath the thin fabric.

Silky soft and hard.

The contradiction had fascinated her, excited her, then and even more so afterwards, when they had gone to bed and she had slid her hands through his hair and he had rolled her under his hard body, his mouth urgently seeking hers—

She blinked the image away determinedly, unwilling to dwell on his memorable skills in that area.

'I was always just background noise.'

He turned then, his dark gaze resting on her face, his brooding, masculine presence somehow filling the massive studio.

'You were never in the background. You lit up the room.'

He took a step closer—too close. Now she could see the contours of his muscles beneath the deep blue shirt and superbly fitted suit jacket.

'Like sunlight. Only you shone all day and night. Sometimes I used to think that maybe you were a star that had fallen to earth.'

His words made her pulse flutter. 'Don't do that.' She glared at him, her cheeks flushed with colour. 'Don't pretend that our relationship was about anything but sex.'

Her voice dried up for a second as her brain unhelpfully reminded her of the sex they had shared. She didn't have words for what it had been like with him. But she didn't need words. Just remembering the scratch of his stubble against her throat as he'd thrust inside her sent ripples of pleasure through her body.

Blanking her brain, she forced her eyes up to his. 'And even that was probably a sidebar. What you really liked was my name.'

'Not true.' He took a step closer. 'I didn't know your name when I saw you in that bar. I didn't know anything about you except that you were the most beautiful woman I'd ever seen.' Reaching out, he caught a stray strand of hair between his fingers. 'You know, if Hera and Athena and Aphrodite had been sitting beside you, I would still have given you the golden apple.'

His touch made her tremble inside. She felt a flicker of heat low down in her belly, as if her body was coming to life, waking from a long hibernation. And suddenly she was tantalisingly aware of his hand with its smattering of tiny hairs, and of the enticingly masculine smell that she associated only with Dante.

There was a temptation to move closer, to lean into his hand and rub against it like a cat, and she hated herself for still feeling that need. She badly wanted to take a step back, put some distance between them, only she was damned if she was going to so much as hint that a part of her still craved him.

Ignoring the traitorous quivering of her body, she

forced herself to hold her ground. 'I don't like apples,' she lied. 'I prefer pears. But I wouldn't expect you to know that because you weren't interested in me. I was just a stepping stone.'

'I thought you didn't want to talk about the past.' His grey eyes rested steadily on her. 'Careful, Talitha, you're breaking your own rules.'

She felt a tingly shiver scamper across her skin as his gaze dropped to the tiny pulse jerking in her throat.

'But then I seem to remember you making a habit of that.'

Cheeks flaming, she flinched inside—a fast, uncontrollable twitch. She knew what he was talking about. Those first few weeks in Milan had been wild, crazy. They hadn't been able to keep their hands off each other. It had been like an addiction, both of them never satisfied, always wanting more.

She breathed in sharply, blinking away a memory of the two of them on the staircase leading up to her hotel room, the fever-heat of his skin, her teeth nipping his shoulder in frustration as she squirmed against the hard swell of his erection pushing against his trousers.

Her fingers twitched into fists. Moments earlier she had wanted a fight. She had wanted to fight him, to hurt him as he had hurt her, but now she just wanted him to go. She needed him to go before she did something stupid. Like hit him.

Or kiss him.

Her chin tilted a little. 'I think you and I have very different memories of our time together, Dante. But, as you've already pointed out, you didn't come here to talk to me. You're here to discuss a strategy for your art collection.'

His gaze didn't shift from hers. 'That's correct.'

'Okay, then.'

She smiled at him coolly and would have marched out with her head held high if Dante hadn't made a slight sideways move to block her.

Her eyebrows shot up. 'What do you think you're doing?'

'I could ask you the same thing,' he said softly.

'I would have thought it was obvious.' Her chest rose and fell in time to the rapid beating of her heart. 'This meeting is over. If you wouldn't mind waiting, I'll go and find my colleague, Arielle Heathcote. She's very experienced—'

'But I do mind.'

Her skin was prickling, and she suddenly felt hot. It was bad enough that he had used her to further his ambitions. She didn't want to be demoted into a minion helping him in the pursuit of his latest hobby.

'What do you mean?' she demanded.

'I mean that you don't need to find your colleague. In this instance, you will suffice.'

She stared at him mutely, her heart hammering against her ribs, his barbed words scratching across her skin.

'You're just saying that to make things difficult. Clearly we can't work together.'

'We can't?' He frowned. 'What's your objection?'

His question sucked the breath from her lungs. He was still maddeningly calm and detached, and she knew that he was toying with her, pressing against the bruise. And suddenly she hated him—and hated herself for feeling another bubbling rush of irritation and anger.

For feeling anything.

'Objections, plural. I have many.'

The change in him was so subtle that if she had been a stranger she might have missed the slight narrowing of his dark eyes as he stared at her in silence.

'Perhaps you'd care to share them with me?'

His voice was still soft but Talitha felt the hairs stand up on the back of her neck. She deliberately hadn't followed his skyrocketing career, but occasionally, usually when she'd spent one too many evenings in, watching box sets and feeling like a modern-day Miss Havisham, she'd looked him up on the internet, and she knew he had a reputation for being someone you wanted as a friend, not an enemy.

But it was too late to worry about that.

'I don't care to share anything with you, Dante,' she said hoarsely, the flickering resentment and misery that had been smouldering ever since he'd walked into the room catching fire. When had he ever shared anything with her? 'You know perfectly well why we can't work together. We have a history, a past.'

He shrugged. 'Exactly. It's in the past. If I'm willing to put it behind me, I fail to see why you shouldn't.'

She gaped at him, rendered speechless by his casual dismissal of her pain.

Put it behind her?

Her hand went instinctively to her throat, as if to protect herself from the impact of his words. Had their relationship really affected him so little?

Surely he must have known how much she'd loved him. Had he no idea how badly he had hurt her? Didn't he care even a little bit? Feel anything?

Her gaze fixed on his superbly tailored suit, the crisp blue shirt and discreetly patterned silk tie. In a word: no.

Dante King didn't do feelings. Particularly not other people's.

Suddenly she wanted to hurl herself at him, pummel him with her fists—anything to make him feel a fraction of her pain.

'We were engaged, Dante. You made a promise to me.'

A forever promise…a perfect moment in time.

Only that was all it had been: a moment.

His gaze slammed into hers and she tensed, her heart lurching as he stepped towards her.

'As did you.'

He was right. Only for her it had been more than a promise. It had been a leap of faith. As it turned out, it had been a leap too far.

'Everyone makes mistakes, Dante.' And she was still paying. Every day. 'Thinking that you and I could ever work was mine. And maybe this time it's business, not personal, but I'm not willing to make the same mistake twice.'

CHAPTER TWO

DANTE STARED AT Talitha in silence. She was wrong. This *was* personal.

Walking into the room, seeing her again after all these years, he had felt as though he had stepped through the looking glass into a world where nothing made sense. For one delirious moment he had actually thought he was asleep, and that all of it—this studio, the paintings, Talitha—was part of some elaborate dream.

It was the shock of seeing her again, he reassured himself grimly. Obviously he hadn't expected to see her.

His pulse twitched.

Maybe if he hadn't spent the last three years doing everything in his power to erase her from his memory then seeing her again might not have hit him so hard. But the shock of her beauty had felt like a bomb blast. Skin as smooth and pale as the inside of a shell…eyes the colour of fresh honeycomb…light blonde hair…and a perfect pink mouth like a rose opening to the morning sun.

Three years ago that was how he'd thought of her: his English rose.

His chest tightened.

Except she wasn't his anymore.

Now she belonged to another man.

He felt a tremor run through his body. That she had broken off their engagement had been agonising enough, but to find out that she had so quickly and casually replaced him still brought an acid rush of misery and resentment.

Had he been just a sticking plaster for her ego? A stopgap to pass the time? Or had it been a set-up from the start? A carefully choreographed illusion designed to get her ex jealous enough to propose? Either way, he had been a humiliatingly willing patsy and Talitha had got her man.

Although she had chosen to keep the St Croix Hamilton name professionally...

But that was Talitha all over, he thought, his anger and frustration spiralling up inside him in a vortex of emotion. She might look like a princess, but despite her aristocratic ancestors first and foremost she was a hard-boiled pragmatist, and while her husband was almost certainly rich, her surname had the country house cachet that opened the right kind of doors.

Three years ago he hadn't really understood that about her. He had been blinded by her beauty, astonished that a woman like her had even noticed him, let alone wanted to marry him. He'd been dazzled by everything about her so that he hadn't really been able to see her properly, much less analyse her behaviour or make judgements about her.

And she had seemed such a good person—wanting the best for him, for everyone.

His stomach clenched, as it always did when he thought back to the moment when he'd realised she had left him. Of course, he had tried calling her, but her phone had been switched off, and as shock and hurt had faded, anger had set in. By the time he had calmed down enough to accept that he couldn't live without her, weeks had passed and she was already engaged.

Hurt and humiliated, he had put the whole disastrous episode out of his head. It was only later that it had started to make sense. When he'd realised that she had wanted the best, and in Milan he had been the best on offer.

Until he'd left. And then she'd gone and found a better 'best'.

And now here she was, doing it for a living.

He gritted his teeth.

In business—in life—he liked to be prepared, and as usual his people had thoroughly researched Dubarry's. But for once he had failed to read their report in full.

It was a rare moment of sloppiness. Inexplicable and unacceptable. And in those first few devastating moments, when he'd seen Talitha and realised the consequences of that sloppiness, he'd been on the cusp of cancelling the whole meeting. But then he'd seen the flush of temper colouring her cheekbones, and the fire in her eyes, and just like that all thoughts of leaving were forgotten.

A knot formed in his stomach. She had no right to be angry. She wasn't the one who had been played like a puppet, then discarded.

But he wasn't the same love-struck fool he'd been three years ago. Then, he'd been in thrall to her. Now he was the one calling the shots, and this meeting would be over when he said it was.

'It's not really your decision, though, is it?' he said softly, his eyes locking with hers, holding her captive. 'As your colleague said, my wishes are paramount. In other words, what I want, I get. And I want you to curate my collection.'

She glared at him. 'You're doing this on purpose, aren't you?'

As her chin jutted forward he had a sudden intense urge to lean forward and cover her mouth with his. 'I'm not doing anything,' he said blandly.

'Yes, you are.' Her eyes flashed with temper and frustration. 'You're doing this because you didn't know I was going to be here, and you don't like being put on the spot, so you've decided to punish me.'

Her choice of words made his chest grow tight, his groin hot and hard. 'If I was going to punish you, *ciccia*, you wouldn't be standing here fully clothed. In fact, you wouldn't be standing at all.'

There was a long, twitching silence.

Gazing over at her pale face, he could see her mind racing, her thoughts tumbling over themselves as she struggled to think of a suitable reply. Finally, she looked up at him, her brown eyes wary and defensive, like a vixen cornered by a stray hound.

'Look, we need to deal with this like grown-ups,' she said stiffly. 'We both know that I can't work for you. Just think about what it would mean. Building a collection takes time. It's an ongoing process. And for me to best meet your needs it would require a connection, an intimacy—'

Her voice faltered and he knew that, like him, she was remembering the intimacy they had shared. His pulse accelerated. Back then, intimacy had meant more than being close; being with her had obliterated the boundaries of skin and bone. They had been like one person, their bodies dissolving, merging with desire. In her arms, even the past had been erased.

Only then she had left him, and she had erased their future too.

'In other words, nothing we haven't done before,' he said coolly.

He heard her take a breath.

'And look how that worked out,' she said.

'It worked just fine until you broke off our engagement.'

His words ricocheted around the silent room like gunfire.

'How can you say that?' She was looking at him in disbelief, as if he had suddenly sprouted scales. 'How can you say that to my face?'

'Quite easily. You were the one to leave.' His shoulders stiffened. The memory of returning to their empty apartment was hauntingly vivid still.

'That's not what happened.'

Banking down his anger, he fixed his gaze on her beautiful deceitful face. 'And what about you, getting engaged to someone else just months after breaking off our engagement? I suppose that didn't happen either,' he said silkily.

She flinched, as if his words had struck her like a physical blow. Her eyes were wide and stunned. 'What are you…? How do you know about that?'

He shrugged. 'People talk.'

Actually, it had been one person in particular talking. The man she had been dating before they met. The man she had gone on to marry. But it had been humiliating enough at the time, finding out Talitha was engaged to someone else. He certainly wasn't about to replay the grim details of that conversation with her now.

'Well, I don't want to talk about it.'

He could feel his face hardening—could feel anger and pain seeping through his body, turning it to stone. After all this time it was still all about *her*, what *she* wanted.

'You left me,' he continued remorselessly. 'You went back to England and you got engaged to the man you were seeing before me. Which was the plan all along, I suppose.'

'I don't know what you're talking about.' She was shaking her head. 'There was no plan.'

He stared at her, anger hammering against his skin like hailstones. What was it about this woman that turned him inside out? It was all he could do not to reach over and shake her, and he tried to remember that he was a business titan who had earned a reputation for never letting emotion govern his actions.

'So what was the problem?' he said curtly. 'Was he dragging his feet? Did he need a little nudge in the right direction? Some off-stage rival for your hand?'

Her eyes flashed with anger, the irises darkening. 'It wasn't like that,' she shot back.

'Tell me, then. What *was* it like?'

What was he like? Did he make your body arch beneath him as you called his name? Did you tear each other's clothes from your bodies like animals?

His pulse was beating out of time, and he wanted to grab her by her arms and demand that she answer, but the words remained locked in his throat.

'It was nothing. It was just a rumour that got out of hand.'

He studied her face. There was more to it than she was letting on, but he couldn't deny the relief which washed over him as she shook her head.

'So you didn't marry him?' He couldn't bring himself to say the name.

'No, I did not. Although that actually comes under the heading of "None of your Business".'

Eyes blazing with fury, she took a step forward, jabbing a finger into his chest. 'In fact, nothing I do is any of your business anymore.'

He reacted instinctively, capturing her wrists, and she took a quick breath like a gasp as the movement tipped her forward against his body.

His pulse jumped, his heart running wild as he stared down into her mute, trembling, upturned face. He could feel the heat of her skin through the thin silk of her dress and suddenly his whole existence was fixed on the ache in his groin. Or rather the need to satisfy it by pulling Talitha closer and kissing her until that quivering fury turned to a different kind of heat.

And then what?

Blanking his mind to the incessant clamouring of his body, he loosened his hands and took a step backwards. He'd lost control one too many times with this woman. It wasn't going to happen again.

Recalibrating his own sense of balance, he straightened his cuffs, then glanced past her, his eyes moving unhurriedly across the artworks, returning to settle on his favourite—a Twombly 'Blackboard' with its distinctive looping lines.

'Let me give you some advice, Talitha. You have a good job with a good company. If you want to keep it, I suggest you learn to separate your private life from your professional one.'

'You can talk,' she retorted. She had clearly recovered her poise and her voice. 'You never stopped working the entire time we were together.'

Heart thumping, he stared at her in mute frustration. 'Because, unlike you, I *had* to work.'

And not just to earn a living. He had needed to build an entire life from the bottom up—an unbreachable citadel that would shield him from the shame and ugliness of his past. Not that he'd expected Talitha, with her trust fund and her friends in high places, to understand that. She had never lived like normal people did: cooking, cleaning, working...

He looked over to where she was standing, fists clenched, eyes watching him warily.

Until now.

'And yet here you are,' he said slowly. 'A wage-slave.'

Although she could just as easily be hosting brunch on the deck of some glossy boat, he thought, his gaze drifting appraisingly over her sweeping yacht-perfect silk dress. 'So, did you get bored of shopping and partying?'

He gazed around the huge studio space. 'Or is this your Hameau de la Reine? Do you come here to play at being a shepherdess?'

Watching her clench her teeth, he was surprised to find that he was enjoying himself. More than enjoying himself. He had been dazed when he'd seen her standing there, but now he felt clear-headed, invigorated, filled with a kind of fierce energy that made him feel almost superhuman.

His heart thudded. Talitha had been right. He had wanted to punish her, to taunt her with his power. Only what had started as just a whim had turned into something more insistent, more purposeful.

The truth was, he'd thought he was over her. But being in her orbit again was making it abundantly clear that she had simply stayed dormant in his blood—like a virus. Why else had seeing her again produced in him such an intense, uncontrollable sexual reaction?

But that was unacceptable. His past was an overcrowded place as it was. Being born into the notorious Cannavaro clan was a legacy he was still trying to outrun. It was why he worked so hard, why he kept his private life out of the spotlight.

It was also why he'd left Talitha behind in Milan.

Letting her meet his parents would have been too risky. All it would have taken was for her to find out he was adopted and then it would have been question after question, each one leading inevitably back to his ignominious birth.

And after what had happened when that man had snatched her bag, he had been even more desperate to get away from her. Losing control like that had not just scared him—it had made him question himself. Question who he was and whether he could tie Talitha ''till death do us part' to that man.

The irony was that when he'd been over in the States he had finally made up his mind to tell her everything—only to return and find her gone.

Even now the thought of how close he'd come to revealing the truth to her made his skin sting with humiliation. He didn't need any more bad memories. What he needed was to confront the past head-on by putting Talitha in her place, and in so doing free himself from any remaining hold she had over him.

'I'm not playing at anything. This is my job.'

Her voice was shaking, and the delicate hollows of her nostrils flared in time with her breathing. He knew that she was fighting to get on top of her temper.

'A job you got on merit alone, I suppose?' he said softly. 'Or did some friend of the family put in a good word?'

She was quivering with fury. 'It doesn't matter how I got this job. It's why I've still got it that counts.'

He let his gaze drift tauntingly across her beautiful angry face, down over the mouth-watering contours of her silhouette. 'And why is that, do you think?'

'It's because I'm good at it. Very good at it, in fact. Not that I'd expect you to believe that.'

He didn't. It was obvious Talitha had batted her eyelashes at Philip Dubarry to acquire her job.

'Why wouldn't I believe it?' His eyes locked with hers. 'As I recall, you did a lot of things extremely well.'

A flurry of pink rose over her collarbone and he felt a tiptoeing rush of excitement as he remembered just how well. Their relationship had been a long, scorching burn of a passion so obliterating and intense that for a short while it had consumed them both.

Was it any surprise that the embers were still warm?

For years he'd told himself that he was done with her, but now he knew he would never be over her unless he faced her on his own terms. He had no intention of re-kindling that fire, of course. But knowing that he could make Talitha jump through a few hoops was immensely satisfying.

Enjoying the feeling of being in control, he held out his hand. 'I think we're done here.'

Ignoring his hand, she raised her head. 'We were done three years ago.'

Wrong, he thought silently, unable to drag his gaze away from the soft, kissable mouth that was currently pressed into a thin line of hostility. *They were just getting started.*

He stared at her, letting the silence between them lengthen, letting the tension mount. 'My people will be in touch,' he said finally.

Her eyes found his. 'I'll tell Arielle to expect their call.'

He heard the catch in her voice, the nervous edge, the flicker of relief, and he paused for a few seconds, as if weighing up possibilities. But really, he just wanted to string out the moment for just a little longer. Give her a chance to enjoy the feeling...

And then take it away.

'That won't be necessary,' he said slowly. 'Like I said earlier, I have no problem working with you. In fact...' he gave her a small taunting smile '... I'm looking forward to it. So, shall we say Friday? One-thirty? I'm staying at the Hanover. We can discuss my wishes in more detail over lunch.'

Her chin jerked upwards and he watched the conflicting emotions flit across her face, anger giving way to confusion and then panic. She was shaking her head now.

'That's not going to happen, Dante, so why don't you stop with all the games?'

He took a step forward, his eyes slamming into hers. 'I'm not playing games, Talitha. Not playing at anything. And neither will you be. You're going to be working. Hard. For me. Unless, of course, you want to explain your reasons for not doing so to your boss. Although I think that might end badly for you.'

Recently he had experienced a dust storm while on business in Saudi Arabia, and the hush that followed this remark reminded him of the long, grainy silence that had followed that storm.

'Nothing to say?' he murmured, knowing he had the upper hand. 'No last-minute tantrum or threat of bodily harm? Then I'll send a car to pick you up.'

And, indifferent to the shocked expression on her face, he turned and sauntered casually out of the room with the same unruffled authority with which he'd entered it.

Shifting against the cool leather, Talitha gazed out of the window, feeling her heart accelerate as the car nosed its way through the lunchtime traffic. She had been rather hoping that this was one commitment Dante wouldn't honour, but when she'd walked out of Dubarry's offices into the bright June sunshine the dark limousine had been hovering by the kerb like a dozing panther.

It was entirely unnecessary.

Given the traffic, it would probably take much the same time, or perhaps even less, to walk the point nine of a mile to the Hanover. But then Dante's motive for sending the car was not about logistics. It was just another little reminder that he was calling the shots.

As the limo took a left into Berkeley Square she stared

enviously at the tourists sprawled lazily on the grass in the familiar oval gardens. Despite being in the heart of London, beneath the canopy of plane trees the garden was a green zone of quiet and calm.

Which was more than could be said for the inside of her head.

Her heartbeat faltered. This week was officially turning into the week from hell. And, given her past, that was saying something.

She silently ticked off the other contenders. There had been the week when she was seven and her father had decided to run off with the mother of her best friend from school. Then fast-forward six months to another week, another bombshell. This time her mother had collected her from school and announced that she was moving to Switzerland before dumping her with her grandparents. A year later her grandmother had died, and since then it had been just her and her grandfather.

Her throat clogged with tears, as it always did these days when she thought about Edward. He was not an overly affectionate man, but he had taught her to ride and shoot, and later how to make a perfect martini and to drive, quietly issuing instructions as she'd rumbled nervously around the estate in the gamekeeper's ancient Land Rover. He had taken her to the opera, and Royal Ascot, and most important of all he had shared with her his passion for art.

She felt her breathing hitch. Everything that was good about her life—about her—was thanks to him, and now she was going to take everything he loved, everything he needed, away from him.

Catching sight of her reflection, she felt her pulse stumble as she replayed her meeting at the bank. A casual observer would only see what she wanted them to see: the delicate features, the careless tilt to her chin. But of course Charles Tait was not just a casual observer. He was an old family friend.

He was also a banker—in fact, he *was* the bank. And it was as the CEO of Taits that he had sat opposite her in his office and told her that he could see no reason other than sentiment to justify extending her grandfather's loan. And unfortunately he couldn't expect that sentiment to be shared by the other directors.

Remembering the apologetic smile that had accompanied his words, Talitha breathed out shakily. Maybe if she hadn't still been reeling from her encounter with Dante the day before she might have rallied, might have fought harder, but as soon as she'd sat down she'd had to press her hands into the arms of her chair to stop the feeling that the ground was tilting beneath her.

She had options. She could sell the townhouse.

Only that wouldn't be enough to save Ashburnham. It would be more sensible to sell the estate and keep the townhouse. Or better still sell both. That had been Charles's advice, and deep down she knew that he was right, but...

Blinking back tears, she tried to keep her breathing steady. She didn't want to cry. Not here. Not now. Not when she was only minutes away from meeting Dante.

Her heart thudded against her ribs and then, before she could change the direction of her thoughts, she was back to reliving the moment she had been trying so hard to not think about.

When Dante had strolled into the studio four days ago she hadn't known whether to scream or cry. It had taken her three years—three, long, miserable years—but she had finally managed to forget what they had shared. Her infatuation, their engagement, his rejection.

Or she thought she had forgotten it.

But by the time he'd strolled out sixty minutes later

it had been as though those years had never happened. Everything had suddenly been cut loose, every memory, every feeling...

Stomach tensing, she replayed those few tense seconds when she'd jabbed her finger into the hard wall of his chest and he had caught her hands and tugged her forward. He had been so close—close enough that she had been able to see the streaks of anger on his high, flat cheekbones, close enough to feel the heat of his skin.

For what had felt like an endless moment she had been rooted to the floor, legs trembling, hands shaky and incompetent. Only it had been more than just his tantalising proximity that had made time come to a quivering halt and her body lose substance. There had been a kind of restrained power and measured control in his grip, so that even as she'd fought to keep her footing, she'd been aware that he was *permitting* her to do so.

The promise to go further, to tip her against him and kiss her to the point of meltdown, made her breath catch in her throat. Had he done so she would have slapped his face and told him exactly where he could put his art collection.

Or would she?

It was a question she had been asking herself ever since he had strolled out of the studio and, truthfully, she still wasn't sure that the answer would be yes.

Her heartbeat faltered a little as the limousine slowed and she caught a glimpse of the Hanover's iconic Art Deco façade.

All week she had been telling herself that she wasn't going to go through with it. Each morning she woke early, planning ways to tell Philip the truth, or as much of the truth as she could bear, and every night she left work having said nothing and feeling diminished by her own cowardice.

Her jaw clenched. She hated being the kind of person who let fear guide her behaviour. Dante might have been just pushing her buttons when he'd said that she needed to keep her personal life separate from work, but she knew he was right. She also suspected that Philip would agree with him.

And, really, was it such a big deal? It would be an hour or two at the most in a crowded restaurant, she thought as the car slowed. After that, in all probability she would never have to see him in person again. According to Philip, Dante conducted most of his business from his offices in New York. Besides, she knew him—and, whatever he might have said to the contrary, he didn't want her to work for him. He had summoned her here today solely because he wanted to rub in the fact that he could. Once he'd had his fun, he'd leave her alone.

So all she needed to do was get through this lunch and then it would be over.

Taking a breath, she smoothed down the skirt of her yellow silk dress, feeling calmer than she had in days.

'Good afternoon, Ms Hamilton.'

As she slid out of the car, a young man in a dark suit stepped forward.

'My name is Thomas. I work for Mr King in London. If you'd like to come this way?'

Smiling stiffly, she followed him inside.

The Hanover was her favourite London hotel.

As a child, she had often gone there for afternoon tea with her grandfather, but she hadn't been for a while, and she was slightly concerned that a recent makeover might have muddied the hotel's character. But, gazing anxiously across the legendary Art Deco foyer, she saw that the renovations were both sensitive and stylish, opulent but not overwrought. Everything looked sharp and clean and bright.

Her relief was swiftly replaced by a spasm of unease as the sleek brunette behind the reception desk glanced over at her curiously.

She felt her throat tighten.

What was she thinking?

Was she looking over because guests for the King suite were a rarity? Or had she sat there day after day watching a steady stream of women pass by on their way to Dante's rooms?

Not that she cared, she thought with a swift stab of anger. *They were welcome to him.*

As befitted a King, Dante was staying in the Royal Suite, and as she stepped out of the lift into the private lobby she lifted her chin like a gladiator on the threshold of the arena.

This was just a job, she told herself firmly as Thomas opened the door, then melted into the shadows. Dante was just a client. Thanks to her grandfather, and to Philip, she had a home, a career, a life. And even if that life overlapped briefly with his again, there was no way she was going to let Dante mess it up a second time.

The suite was every bit as opulent as its name suggested. *Rouge noir* velvet and sumptuous silks blended regal grandeur with contemporary comfort. But she barely registered her magnificent surroundings. Instead her entire attention was fixed on the man standing by the window.

He had his back to her. Deliberately? But of course, she thought, her mouth thinning in irritation. This whole charade was a deliberate show of power.

She gritted her teeth. In the past, like most people in love, she hadn't noticed his flaws. Or rather she had made them into positives, even telling herself in those moments when she'd felt him withdraw from her that they were proof of his sensitivity rather than evidence of his indifference.

But she wasn't that same dazzled, love-struck young woman anymore, and whatever power Dante had over her was temporary—*hopefully*. It existed only within the realms of a work-based relationship. She had moved on emotionally and physically.

He turned towards her and, looking at his mouth, she felt her pulse stutter. A betraying colour flooded her cheeks as she remembered again that moment in the studio and her body's traitorous response to his.

It was just a tic, she reassured herself quickly. An urge triggered by some muscle memory from the time when they hadn't been able to keep their hands off one another. But it wouldn't happen again.

'Talitha.'

He didn't smile, or make any attempt to shake her hand, instead he just stood there, gazing intently at her in a way that made her feel suddenly and acutely conscious of the beating of her heart and where the silk of her dress clung to her body.

'Dante,' she replied with a curt flick of her head. 'Wouldn't it have been easier just to meet in the restaurant?' she asked stiffly.

His mouth curved almost imperceptibly. 'Yes, it would. If we were eating there. But I thought it would be easier to have lunch here. We have a lot to discuss. This way we won't get interrupted.'

She couldn't stop her eyes from darting around the vast suite as her stomach gave a lurch that had nothing to do with hunger. Eat here. With Dante. *On her own.*

She cleared her throat, her body prickling with panic. 'That wasn't what we agreed.'

He was studying her face. 'You don't need to be scared of me, Talitha.'

'I'm not,' she said quickly—too quickly, she realised a moment later as the corners of his mouth tilted up fractionally.

'So, it's yourself you're afraid of?'

She felt the tension in her stomach wind tighter as he walked towards her. 'I'm not going to dignify that with an answer,' she snapped as he stopped in front of her. 'I'm here to work.' She lifted her eyes challengingly. 'Unless, of course, you've changed your mind.'

'I haven't.' He gestured towards a table set for lunch. 'So perhaps we should sit down, and you can talk me through the process of building an art collection while we eat.'

She was still on edge, but it was easier, she found, to talk to him now she was following a script. And while they ate—a delicious herb-crusted rack of lamb, Jersey Royals, heritage carrots and pea purée—she explained everything from sourcing artworks and confirming authenticity and provenance to shipping and storage.

He asked a couple of questions but seemed distracted. His gaze kept drifting away from hers, and she was suddenly glad that lunch would soon be over. She didn't want to be reminded of how it felt to be not enough to hold his attention.

The waiter had returned with dessert. Or rather dessert for her. Glancing down at the plate, she felt herself blushing. It must just be a coincidence. Dante couldn't have remembered.

There was a beat of silence and, looking up, she felt the blood pulse through her body.

'*Budini di riso fiorentini.* With a coconut sorbet,' Dante said softly. 'I asked the kitchen to make it.'

He shifted back in his seat, and now she was the focus of his gaze. Her hand felt clumsy against her water glass. Beneath the sudden rapid beating of her heart she could hear the faint hum of traffic from the street outside and suddenly she was scared. Not of him, but of herself, and how vulnerable she still was to him. Only he must never guess...

The dessert was delicious. Soft and creamy but light, with a fresh citrus tang.

'Is a bespoke menu on offer to all the guests?' she asked crisply. 'Or does it only come with this particular suite?'

He didn't answer immediately. His eyes held hers, the grey of the irises dark and impenetrable like flint. 'No, it comes with being the owner of the hotel,' he said at last.

Her mouth didn't quite drop open, but she knew she might as well have had a speech bubble filled with exclamation marks coming out of the top of her head. 'This is your hotel?' She didn't recognise her voice. It sounded high and hoarse. 'I didn't know you owned a hotel.'

'Hotels. Plural.' He stared at her for a moment, and then added, 'I have many. Shall we take our coffee on the terrace? England has so little sunshine, it seems a shame to waste it.'

Before she had a chance to reply he stood up and walked across the suite to where sliding doors led onto a private balcony. Gritting her teeth, she followed him.

Wow, she thought silently, momentarily lost for words. It was like having your own exclusive viewing platform over London. She made no move to sit down in the L-shaped seating area, choosing instead to brace herself against the railing.

Having dismissed the waiter with a nod of his dark head, Dante joined her. 'You seem surprised by my expansion into the hotel industry.'

She turned to face him, scowling. 'I thought crypto currency was your thing.'

He shrugged. 'It is. But I thought it wise to diversify,

so as well as hotels I own other property, a film studio, and several newspapers. In fact, I have quite a few business interests in the UK, including—'

'Congratulations!' she interrupted him curtly. It was what he'd wanted when they were together. Money. Power. Prestige. Global domination.

Even in its embryonic stages it had consumed his life, their life together. But they weren't together now, and she didn't want to hear about the empire that he'd chosen over her.

'You must be very happy.'

He had picked up his cup and, taking a mouthful, he pulled a face. 'I would be if I could get a decent cup of coffee,' he said mildly. 'I need to speak to the kitchen about the beans we're using. This is too fruity, too acidic. A true espresso should be nutty, chocolatey, a little earthy. I think maybe I need to make a trip to Italy.'

She returned his gaze coldly. 'You should. And sooner rather than later.'

'I'm glad you think so.'

Something was happening. His eyes were fixed on hers as if he wanted to commit this moment to memory.

'I can't think why,' she said, not understanding but wanting to be free of the focus of his gaze. 'What you do and where you go has got nothing to do with me.'

She felt the tension throb between them in the silence that followed her words and suddenly she was holding her breath.

'Oh, but it has,' he said smoothly. 'I'm going to Italy and you're going to come with me. You're going to come and stay with me at my house in Siena.'

CHAPTER THREE

THIS TIME HER JAW did drop. Not just metaphorically but literally. She felt a lurch almost like vertigo.

Her heart was thumping hard against her chest, and the dampness of her hands had nothing to do with the sunlight beating on her back. If she hadn't been so appalled by his suggestion she might have laughed. Go with him to Italy? Stay in his home?

She stared at him in silence, momentarily deprived of speech by his spectacular disregard for her feelings and the absence of any emotion on his part.

'Are you out of your mind? No.' She shook her head emphatically. 'That's not going to happen.'

She didn't want to stay in his home as his employee. She didn't want to have breakfast with him in the mornings and dine with him in the evenings in some horrible parody of what their married life might have been like if he had meant the words of love he'd spoken to her in Milan.

It would be too painful.

Being so close, only not close at all...

She shook her head again. 'Working with you is bad enough as it is. I am not going anywhere with you. And I am absolutely *not* going to be staying in your home.'

There was a long silence. Dante's gaze didn't flicker, but she saw a dangerous glitter in his dark eyes and she flattened her body against the railing, trying to create more distance between them as he took a step towards her.

His expression was serious, almost sombre. 'But earlier you said that the relationship of an artwork to its location requires careful consideration.'

Her fingers trembled against the railing and in that moment she hated him—hated how he could so effortlessly recall her words and use them against her.

'Actually,' he went on, staring at her as if he was testing her, 'you said that it was *crucial* to balance the works with their surroundings.' His expression was unreadable. 'And that it would require a site visit for you to fully understand the space.'

She dragged her gaze away from the glitter in his eyes. *She had said all those things.*

Worse, she had been proud of her professionalism. But that had been when she had thought her part in this pantomime was almost over. It had never occurred to her that she would be the one doing a site visit.

And she wouldn't be.

Even if it meant losing this job.

'You're wasting your time, Dante.' Heart beating painfully fast, she lifted her chin. 'And don't think you can pull the *what-would-your-boss-think?* card this time,' she said bitterly. 'I'm done with being threatened by you.'

He was watching her steadily, his grey eyes cool, clinical, almost as if she was an exotic creature that he was studying.

'I'm not threatening you,' he said quietly. 'I don't need to. You will come to Italy, Talitha. In fact, you'll be eager to come,' he continued, his tone conversational. 'You see, as I tried to explain earlier, I have extensive business interests here in England.'

Her heart was banging uncomfortably against her ribs.

What was that supposed to mean? And why did it sound like a threat?

Wishing she could read his thoughts, she stiffened her shoulders. 'You know, this international man of mystery routine is wearing a little thin, Dante.'

He was still staring at her in that same assessing way, infuriatingly calm in the face of her growing anger and frustration. Trying to calm herself, she reached out and picked up her coffee cup with a shaking hand.

She could feel something stirring in her. Only Dante had ever looked at her with such intensity. It was as if he was peeling back her skin, reaching inside her, claiming her. The hairs on the nape of her neck rose. How did he do it? And what was he thinking when he looked at her like that?

But she knew what he was thinking because she was thinking it too, and she knew that if she closed her eyes she would almost be able to feel the weight of his body overlapping hers.

His mouth.

His hands.

His—

Her belly clenched. Just remembering sent fluttering ripples of pleasure over her skin, so that for a moment she forgot where she was and why she was there. Breathing was an effort, thinking an impossibility. She was lost, swept away by the sudden heat in her veins and the slow, hypnotic pounding of her heart.

From somewhere down below a cacophony of car horns cut through her thundering heartbeat and, twisting her traitorous body away from the pull of his gaze, she said quickly, 'If you've got something to say, I suggest you stop speaking in riddles and just say it.'

He watched her: steady, patient, absolutely focused. He knew she was on edge. Knew that she was cornered.

'I'm a non-executive director for several companies,' he said finally. 'Including a private bank which I think might be of particular interest to you.'

The cup in her hand felt suddenly slippery and she put it down clumsily, slopping coffee into the saucer.

He waited a moment, and then he said quietly, 'Charles Tait is a good man.'

Slowly, like in those nightmares where your body refused to run from the monster, she stiffened her shoulders and forced herself to look him in the eye.

'How dare you? My account with Taits is private. You have no right—'

'I have every right.' His handsome face was impassive, but his voice crackled with authority. 'As do the other directors. Your debt is not some little bar tab, Talitha.'

His spare, brutal summing up of her finances made her flinch inside.

'Do you think I don't know that?' she snapped.

'So why haven't you dealt with it before now?'

A shiver raced through her as his face hardened.

'This isn't something you can just walk away from.' There was flint in his voice now. 'Your family owes a lot of money, and you have no way of paying it back—now or in the foreseeable future. Or did you think you could just toss that pretty little head of yours like a show pony and it would all just disappear?'

She passed a hand over her face, as if somehow that might brush his words away, and she heard him sigh.

'If it's any comfort, I didn't know you were a client when I accepted the position with Taits.'

It was no comfort. Her skin felt as if it was on fire. For months now she had been maintaining a perfect façade. It was all she had left. And that Dante, of all people, should know the truth made her feel sick.

'Why are you doing this?' Panic was rising inside her

like a tidal wave, and despite all her efforts she couldn't stop her voice from shaking. 'Don't you think I've been punished enough?'

No, was the obvious answer to that question. But, watching Talitha wrap her arms around her body, Dante found himself hesitating. Wading through the St Croix Hamilton family's chaotic financial history with Taits, he had felt something pinch inside him. She was paying the price—metaphorically and literally—for her parents' incompetent and irresponsible spending habits.

But he refused to soften towards her. Talitha was hardly blameless. Up until last year she had never had to work for a living. Never had to lift a finger. She'd spent money like she did everything else—unthinkingly, and with the assumption that she deserved the best on offer.

His jaw tightened.

Talitha was spoiled and thoughtless and ruthlessly self-centred. She had used him and then discarded him.

She had no idea what it had taken for him to let down his guard. He had let her get closer than any other woman, trusted her more than any other woman, and what had she done but throw it all back in his face?

So *no*, to answer her question, she hadn't been punished enough.

But he was not about to reveal how badly she had hurt him.

He turned his head, letting his gaze drift across the London skyline. 'Actions have consequences, even for the St Croix Hamiltons of this world. Your family has been living on borrowed time. And borrowed money.'

The bank should have acted sooner—no doubt they would have done so with anyone else. His stomach twisted. But it was completely obvious that Charles Tait was smitten with Talitha.

'So you thought you'd put the clocks forward, did you?' Her voice was barely above a whisper. 'Hasten our demise? That's why you wanted this stupid meeting? To gloat?'

He dismissed her accusation with a careless lift of his shoulders. 'I'm not here to gloat, Talitha. I'm here to discuss my art collection. But I'm happy to give you some independent advice, if you wish.'

'Advice?' She gave a humourless laugh. 'I don't need any advice from you. I know what I'm going to do.'

She didn't: he could hear the uncertainty weaving through her voice.

'I see. So you've decided to sell the estate?' he said smoothly.

'No. That's not going to happen.' There was a jagged edge to her voice. 'I'm going to sell the townhouse.'

God, she was stubborn, he thought, watching her. *And out of her depth.*

Even before he'd been able to talk, he had known that life was dog-eat-dog. It was hard and brutal and ugly. For a moment he stared past her, remembering the childhood he had discarded, the past he had buried beneath the lies he'd told himself and other people.

But what would she know of that? Living as she had with horses and cooks and gardeners, untouched by poverty and tragedy, never once thinking about the way other people clawed their way from one day to the next.

Glancing sideways, he studied her profile: the clean, curving jaw, the finely drawn arch of her eyebrows, the soft, pouting mouth. His gaze lingered on her mouth. Her lips were full, and painted a soft, dusky rose that he happened to know matched the colour of her nipples exactly.

He felt his groin grow hot and hard. Somewhere at the margins of his brain he could clearly see Talitha, naked on the bed in his apartment in Milan, her sun-saturated body arching up to meet his, her small, high breasts as warm and tempting as the white-fleshed peaches that they'd bought in the market and fed to each other in the bath.

Blanking his mind, he turned towards the cooling view of Hyde Park, where a few riders were trotting their ponies down the broad, sandy track of the Row. Nearby, he could see groups of Household Cavalry exercising their horses. There was a comforting order to the regimented progress of their blue and white jackets and distinctive jaunty red plumes.

'That won't be enough to satisfy the bank,' he said curtly, turning to face her. 'Surely Charles made that clear? Selling the estate is the only possible option available to you, and even then you'll probably still have to sell the townhouse too.'

She leaned forward, her eyes flashing with anger and frustration, and some other emotion he couldn't place. 'I'm not selling the estate.'

'It's just a house, Talitha. You can buy another one.'

'It's not just a house. Ashburnham has been in my family for generations. Selling it is not an option.'

His gaze shifted from her face to her tightly clenched fists, and the acid taste in his mouth burned all the way to his stomach. That was what mattered—what had always mattered most to her. Her estate. Her ancestry. Her name.

Not people.

And certainly not some nobody from a Naples slum.

'In that case, you might want to consider being a little more flexible,' he said coolly.

They gazed at one another, wary and unsmiling.

'What is this really about?' she asked at last.

Before he could stop it, he felt his body respond to her question. His gaze dropped to the tiny pulse beating frantically in her throat, and then lower still to the slim curves of her breasts beneath the yellow silk.

He shrugged. 'I told you. I want you to come to Siena.'

She raised her head. 'And I told you that's not going to happen.'

There was still a quiver of defiance in her face but the smudges under her eyes made her look young—too young to be dealing with a mess of this magnitude on her own. It wasn't as if she was some hotshot business-woman—hell, she hadn't even had a job up until a few months ago. So where were the grown-ups? Her parents? Her grandfather?

'You don't know what I'm offering,' he said softly.

Leaning back against the railing, he watched a flush of colour spill across her cheeks.

'Whatever it is,' she said hoarsely, 'it could never be enough to tempt me into going anywhere with you.'

He put down his half-drunk cup of coffee. 'Really? Given your financial predicament, I would have thought you would be keen to clear your debts.'

She was staring at him blankly, her brown eyes wide with shock, or confusion, or maybe disbelief. 'What are you talking about?'

There was a silky sheen of perspiration above her upper lip and a few strands of hair had come loose from her ponytail. He had to tense the muscles in his arms to stop himself from reaching over and tucking them be-hind her ear.

'That's what I'm offering. You come to Siena and I will square your debt with the bank. Nobody will ever know how close you came to being another poor little ex-rich girl playing in the cinders. You get to keep the family seat and the St Croix Hamilton image intact—and I know how much having the perfect shopfront matters to people like you.'

There was a long, gritty silence. Her face was pale and still, like a stone statue, and he could see her mind racing, turning over his words, weighing them up, examining them.

'Why would you possibly want to do that?' she asked finally.

His gaze touched her blonde hair. He remembered what it felt like to wrap its glossy length around his hand, how he would tangle his fingers through it and pull back her head to expose the curve of her throat to his mouth. *That was why.*

All week he had slept badly, his conversations with Talitha and Charlie replaying endlessly inside his head, blurring into one another.

Nothing he did seemed to make any difference.

Not even work.

His spine tensed. He'd had to force himself to concentrate. His mind had kept drifting off, only to make its way inevitably to Talitha, and then this morning he had woken and for the first time in days had felt clear-headed—almost as if he'd woken from some feverish dream.

He'd known what he needed to do to get her out of his head once and for all.

It was simple. He would make her come out to Italy and work for him. Give their relationship a distance and a formality that would override the frenzied passion of their short-lived affair and the pain of her betrayal.

Keeping his expression intentionally bland, he shrugged. 'Because I want you to curate my collection and that's what it will take to get what I want.'

The smudges under her eyes looked darker, but her gaze held his as she shook her head. 'So basically you're holding my home to ransom,' she said shakily. She shook her head. 'My answer is no.'

Of course it was, he thought, torn between exasperation and admiration. Most women in her position—most men—would be biting his hand off, but Talitha had a mile-wide streak of stubbornness equal only to his.

He shook his head. 'As usual, you're turning something simple and straightforward into a drama.'

She gave him an icy glare. 'You want simple and straightforward? Then how about goodbye? Or, better still, *ciao*?'

'*Ciao* also means hello, *ciccia*,' he said softly. 'Another reason for joining me in Siena. You get to practise your Italian.'

He felt lightheaded, but also exhilarated, like a diver on the Fiordo di Furore, looking down into the Tyrrhenian Sea.

'Unless, of course, it was a slip of the tongue.'

He watched her bite into her lower lip, suddenly aware of nothing beyond the beating of his heart and the darkening of her irises. As the silence between them lengthened, he felt the tension mount.

Finally, she blew out a breath. 'Look, Dante, me working for you, my loan from Taits—none of that changes the fact that I don't want to be a part of your life anymore. So why can't you stop trying to be a part of mine?'

He heard the flicker of emotion in her voice, the frustration, the conflict and the hunger. Could feel his own hunger pulsing in every cell in his body. His eyes locked with hers and then dropped to her mouth, lingering there before rising again to meet her gaze.

'I could, but it would inconvenience me to do so. I'm a very busy man, Talitha, and as you so rightly said, building an art collection requires a connection, an intimacy. We have that already, so why would I waste time recreating that with a third party?' He hesitated, letting his voice drop to a speculative murmur, 'Unless, of course, you still have feelings for me.'

'Feelings?' She took a step forward; she was trembling. 'I don't feel anything for you. Except an immense longing for you to disappear back under the stone you crawled out from. I mean, given what happened between us, what else could I be feeling?'

There was a beat of silence.

Afterwards, he tried to remember who made the first move. Perhaps he leaned into her, or perhaps she reached for him. But one moment they were standing opposite each other, not touching, and the next his hand was wrapped around her waist and Talitha was clutching his shirt as if it was a life jacket.

She took a quick breath like a gasp as his other hand found her face, his fingers moving gently across her cheek, tangling roughly through her hair so that it fell heavily to the base of her neck. He felt her mouth open under his and then she was kissing him back, the pale curve of her body swooning against his so that he could feel the taut tips of her nipples through his shirt.

He made a rough sound in his throat. His desire was raw. Unrestrained. Unthinking.

Behind him, the London skyline was moving in slow, tilting circles, like a huge panoramic kaleidoscope. Nothing had substance, nothing made sense—except Talitha and the wave of shivery pleasure building inside him.

His thighs moved between hers and heat exploded in his groin as she squirmed closer to where his erection was pressing against his trousers. Its hardness was too much to bear and he pulled her hips closer still. Lifting her hair from her neck, he found the pulse in the hollow beneath her ear, tracing its progress along her collarbone with his mouth. And then his hand moved up to the curve of her breast, his fingers sliding beneath the thin silk of her dress to find hot bare skin.

Her lips parted and she let out a low, scratchy moan…

What the hell was he doing?

Abruptly, he drew back, ignoring the protests of his body. Talitha was staring up at him, looking as dazed as he felt. Her face was flushed, her lips pink and swollen from his kisses, and she was trembling slightly. As if she'd been standing in the middle of a storm.

And she had been. They both had. A storm of passion.

Dizzily he braced himself against the railing, trying to quiet the chaos in his body. He hadn't lost control like that in years. Not since the first time he had set eyes on Talitha, in fact.

He felt his stomach clench. Ever since he'd walked out of Dubarry's he'd imagined kissing her—or rather he had thought about how he would look deep into her eyes, hold her close, and then show both of them that he was able to resist her.

It had all gone perfectly during the rehearsals inside his head, but when it had come to the actual performance he had weakened, her proximity lighting the touchpaper of his libido. His body had reacted to her as it had always done, so that he'd only had to touch her full, soft lips and he'd been drowning in pleasure.

Blanking his mind against how badly he wanted that pleasure to continue, he said coolly, 'I hope that answers your question.'

Her chin jerked upwards, almost as if he had slapped her, and just for a moment he wanted to take back his words. But then he remembered his silent apartment and the simple diamond engagement ring he'd given her sitting on the kitchen table, no longer a token of endless love but a wordless circle of rejection.

'My answer is the same,' she snapped. 'I'd rather clean toilets than be in debt to you.'

'So you don't need the money? You don't want to save your precious Ashburnham?'

Her face flushed. 'Not if it means doing a deal with the devil.'

'In that case,' he said softly, 'would you like me to put in a good word with Housekeeping? I'm sure they could find you some hours to suit.'

'Go back to hell, Dante,' she said tightly. Snatching up her bag, she spun round and stalked across the terrace. 'And this time,' she called over her shoulder, 'why don't you stay there?'

Stepping out of the shower, Talitha grabbed a towel and briskly rubbed her skin dry.

After leaving the Hanover she had called work and said that she had a migraine. She hated admitting to herself that Dante had got under her skin, but she had been too on edge to face everyone at the office. Too worried that they would somehow sense what had happened with him.

Or rather what she had allowed to happen with him.

She caught sight of her reflection in the mirror. She looked like she always did, so probably they wouldn't have noticed anything. But she felt different. Wound up. Jittery. *Ashamed.*

Her insides tightened. She should have stopped him. *Correction:* she should have stopped herself.

Because, much as she would like to blame Dante for what had happened on the terrace, deep down she knew that she had been as responsible as him for that kiss.

Only of course they'd had very different motives.

She had kissed him out of need, out of compulsion, meaning in that moment not to kiss him had been beyond her conscious control. But Dante had kissed her for the same reason he had broken off the kiss. To prove a point. To prove he could. To satisfy his curiosity and confirm what he had thought three years ago—that she was not enough to make him want more.

It had been a demonstration of power, not a helpless surrender to a desire that seemingly refused to die.

She grimaced and, seeking a moment of darkness and oblivion, closed her eyes. Instantly she could feel his mouth on hers, his fingers in her hair, his hand cupping her breast—

Her nipples tightened beneath the towel and her eyes snapped open. She banged her own hand against the side of the shower cubicle in frustration.

She was such an idiot.

How, after everything that she knew about him, could she have reacted as she had? But one touch was all it had taken for her to melt on the inside and into his arms. Even now, after she had spent half an hour washing every trace of him from her body, her skin was still prickling where he had touched it and she felt hot and restless and conflicted.

Somewhere in the house a clock chimed six and she bit her lip. She needed to dry her hair and change, otherwise she would be late. Stepping into her dressing room, she selected a simple cream dress, towel-dried her hair and smoothed it into a bun, and slipped her feet into a pair of low court shoes.

Gazing at her reflection, she breathed out shakily. Like most people after a day at work, she would much rather throw on a pair of tracksuit bottoms or shorts and a T-shirt, but sticking to a routine and making as few unnecessary changes as possible was one of the things Dr Nolan had suggested to help keep her grandfather calm.

And Edward liked to dress for dinner and have a gin and tonic at six-thirty.

She felt a sudden stab of anger. Only what was the point of bringing her grandfather a gin and tonic every evening when she was going to be making him homeless any day now?

But of course Dr Nolan didn't know about that unwelcome but necessary change that was looming.

Her anger faded as she walked into the drawing room and caught sight of her grandfather. He was sitting outside on the terrace, his snowy hair just visible beneath his Panama hat, his head tilted towards the radio.

'Hi, Jill. How's he been today?' she said softly.

Jill was one of Edward's two live-in nurses. She worked alternate shifts with her colleague Michael. They were both specially trained in dementia care and had been looking after her grandfather for the last year and a half.

'He was good this morning. A bit confused this afternoon...you know, asking for your grandmother. But he's looking forward to his gin and tonic.'

She mixed the drink and made her way into the early evening sunlight.

'Hi, Grandpa.'

As Edward St Croix Hamilton looked up at her, she felt a tug on her heart. At eighty-one, he was still a handsome man, with fine features and the same clear brown eyes she met every day in the mirror, but there was a fragility to him now that had never been there before.

Leaning forward, she gently kissed the papery skin of his cheek. He smelled of the old-fashioned shaving soap he used and the cologne that her grandmother had always given him.

'Pamela?'

At the sound of her voice he looked up, smiling warmly and, swallowing past the lump in her throat, she crouched down beside him. 'No, Grandpa, it's me. Talitha.'

She made herself go on looking into his eyes, waiting, hoping that he would remember.

'Talitha…' He was staring at her as if he was seeing her through a fog.

'Yes, it's me, Grandpa. I've got your gin and tonic.'

'Is it that time already?'

She nodded, smiling. 'I made it just as you like it. Three to one ratio of tonic to gin. Lime, not lemon and plenty of ice.'

'Good girl. Just don't tell your grandmother.'

He looked so pleased with himself, like the man in his wedding photos, and, still smiling, she picked up his hand and squeezed it. Her grandmother had died nearly seventeen years ago, but that was another of Dr Nolan's rules. Avoid correcting the patient.

While he sipped his drink she read to him from his newspaper, steering clear of the actual news and concentrating instead on the racing pages.

'It looks like Jimmy's got a runner in the two-thirty at Cheltenham,' she said, scanning the runners and riders for the next day's races. Jimmy Vincent was the son of her grandfather's former trainer, and fortunately he had the same name as his father, therefore avoiding any confusion in his mind. 'Would you like to have a little flutter?'

He didn't reply, and then she felt his hand squeeze hers.

'It's good of you to move back home, Talitha. I know you must miss your life in London.'

'Not at all,' she protested. 'I love Ashburnham. It's my home. Our home.' She glanced away to where a trio of fallow deer were cropping the grass beneath the spreading branches of a horse chestnut tree. 'It's so beautiful.'

'It is, isn't it?'

She turned back and felt her smile freeze. She stared at him, stricken. Tears were rolling down his cheeks.

'I don't think I could be happy anywhere else.' His

face puckered. 'Promise me—promise me that we can stay here.'

Her chest hurt so badly it felt as if she had swallowed rocks. 'We're not going anywhere, Grandpa.' Her voice cracked a little and she cleared her throat. 'This will always be our home. I promise.'

They ate early, as usual, and she watched him carefully throughout the meal, keeping the conversation light and free-moving. To her relief he seemed to have completely forgotten his earlier distress.

But she hadn't forgotten.

And as soon as her grandfather was safely tucked up in bed she made her way to the library, pulled out her phone and, before she had a chance to change her mind, called the number that Harriet had given her for Dante.

She wasn't expecting to talk to him in person. Men like Dante didn't answer their phones. But that was fine. She would leave a message, and if necessary, she would go to the hotel and speak to him in person.

But she didn't have to do either of those things.

'Talitha.'

Around her the book-lined walls quivered, and hearing Dante say her name rendered her momentarily speechless, but then she remembered her grandfather's tears and, lifting her chin, took a deep breath.

'Is your offer still open?'

'It is. Have you changed your mind?'

He seemed utterly unfazed by her call, and for a moment she wavered.

'You will come to Italy,' he'd said. *'In fact, you'll be eager to come.'*

And now here she was, calling him back.

She swallowed past the panic building in her throat. He was always one step ahead of her. Still ruthless and single-mindedly pursuing his goals. And she was still hopelessly out of her depth.

But she had made a promise to her grandfather. And, unlike Dante King, she kept her promises. Going to his home, seeing the life he had built without her, might put an end to all the lingering regrets, the 'if onlys' that had stalked her for the last three years. Maybe then she would finally be free of the past.

'Yes, I have,' she said firmly. 'I've decided to come to Siena with you.'

There was a slight pause, and then he said quietly, 'I'll send a contract over.'

The line clicked as he hung up.

CHAPTER FOUR

PUSHING OPEN THE SHUTTERS, Talitha blinked dazedly into the early-morning Italian sunshine. She might have sold her soul to a devil, but it was her first morning in Tuscany and for a moment she forgot about everything that had happened over the last week and just enjoyed the view.

The sky was a brushstroke of brilliant endless blue, with not even a wisp of cloud in sight. The housekeeper, Angelica, had warned her that there would very likely be a *temporale* heading their way—but not today, she thought, glancing up at the sky again to where a bleached yellow sun hovered over the distant terracotta rooftops of Siena like a giant beach ball.

Up until that moment she had thought that nothing manmade could compete with the beauty of a perfect summer's day. But she'd been wrong.

Her gaze dropped down to the wisteria-covered walkways meandering between box-edged geometric beds of lilies and irises and the pergolas swathed in climbing roses. Over a dusky-pink brick wall the geometric precision softened into meadows of wildflowers, stretching out to a gleaming mass of water fringed by a forest of trees, and then onwards to khaki-coloured olive groves and vineyards.

It was a glorious view and, according to Angelica, all of it belonged to Dante.

She blew out a breath. If only she was here on holiday. She would love to mooch around the gardens and then take a trip into Siena and wander the medieval streets like an ordinary tourist. But she wasn't here to wander, and she certainly wouldn't be doing any sightseeing. She was here to work.

When that was done, she would go back to her life in England. Not the same life, though. She wanted to make a few changes. Sell the townhouse. Talk to Philip about her future.

One thing was certain. There would be no more jumping through hoops for Dante King. In fact, hopefully this would be the last time she ever had to see him.

Assuming she did actually see him.

She felt a beat of anger pulse across her skin. If she had needed proof that she was right about the man she had come so close to marrying then she had it now. It was typical of Dante, she thought irritably. He had been the one pushing to make this happen. And here she was, in his beautiful seventeenth-century Baroque home. Only the man himself was nowhere to be seen.

Pulse accelerating, she watched a lean black cat stalk a pale lilac petal across the terrace.

It was different from when they'd been in Milan. Then she had loved him so much that whenever he'd taken his hands off her she'd felt his absence like an actual physical emptiness, as though someone had scooped out her insides. Now her pride was the only casualty; she had a niggling sense that she was being played with like a puppet.

Her mouth thinned. They were in different places, and both of them were different people now, but one thing hadn't changed. She was still marking time, waiting for him to return.

The steward had been apologetic as she'd stepped into Dante's private jet. Signor King was very sorry, he said, to miss the opportunity of accompanying Signorina Hamilton on the flight, but he had been unavoidably delayed.

It had taken several seconds for the full implication of his words to register, and when they had any lingering doubts as to where she stood and why he had kissed her had been instantly resolved.

She had been right: that kiss had had nothing to do with passion. It had been about putting her in her place, having the last word.

Cheeks flaming, she remembered how eagerly she had pulled his hard body against hers. How for those few frenzied seconds she had imagined it was real.

It was maddeningly frustrating—not to say humiliating—to find out all these years later that her attraction to him hadn't become any less. But in a way wasn't it a good thing? Knowing that he was prepared to ruthlessly manipulate the chemistry they'd once shared would surely make it so much easier to keep her wayward physical response to him in check?

And she clearly needed all the help she could get.

She showered quickly, leaving her hair loose to air-dry, and then stared at her clothes, a prickle of resentment spreading over her skin. She would have much preferred to wear something casual, but after what had happened on the terrace at the Hanover she wanted to make it clear that she was here to work, so she had packed accordingly.

Only it was so hot.

In the end she chose a pair of navy tailored Bermuda shorts with a pale pink wrap blouse and tan-coloured gladiator sandals. She always wore the watch her grandfather had given her for her twenty-first birthday, but she wore no other jewellery aside from two pearl studs that showed when her hair fell away from her ears.

As she made her way downstairs, she felt her nerves dance back to life. It was just four days since she'd called

Dante and told him she'd changed her mind, and she still couldn't quite believe that she was here. Everything had been arranged with head-spinning swiftness.

After finally agreeing to Dante's request, she had been slightly anxious that Philip might veto the trip on such short notice, but her boss had practically purred with joy when he'd heard that she was doing a site visit. A site visit meant the client was serious. More importantly, it meant he was going to spend serious money.

Telling her grandfather that she was going to be away for a few days had made her anxious for different reasons. Fortunately, she'd caught him on one of his good days. He had taken it well, and she had left strict instructions for Jill and Michael to call her if anything happened.

And of course there had been none of the usual fussing around flights or hotels.

A pulse skimmed across her skin as she made her way downstairs. She had been on private jets in the years before Dante. But it felt like a lifetime ago now. Back then she had been footloose and fancy-free; utterly and blissfully unaware of the true cost of anything.

She felt her stomach twist.

Was there a price for relinquishing your pride? If so, then she was paying it. But she would willingly pay any price to make sure her grandfather was safe and happy, and that was why, in the end, she had agreed to come here. To keep the wolf from the door.

Picturing Dante's handsome face, his grey eyes narrowed on hers, she felt her heart begin to thud rhythmically. Keeping the wolf from the door was all well and good when you were in your own home, but right now she was in Dante's. And how could she keep the wolf from the door when she was living under his roof?

'*Buongiorno*, Signorina Hamilton.'

Angelica greeted her warmly as she reached the bottom of the stairs.

'I hope the bed was comfortable, and that you slept well, *signorina*.'

'Yes, thank you,' she lied.

Dante might not have been in the house, but he had roamed her dreams freely, his face drifting unchallenged through her subconscious, and she had woken at one o'clock, then three, tangled in the sheets, her body twitching restlessly.

But obviously she wasn't going to tell the housekeeper that. Angelica had done everything possible to make her feel welcome, and it wasn't her fault that her boss had been put on earth to torment Talitha.

'I thought you would like to breakfast on the terrace.'

Talitha smiled. 'That would be lovely,' she said truthfully.

Breakfast lately had been a snatched piece of toast and then a take-out coffee when she got to work. Breakfast Villa Bencivenni-style was a little more elaborate. *Bomboloni* filled with *crema*, sticky, flaky, caramelised *sfoglie*, apricot jam *crostata*, cut into large squares, powdery *millefoglie*…

'You don't like it?' Angelica was staring at her with concern. 'I can have Antonio do pancetta with some eggs, if you prefer.'

'No, this is perfect,' she said quickly. 'I'm just trying to make up my mind.'

In the end, she chose a *cornetto integrale* with a *caffè* latte. The pastry was delicious, sweeter and softer than its French counterpart, but it was the coffee that most surprised her. It was nutty, with a dark, caramel sweetness, and after one mouthful she found herself reluctantly agreeing with Dante.

She could have sat there all morning, just drinking

coffee and gazing at the mesmerising view, and once again she found herself wishing she was simply on holiday. But the sooner this was done, the quicker she could go home.

Wandering through the house, she felt her heart lurch. *So this was what Dante had been chasing all those years ago. This, not a life with her, had been his goal.*

Having grown up at Ashburnham, she was used to elegance and tradition—and, despite the paint flaking off the window frames and the dust motes spiralling up to the ceilings, her home still had a tarnished grandeur.

But even when Ashburnham was picture-perfect, it would be no competition for the Villa Bencivenni's palatial opulence.

The walls were mostly bare, but there was a museum-worthy collection of Murano glassware, Foggini chandeliers and Limoges porcelain. And with its gallery-sized rooms, and soft, natural light filtering through the deep-set windows the villa was a gift for any curator, so that despite her irritation with Dante she felt a quivering excitement skate across her skin.

There was a Francis Bacon that would sing in the exquisite cream-coloured drawing room, and she had the perfect Ellsworth Kelly diptych in mind for the incredible dining room, with its vast vaulted ceiling.

She scowled at a priceless bronze figurine of Amitayus, sitting serene and oblivious on an antique walnut credenza. Obviously she would need to run all that past Dante when—*if*—he ever decided to turn up.

After a quick lunch break she got straight back to work and, despite her reservations about coming to Italy, she couldn't deny that it had been worthwhile. But by the middle of the afternoon she found herself wandering from room to room and then out onto the terrace, twitching with frustration.

Dropping down into one of the teak armchairs, she stared across the beautiful gardens, trying to ease the stabbing tension between her shoulder blades. This was supposed to be a collaborative process—a curator was as much a sparring partner as an advisor—only with Dante absent she couldn't spar on her own. And all this waiting around was giving her flashbacks to Milan.

'Having fun?'

The deep, masculine voice took her by surprise and she froze, her eyes narrowing on the man silhouetted in the doorway. The silhouette lingered for a moment and then Dante stepped into the light. In his dark suit, crisp white shirt, knitted tie and black leather shoes, he looked utterly out of place among the soft green foliage and bright sunlight.

She blinked. 'I didn't know you'd arrived.'

For a moment his slate-coloured eyes locked with hers. 'Evidently,' he said coolly. 'Why else would you be out here topping up your tan instead of doing what you're being paid to do?'

Watching a flush of pink spread across Talitha's cheeks, Dante felt anger flare beneath his skin. Arriving at the villa, he'd assumed he would find her working, or at least dressed for work. But here she was, wearing some whimsical pink confection and shorts that showed off her long, lightly tanned legs, with her blonde hair loose and spilling over her shoulders.

But should he really be surprised?

A work ethic was simply not part of her DNA.

His shoulders tensed. It was not part of his DNA either, but that was where the similarities between him and Talitha began and ended.

She had nothing to prove, nothing to outrun. On the contrary, her name had gifted her a Sybaritic life among the gods. Thanks to his name—his *real* name—people had judged him from birth, applied a label and then turned their backs on him.

Not that Talitha had needed that knowledge as an excuse to turn away.

He felt his stomach clench, remembering how close he had come to telling her the truth about his childhood, about his family.

He was lucky; he had been given a way out. But he had known right from the start that he couldn't rely forever on luck to stop him from being pulled back into that world. Luck was too fickle, too random. He needed something he could rely on. Something that would mean nobody would ever connect him with the baby born in a prison cell in Naples.

And that was why he worked and why he would keep on working. Not for money, but for what money could buy. He was rewriting his DNA, erasing the past, defying the legacy of his family, one penthouse and one private jet at a time.

It was a long journey, but he had only strayed from his path once. When he'd met the woman standing in front of him now, and had stupidly thought he could have it all.

Thanks to her, he knew that wasn't possible.

'I was working,' she snapped. 'I've been working all day. I was just taking a break.' Her eyes narrowed. 'But it would be difficult for me to do much more than I have without the client present. That's you, by the way, in case you've forgotten.'

Ignoring the sarcasm in her voice, he shrugged. 'I have offices all over the world. That means a twenty-four-hour working day. Something came up.'

That was a lie. The truth was that he had deliberately chosen not to fly with her. After what had happened in his suite, spending two hours with Talitha in a confined space had seemed like the very definition of a bad idea.

Not that he was worried it would happen again. But he'd been more shaken than he cared to admit by the kiss they'd shared.

By how it felt to have her in his arms again.

His pulse beat a little faster. After she'd stormed out he'd been furious with himself. He had lost control *again*, and in a few frenzied, mindless minutes undone three years' worth of the effort he'd made trying to forget her.

She had tasted so sweet. The temptation to give himself up to her sweetness had been almost more than he'd been able to bear...

And that was the worst part.

He should find it easy not to want her. After all, he knew her. He knew what she was like. Talitha had used him, then left him—not high and dry, but drowning in disbelief and despair. How could he know all that, and feel this angry, and yet still be so physically drawn to her?

'You don't need to tell me how busy you are, Dante,' she said crisply. 'Or remind me that with you business always comes first.'

His jaw tightened. It had been her constant complaint in Milan. That he had to work, that he wouldn't play hooky. Although he had, on more than one occasion, and each time it had physically hurt to pull his body away from hers and return to the office.

Remembering those stolen hours in his apartment, he felt his groin harden. They'd had sex on the bed and in the shower, on the floor and even out on the balcony. But it had been more than just bodies moving. It had been transformative. He lost himself in her, and for the first time in his life he had forgotten who and what he was.

Talitha chose that moment to lean forward and brush a petal off her ankle. The movement made the neckline of her blouse gape invitingly away from her skin and his breathing jerked as he caught a glimpse of her breast and a soft, rosy nipple.

Gritting his teeth, he brought his mind back to the matter in hand. 'You appear to be a little confused, Talitha,' he said curtly. 'I'm not just buying pretty pictures to hang on my walls. For me, this is business. It's an investment, exactly like any other, and as with any other investment I'm looking to make a profit. It just so happens that on this occasion I'm investing in culture, not condos.'

'Art is nothing like a condo,' she protested. 'It's a creative vision. Art defines beauty. It can be provocative and confrontational or stimulating and desirable. A condo can't do that.'

No, it couldn't, he thought, unable to look away from the fire in her eyes. But none of that mattered. Nor did making a profit. No, the reason he wanted an art collection was, ironically, down to Talitha.

It had been a hot day, and he had been trying to finish off some work at home, but Talitha had had other ideas. Pulling off her clothes, she had turned off his computer and climbed onto his lap.

'Nobody should work on a day like this, Dante. Just buy a painting instead.'

She had pressed her hand flat against the swell of his erection.

'Trust me. I know what I'm talking about. Art is worth more than you pay for it. It rises above money and makes people look at you with respect,' she'd said, between kisses.

She was right. Owning art put you on a different level. It put you out of reach, cloaking you with a kind of protective colouring. A bit like the 'razzle dazzle' camouflage used on warships in the Second World War.

He shook his head. 'Art is money on a wall.'

Her chin lifted. 'Not everything in life is about money, Dante.'

His eyes held hers. 'Easy to say when someone else is paying the bills,' he said softly.

Two stripes of colour flared along her cheekbones.

For a moment the only sounds were the faint splashes of water off stone from a nearby fountain.

'Then I suggest we get back to work, Mr King,' she said at last. She gave him a haughty stare. 'After all, time is money. *Your* money.'

Seriously?

It was that snooty little stare that did it. How could she look down her nose at him when it was his money that was getting her off the hook with the bank? This was the Talitha he knew, he thought savagely. The entitled little rich girl used to bewitching every hapless man who crossed her path, greedily helping herself to jobs and bank loans as if they were sweeties, with never a thought of lifting a finger in return.

Only she wasn't rich anymore.

He took a step towards her, holding on to his temper by a hair-fine thread. He kept talking about being in charge—perhaps he should behave as if he was.

'Don't push it, *ciccia*. You might be able to twist every other man with a pulse around your little finger, but I'm not like every other man. There's going to be no more favours, no more special treatment. If you want to keep your house then we're going to do things my way. Are you listening? Am I making myself clear?'

He snapped his fingers in front of her face, and as her eyes flew to his he felt a rush of satisfaction. This was why she was here. So that he could redress the balance of their relationship. See her in her true colours rather than through the distorting lens of her sensuality. Then, finally, he would get her out of his system.

She stared at him as if he was something she needed to wipe off her shoe. 'As crystal,' she said stiffly.

The rest of the day was one of the least satisfactory he had ever spent 'working'.

They sat at right angles to one another in the drawing room, their knees practically touching, but Talitha barely acknowledged his presence. Aside from when she was talking about specific works of art she spoke almost entirely in monosyllables, even during lunch.

The only time her frostiness thawed was when Angelica came into the room. Then he had to endure the sight of her blessing his housekeeper with one of her dazzling, irresistible smiles. But other than that her nose was glued to her laptop.

Surprisingly, this didn't please him as much as it should have done. More surprisingly still, he realised that she had been telling the truth when she'd said that she was good at her job.

As he'd suspected, she hadn't had an interview for her position at Dubarry's—not a formal one anyway. He'd learned that the other day, when Philip Dubarry had let slip that he was a friend of her family. But she was exceptionally well-informed, focused, and passionate about art. Far more so than the average pretty rich girl who had studied history of art at the Courtauld.

He wondered how and when she had picked up her knowledge. Back in Milan they had never talked much. Or rather *he* had never talked. Talitha had talked all the time, but not about anything like art. Mostly it had been about what she had done during the day and the people she knew. She'd seemed to live entirely in the present, with no plans for the future and no apparent interest in the past, and that had suited him fine.

It had more than suited him. He'd been captivated by her.

Afterwards, when it had all fallen apart, he had characterised her as careless. A beautiful, fickle child who needed constant entertainment, playing with things until she got bored and then smashing them and retreating behind her money.

But it appeared there was more to Talitha than he'd suspected.

'I like this Kiefer.' He twisted his laptop around to face her. 'But I also like this Freud. Do you have an opinion on which would work best in here?'

She glanced up at his screen, her mouth forming a pout. 'The Freud,' she said tersely.

'I prefer the Kiefer.'

'Okay,' she said tonelessly.

He shifted back in his seat, his eyes lingering on her pouting lips. 'Why shouldn't I choose the Kiefer?'

Her eyes didn't budge from her laptop. 'The Freud is a known commodity. Financially it's a less risky purchase.'

'But if you took money out of the equation?'

Now she lifted her chin, taking the bait as he had known she would. 'You can't,' she said sweetly. 'Art is just money on a wall.'

He let a beat of silence bounce between them.

'It's also a creative vision that defines beauty,' he said softly. 'Art can be provocative and confrontational or stimulating and desirable.'

A bit like Talitha herself, he thought, as she stared up at him warily.

'That's my opinion, not yours.'

Their eyes locked. 'So change my mind. I want you to change my mind.'

She licked her lips and her pupils flared, the black swallowing up the brown, and he felt a swooping, vertiginous rush of desire as she seemed to sway towards him. This close to her, he was intensely aware of the light floral perfume she'd worn in Milan, and he could feel his body reacting viscerally, hungrily, to the memory of how he'd loved to slowly peel off her clothes and inhale her scent. All of her scents.

A shadow crossed in front of the window: his gardener, Mauro.

'That's not my job.' Blinking, she sat up straighter.

'You're here to guide me.'

'Yes, but you've made your motivation clear. You want investment pieces. Reliable heavyweights.' There was a sharp-edged, brittle tension to her voice. 'You're risk-averse.'

'Not true. I'm happy to take risks. I just don't like being played for a fool.'

Her eyes narrowed. 'You're many things, Dante, but a fool isn't one of them.'

He stared at her in silence. He'd been a fool for her. Tongue-tied, dazed. More like a stuttering adolescent than a man. Was that why she had walked away? Or had she never meant it to last?

'Why didn't you marry Ned Forester?'

As she looked up at him, her eyes widening with shock, he felt his heart beat a little faster as he realised that he had spoken out loud. But, dammit, why shouldn't he ask?

She stiffened 'I don't—I don't want to talk about that.'

Misery wrapped around his throat. In other words, she had been in love with another man the entire time she'd been with him.

'Tough. Because I do,' he said. The edge in his voice

was an unmistakable reminder that he was calling the shots. 'And I think you owe me that.'

Talitha stared at him, her heart pounding so hard that it hurt. '*Owe* you?' she echoed. Did he think that by clearing her debt he somehow owned her, body and soul?

She thought back to that treacherous chasm of lost time a moment ago when he had stared so deeply into her eyes that she had forgotten to breathe, and her thoughts had lost shape, and her pulse had been drumming hard for danger. They had been seconds away from kissing again. Truthfully, she might be still vulnerable where her body was concerned, but her soul was strictly off-limits.

'I don't owe you anything, Dante.'

Her skin was prickling. Just seconds earlier she had actually thought he was taking her seriously, and that they might be able to work together. She'd even thought he might have drawn a line under their relationship and was starting to see her as an okay person.

She swallowed, not wanting to dwell on her stupidity. 'We have an agreement, and I am here now fulfilling the terms of that agreement.'

'Did he ask you to marry him again? Or did you ask him?' he went on remorselessly, as if she hadn't spoken. 'Did you break it off? Or did he? Did—?'

'Stop! Just stop it, Dante.' She slammed her laptop shut. 'He asked me. I bumped into him when I got back from Milan and we saw each other a couple of times.'

His jaw tightened. 'You mean you slept with each other.'

It was a statement, not a question, and she felt a rush of anger. 'No, I didn't sleep with him. I haven't slept with anyone since you.'

Dante was staring at her as if he didn't recognise her. 'I don't believe you.'

'I don't care,' she snapped. 'I'm not here to change your mind, Dante. I'm just telling you the facts.'

'And according to those facts he was your boyfriend.'

'No! We met up maybe three times as friends,' she corrected him. 'It wasn't romantic. Not for me, anyway,' she admitted. 'And I truly thought Ned felt the same way. But he didn't, and he asked me to marry him again, and...' she swallowed '...and this time I said yes.'

'I thought you were just friends.'

Her heart thudded heavily in her chest as his eyes slammed into hers. 'We were.'

'So, what? You needed a little ego-boost?'

The cool disdain in his voice made her skin sting. What she had wanted was a shoulder to cry on, but then Ned had been so sweet, and just for a moment she had weakened.

She gave a slight shake of her head. 'It wasn't like that. I knew I didn't love him, and that I didn't want to marry him, and I should have told him immediately.'

'And yet you didn't.'

She felt his narrowed gaze on her face.

'Strange. I would have thought it would be easier the second time around. I mean, you'd already had practice in telling a man you didn't love that you didn't want to marry him.'

Her heart twisted. *Was that what he thought? Hadn't he known how much she loved him?*

She almost asked him that exact question—but what was the point? It was too late. They'd moved past a time when it could have made a difference.

'Something happened and...' She faltered, remembering the phone call, her grandfather's panicky voice. 'Something came up and I didn't have a chance to speak to him. By the time I did, he'd already told a few people.'

For a moment she thought about telling him the truth.

Every detail. From how her father had squandered the family money to her grandfather's dementia. But thanks to his role at Taits he already knew way more than she wanted him to know about her private life.

'Why does any of this matter anyway?' she asked, lifting her chin, anger splicing through her.

Why did he get to push her on this? And what about the part he'd played in the disintegration of their relationship? Suddenly she wanted to hit him—hurt him as much as he had hurt her and was still hurting her.

'We'd split up by then. But I suppose you don't want to talk about that.'

His eyes held hers, narrow, dark, challenging. 'Do *you* want to talk about that?'

Her stomach clenched. Maybe for a short time he'd thought himself in love with her, but she knew he hadn't loved her in a swooning, always and for ever kind of way. She had known that the moment he'd told her he was going to visit his parents on his own, had understood then that he wasn't serious.

But did she want him to say it to her face?

She was suddenly shaking inside. Even the idea of it made her feel sick.

Feigning indifference, she shook her head. 'No, I don't.' She waited a beat and then, avoiding his eyes, opened her laptop.

Work was her ticket out of here, and right now that was the only thing she truly wanted. To go home. Her fingers stilled against the keyboard. In the meantime, she was just going to have to find a way to get through the next few days without either kissing or killing Dante.

CHAPTER FIVE

'TALITHA, HAVE YOU had a good day?'

Hearing her grandfather's voice, Talitha squeezed the phone tighter and for the first time since arriving in Siena felt her body relax.

She dropped down into one of the linen-covered armchairs by the window. Thankfully, after their confrontation in the drawing room, Dante had retreated to his study. She had spent the rest of the afternoon on the phone, negotiating a price for the Kiefer and the Freud he'd selected.

Ordinarily that would be a cause for celebration, but when he'd finally emerged for supper he had simply nodded. She had half expected him to start interrogating her again, but they'd eaten in near silence and the meal had been over within an hour. Afterwards he had returned to his study, and she'd scampered upstairs—to 'decompress', as Philip liked to say, when he came back from seeing a particularly challenging client.

It was still early, and in a parallel universe she might have stretched out on the exquisite pink velvet chaise-longue and read a book, or simply stared at the view. But after the day she'd had she wanted, *needed* to remind herself why she was putting herself through all of this.

'It's been wonderful, Grandpa,' she lied. 'The weather's perfect and I had the most delicious mushroom *cappelletti* for supper tonight.'

That, at least, was true. From the starter of pan-fried scallops on a pea cream to the delicately flavoured coffee mousse for dessert, the food had been mouth-wateringly good.

'And when will you be home?'

There was an anxious note in his voice now and she felt a buzz of panic in her bones. Had he forgotten she was in Italy?

'Soon,' she said carefully. 'But I need to finish this job in Siena. For Philip.'

She could picture her grandfather's face, the crease in his forehead as his ravaged brain tried to make sense of her words.

'Yes, I remember now,' he said more firmly. 'But you must have free time, so tell me, have you been to the Duomo?'

'Not yet, Grandpa.' With relief, she let out the breath she'd been holding. 'I've only been here a day.'

'But you must go, Talitha. It's dazzling. A triumph of Romanesque-Gothic architecture…'

Tucking her legs to the side, she leaned back and let him tell her about the intricate white, green and red marble façade of the Duomo, its elaborate Nicola Pisano pulpit and the sculptures by Michelangelo, Donatello and Bernini.

Sometimes when he was like this, so calm and so lucid, she could forget that he had Alzheimer's. But she knew that, in the early stages at least, memory problems were intermittent, and Dr Nolan had warned her that as the illness progressed he would get more confused and start to have increasing trouble organising his thoughts.

And that was only the beginning. In the future he might experience a change in personality and struggle to recognise friends and family members. There were drugs that could help, but at the moment there was no cure, and his deterioration was inevitable. The only question was over the speed at which he'd decline.

All she could do was make his daily life as comfortable and steady as possible. Having a routine and familiar things around him would help him to feel secure. In other words, he needed to keep on living at Ashburnham, and now thankfully that was possible.

If she did nothing else in her life she could be proud of that, she thought, her throat tightening a little as she said goodbye.

By the time she had written up her notes the sky was turning a deeper shade of blue at the horizon and a pale, pearlescent moon had finally ousted the sun. Reaching under her pillow, she pulled out her pyjamas. She had bought them specifically for the trip and they were perfect.

By 'perfect' she meant boyish and practical. In other words, nothing like the wisps of lace-edged silk and tulle she'd worn the last time she was in Italy.

With Dante.

And just like that, almost as if he had been waiting in the wings, Dante was inside her head and she could see him lying on the bed, his arm folded behind his head, those bewitching grey eyes soft and hazy with desire, his beautiful golden body stretched out like a dozing lion against the tangled sheets.

She pressed her hand across her mouth, felt her breath damp and shaky against her fingers. She had promised herself that she wouldn't think about him here in her room and she had been doing just fine.

But she was in Dante's house, so of course it was impossible to escape. Even inside her head.

Especially inside her head.

Her mind clicked slowly through the day: his sudden appearance in the garden, the near silent lunch, and then that interrogation in the drawing room followed by a near silent supper.

And don't forget that moment when you almost kissed again, an accusing little voice whispered in her ear.

She turned and walked swiftly across the room towards the open window, as if by doing so she could somehow outrun the memory of that moment.

But who was she trying to kid? She would have more luck evicting Dante from his home. And as for thinking that a pair of pyjamas could somehow neutralise the fact that he was sleeping under the same roof as she was—

Her eyes narrowed.

Except that he wasn't sleeping.

Or not at this moment in time anyhow.

She edged behind the filmy muslin curtains and stared down into the garden. A figure was silhouetted against the pale stone balustrade, head bowed, walking slowly back and forth across the flagstones.

As if sensing her gaze, Dante glanced up at the window and she shrank back into the shadows. For a second she almost felt as if she was floating. She couldn't feel her limbs, and the breath seemed to have left her body. Then he turned and walked in the opposite direction, and she exhaled shakily.

It must be nearly one in the morning. So what was he doing? Her lip curled. Given that he was still dressed in his suit, minus the tie, probably working. More master of the universe stuff, she thought irritably.

Heart thumping against her ribs, she watched as he stepped off the terrace and walked down one of the paths. Only he didn't look like a man straddling the world like a colossus. On the contrary, he looked more like Atlas.

There was something oddly vulnerable about the set

of his shoulders, and she wondered why it seemed so familiar.

And then with a jolt she remembered.

It had been after her grandmother's funeral. All the guests had gone home, and she'd been supposed to be in bed—only she hadn't been able to sleep and she had crept downstairs. Her grandfather had been sitting, not standing, on the terrace, his head bowed as if an immense burden was crushing him.

Her heart pulsed in her throat.

But her grandfather had been hurting. He had just lost his wife of forty years. His only son had abandoned not just his family but his duties, disappearing off to the Caribbean to fritter away the Hamilton fortune.

Dante had an enviable life. *Didn't he?*

There was only one person who could answer that, but even if she had been in a position to ask him she had learned from experience that direct questions were not a hugely successful method of eliciting information from Dante.

Watching him turn again and pace back along the path, she nibbled her thumbnail. She'd been so caught up with hating him, and then with trying to quell her attraction to him, that she had forgotten he was a person.

But Dante was nothing like her grandfather, and thinking about him in that way wasn't clever. The last thing she needed was a reason to care about him. Besides, it was none of her business, she told herself as Dante was swallowed by the darkness. Not anymore. Not ever again.

Rolling over onto his side, Dante reached out and fumbled on the table beside his bed for his watch. He squinted at the face and then his eyes widened with shock.

Surely it couldn't be that time! He never slept this late. Throwing back the covers, he stood up and stalked across the room to the bathroom and into the shower, seething with frustration.

As the cool water hit his skin, he flinched.

Back in London, when fate had thrown them together, he had been forced to acknowledge that he and Talitha had loose ends to tie up. Bringing her out here, forcing her to be at his beck and call had seemed like an appropriate punishment for what she'd done, and he'd been looking forward to making her squirm.

Now, though, he was starting to think that he had made a catastrophic error of judgement.

His mouth twisted. It wouldn't be the first time where Talitha was concerned.

Slamming off the water, he snatched a towel, drying himself as he walked into his dressing room. He pulled open a drawer with unnecessary force, and as it sprung out it caught his knuckle.

'Porca puttana!' He slammed it shut.

He had wanted to turn the tables on her, prove to himself, and to her, that this time he was calling the shots. And theoretically he was.

Except if he was in charge then how come he kept losing control?

First at the Hanover and then again in the drawing room. Both times he had been pulled into a twisting tornado of emotion, his anger and frustration and desire whipping at his senses so that he hadn't known left from right or up from down.

This unwelcome and ungovernable explosion of emotion was not part of the plan. Nor was having sex with Talitha.

So why was it all he could think about?

He stared blankly at the rows of handmade suits and shirts, his temper fizzing. After supper he had shut himself in his study and tried to blot out the day, but each time he'd stared down at the screen of his laptop he had seen Talitha's face.

Everything she did and said seemed designed to confound and contradict what he believed to be true about her. Like when she'd told him she hadn't slept with anyone else. Of course, she had to be lying. Although she had no reason to.

He swore under his breath.

He was doing it again. Letting her get inside his head. Just as he had done last night, so that it had been the early hours of the morning before exhaustion had brought him a few hours of oblivion. And now he was running an hour late.

Grabbing a pair of chinos and a polo shirt, he dressed in minutes and made his way downstairs.

It was his own fault. Bringing her here had been a spur-of-the-moment decision and he didn't do those. They were too high risk and, as Talitha said, he was risk-averse. And as for picking over the bones of their relationship—

He gritted his teeth. No good ever came from revisiting the past—he knew that. In fact, putting as much distance between himself and his childhood had been the driving force of his life. And yet with Talitha he just couldn't seem to stop himself. He was like a child picking at a scab.

Maybe it was because she so obviously didn't want to talk about it. His chest tightened. For the equally obvious reason that he'd been in the right and she in the wrong.

'*Buongiorno*, Angelica. Just a coffee, please,' he said, stepping out onto the terrace.

Outside of the house's thick walls the air was heavy with heat and scent, so that it was almost like walking into a perfumed sauna. He stared upwards assessingly, shielding his eyes from the sun. There were no clouds, but the sky was a different kind of blue today and he could feel it—in fact he was certain of it. A storm was on its way.

'Looks like we're going to see some rain,' he said.

'*Si*, Signor King. There is so much tension right now. It is impossible to think, to go about one's business. Soon it will be too much, and it will snap, and then it will be better.'

Glancing over to where his housekeeper was innocently pouring his coffee, Dante felt his skin tighten. Was she still talking about the weather?

A pulse beating across his skin, he turned and, gazing across the empty terrace, said casually, 'Angelica, have you seen Ms Hamilton at all this morning?'

Handing him his coffee, Angelica nodded. '*Si, signor.* She was up very early. She asked to see the original plans of the garden. And then I think she went to look at *il tempio di Diana*.' His housekeeper frowned. 'She was most excited when I told her that the statue was missing.'

Now it was his turn to frown. And as Angelica disappeared back inside the house he felt a tug of curiosity. Why would anyone be excited by that?

Heartbeat accelerating, he put down his untouched coffee, and before he realised what he was doing he was walking away from the house towards a just visible patch of shimmering water.

It was a thirty-minute walk to the ornamental lake.

He got there in twenty.

He loved everything about his home, but the lake was not only his favourite place on the estate, it was probably his favourite place in the world. Here more than anywhere he felt safe…out of reach.

In truth, it was more of a pond than a lake. Shallow enough for a person to stand up in most places, it was edged by weeping willows and alders, and its smooth surface was stippled with water lilies. At its centre was an island, and in the middle of the island was a colonnaded temple—*il tempio di Diana*.

Diana herself had gone missing—stolen many years ago.

His breath caught in his throat. But today it seemed she had returned.

Wearing a sundress in some kind of filmy white fabric, her hair piled loosely on top of her head, Talitha was standing side on to him, one foot resting on her calf as if she was performing a tree pose. She had a sketchbook in one hand and a pen in the other, and her forehead was creased in concentration.

As he stepped forward, a twig cracked beneath his foot. It sounded like a pistol going off. She spun round sharply and he got a glimpse of wide brown eyes as she almost fell over.

'What are you playing at?' Recovering her balance, she glared at him.

'I could ask you the same thing.'

There was a long silence, and he got the sense that she was biting back her irritation when she said stiffly, 'I'm drawing the temple.' Glancing away, she stared across the lake. 'Is it possible to get over there?'

'It is. There's a boat. I'll show you.'

He led her to the boat in the boathouse, slotting the oars into place as she stepped in.

'What are you doing?' Her eyes widened as he dropped onto the bench opposite her and picked up the oars.

'Coming with you, obviously,' he said blandly. 'Somebody needs to row.'

Her lip curled. 'I can row a boat.'

'Not that in dress, you can't. Not if you want to keep on wearing it anyway.'

She gave him another of those haughty little stares,

and then, scooping up her skirt, swung her legs over the bench so that her back was facing him.

His gaze snagged on the hollow at the hairline of her neck, sending heat skimming across his skin.

Being alone with Talitha on an island, with her in that dress, was an extraordinarily bad idea. Every instinct he had was screaming at him to turn the boat around. But instead he carried on rowing, and it was easier than he thought to lose himself in the rhythm of lifting and dipping the oars into the cool, clear water.

'Is it all right to go inside?' she asked as he tied up the boat and helped her onto the island.

He nodded. 'Be my guest.'

If the length of her hem wasn't distraction enough, she had paired the dress with those sandals that wrapped around and up the leg, and as he watched her weave between the columns he felt such a throb of desire that he had to walk away to compose himself.

Only now, having walked in opposite directions, they met head-on.

She stopped first, her eyes fixing on his face, and he saw her shoulders straighten.

More to maintain the upper hand than because he wanted to see, he held out his hand. 'May I see what you were drawing?'

After a short, appraising silence, she handed him the sketchbook.

To his knowledge, Talitha had never drawn anything during their entire relationship. Now, looking down at her sketch, he wondered why.

'I didn't know you could draw.'

Her eyebrow rose into an arch as perfect as any at Rome's Colosseum. 'I could fill a library with books about all the things you don't know about me, Dante.'

He let that go. Flipping over the pages, he saw that she

had drawn all the downstairs rooms of the villa, and that the first sketch had been just that—a sketch. The others were finished and they were good. More than good. They were mesmerising. The brushstrokes seemed almost to float on top of the paper, so that rather than obscuring the shape and form underneath they brought them to life.

'So you fill in the colour later?'

She nodded. 'It helps. I don't have a very good visual memory.' Her eyes darted to his face: a tiny, tentative upward flick, so quick he thought he'd imagined it, and then a flush of colour crept upwards over her cheekbones.

'But you take photos?'

Another nod. 'Yes, because nothing can beat the precision of a photograph. But this isn't about accuracy—it's about preserving the mood of an interior, even if there is a photographic record.'

'And why do you need to preserve the mood?'

'Because, for me, mood is as important as scale or light. If you get it right the art breathes; you give it life.'

Her voice had changed. There was a seriousness to it now. He realised with shock that he had misread her again. Curating was more than a job to her. She cared.

He stared down at her, a pulse of excitement beating down his spine. 'May I keep these?'

She blinked. 'I don't usually— I mean, they're just something I do for myself.'

'Is that a no?'

She hesitated. 'Maybe I could do you copies,' she said finally.

'I'd like that.' He flipped back through the sketchbook to the Temple of Diana. 'What's this?'

At the centre of the temple she had drawn an outline, the cross-hatched body incomplete, yet recognisably female.

'It's Diana. It's a futuristic interpretation of a Roman-esque statue by an Italian artist called Stefano Riva.'

'I like it. What's it made of?'

'Stainless steel.'

He stared down at the figure, then back to the bare plinth where the original Diana had stood. It was perfect.

'Can we get it?'

'I think so. He's an emerging artist, so prices should be well within the budget.' She gave him a small uncertain smile. 'It's actually coming up for auction on Thursday, at Sotheby's in Milan.'

Milan.

His body tensed and he stared down at her, looking for a flicker of emotion in her beautiful face. But he saw nothing, and he felt his jaw set tight. That she could so easily consider a return to the city where their relation-ship had imploded was more proof of how little it—*he*—had meant to her.

She might be happy to return, but he wasn't. And as for an auction…

He felt his stomach clench. After all these years it was unlikely that anyone would connect crypto-currency bil-lionaire Dante King with the Dante Cannavaro who had grown up in a Naples slum, but here in Italy, even more so than in the US, he avoided public appearances.

He handed back the sketchbook. 'I don't have time to go to an auction.'

'I wasn't expecting *you* to go.'

The startled expression on her face made his jaw tighten and he felt the ground ripple beneath his feet. Back in England, his plan had been simple. He'd wanted to bring Talitha to heel, curtail her as he'd failed to do in Milan. So why, then, did it feel as if she was still out of reach?

He knew why. She might be doing it under the guise

of being very efficient, very professional, but she was trying to avoid him. Suddenly he was fighting to get on top of his anger.

'My apologies,' he said coolly. 'I expressed myself badly. What I meant to say was *you* don't have time to go.'

Talitha stared at him mutely. Her heart was pounding so hard that it was making her body shake.

She was such an idiot. Last night, watching him prowl the garden in the darkness, she had actually been worried about him. Despite everything that had happened, everything he had done, she'd let herself care.

But she was done caring for this infuriating, judgemental man. He had hurt her on so many levels and she wouldn't be hurt by him anymore. She certainly wasn't going to let herself slide back down into that place she'd been three years ago.

'This was your idea, Dante,' she hissed. 'You insisted that I come out here. Yet all you want to do is bring up the past—and we could have done that in London. I'm trying to make this work, but I'm starting to think you're not really committed to building a collection at all.'

She was getting out of breath, but she couldn't stop herself. Anger was swelling inside her, filling her up so that suddenly she was no longer a person but an outlet for her fury.

'But I suppose I shouldn't be surprised. You always had commitment issues. Why should this be any different?'

His eyes locked on to hers. 'That's not how I remember it.'

'Then you must have a very selective memory. Or have you forgotten what happened in Milan?'

He took a step towards her, and she could see the anger smouldering in his eyes.

'Oh, no. I remember everything that happened in Milan. I remember saying goodbye to you, and texting you from the airport. I remember walking back into the apartment three weeks later and you being gone. I remember there being no note.'

'There was nothing to say,' she snapped. 'You said it all by going to America *without me*. Going home to your family *without me*. You didn't want me involved.'

He shook his head. 'Not this again.'

'Yes, "this again",' she snapped.

'Why would you go with me, Talitha?'

All of a sudden she felt as if they were back in Milan. He was looking at her with just the same mix of frustration and caution. She could almost feel him closing himself off from her.

'We'd been dating for four months.'

'We weren't *dating*, Dante. We were engaged.' Her heart was hard and heavy in her chest. 'And your mother was in hospital.'

'It was cataract surgery. She didn't even have an anaesthetic. There was no need to drag you halfway around the world.'

She gave a brittle laugh. 'You wouldn't have been dragging me. I wanted to go with you.' She had wanted to be there for him. Only of course that had been the last thing he'd wanted.

'So you said at the time.' The ice in his voice burned her skin. 'And yet strangely, twenty-one days later, you left me. So perhaps we should be talking about your commitment issues, not mine.'

The memory of those weeks—her frantic phone calls, the crushing uncertainty and confusion—made her shake inside. 'Don't you dare make this about me. You didn't call me or answer my calls for days.'

'I only waited because—'

She interrupted. 'Because you were too busy further-ing your career.'

Meeting people she had introduced him to.

A muscle flickered in his jaw. 'I didn't plan that, but I wasn't going to turn down the opportunity.'

'And you can't see why I might have had a problem with that.'

'A problem! You upped and left me.' The frustration in his voice turned Dante's words into a rasp, like a blade scraping across a stone.

'No, I didn't. I sat around like a mug and waited.'

Even though she'd known that he didn't care for her the way she cared for him, she had loved him so much she would have waited until the end of time.

'Only then I bumped into Nick Coates, and he told me he'd met up with you in New York. *At the office.*'

Doing what mattered to him the most.

'I met up with him for you—for us.'

Pain cut through her anger. 'There was no "us", Dante. There was only ever you.'

His face hardened. 'So in Milan, when we walked around the city until dawn the night we first met, was that about me or was it about us? When I brought you breakfast in bed and we ended up staying there all day— was that about us?'

Yes, she had thought so, at the time, and even now she wanted it to have been...

She felt suddenly exhausted. What was the point of any of this? Dante had made up his mind about what had happened a long time ago, and no amount of analysing the past was going to change his opinion of her.

'It doesn't matter anyway,' she said dully. 'I don't even know why we're talking about it. There's no going back.'

The journey over to the island had been tense but, if anything, the return trip was even more strained. She sat facing away from him again, it was easier that way, but she could still feel his gaze drilling into her back.

She frowned. He had stopped rowing. 'What is it?' Turning, she felt her muscles tense. His eyes were locked on her face.

'You should have waited for me,' he said.

'I told you. I did.'

'Why didn't you wait longer?'

Pain seared through her. She had been exhausted, and desperate not to lose him, but scared of how easy he'd found it to cut her out of his life. Just like her parents had done—like they still did.

Tears pricked her eyes and, hating how he still had the power to anger her and hurt her like no one else, she answered without thinking. 'Because when people go, they don't come back. I didn't need to waste any more of my life waiting around for someone who could so easily forget me.'

She had done enough of meeting her parents halfway, only to realise all the effort was on her side and not theirs.

His gaze was intent. 'What people?'

She felt panic slither down her spine. She didn't need his judgement. Or, worse, his pity. 'It doesn't matter,' she said quickly.

Her eyes darted past him to the bank of the lake, and for one mad moment she actually considered jumping in and swimming back. But something in his face told her that she would be wasting her time, and that he would be relentless in his pursuit of an answer.

Taking a breath, she said quickly, 'When I was seven, my father went off with the mother of my best friend from school.' She swallowed past the lump in her throat. 'A few months later my mother dropped me off at my grandparents for the holidays. Neither of them came back.'

A silence stretched out between them.

His face was like stone. 'That must have been painful. Do you see them now?'

She looked away, not wanting him to see the tears in her eyes that would reveal how much the revelation was costing her. 'My father, almost never. My mother, maybe once every two or three years. I don't fit in with their lives, and that's fine. I'm not a child.'

She had spent so long trying to be strong and independent, pretending to everyone that everything was fine. It was strange finally saying the words out loud. And oddly, a relief.

'And you thought I was like them?'

Her heart contracted. *Yes.* Except it wasn't that simple.

Maybe it would have been different if one of her parents had stayed. Losing one parent was unfortunate, but to lose two looked a lot like a pattern. And the only common denominator was her. She was clearly the problem, and deep down she had always been waiting for him to discover the real Talitha—the one who was not worthy of being in his life.

She just hadn't expected it to happen so quickly.

'Maybe subconsciously,' she said. 'I don't think I was rational about it.'

There was no 'think' about it. Why else, aside from a complete loss of reason, would she have proposed to him?

After witnessing the devastating erosion of her parents' marriage she had been adamant that she would never marry. Right up until the moment she'd met Dante, and then she would have done anything to keep him—including propose to him.

'Why didn't you tell me?' he asked quietly.

She stared at him, shivering inside. More importantly, why had she told him now? Why stir everything up after all this time?

'It never seemed to be the right time.' Her focus had been on the present with him, never the past.

His face stiffened and she thought he might be about to cross-examine her, unpick her motives, but instead he said quietly, 'I don't understand how someone could treat a child like that. Especially a parent. It's unforgivable.'

Glancing up, she felt her throat clench. Even in profile she could sense his discomfort. But how could someone like him understand? He came from the archetypal Italian family. One adored child. Two doting parents. And he was a son as well.

'Some people just aren't meant to be parents.'

'No, they're not. But you deserved better. A lot better. I'm sorry.'

She stared up at him in confusion. Whatever she had been expecting him to say, it wasn't that.

'I'm sorry,' he said again, and this time he reached out and laid his hand over hers.

Her heartbeat stumbled. His hand felt warm and firm, and it seemed to heal a little of the pain she had carried for so long. 'It's okay. It was a long time ago.'

'I wasn't talking about your parents. I was talking about how I behaved.'

He was staring at her so intently she felt his gaze like the touch of his hand on her face.

'I didn't mean to hurt you, Talitha—'

He broke off, glancing upwards. She felt the air shiver, registered that the surface of the lake had turned dark, and then a few, fat warm raindrops fell from the sky and it started to rain hard. Seconds later torrents of water were sheeting down, dancing off the lily pads and drenching them in seconds. Above them the bruised sky bellowed like an angry god, and she gasped as a fork of light splintered the blue.

Lifting her face, she closed her eyes, conscious of

nothing but the warm water and the snatch of her breath. And then, just like that, the rain stopped. Squinting through damp lashes, she looked across the lake to see a rainbow, arcing above the meadow like an iridescent bead curtain.

But only for a moment, and then she turned back to Dante.

'I never want to hurt you,' he said quietly, and only then did she realise that their knees were touching.

She turned towards him slowly and felt all the air leave her body. He was staring at her so intently that she couldn't move out of his gaze, and she was suddenly acutely conscious of how her dress was clinging to her body, the soaked fabric revealing not only the lace of her bra and panties but the outline of her taut nipples.

Something stirred low down in her pelvis.

His clothes were wet too, his shirt sticking to his powerful body so that she could see the contours of his muscles.

Mouth dry, she lifted her chin and his eyes locked with hers. And then her pulse stalled as he reached out and smoothed a strand of damp hair behind her ear. His thumb strummed against her cheek and for a moment they just stared at one another. And then she leaned forward and kissed him.

She felt heat rush through her as his fingers slid through her hair and he drew her head back with a tug, his mouth covering hers, his lips and tongue urgent.

Her belly clenched, tightening around the ache building there, and then he was pulling her closer, the hard muscles of his arms wrapping around her, pressing her against his chest, and the heat flared into something fierce and demanding.

CHAPTER SIX

SHAKING WITH DESIRE, she shifted against him and he lifted her onto his lap, the movement causing the boat to judder alarmingly. Neither of them cared. Nothing mattered except the touch of his hands, the jagged rush of his breath, the rasp of his stubble against her face.

He was kissing her wet neck now, and then his hands slid over her shoulders, pulling down the sleeves and the straps of her bra, exposing her breasts to the warm, damp air as the boat spun in slow, sweeping circles.

But only for a moment. And then his mouth latched onto the nipple and she felt her body come to life. She arched against him, feeling the hard press of his erection, feeling an answering wetness between her thighs that had nothing to do with the rain.

Breathing out raggedly, she pushed his shirt up from his trousers, tugging at his belt buckle, a grunt of frustration breaking from her lips as her damp fingers slipped against the zip and then finally—thank goodness—finally she freed him.

The feel of him took her breath away. He was so hot and hard. Her fingers trembled against the smooth, pulsing length of him, and then he was pushing aside the scrap of lace between her thighs, and she felt his hand move between them, unerringly finding the taut bud of her clitoris, touching her, caressing her in a way that made her breath clog.

She shuddered, pressing closer, wanting more, needing more, needing the ache inside her to be answered. Her eyelashes fluttered shut and, lifting her hips, she opened her legs, stroking the taut, swollen head of his erection back and forth against the slick heat, a little deeper each time. And then he was pushing inside her.

Someone moaned; she had no idea if it was him or her.

They were clinging to one another as if they were drowning. His hand was clamped against her back, drawing her closer, bodies moving in tandem, their edges blurring.

His pulse was filling her head. Her skin was hot. She was melting into him. Flames were dancing inside her eyelids and she was lost to everything but the heat and the urgency of her desire as she felt him grow inside her, swelling, filling her.

A streak of fire snaked through her and she reared against him, her body tightening on the inside as he thrust upwards, the friction building, hotter and hotter. She took a breath, her pulse beating out a drumroll of need, rocking her hips, chasing the fierce white heat, her pulse quickening as he thrust deeper and harder. And then she jerked against him, her body gripping his tightly, so tightly, her back flexing beneath his hands, muscles spasming in a breathless frenzy of pleasure.

He groaned her name, his body arching, his fingers tightening in her hair, his breath hot against her throat as he slammed into her, shuddering convulsively.

Body twitching, she leaned into him limply, her sweaty skin sticking to his face. His jerky breath was hot in her hair, and beneath the thundering of her heart she could just about hear the sound of insects hovering above the water.

She could have stayed there for ever with her eyes closed. The sun was warm on her back, her body felt soft and sated, and Dante's hand was deliciously heavy, draped around her waist. But she knew she should move.

And not just because someone might come along at any moment and catch them *in flagrante*.

Muscles clenching inside, she squeezed her eyes more tightly shut.

There were two ways of dealing with this situation. Two possible things that could happen next but only one which should. Obviously the thing that wasn't going to happen was the two of them tearing at each other's clothes and mating like animals in the open air again.

That left only one alternative. To tell him firmly and clearly that this was a crazy thing to have done, and the best and the only thing to do now was to move forward as if it hadn't happened.

'I didn't ask—'

Dante's voice cut through her thoughts and she felt his hand lift away from her body as she sat up straighter. With a jolt, she realised he was still fully dressed and, suddenly acutely aware of her bare breasts, and how her dress was rucked up above her thighs, she felt heat flame in her cheeks.

He probably couldn't believe his luck. Not only had he managed to take her with next to no disruption, but she had spurred him on, clutching his erection as if she had never held one before, climbing up to straddle his muscular body in her hunger.

Remembering the noises she had made, and how frantic she had been, she felt another wave of heat wash over her body and, clutching at the front of her dress to cover herself, she clambered back onto the other bench.

Leaning forward to smooth her skirt, she let her hair fall in front of her scalded face. 'Ask what?'

She heard the rasp of his zip. 'If you were protected.'

Protected! She glanced up at him, blinking. Thankfully, she was. But it had all happened so fast that truthfully it hadn't even crossed her mind.

Trying to keep her voice steady, she nodded. 'Yes, I am.'

She had thought he would be relieved but, glancing up at his face, she saw that there was tension around his mouth.

'Good,' he said at last. 'And you don't need to worry about me. I'm careful.' He hesitated, his voice stiffening. 'I suppose we should talk about this.'

If she hadn't been so shocked she might almost have laughed.

Dante was offering to talk.

When they'd been together it was what she had wanted most, but he'd always held a part of himself in check. Only now it was happening she could feel herself shying away from the prospect of discussing her blatant, febrile need.

Tearing her gaze away from his dark, perfect profile, she said quickly, 'I don't think that's necessary. I mean, it's not as if it's going to happen again.'

Dante stared at her in silence, his muscles aching with the effort it was taking not to pull her against him and prove her wrong. But that would mean revealing how badly he wanted her, and he had got close enough to embarrassing himself already today.

He'd been so eager and hard for her that he'd only just managed to hold himself back until he was inside of her. Worse, he'd been so caught up in his hunger that he'd actually forgotten about a condom.

Staring past her, to where the drenched landscape

shimmered in the sunlight, he tried to persuade his famous and feared *sang-froid* to return.

The whole encounter had lasted less than five minutes, but he had felt it with the obliterating force of a thunderbolt. Just like in Milan, there had been a oneness between them, so that in those few frenzied moments it had been impossible to say where he stopped and she began.

But that was how it was with Talitha.

How it had always been with Talitha.

And he wanted her again—wanted her already, wanted more. He wanted to touch her, caress her, lick every inch of her skin, mould her body against his.

He felt his blood pound, hot and fast.

She wanted the same. So why not kiss her again? Why not go back to the villa and up to her room and strip her naked? Keep her there until he'd exhausted this hunger they had reawakened.

There was such a terrible, tempting logic to that idea that he had to clamp his hands beside his thighs to stop himself from reaching across the boat for her. But that itself proved how off-key his thinking was right now. He'd already made enough mistakes with this woman, letting passion override common sense, believing love could surmount all obstacles. He didn't need to make any more.

'Agreed. Sex with the ex has a certain *piccantezza*,' he said coolly. 'But I think that particular itch has been sufficiently scratched now.' Reaching past her, he took hold of the oars and lowered them into the water. 'We should probably be getting back.'

She nodded. 'I think so.'

She glanced away as she spoke, and her voice was smooth and chilled like vintage champagne. Something tightened inside him. He should be relieved that they were on the same page, but instead he was stung by just how quickly and easily she could dismiss their frantic coupling.

'You would never have told me, would you?' He stared at her steadily. 'About your parents.'

Her eyes narrowed. 'Would you have wanted to know?'

'Of course.'

There was a beat of silence, and then she breathed out shakily. 'What do you mean, "of course"? You weren't exactly into sharing. You still aren't.'

He stared down at her. 'You moved into my apartment in Milan. You're staying in my home now. I'd say that makes me pretty good at sharing.'

Her arms were folded in front of her like a shield. 'I don't mean *things*, Dante. I mean feelings—all the stuff going on in your head. Like why you were pacing around your garden in the middle of the night.'

There was a long, quivering pause. 'I'd been working for hours,' he said at last. 'I needed some fresh air.'

As answers went it was perfectly plausible, but as he watched her shoulders stiffen he knew that Talitha was not convinced.

But what was he supposed to say? He could hardly tell her the real reason he had been prowling around the garden in the dark. Although three years ago he had come close—closer than at any time before or since. Besotted and reckless with love, he had been on the verge of telling her everything about his family.

His biological family.

It was the first time he had even imagined sharing the truth with anyone, and he had been so scared. That was why he had agreed to meet with Nick Coates in New York. He had wanted to have something to show Talitha—something to cancel out the ugliness of his past. Proof that although he shared their bloodline he wasn't a Cannavaro, that he was different, that he could take care of her.

That she could trust him.

Only as it turned out, he hadn't been able to trust her.

His stomach clenched and he gripped the oars, his fingers tightening around the leather handles as if to anchor himself. But of course, it wasn't as simple as that. And it didn't sit well, finding out that he had misjudged her. Or that she had imagined her only option was to run back to England.

Thinking back to what Talitha had told him about her parents made his throat tighten. He felt ashamed. No wonder she had run from him. He would have run too.

A knot was forming in his stomach. He had run—and was still running. Running from the past, and running from the fear of who he might become if the past caught up with him.

And with both of them running it was hardly surprising that they had ended up so far apart. Or that they had wrecked everything.

Not quite everything, he thought, his body tensing, thinking back to the velvet heat of her mouth on his.

His shoulders tensed as he drew back the oars. That was his fault too. The predictable result of an abstinence that had stretched on far too long. He should have found some other woman to satisfy his physical needs, but that was easier than it sounded. Talitha might have walked out of his life in Milan, but whenever he had thought about sex, or considered seeing someone else, it had been her face that swam inside his head, her soft, pouting mouth begging him for release.

His breath hitched, his groin hardening with a surge of testosterone, and as he shifted against the hard wooden bench, he swore silently. How was that even possible?

But he knew from experience that it wasn't just possible with Talitha—it was inevitable. One touch was never enough.

Cursing himself silently for his weakness, he concentrated the throb of his libido on the task in hand, rowing back across the lake with smooth, efficient strokes, slicing through the lily pads with an almost savage pleasure. Inside the boathouse, he climbed out swiftly and held out his hand. She took it, then hesitated, her eyes darting back to the boat.

'My sketchbook—' She reached down and fumbled beneath the thwart, then stood up slowly, biting her lip.

Water dripped from the pages; the beautiful crisp sketches looked more like Florentine marbled paper.

He stared down at it, felt something wrenching inside him, and without thinking he reached out and touched her hand.

'Don't.' She jerked her arm away.

'Talitha...'

'Just leave me alone, Dante.' He reached for her again but she swerved past him, ducking out of the boathouse, and he watched the pale soles of her shoes as she ran across the meadow and disappeared from view.

Reaching the villa, hot and out of breath, Talitha felt her legs stiffen and slow. She had hoped to slip inside unnoticed, but the housekeeper was waiting anxiously on the terrace, a folded umbrella tucked under her arm.

'Hi Angelica.' Smoothing her damp dress, she pinned a smile on her face.

'Signorina Hamilton... Thank goodness.' The housekeeper's eyes widened as they took in Talitha's dishevelled appearance. 'But you got caught in the rain.'

'It's fine, really. I'm practically dry now,' Talitha lied, feeling suddenly self-conscious about her clothing. Had she fastened everything up? Or was something on show that shouldn't be?

Angelica tutted. 'I should have sent Mauro to look for you with the buggy.'

Talitha felt her cheeks burn. Even the idea of Mauro witnessing what had happened on the boat made her stomach churn. The last thing she needed was that moment of weakness existing independently of her and Dante.

As if Angelica could read her thoughts, she glanced past her. 'Did Mr King find you?'

She felt her heartbeat trip over itself.

Yes, he had found her.

Or, to be more accurate, they had found each other. And, much as she didn't want to admit it, even to herself, on some subconscious level at least she knew that the two of them had conspired to make that happen.

Dante could have asked Arielle to curate his collection.

He could have put her up in a hotel in Siena, not in his home.

And she could have insisted on staying in a hotel. Or gone to the island another time, on her own.

Instead, she had kissed him, and then she'd had sex with him.

'He did. He had something to do,' she said vaguely. Her jaw was aching now with the effort of smiling. 'I think I might go and tidy up. Could you tell Mr King that I'll catch up with him later?'

Still smiling, she escaped up the stairs. Closing the door behind her, she let her smile fade and sank shakily to the floor.

The sodden sketchbook slipped from her fingers. She couldn't quite believe what she had done—what *they* had done. After that kiss in the Hanover she had known that Dante was playing with her.

Only they hadn't been playing in the boat.

She pressed her knees together, felt the muscles of her legs tightening around the stickiness and the ache between her thighs.

It had been real.

Hot and primal and irresistible.

Her heart thumped against her ribs as she pictured the dark fire in his eyes as he thrust inside her. Sex hadn't been part of the plan, but that blazing hunger had transformed him into the man she had fallen in love with.

So of course she'd had sex with him.

Only it shouldn't have happened.

Just as she shouldn't have told him about her parents.

A breeze from the balcony drifted across her face and she put her hand to a cheek that now burned for a different reason.

Three years ago he had left her behind in Italy to go and see his family in the States. And whatever he said now, about their not knowing each other for very long, it had been glaringly obvious that he didn't want to share his life with her. Nothing had changed. Look at how he'd fobbed her off when she'd asked why he'd been walking in the garden.

Remembering how she had watched him from the window, she felt her skin tighten. She had been idiotic enough to feel sorry for him, but no more. Dante had broken her heart and if that wasn't enough he had blackmailed her into coming out here.

And yet you just had sex with him as if none of that mattered, said an accusing little voice inside her head.

She hugged her knees to her chest.

On every possible level it was wrong, and yet she

still couldn't imagine a timeline where it wouldn't have happened.

Staring blindly across the room, in her head she saw the moment when he had slipped her dress from her shoulders, saw his hands moving feverishly over her hot, bare skin, and she knew that if she closed her eyes she would almost feel Dante's mouth on her breast.

She licked her lips, feeling the softness and the soreness. Hadn't she learned anything? Surely she knew better than to get too close to the flame.

Situations changed: people didn't. Everybody was on a fixed path. The good ones, like her grandparents, were always there for you, always trustworthy and reliable. The rest might converge briefly with you on your journey, but believing you were their destination and not just a stop enroute was a mug's game.

Her parents had taught her that lesson again and again. Only it was difficult not to keep hoping that the next time would be different.

Glancing down, she caught sight of a red mark on her collarbone, where Dante's stubble had rasped against her skin, and a ripple of desire pulsed across her skin.

It was even more difficult when there was a lingering echo of attraction.

But she couldn't ignore the truth. Not this time.

When it came to the crunch, when he'd had the choice to have her by his side, he hadn't wanted or needed her. He'd been too busy building his empire.

She took a quick, hot shower, turning the jets of water on full, washing away every trace of Dante from her body, wishing she could do the same with her mind.

Smoothing her hair into a low ponytail, she picked out a pale green dress with bell sleeves and a pair of nude heels for added height. After days of wearing sandals they felt a little on the tight side. But she didn't care. In fact, it was probably a good thing. Pain was just what she needed to clear her head.

And she needed a clear head to set up a telephone bid for the Riva statue.

A hollow ache spread beneath her ribs. She was so excited about the statue that she had actually been prepared to go to Milan—back to the city where she had let passion override common sense, and paid the price.

Only even now there was a certain twisted appeal to the idea. She could see how returning alone might offer a kind of closure. But his blunt refusal to let her go had simply confirmed that this entire trip was just an opportunity for Dante to punish her.

As if he hadn't already punished her enough.

She was just checking the reserve price in the catalogue when her laptop screen abruptly turned black. Glancing down at the battery icon, she swore softly. How could she have let that happen? And then she swore again, this time more loudly, as she realised that she had left her charger in the drawing room.

Gritting her teeth, she stalked across the room and wrenched open the door.

'What the—?'

Her heart thumping wildly in her ears, she rocked back on her heels with shock.

Dante was standing in front of her door, his arm frozen in the act of knocking.

A prickling heat darted across her skin. Unlike her, he hadn't bothered changing his clothes, and his slightly crumpled appearance instantly conjured up an image of the two of them coupling frantically in the boat.

'Sorry, I didn't mean to startle you,' he said.

There was nothing in his voice—no stress, no hint of intimacy—to suggest that anything had even happened. Instead, he sounded perfectly composed. She clenched her hands by her sides, no longer squirming but indignant. Clearly he had no regrets or concerns about what they had done.

'I wanted to give you this.'

He was holding a bunch of folders and, reaching between them, he extricated a box.

'What is it?'

'It's a sketchbook. To replace the one that got ruined in the rain. I know you need it to work.'

She stared at him, shaking inside with the force of her indignation and hurt. Unbelievably, and yet entirely predictably, he had already moved on from their sexual encounter to what mattered to him most.

Work.

Part of her wanted to ask how he could do that. But she wasn't going to reveal the depth of her hurt or let him think that it had meant more to her than it had to him.

'You didn't have to do that. I have a spare one.'

Could she sound any more ungrateful?

Very slowly, he lifted his gaze to meet hers. 'I know I didn't have to.' There was a dangerous edge to his voice, like sharpened steel sheathed in silk. 'I wanted to.'

And what Dante wanted, he got, she thought, swallowing past the ache in her throat. And he wanted copies of the sketches she'd made.

Ignoring his outstretched hand, she folded her arms in front of her body. 'Why? So you can throw it back in my face afterwards? Chalk it up as another example of my bad character? Well, you didn't need to bother. I already know what you think of me.'

Her eyes snagged on the bare skin of her finger, where she had briefly worn his engagement ring.

How little he thought of her. How easily he'd been able to forget her.

It was going to rain again. The air felt thick, and behind her the bedroom was growing darker. She felt panic grab her by the throat. She felt exposed, trapped by her own stupidity and a feeling of there being no way out.

'I thought you were upset. I just wanted to do the right thing.'

There was a note she didn't recognise in his voice and she looked up at him in confusion, noticing the flattened mouth and the tension in his shoulders. But she was done with caring about what was going on inside Dante's head. He'd cured her of that.

'You? Do the right thing?' Her mouth twisted. Right or wrong was irrelevant. He didn't do anything unless it suited him. 'I don't think that's genetically possible, Dante.'

His eyes darkened like the surface of the lake when the clouds had moved in front of the sun. He stared at her in silence for a few pulsing seconds, and then he put the box down on the table with a gentleness that made something pinch inside her.

'I have no use for a sketchbook. So if you don't want it then perhaps you can give it to someone else. I'll leave you to get on with your work.'

He turned and walked away before she could reply and she stared after him, a hard, heavy lump filling her throat. Aside from the more glamorous setting, and a few changes to the dialogue, it was essentially a replay of how he'd left her in Milan.

In other words, a masterclass in equivocation.

Fizzing with frustration, Talitha stalked back into her bedroom and slammed the door.

She was so done with his arrogance, and his assumption that everything should be done his way, and by how he was so ready to judge her but so reluctant to face his own faults.

And yet there was something about him that tunnelled

deep beneath her anger. Something that made her heart squeeze painfully tight, so that even though she knew she was in the right, and he was in the wrong, she felt bereft.

She stopped in the middle of the room.

He had destroyed their love. Why, then, did he still have the power to make her care? It didn't make any sense. But then nothing about her response to this man was logical.

She snatched up the box with hands that trembled slightly. She slid off the lid and, pushing aside the cappuccino-coloured tissue paper, lifted out the sketchbook. Pulse dancing, she walked a few paces and sank onto the bed. Bound in supple leather, it was the most beautiful sketchbook she had ever seen.

It would be stupid to read anything into it. He probably hadn't even seen it. Just asked Angelica to find a replacement. She ran her fingers lightly over the pale green silk endpapers and then glanced down at her dress. Except *eau-de-nil* was her favourite colour.

A coincidence, then?

She bit her lip. Why did everything have to be so complicated with him? Just when she was happy hating him, despising him for being so cold-blooded and remote, he did this.

He was so confusing. He made her confused.

She glanced down at the sketchbook. But, whatever Dante's motives, this was still a gift. Remembering her graceless remark when he'd held out the box, she felt a sharp nip of shame.

Her grandfather would be appalled. As a child, she had been required to write thank-you cards promptly after every birthday and Christmas, and she knew that, for Edward, thanking someone for gifts, hospitality, favours, was not optional, but an absolute necessity.

She had been so wrapped up in this emotional tug

of war with Dante she had lost sight of what it meant to be Edward St Croix Hamilton's granddaughter. But he was the reason she was here, and she wasn't going to let him down.

It took her over an hour to redo the sketch of the drawing room, but she was more than satisfied with the result. The paper in the sketchbook was of such good quality that it gave a wonderful depth to the gouache.

She felt calmer now. More in control. *More herself.*

Ready to face Dante.

Or so she thought. But as she rounded the corner to go downstairs her footsteps faltered. Dante was walking out of his bedroom, a phone clamped against his ear.

He said something in Italian she didn't understand and hung up.

'I didn't mean to interrupt you,' she said quickly.

'It wasn't important. Do you want me for something?'

Her pulse twitched, and she felt heat ripple across her skin as her brain offered up several all equally X-rated answers to that question.

She hesitated. 'Actually, yes. I wanted you to know that I've just finished redoing the painting of the drawing room.'

'You still think that's why I gave you the sketchbook?'

His voice was cool and even, but his eyes had narrowed fractionally, and she felt her earlier certainty bleed away. Why had she thought this would be simple?

'Yes... No... I don't know. But that's the point,' she said quickly. 'It doesn't matter.'

There was a silence. Then, 'So what are you saying?'

What was she saying? Head spinning, she groped for the words. 'Thank you. I wanted to say thank you. That's all.'

'Wait.'

The tension in his voice stopped her as she turned away.

'You wanted to thank me?'

His hesitancy caught a nerve. But why did she care so much what he thought of her? 'You're not the only one who wants to do the right thing,' she said quickly.

'Talitha...'

Her body quivered with the effort of facing him. 'I'm not looking for a fight, Dante.'

A muscle flickered in his jaw. 'I'm not either.'

She gave a shaky laugh that almost became a sob. 'And yet somehow we always end up fighting.'

There was another silence.

'Not always,' he said quietly.

Her gaze skidded towards his face and she shook her head. She had to think about him without any reference to the past or the pull of their hunger.

'We can't... I can't—' She shook her head again as he took a step towards her.

'Would it help if I told you that I want you so badly I can't think straight?'

The bluntness of his words made her breath catch fire. 'And I want you,' she admitted.

She knew she was giving away too much, letting him know the power he wielded, but somehow it seemed important to be honest with him.

'Only wanting isn't enough. I know people say it is, and it was for me in the boat. But that was different. It wasn't planned.'

It had been pure animal desire—a force of nature. Wild and mindless and excusable. But consciously choosing to have sex with a man who didn't like her, much less love her, was just too cold-blooded.

His eyes didn't leave hers. 'So what are you suggesting? That we just ignore it? Walk away?'

Something in his voice made her chest ache so that she could hardly breathe. 'You want it to be just sex. But it isn't. It can't be because of what happened before. And in case you've forgotten that didn't work for either of us then, and nothing's changed.'

'Everything's changed. We're different people now.'

Had it? Were they?

'Okay, then, if you're different tell me something true about you,' she challenged. 'Something I don't know.'

He stared at her in silence, his eyes distant, his expression shuttered, and she felt a sick lurch in her stomach. With all her heart she wished that she could take it all back, return to her bedroom, to England. She could no longer even remember why she was doing this.

'I came after you,' he said quietly. 'After I got back to Milan, I came to London to find you.'

CHAPTER SEVEN

TALITHA STARED AT DANTE in stunned silence.

A part of her wanted to accuse him of lying, but she knew from the tension radiating from his body that he was telling the truth.

'When…? How—?'

'About a month after you left. I made up some story and got your address from Nick, and then I flew to London and went to the townhouse.' He stared past her as if was looking back in time. 'I bought you roses. Only when I knocked on the door a man answered.'

She felt her heart stall. *Ned.* Dante had met Ned.

'He thought I was delivering flowers, and when I said that they were for you he said that it was okay to leave them with him because he was your fiancé.'

Her breath was clogging her throat. There had been flowers, lots of flowers, before she'd had a chance to speak to Ned. She could remember being appalled that she had let it get so far.

His mouth twisted. 'I didn't correct him. There didn't seem much point.'

She felt dizzy, as if an earthquake had shaken the landscape and everything she'd thought she knew—everything that had seemed so solid and unchangeable—now looked completely different.

'I didn't know,' she said hoarsely.

A band was tightening around her ribs. She felt as if she'd had a terrible dream and was trapped in it.

What had they done? What had *she* done?

'I know.' He spoke so quietly that his words were nearly drowned out by the sound of the thundering rain.

There was a silence.

'I know you've spent the morning telling yourself what happened on the lake was a mistake, because I have too,' he said at last. 'Only I can't stop thinking about you. You're always there in my head. When I wake you're lying there beside me. I can't get undressed at night without undressing you too.' He cleared his throat. 'I'll walk away if that's what you want. But I don't think either of us will ever be free until we let this…' his eyes captured hers, holding her, letting her know what he wanted '… run its course.'

Her heartbeat was filling her head.

Dante had come after her.

She had been wrong about that, just as he had been wrong about her being engaged to Ned. It was exactly like one of those Shakespearean plays, with confusing titles and complicated plots about mistaken identity, where everyone ended up with the right person in the end.

Except she and Dante were neither with nor right for each other.

From somewhere above came a low, warning rumble.

She shook her head. 'We can't go back. It's too late. What we had…it's gone.'

'I'm not talking about going back.'

He took a step closer, the intensity in his eyes rooting her to the spot. Now there was only a hair-fine gap between them.

'The past has no bearing on this. It'll be like we never met. We'll just be two strangers hooking up in a bar.'

His words caught her off guard.

Two strangers in a bar.

That was when they had worked. When it had been just a blur of sex and food and sleep and sex. When it had been a no-strings holiday affair in the sun. Before fear had entered the relationship.

Her fear. That he would leave her. That history would repeat itself.

But there was nothing to fear in what Dante was suggesting now. The past had been erased and the future too, and this time she knew what she was getting into. This was passion, not love, and instead of feeling scared of the uncertainties she felt powerful, and for the first time in their relationship his equal.

There was a tension in the air, cocooning them, pushing them together, and a tingling quiver of anticipation ran through her as he held out his hand.

'Hi, my name is Dante.'

She was shaking inside. It felt as if her life was on a pivot. Except this wasn't her life. This was make-believe.

She took his hand, playing along. 'Talitha.'

'Beautiful name…almost as beautiful as that dress you're wearing. That green is perfect on you.'

'It's called *eau-de-nil*. Water of the Nile.'

His gaze touched her like a caress, a shadow-smile pulling at his mouth. 'You're very precise about colour.'

She shrugged. 'I curate art. Colour matters to me.'

'Really? That's such a coincidence. I need a curator.'

As he spoke he took a step closer, and she felt a pulse start to beat between her thighs.

'Wait—how does this work?' She didn't recognise her own voice. 'I mean, how far are we going to go?'

She couldn't meet his eyes for fear she might be imagining it all, but then he raised his hand to her chin, tilting her face up, and she saw only certainty and a need as legible as her own.

His eyes rested on her face, the grey irises boring into her. 'All the way,' he said softly and, leaning forward, he slid his arm around her waist and covered her mouth with his.

He felt his blood turn to air.

Talitha's lips were cool and soft and, maybe because they were playing at being strangers, he was strangely reminded of the first time they'd kissed. There was the same sense of almost shock, of knowing that this was different, that it was more than just a kiss.

It was an acknowledgement of something intangible but undeniable. A communion of need.

Hunger shivered inside him and he moved his mouth across hers with deliberate slowness, taking his time. His hands slid over her ribs, moving up to her breasts. His fingers circled the nipples and the sudden quickening of her breath made all the blood in his body surge to his groin.

She swayed against him and he felt the slide of her thigh between his legs, and then her hands moved under his shirt as they had earlier, pulling him closer and they waltzed backwards into his bedroom, like the last dancers on the floor at the end of the night.

Heart pounding, body aching, he pushed the door shut. Outside, the sky was a smouldering grey, like a fire that at any moment might catch alight, and the air was thick with moisture. In the gloom of the room, her eyes were a shade darker than normal, her skin gleaming like Carrara marble.

'Talitha…' he murmured, his voice splitting in a kind of groan. *'Sei molto bella.'*

She reached out and touched his face, her fingers feathering over the line of his jaw. 'You have a beautiful face.'

'It's just bones.'

Turning his cheek, he kissed her hand, heat flaring across his skin as her eyelashes fluttered. He stepped closer, his fingers sliding through her hair, lifting it from her neck, his mouth slipping over the doe-soft skin of her throat to the pulse beating feverishly beneath her ear.

'Undress me…'

Her words, spoken breathlessly, made his body harden so fast he thought he might black out and, reaching out dazedly, as if in a dream, he unbuttoned the front of her dress and he let it slide from her shoulders, slipping to the floor and pooling at her feet.

She was wearing no bra and he stared at her nipples, watching the tips harden in time with the jerky beat of his heart. He saw that her hands were trembling slightly. His own hands shook too, as he drew her cream-coloured panties over her hips and down her thighs to join her dress.

Heart thudding, he stared at her in silence, heat swarming over his skin.

'Now you,' she said hoarsely.

Kicking off his shoes, he yanked his shirt over his head. Then he unzipped his trousers, grimacing as he pulled them down past the erection bulking against his boxer shorts.

Their eyes met, and then he picked up her naked body and carried her over to the huge bed.

It was different from the last time. That, as Talitha said, had been unplanned. Hunger had slammed into him with a force that had knocked all thought, all memories of the past and doubts about the present, from his mind. Everything about it had been urgent, intoxicating, acute—rising up from a place where it had been dormant so long it might reasonably have been assumed that it had lost its vigour, its potency.

But it had been like a spark flaring in his blood. They

had crashed together like storm clouds, their hands clumsy as they'd tried to get past the barrier of their clothes and skin. They had kissed as if they were dying of thirst, held each other as if there would be no tomorrow, her soft body moulding to his hard muscles.

But this time he took his time, sliding down her body, feeling her shiver and shift beneath him as his fingers caressed her breasts, her stomach, and then the triangle of tiny honey-coloured curls.

He lowered his mouth, tracing a line with the tip of his tongue down to part her legs. *'Amo il tuo sapore,'* he murmured.

She moaned, her fingers tightening in his hair as he pressed the flat of his tongue against the quivering, tight bud of her clitoris. His hands gripped her thighs as she started to writhe beneath him. He could hear her ragged breathing, feel the shudders racing across her skin, and then she tensed against his tongue, her body arching upwards.

Her hands fluttered against his shoulders and he pulled her down the bed, stretching her out beneath him, grunting as her fingers reached for him. He grabbed her wrist. He was so close now. One wrong move and he would lose what little control he had left.

Heart thundering, he lifted her hips slightly and pushed the blunt head of his erection inside her, the breath twisting in his throat as she locked her legs around his waist. Bracing his elbows at the shoulders, he started to move, slowly at first, then faster, losing himself in the liquid rhythm of their bodies until their skin was slick with sweat.

The blood was pulsing through his body like an express train. Placing his hand palm down on the mattress, he lifted her up, pressing her body against his in a seamless intersection of flesh and sweat. And then he heard her gasp his name, and the hot whisper of her breath tipped him over the edge and he thrust upwards, spilling into her with a groan of ecstasy.

He let his head fall forward against the hot, damp skin of her throat and then, breathing unsteadily, lifted his weight and rolled over, taking her with him, just as he'd used to do. He wasn't ready to open his eyes yet. Instead he lay still, lost in the steady pounding of the rain and the feel of her soft body curled around his.

Later—he wasn't sure when—she stirred against him and he realised he was still inside her. Still holding her close, he eased himself out. Her hand flexed against his stomach and he glanced down at her naked body, his eyes tracking along the curve of her hip.

His breath caught in his throat. This wasn't part of the plan, and yet now that it had happened he felt calmer than he had for days. It wasn't just the sex—although 'sex' felt like too mundane a word for something that had tilted his entire world on its side—it was the certainty. That was what had dogged him for so long. The sense that everything had been left hanging, unspoken, unresolved—just as if they'd both got up one morning and walked out of the apartment, leaving their clothes behind and the door wide open.

This arrangement would finally close that door.

Talitha shifted in her sleep and he glanced down at her, his eyes snagging on the dark smudges beneath her sooty lashes. Even against the crisp white pillows she looked pale, and he felt his stomach clench.

One thing was certain: he had lost all interest in punishing her. She had already suffered enough. Remembering the strain in her voice as she'd told him about her parents, he felt his skin tighten with shame. It hadn't been intentional, but he had hurt her in Milan. Pushing her away because of his own fears, never once thinking that she might be acting in self-preservation.

His mouth twisted.

Knowing what it would cost him to tell Talitha about his past, he could only imagine what it must have taken for her to reveal the truth to him—and yet even after she had bared her soul he hadn't been man enough to admit the part he'd played other than to say that she deserved better. What she really deserved was the truth.

Outside, the rain had stopped again, and he stared across the room, watching the day gain in beauty with every passing second.

He hadn't set out to lie to her. In the beginning, he had been swept off his feet in a rush of passion.

Then, when he'd realised who she was, it had been easy to persuade himself that not telling her about his birth family was no big deal. That there was a major difference between not revealing something and actually concealing it.

Then two things had happened. Talitha had proposed, and on the way back to his apartment after a night out someone had grabbed her handbag.

He felt the muscles in his arm bunch. He had chased after him, cornering the man in a side street, the blood roaring around his body. As he'd wrestled the bag free the thief had swung wildly, catching him on his mouth, and he'd hit him unthinkingly, his fists acting outside of his will.

Even now he could remember the white-hot fury that had engulfed him. The urge to keep hitting and hurting had been like a jackhammer pounding through his body, but somehow he'd found the willpower to push the man away, holding back his rage until he was out of sight. And then he'd punched the wall until the pain in his hand had blotted out the pain in his head.

Afterwards, with the sound of bone on brick still ringing in his ears, he had been appalled—not just by the suddenness with which he had lost control, but by Talitha's distress when he'd returned with her bag and she'd seen his bloodied knuckles and cut lip.

Back at the apartment, he had looked in the bathroom mirror and seen a stranger staring back at him. Except the stranger had had a name: *Cannavaro*.

He had been repulsed, and terrified, and when his father had called the next day, to remind him about his mother's operation, he had instantly decided to go home, to get far away from Talitha. It had been the only option.

But for Talitha to understand that he'd known he would have to explain why—and that wasn't going to happen.

Only he didn't like knowing that he had made her feel as worthless as her parents...

'What are you thinking?'

Talitha's voice, drowsy with sleep, snapped his thoughts in two and, gazing down, he blanked his mind.

'I was—' he began.

But then, sitting up slightly, she pressed her fingers against his lips. 'Actually, don't answer that. I don't need to know, do I?' she whispered. And, reaching out, she looped her arm around his neck.

He felt his body throb with excitement as she pulled him closer.

It was nearly lunchtime when they finally managed to prise their bodies apart and pull on their clothes. Having done some remedial work with lipstick and eyeliner, Talitha joined Dante outside on the terrace for lunch.

'Here, let me.'

He pushed in her chair, his fingers brushing against her shoulders, and she felt a wave of anticipation ripple inside her.

Lunch was delicious, but she barely registered the food. She was too busy retracing the steps that had brought her to this moment with Dante.

Picking up her wine glass, she stared across the terrace. She felt as if her brain had split into two halves. One accepting, revelling in what it had felt like to feel the flex of his back beneath her hands and his quickening breath against her throat as he'd thrust hard and fast inside her. The other struggling to believe that she was giving herself to Dante again.

But all she was really doing was treating like with like, she thought defensively. Triggering her body's natural defences by administering a small, controlled dose of what was making her ill.

In other words, she was immunising herself against Dante.

And right now it felt good.

It felt better than good.

It felt as if she'd been let out of a cage.

The next two days and nights passed as if she were in a dream. Not once did she allow herself to think beyond the moment.

Not that thinking was her priority.

Now that the tension between them had an outlet, it was as if a dam had broken. Her hunger for him gnawed at her constantly. Whenever he was near she found herself looking at him. If he was within touching distance she couldn't not touch him.

One time, when she had gone upstairs to double-check the exact colour of one the bedroom walls, he had come to find her. She had pulled him through the door, undone his trousers, and he had lifted her skirt over her waist and pushed into her, standing up, both of them shaking like teenagers.

Except she wasn't a teenager. She was an adult with re-sponsibilities—including, first and foremost, her grand-father. And, although she knew he was safe and being cared for, she couldn't help feeling guilty that she was wantonly spinning out these hours of pleasure with Dante rather than rushing back to England.

'What time did you say the auction was today?' he asked.

They were eating lunch on the terrace. Or rather she was eating. Dante had barely touched his food.

'Three o'clock.'

Turning her gaze towards him, she felt her heart spin like the boat on the lake. His grey eyes were staring at her steadily and the dark silky hair falling carelessly across his forehead only accentuated the sculptural perfection of his features.

Her heart skipped a beat. She had fallen in love with that face—but this wasn't about love. It was about sex and satisfaction and working him out of her system.

She gave him a small half-smile. 'Don't worry. I've set up a telephone bid.'

There was a beat of silence, and then he said quietly, 'Then you'd better cancel it.'

Her smile froze to her lips. 'I don't understand. I thought you liked the sculpture?'

'I do.' Pushing back his chair, Dante stood up and held out his hand. 'Which is why I want to be there in person.' His eyes locked with hers. 'With you. If you'll come with me?'

She stared at him, warmth tingling though her body at his words—or rather his phrasing of them. It was an invitation, not an order.

Standing up shakily, she took his hand. 'I'd like that very much…but haven't we left it too late?'

'By car, yes.'

His fingers tightened around hers, and as she watched his mouth curve up into a smile, suddenly the sun was not the brightest star in the universe.

'But we're not going by car. We're going by helicopter.'

The flight took exactly eighty minutes, and it was the perfect way to see the Tuscan countryside, Talitha decided, as they flew over cypress-lined roads, rolling green hills and golden fields dotted with sunflowers and medieval hilltop villages.

A limousine met them at a private airfield, and in no time at all they were heading through the city centre of Milan, past the upmarket boutiques in the Via Montenapoleone.

There was already a crowd outside the auction house, and as the limo slowed Talitha felt her pulse skip. Despite being a curator, she didn't actually go to that many auctions. Most of her clients opted to buy and sell privately, and there was some sense in that. But there was nothing like the rush of walking into a crowded saleroom.

'You're excited,' he said softly.

She felt her face grow warm. 'I am,' she admitted. 'I know we're not in Rome, and this isn't the Colosseum, but auctions are a lot like a gladiatorial contest. But with paddles instead of maces.'

'And an auctioneer for an emperor?' he suggested.

She smiled. 'Exactly.'

He held her gaze. 'So, how do we do this?'

We. Feeling a disproportionate throb of pleasure at Dante's use of the word, she glanced over at him. She still couldn't quite believe that they were here. He had seemed so adamant before, and she knew he was fanatical about his privacy. What could have changed his mind?

'You keep your head down and I keep my head up. Trust me. We'll get your Diana.'

She had expected him to keep his distance, but as they joined the throng of people making their way into the auction rooms she felt his hand clasp hers. Maybe he wanted to share the drama of the moment. There was something almost operatic and Baroquely brutal about the assembled collectors and speculators, circling their prey beneath the glittering chandeliers.

'Sold at two hundred and twenty-five thousand dollars!'

She glanced up, breathing in sharply as the auctioneer banged down his gavel with a flourish. Slipping between the rows of seats, she picked up the sales brochure and sat down. Dante's hands rested casually in his lap, but she could feel his iron-hard thigh pressing against hers.

'This is it,' she whispered, watching the porters carrying the covered sculpture. She felt her pulse jerk in her throat as the cover was removed, and suddenly she was shaking inside with excitement, willing the auction to begin.

'*Signore e signori*—ladies and gentlemen—next we have Lot Nineteen, an exciting opportunity to acquire a sculpture of Diana by Stefano Riva, from his New Renaissance series. I will commence the bidding at forty-five thousand dollars.'

As she'd expected, the bidding was seamlessly smooth and dizzyingly fast. Like a conductor without a baton, the auctioneer expertly read the room, shaping the emotions of the crowd as the price rose inexorably.

'We have three hundred thousand dollars—'

Talitha raised her hand, her pulse hammering inside her head. Bidding took nerves, courage, but freed from the financial constraints that dogged her everyday life she was enjoying herself.

'Three hundred and thirty thousand dollars, ladies and gentlemen, and three-fifty against you on the phone.'

Around her there was a gasp, and some applause as the bid jumped to four hundred thousand.

Pulse accelerating, she raised her hand.

'On the floor, four hundred and twenty thousand. I have four hundred and twenty thousand. Fair warning at four hundred and twenty thousand...'

The gavel hit the wood and applause filled the sale-room.

'Sold at four hundred and twenty thousand.'

Talitha felt a surge of exhilaration. People were turning to congratulate her.

'Well done,' Dante said softly. 'And thank you.'

His hand brushed against hers, and impulsively she reached out and touched the stubble-shadowed curve of his jaw. 'Thank you for changing your mind.'

'You changed my mind.'

She had? For a moment she was going to ask him how, but then she stopped herself. Strangers in bars didn't get to ask those kinds of questions.

'I'm glad.' She bit her lip. 'Do you think I could change it again? Because there's a beautiful John Hoyland that would work perfectly with the Freud. And a Damien Hirst I think you'd love.'

They stayed. And bought not just the Hoyland and the Hirst she'd mentioned, but another Hirst and a vivid yellow canvas by Maria Azzurri.

As they walked out into the warm early evening, she glanced past him, expecting to see the limo but there was no big car idling alongside the pavement.

'I thought we might go out to dinner,' Dante said quietly. 'Just something simple.'

In the past, 'simple' would have meant pizza, or a bowl of saffron-tinted risotto at a local *trattoria*.

Today, Dante's idea of something simple was a table in the two-Michelin-starred restaurant Locanda Luzzi, owned by chef of the moment Enrico Luzzi. No more than twenty diners could fit in the minimalist room, and as well as beautifully balanced dishes the service was the perfect ratio of discretion and professionalism.

'I thought there was some crazy long waiting list for dinner reservations here,' she said as they sat down next to the famous glass wall that opened on to the courtyard of a historic *palazzo*.

He held her gaze and she made a mock awe-struck face. 'Oh, this is one of your many assets.'

Not her favourite one, she thought, a pulse of heat beating across her skin as he nodded slowly.

'Rico was working in another restaurant I own. He impressed me, so I set him up in this place.'

She glanced assessingly around the dining room. 'So this is what? Money on a plate?'

He laughed, and her body seemed to fold in on itself as he reached across the table and caught her hand, his thumb brushing the underside of her wrist.

'I deserve that.'

'Yes, you do.' She smiled. 'It's okay. Your secret is safe with me,' she said softly.

She felt his fingers flex against her skin. His face stilled. 'My secret?'

Glancing over her shoulder, she lowered her voice conspiratorially. 'I know your art collection is actually about the art, not its market value.'

He held her gaze, and then his face shifted and the tension she hadn't fully registered until then faded as he smiled slowly. 'And that's down to you. You made me connect with it in a way I would never have imagined I could.'

A warm golden glow was wrapping around her skin and a feeling of intense happiness rose up inside her. 'My—'

She'd almost said *my grandfather* but stopped herself just in time. Why make it personal? Her grandfather wasn't a part of this, and she didn't want him to be. In fact, she needed to keep him and Dante separate. Her relationship with Dante was pared down to the bones of sex and money. Her grandfather was everything else.

'Your what?' Dante prompted.

She glanced over at him, grateful for the distraction. 'My belief is that you don't own a collection just by looking and appreciating. You have to feel it. You have to feel saudade, you know... You have to be dizzy with longing.'

His eyes locked with hers. 'I think I can do that,' he said softly.

The nearness of his clear grey eyes overwhelmed her, and for a moment she forgot what they were talking about. She forgot that they were in a restaurant with other diners. Suddenly there was just him, Dante King, the man with the sweetest smile and eyes like flames.

'Are you hungry?'

When she nodded, dumbly, he summoned the waiter with a brief nod of his dark head.

'Then let's order.'

Squashing a stray thought about how easy this was— talking, teasing, spending time with him—she glanced down at the menu. 'What do you normally have?'

There was a pause. 'I don't normally have anything. This is the first time I've been here,' he said finally. 'In fact, this is the first time I've been back to Milan since... Well, since we broke up.'

She blinked, her heart squeezing at his words as the waiter took their orders. But she was reading too much into it. Dante's career had not just taken off after they'd split—it had turned him overnight into a member of the richest one percent of people on the planet, with offices and homes all over the world.

'You've been very busy,' she said carefully.

'Signor King?'

The waiter had returned with their pasta and she turned, eager to be distracted from the sudden tension between them. Her eyes widened. 'Champagne?'

'Of course. We have something to celebrate.'

We again.

She ignored the twitch of her pulse and smiled as the waiter popped the cork discreetly. 'I'm glad you think so.' She held out her glass, smiling. 'Congratulations! You have the makings of a very fine collection.'

'Once again, that's thanks to you.'

His dark gaze settled on her face and she took a sip of champagne, lifting the glass to hide the sudden flush in her cheeks.

'You were right. You are very good at your job.'

Dante wasn't smiling, but there was a softness in his eyes that made her heart beat loudly for no reason. Watching him pick up his fork, expertly twirling it in his spaghetti before lifting it to his mouth, she said, 'I should be. I've been going to auctions since I was a child. In fact, I won my first auction when I was seven.'

Ignoring the urgent little voice at the back of her brain, telling her to change the subject, she felt her heart lurch, remembering her excitement. It had been a Gustave Doré woodcut of Cinderella for an unpublished volume of fairy tales. Now it was the only remaining picture in her bedroom at Ashburnham.

'Did your parents take you?' he asked.

She shook her head, her insides tightening with a panic she could neither explain nor stop. 'They both hate art.'

Although her father wasn't averse to taking it and selling it off when he needed the money.

His eyes were studying her face, considering her answer, and to stop the next inevitable question she said quickly, 'My grandparents used to take me, and then...'

She hesitated, feeling a familiar ache spread inside her. 'And then, after my grandmother died, my grandfather took me on his own. It gave us both something to do.'

She'd said it too quickly. It had sounded harsh.

'When did she die?'

'When I was eight.' Her hands shook as she tried to cut up her chicken and she felt the exhilaration of winning the auctions ooze away. Talking about her parents was one thing, but she didn't trust herself to talk about Edward without crying.

'So your grandfather raised you? He took care of you?'

She nodded. And now he needed her to take care of him, and soon he wouldn't even know who she was. She would be lost to him and he to her.

It wouldn't be the first time she had been cut out of the life of someone she loved, but her grandfather was the first person who'd loved her back. And still loved her—even though dementia was destroying his brain.

She could feel her composure slipping, and suddenly she wished that they had just gone back to the villa. There, the rules of their arrangement felt clearer, somehow. They ate, and worked, and while they ate and worked they looked at one another. And when looking wasn't enough they went upstairs and had sex. Up until now they had been careful not to extend their conversation beyond what happened in the bedroom.

'Talitha?'

Dante was looking at her intently, and she had a sudden hysterical urge to laugh. All the time they'd been together she had wanted to know what he was thinking and feeling. Was this how he'd felt then? Cornered and exposed and alone?

But she knew he had never felt like that—because Dante didn't understand fear or failure. If something got in his way, then he found a way to eliminate it from his life. That was, after all, why he had suggested this lunatic arrangement with the two of them pretending to be strangers.

And she had gone along with it.

'Yes. He took care of me,' she said, in a voice that trembled slightly. 'So what? I know your family is cookie-cutter-perfect, but it's not a big deal.'

'I didn't say it was.'

'Then can we please change the subject?'

His eyes narrowed. 'What would you like to talk about?'

The easy intimacy they'd had moments earlier was fading, but she didn't care. In fact, she welcomed the edge of anger in his voice.

'Actually, I don't want to talk to you about anything, Dante. You and me—that's not what we're about, remember? We're just two strangers from a bar having sex.'

The dining room was suddenly very quiet.

Dante held her gaze. 'In that case, I think we'll skip dessert.' Eyes still resting on hers, he signalled to the waiter. *'Il conto, per favore.'*

The flight home was completely silent.

When they reached the villa she didn't wait for the driver, but yanked open the car door herself and ran lightly up the steps into the house.

Dante caught up with her outside her bedroom. 'What the hell are you playing at? Embarrassing me in a restaurant I own.'

She spun round to face him, her eyes wide with fury. 'I'm sorry if I embarrassed you, Dante. But if that's all you're worried about then your worries are over.'

'Cazzo!' He swore explosively. 'What are you talking about now?'

'I'm talking about *this*—this version of us. It's ugly and dishonest and wrong, and I don't want to do it anymore.' Suddenly she was fighting the beating of her heart, and she heard herself say hoarsely, 'The site visit is done and so are we. I'm going home tomorrow.'

And before he could open his mouth she slammed the door in his face.

CHAPTER EIGHT

As HE HEARD the key turn in the lock, Dante stared at the door in stunned silence, fury and frustration dancing across his skin like flames across a forest floor.

His head was spinning.

It made no sense, her turning on him like that.

He had been unsure about the trip right up until the moment he'd invited Talitha. It hadn't just been his dislike of public places. He liked this new understanding between them, and he'd childishly feared that it would somehow break the spell between them if they went outside the villa's protective charm and ventured into the real world.

But they had spent a perfect day together, reaching for one another as the first grainy light of dawn slipped into the bedroom, then flying to Milan after lunch for the auction.

He breathed out shakily. In truth, he had barely registered any of the artworks being carried in and out of the room. He had been too busy watching Talitha, drawn to the flush of pink colouring her cheeks, the glitter of excitement in her eyes and the curves of her body in that stunning Chinoiserie dress.

She'd looked beautiful—so beautiful that he'd kept forgetting to breathe. And everything had seemed easy between them—easier than it had ever been in Milan before, when he'd been on edge the entire time, thinking about how she would react if and when he told her the truth about his childhood and his family.

Only now she was the one holding back. He was here, locked out of her life—not just metaphorically, but literally—and tomorrow she would go back to England.

His chest tightened. He had deliberately avoided confronting the issue of her leaving, letting each day pass, choosing not to keep a tally.

It shouldn't matter. He shouldn't care. He shouldn't have even felt the need to follow her upstairs.

But he hadn't been able to stop himself from going after her. Or standing here like some thwarted Romeo outside her door. Because he was angry, he told himself quickly, and that was Talitha's fault. She was the one who had provoked the fight, even though she'd told him she didn't want to fight any more.

Turning away from her door, he caught sight of the moon through the landing window and felt his heartbeat slow as he walked towards it.

That wasn't the only reason he'd followed her. This time there had been a brittleness to her anger—a pain that went deeper than their stupid argument in the restaurant. He'd heard it in her voice. More importantly, she'd heard it too, and that was why she had provoked a fight, so she could hide behind her rage.

He sat down on the window seat and let his head fall back against the wall.

Only what was she hiding?

He didn't know how long he sat there, or when he dozed off, but he jerked awake with the sudden, immediate knowledge that he was not alone.

'Dante?'

Talitha was standing beside him, her face pale in the moonlight, her pupils wide like a startled doe. She was barefoot, but she was still wearing the beautiful black Chinoiserie dress from earlier.

'What are you doing?' she asked.

He shifted, stretching out the crick in his neck. 'I guess I must have fallen asleep.'

She stared at him in silence. 'Why are you sleeping out here?' she said at last.

His eyes rested on her face. She sounded calm, but he could tell from the way her shoulders rose and fell that she was fighting to stay on top of her breathing.

He felt his stomach knot.

Talitha wasn't the only one hiding herself. He was hiding too. He had heard how upset she was, but chosen to ignore it, telling himself that he hadn't signed on for her pain.

The knot in his stomach tightened.

His entire life he had been ashamed of who he was. But this was the first time that he'd felt more ashamed of who he was now than where he had come from, and shock and self-disgust made him do something he hadn't been intending to do.

He told her the truth.

'I didn't want to go to bed on my own. I like holding you when I sleep.'

She looked past him at the moon, one arm curled across her stomach as if she had a pain there. He couldn't blame her for choosing the moon over him. The moon hadn't blackmailed her into coming here. Or offered up some role-play in lieu of an actual honest conversation.

'I'm sorry, Talitha,' he said quietly. 'I keep hurting you and I don't want to.'

'That's not true.' She shook her head. 'Everything you've done has been to hurt me, to punish me for leaving you in Milan.'

'In the beginning, yes,' he admitted. 'I was angry. But

I'm not angry with you now. I'm angry with myself. For trapping you into doing something you didn't want to do.'

She looked down at her tightly linked hands. 'You didn't trap me into having sex with you. I wanted to. I still do. I thought I could put the past to one side. It's not like I haven't done it so many times before. Only—' She stopped for a moment and swallowed, 'I don't know why, but I can't do it with you.'

She still wasn't looking at him, but through the curving arc of her hair he saw a tear slip down her cheek.

'*Talitha...*'

In the space of a heartbeat Dante stood up and wrapped his arms around her. A sob caught in her throat and she stiffened against him, and then he felt her body slacken, her face distorting as she dissolved into tears.

His throat squeezed tight. He had never seen Talitha cry before, and hearing her pain almost broke him in two. Cupping the back of her head with his hand, he pressed her closer, gently stroking her back. Gradually her sobs subsided and, still holding her close, he dropped down on the window seat and pulled her onto his lap.

For a long time he sat there, cradling her against him, until finally she breathed out shakily. 'I'm sorry about before. In the restaurant.'

'You don't need to apologise, *ciccia*.' His fingers tightened against her back. The pain he had been trying to avoid was eating him up inside. 'I deserved everything you said and more. You were right. I didn't think it through. I was just so desperate for it not to be a one-off.'

'I know, and I understand—I do. Desperation makes people do stupid things.'

Her voice sounded a long way away from him and, watching her hands clench in her lap, he thought back to what she had just said a moment earlier, about putting the past to one side many times before.

'Look, Talitha, I can completely understand why you wouldn't trust me,' he said carefully, knowing that he was treading on sensitive ground. 'I wasn't and I haven't been there for you.' He stared down at the top of her head, willing her to trust him, to give him a chance. 'But I'm here now.'

His breath twisted in his throat. How could he ask her to trust him? He had never once been honest with her about his own past, his fears, his motives. But, blanking his mind to the hypocrisy of his words, he brushed his lips against her hair.

'I'm here, and I'm not going anywhere.'

But Talitha was still looking down at her hands, and he knew with a sharp, accusatory sting of pain that he had failed her again.

He felt suddenly bone-tired and, glancing out of the window, saw that the sky was growing lighter. She must be exhausted too.

He was about to suggest that she go to bed when she said quietly, 'After my parents left, I was desperate for them to come back for me. One day my mother just turned up, out of the blue.'

She was telling it like a story, but he already knew from the stress in her voice that it would be one without a happy ending.

'She told me she wanted me to live with her and that it was all worked out. She just needed me to talk to my father first, about her spousal maintenance. Sometimes it would be my father who got in touch. Once he came to collect me only instead he took a couple of paintings and left me behind. It was always the same promises—just with different conditions attached.'

Talitha looked up at him then, and the hurt in her eyes took his breath away.

'But they didn't keep their promises.'

He clenched his teeth. *Any more than I did*, he thought.

She shook her head. 'At the last minute there would always be some reason why it couldn't happen, and I made excuses for them. I wouldn't let go. I just kept giving them another chance. And then another. I thought that if I met them halfway—usually more than halfway—then I could make it work.'

He heard her swallow.

'And then I met you. I wasn't looking for a husband. I wasn't even looking for a lover. But I couldn't not be with you. I thought it was just sex, only then I realised I was in love with you.'

She bit into her lip.

'And I was so happy, but I was also terrified. I didn't think you would love me…that I was lovable. That's why I proposed. So that there would be something more than just me tying us together. Only then you went back to America without me, and I knew nothing would ever be enough.'

He hated the pain in her voice—hated that he had contributed to that pain. 'I'm sorry, Talitha.'

'It doesn't matter now. I just want you to understand why I did what I did.'

He understood everything. Her parents had made false promises, put their needs above hers, and he had done the same. And now he was doing it again. Suggesting they act like strangers in a bar, even though they had once been engaged to one another.

'Do your parents know what they did to you?' he asked.

For a moment he thought he'd pressed too hard against the bruise, but then she shook her head again.

'But what I said before, about not fitting in with their lives, that's wrong. They don't fit into mine. Not anymore. It's their fault we almost lost Ashburnham, and I will never forgive them for that.'

He cleared his throat. 'You've put that right.'

'No, you've put it right. But there's some things I can't put right. Like how I treated my grandfather.' Her voice wavered. 'Whenever they turned up or called me I would forget all about him.' Her eyes were filled with tears. 'Even though he was always there for me.'

His hand stilled against her back. Like his adopted parents had been there for him. They were still the only people he truly trusted. They alone knew the damaged, partial person he had once been, and they loved him anyway.

He cleared his throat. 'You're his granddaughter; he loves you.'

'And I love him. He's been so much more than a grand-father. He's been a parent and a mentor. He taught me about art and beauty and he made me feel safe. He gave me love and encouragement and a home.' Her mouth was trembling. 'Back in London you said that people like me care about having a perfect shopfront, but I would have sold Ashburnham years ago if I could. Only I can't.'

Picking up her hand, he gave it a squeeze. 'There are people who can take care of that for you,' he said gently. 'You wouldn't need to get involved.'

'It's not that.'

She shook her head, and again he saw the sheen of tears in her eyes.

'I can't sell it because it's not just my home, it's my grandfather's too. It's the only one he's ever known. Only soon he won't know it at all. Soon he might not even know me. Because...' She hesitated. 'Because he's got dementia.'

Dante stared down at her in shock. He felt as if some-one had pushed a knife into his chest.

'Some days he's fine and then others…' Her face quivered. 'He gets so confused and scared. I think probably it was happening some time before I noticed, but I thought it was just him getting old. And then he had a car accident on the estate, just after I got back from Milan.'

She took a deep breath.

'That's why I didn't get to tell Ned that I couldn't marry him. Grandpa wasn't badly hurt, but when the doctor talked to him he didn't even know what a steering wheel was. It was like he'd forgotten.'

Her voice wobbled a little, and Dante felt the knife in his chest twist.

'And now it's just getting worse, and I know I can't stop it, but I'm not going to let anyone push him out of his home. I don't care who it is or what they threaten.'

'Shh…it's okay.' Grabbing her arms, he held her firmly, his eyes fixed on hers. 'Nobody is going to push him out of his home, *ciccia*. Not now. Not ever.'

Scooping Talitha into his arms, he carried her into her bedroom, undressed her and helped her into her pyjamas.

'Into bed,' he ordered. He tucked the sheet around her body and, leaning over her, kissed her gently. 'I'll see you in the morning.'

Her hand caught his wrist. 'I thought you liked holding me while you slept,' she murmured.

'I do.'

Her eyelashes fluttered against the smooth curve of her cheekbone. 'I like it too.'

As he slid in beside her she fell asleep immediately. Gazing down at her face, Dante felt as if he would never sleep again.

Not that he deserved to.

He had behaved appallingly. Intent on obliterating both her and that sense of unfinished business between them, he had happily used the part she'd played in their shared past to justify his actions, never once stopping to question anything.

Only he'd been wrong about so much.

And instead of freeing himself from those last hints of doubt he was veering off course, straying into new and uncharted territory where Talitha was no longer the spoiled, self-centred darling of the London social scene he'd always imagined her to be.

On the contrary—he knew now that she had overcome her parents' rejection to become a strong, successful woman in her own right. And, far from being self-centred, she was caring for the man who had raised her, fighting her grandfather's corner with the ferocity of a tigress.

He stared down at her in the darkness. Her breathing was so soft and her hair was a swirling golden teardrop against the pillow.

He wanted her.

He wanted her even more now than he had that first night they'd met. Even more terrifyingly, he didn't just want her body. He wanted to see her smile, wanted to *make* her smile, to make her happy.

His jaw tightened. First, though, he was going to have to persuade her not to go back to England...

Stepping out of the shower, Talitha wrapped a towel around her body, grabbed another from the pile, and began drying her hair.

At least that was what her hands were doing.

Her head, though, was replaying what had happened last night, from the moment Dante had caught up with her outside her room to when he'd climbed into bed beside her and held her as she fell asleep.

She had woken to find herself alone, and her heart had filled with a kind of yearning surge as she'd remembered the press of his body and the gentle caress of his hand as he stroked her hair.

In the restaurant she had felt so trapped. Not just by the present, and the mess she had made of coming to Italy with Dante, but by the memory of all those times when she'd believed her parents' lies.

She had never told anyone before. Obviously her grandfather knew, but she had been too ashamed to admit it to other people. Too scared that she might draw attention to whatever it was that her parents had seen in her that had made them walk away.

And she wouldn't have told Dante last night, only the walls had been closing in on her. Needing space and fresh air, she'd decided to go downstairs and sit on the terrace. And when she'd unlocked the door he had been there, his big body wedged uncomfortably on the window seat, like a faithful hound.

Like Bluebell, in fact, who sat and steadfastly watched the front door whenever her grandfather left the house without her.

It had caught her off guard, so that before she'd been able to stop herself she had walked over to him—and then, of course, he'd woken up.

Her heart skipped. Dante had been sweet and patient and gentle in a way that had reminded her so much of her grandfather she didn't know now why she had been worried about telling him the truth. What she did know was that she might have unlocked the door to her bedroom, but Dante had unlocked the door to her past.

And now her secrets were free. Like caged birds they had simply taken flight. And she felt calm, happy and whole in a way that she hadn't for weeks...maybe months.

Frowning, she bit her lip. *Make that years.*

'You're up.'

She turned, her heartbeat faltering. With most people,

after your brain had processed and memorised their features, you stopped looking, but with Dante the more she looked at him, the more there was to enchant her.

'Yes. I was just about to get dressed—' She broke off, her gaze following his as it panned slowly around the empty wardrobe and shelves. 'Only I forgot I packed everything last night.'

In her pain and despair she had been like a mindless force of nature—a whirlwind snatching up neatly folded T-shirts and shorts, blindly tugging dresses from their hangers and tossing them into her suitcase.

There was a short silence, and then he reached out and touched her cheek gently. 'Please stay. I know you need to go home, but could we just have this last day together? There's something I'd like to do with you today. Somewhere I'd like to take you.'

Talitha stared at him, her heart thudding unevenly. Inside her head she could see her and Dante moving as one, their bodies coalescing as day became night, the hazy afternoon sunshine shifting into liquid moonlight and then back into a grainy dawn, like in those time-lapse films used in nature programmes on TV.

And then she thought back to the moment in the restaurant when she had felt so cornered and diminished.

As if he could read her mind, Dante shook his head. 'I don't mean like before. I know that isn't what you want, and I don't want it either. I don't think it can work if we're not ourselves. The real you and me.'

The real you and me.

In the aftermath of her confession there seemed to be poetry in his words. And a finality, she thought, her chest tensing at the thought that today would be her last day here with Dante.

'The real you and me, but better,' she said slowly, pushing aside the flutter of pain and sadness. 'Now everything is straight between us and there's no more secrets or lies like there was before.'

Something shifted in his eyes—or she thought it did. But when she looked again it was gone and he was nodding slowly, his thumb caressing her cheek in a way that made her tremble inside.

'No more secrets or lies,' he agreed.

'So what is it? What are we doing today?'

'I have a horse running in the Palio, and I would really like you to come and watch the race with me.'

She felt her skin contract as his thumb brushed against the corner of her mouth.

'I thought you might bring me luck,' he said.

The Palio. She had heard of it, but only half believed it was real. A horse race in the centre of Siena? How was that even possible?

'I'd love that,' she said quickly.

His lips curved into one those minute almost-smiles. 'Just don't tell anyone I called it a race. It's actually the most intense, lawless, crazy ninety-second contest of horsepower and pride on the planet.'

She reached up and touched his face, her fingers moving from the stubble of his jaw to the silken softness of his hair. 'It sounds right up my street,' she teased. 'What time do we need to be there?'

'Some time in the afternoon.'

'So I don't need to get dressed just yet?' she said softly, feeling a pulse starting between her thighs as his pupils flared.

'Not yet, no.'

'In that case…' She unhooked the towel and let it fall to the floor. Heard him suck in a breath and felt her nipples tighten in anticipation.

There was a thrill in seeing him so aroused, knowing she had the power to arouse him. And, holding his gaze, she let her hand slip down her naked body to the curls between her thighs.

His eyes hardened, grew hotter, and then he leaned forward and kissed her hard—a searing, open-mouthed kiss of hunger and possession. And then, still kissing her, he picked her up and carried her back into the bedroom.

Tilting his head back, Dante gazed up at the vaulted star-spangled ceiling of the Santa Maria Assunta, his throat tightening. The last time he had been here was as a child, with his new adoptive parents Connie and Robert King. They had held his hands in theirs—not so tightly that it hurt, but tightly enough for him to know that they would notice and care if he was not there.

It had been an epiphany—an understanding of what a parent could be. What a parent *should* be. Even now, more than two decades later, he could still remember his relief and gratitude that they had found him, and he would associate that feeling of being found with this city for ever. It was the main reason he had chosen to buy a home here.

Only it was Talitha's hand in his now, and he felt a rush of thankfulness that she had stayed, and that she was here with him now, and that everything was good between them.

Something twisted inside him. But what exactly did he mean by 'good'?

'The real you and me, but better.'

That was what Talitha thought—what he had let her think. But he had lied. The real Dante was a liar and a coward. And that was why he had decided this morning as she'd slept to ask her to the Palio.

He couldn't tell her the truth. But this was as close as he could get. He was peeling back a layer, sharing a part of himself that had nothing to do with work or his carefully curated image.

'Isn't it beautiful?'

He felt Talitha's fingers tighten around his and, glancing down at her face, saw that there were tears in her eyes. He nodded, but for him nothing could compare with her beauty. And he didn't just mean the beauty of her bones, but something deeper and more intrinsic—a sweetness and a strength that was more dazzling than any of the cathedral's luminous frescoes or the paintings that would soon be hanging in his home.

She bit her lip. Her eyes were soft and hazy, like the sky at dawn. 'Do we have time to go round and look at everything again?' she asked.

Drawing her against him, he kissed her softly. 'We have all the time in the world.'

They ate lunch at a small *trattoria* in Banchi di Sopra. While they ate, Dante told Talitha about the Palio.

'It's actually two races. One in July and one in August.' Picking up his bread, he tore off a piece. 'It dates back to the thirteenth century—only then they used to race buffaloes.'

She screwed up her face. 'That sounds like a terrifying idea. Does *palio* mean buffalo, then?'

'Good guess, but no.' He smiled. 'It means banner. The race is held to honour the Virgin Mary, and the *contrada* who wins the race gets the banner painted with her image.'

'And the *contrada* is the jockey?'

Still smiling, he shook his head. 'A *contrada* is a district of the city. My horse is racing for Aquila—the Eagle—but Siena has seventeen districts in total, and they have an all-consuming on-going rivalry. It all comes to a head at the Palio. Bribery is rife, and horses have been drugged and jockeys kidnapped. But the race is the most dangerous part. Every year jockeys get hurt—horses too.'

She bit her lip. 'Aren't you worried your horse will get hurt?'

Catching sight of her expression, he picked up her hand and pressed it against his mouth. 'A little. But he's compact and very fast—a real *piazzaiolo*. And there's a saying in Siena: *il Palio è vita*. The Palio is life. It might only last ninety seconds, but it's talked about all year, and it's a great honour to have a horse chosen.'

Leaning across the table, she touched his face. 'You deserve it,' she said softly.

His eyes found hers. 'For what?'

'You're a good man.' She took a breath. 'Paying off the loan doesn't just get the bank off my back, it means my grandfather can keep his home, and I'll never forget that, so thank you.'

Her words echoed inside his head as they made their way through the clogged streets. If concealing the truth from Talitha already made him feel shabby, it was nothing to how he had felt when she looked up at him with those huge shining eyes.

And it wasn't just guilt and self-loathing picking at him. There was something final in what she'd said—a kind of unspoken goodbye—so that even though he knew today was their last together, it made it much more real.

He had a sudden urge to pull her away from the surging crowds and tell her that he was sorry, ask her to forgive him.

'What is it?' Talitha was looking up at him, and her excitement of earlier was tinged with uncertainty. 'Is everything okay?'

He felt a spasm of guilt. This was her day. He was not going to ruin it by— By what? Asking her to stay? Offering something insultingly partial and second-rate like he had before? That wasn't going to happen.

'I'd forgotten how many people there'd be,' he lied.

'Will we be able to get in?' she said anxiously.

Dante nodded. 'Some friends of my parents—Gianni and Angela—live in one of the houses in the Piazza del Campo. They've invited us to watch the race with them.'

The Continis were actually two of his parents' oldest friends, and up until a few days ago he wouldn't have considered letting Talitha meet them. But today was an exception. He wanted to share this small part of his life with her. And it wasn't going to be a quiet dinner, with lots of questions and reminiscences. The Palio was a theatrical onslaught on the senses. With so much going on there would be no time for much more than pleasantries.

He ran his hand gently down her arm. 'You don't mind, do you? It's just a bit of an endurance test doing it any other way, what with the crowds and the heat.'

Momentarily lost for words, Talitha shook her head. She was stunned. Had Dante really just said that he was taking her to meet some friends of his parents?

Her heart pounded in her throat. She had thought he was just taking her out for the day, but this was different: this was personal. He was letting her into his world. The same world he had excluded her from all those years ago. And not begrudgingly or by chance. He had invited her. It was his choice.

'I don't mind at all,' she said quickly.

By the time they reached the Continis' house her pulse was racing. With such short notice she had no expectations, and yet as soon as she met them she couldn't imagine them being any other way. They were almost exactly her idea of the archetypal Italian *nonni*.

They were sweetly excited to meet her, and judging by the flurry of emotional Italian accompanied by so many kisses she lost count, they both doted on Dante.

'Talitha…such a pretty name. You must sit here, in

the shade,' Angela said, glancing anxiously up at the sun as she led Talitha onto the balcony. 'Dante, go with Gianni and get some water,' she ordered. '*Una caraffa. It is already so hot.*'

It was blisteringly hot and, glancing down at the boiling sea of spectators crushed into the *conca* in the centre of the track, Talitha was grateful to be up so high, where there was at least a whisper of a breeze.

'Thank you so much for inviting me. It's a wonderful view. Like having a box at the opera.'

'Thank you for bringing Dante.' Angela beamed at her. 'Always we ask him to come, but he is so busy with work. This is the first year he comes—and with such a beautiful girl. I cannot wait to tell Connie. She will be so happy.'

Talitha felt a giddiness that had nothing to do with the heat or the height of the balcony. All she really knew about his background was that he had emigrated to America from Italy when he was a child. Now, after all this time, to suddenly meet someone who knew Dante and his family was like waking up after a long journey to discover she had finally reached a longed-for destination.

There were so many questions she wanted to ask, but before she had a chance to ask any of them Dante and Gianni returned.

'This is the Corteo Historico,' Dante said softly as he sat down beside her, his body brushing against hers.

Down in the square, carts pulled by oxen and hundreds of people in historical costumes, many on horseback, some drumming, some waving flags, began to walk slowly around the track.

'It's incredible,' she whispered, twisting to look at him. 'Imagine having all this on your doorstep. No wonder you wanted to live here. Or do you have a more personal connection to the area?'

She wasn't sure how he would react, but after a moment he nodded slowly. 'Yes, I do. This is where my family is from.'

The sun dipped lower, and then the pigeons on the nearby roofs scattered into the sky as the boom of a cannon filled the air. Abruptly the crowd grew quiet as the jockeys in their brightly coloured clothes rode into the *piazza*, the horses jostling one another, skittering backwards and rearing up.

Talitha turned to Dante. 'They don't have saddles.'

He shook his head. 'Don't worry. They have helmets and—' he pointed towards the mattresses piled against the walls of the houses '—there are some safety measures.'

She nodded. 'So which one is yours?'

'The jockey in yellow on the grey horse. The jockey is Luigi Sarratorre. They call him La Patella—the Limpet—and the horse's name is Argento Vivo.'

He had barely finished speaking when the rope dropped and they were off. The crowd roared. There was a clattering blur of hooves and colour and then a furious, scrambling rush. Two horses went crashing into the mattresses at the Curva di San Martino, losing their riders in the process, but the Limpet clung on.

Now they surged round a hairpin corner, galloping with power and purpose. Talitha could hardly breathe. It was the last lap. Everyone was standing and screaming, including her, as the rider in yellow nudged his horse on, and as he crossed the finishing line the *piazza* erupted. People were hurling themselves onto the track, crying, clutching one another, and she was clutching Dante.

His eyes were blazing.

'You won! You won!' Her voice was hoarse, and her heart felt as though it would burst. She found his mouth and kissed him fiercely. 'You won the Palio.'

Nodding slowly, almost as if he didn't believe it, he reeled her in towards him. 'How could I lose?' he said softly. 'You're my lucky charm. When I'm with you, everything is right.'

She knew he was talking about the race but, caught in the shared intensity of his triumph, she looked up at him, dizzy with heat and happiness and love.

Love.

Her pulse was pounding hard in her head and she felt her fingers slip against his skin. She couldn't be in love. But she knew that she was.

It was why she hadn't been able even to think about seeing another man. And why she had agreed to come to Siena. She loved him, had never stopped loving him, and accepting that filled her with an inviolable calmness that was at odds with the wild delirium around her.

Her longing to tell him was so powerful she felt almost sick, but there was no time. Dante was already pulling her back into the house and down the stairs into the street, and now they were joining the river of people heading uphill to the Duomo.

CHAPTER NINE

It was her second visit of the day to the cathedral, and it seemed impossible to Talitha that so much could have changed in such a short time. Not outwardly—although, given the heat and the amount of shouting she had done, that too. But it was a change she felt in herself...in her heart.

Just a few hours ago the cathedral had been still and silent, and she had been dazzled by the serene beauty of the eight-hundred-year-old building. Now it was filled with a jubilant crowd from the Aquila *contrada*, all singing thunderously and waving their yellow and black flags, and the air was thick with heat and sweat and triumph.

Her senses were on overload, and yet she was conscious only of Dante's muscular body, curving protectively around hers. But had anything changed for him?

At that moment the winning jockey was carried into the nave on the shoulders of several young men, and the crowd sang a 'Te Deum' as he received a blessing from the Archbishop.

Then it was over, and she and Dante made their way out into the street hand in hand. When an old man with a tear-stained face stepped forward and clapped him on the back she made herself ignore how it felt almost like a wedding.

Turning, she looked up at Dante and smiled. 'So, what happens now?'

'We celebrate,' he said softly.

They met Angela and Gianni for a huge dinner in the Aquila district's main square. At night the city was magical, and it was a loud, boisterous evening, with plenty of good food and wine, all accompanied by the smell and smoke of firecrackers and songs and drumming from the still celebrating *contrada*.

As he was the winning *cavallaio* a lot of people wanted to talk to Dante, and when yet another group of men came up to congratulate him she turned to Angela and said, 'Everyone is so happy. I can't think of anything in England when people would be so full of joy. A royal wedding, maybe...'

Angela smiled. 'The Palio is more than a race,' she said, her words echoing Dante's. 'It is the day when the city stops to scream and cry and cheer. Mostly scream and cry.' She patted Talitha on the hand. 'But today we cheer, so I think you must come back next year. The last two times Dante's horse comes second.'

Talitha laughed. 'At least it didn't come last.'

As she shook her head, Angela made one of those hand gestures that Italians were so fond of. 'In the Palio, the losing horse is not the one that comes in last, but the one that finishes in second place. But this year we won. *He* won.' Leaning forward, she whispered, 'Don't worry, *mia cara*! It took me a long time too.'

Talitha frowned. 'What did?'

'To understand why the Palio matters so much. But after fifteen years I know now that the people of this city belong to their *contrada* first, then to Siena, and lastly to Italy.'

Talitha stared at her in confusion, the memory of her

conversation with Dante quivering in her mind. 'You're not from Siena?'

Angela shook her head. 'No, no, no. We moved here for Gianni's job, but we were both born and grew up in Naples. Like Connie. And of course Dante.' Her face softened. 'I lived on the same street as Connie and went to the same school. We saw each other every day until she moved to America with Robert.'

It was suddenly difficult for Talitha to breathe, to sit up straight. What had started as an itch beneath her skin— the kind that was so tiny it was impossible to decide if it was even real—was now a prickling sense of panic spreading over her skin.

She tried to think of some sensible, reassuring explanation. There must be a mistake. Angela spoke very good English, but maybe something had got lost in translation. Probably they would laugh later at the mix-up.

Or perhaps she had misunderstood what Dante had said to her.

Her throat tightened. But she knew that she hadn't.

There was a huge cheer from the other end of the table, and as Angela glanced over her shoulder Talitha picked up her glass clumsily and drank her wine. But no amount of wine could change the facts.

Dante had told her that his family was from Siena.

Why would anyone lie about where they came from?

The question remained unanswered throughout the speeches and the toasts that followed. In time with the ragged thud of her heartbeat, Talitha went through the pantomime of smiling and raising her glass and cheering, but she barely registered anything other than the ache of confusion and sadness in her chest.

In the car on the way home she had to look away from him. She would have been hurt at any time, but to find out today, after they'd seemed so close, made her feel ill.

When they reached the villa she didn't go upstairs, but went straight to the kitchen and filled a glass with cold water from the tap.

'Is everything okay?'

Dante's hand against her back felt cool and firm, and she could hear the concern in his voice. More than anything she wished that she could just rewind the last hour of her life—go back in time to when she had let hope flower in her heart, before Angela had snatched off her rose-tinted glasses.

If only she could just pretend.

But there had already been too much pretending.

She shook her head slowly. 'No, it's not. But I can't blame anyone but myself.'

There was a long silence. 'You're going to have to help me, Talitha. I really don't know what you're talking about,' he said finally.

'Help you?' She lifted her eyes 'Of course. I mean, that's what we were always about. Me helping you. Why should this be any different? After all, nothing else has changed, even though you stood there this morning and told me that you wanted today to be about to be the "real" me and you.'

His expression didn't change, but she felt his mood shift like scenery behind the curtains at a play.

'I meant what I said,' he told her.

'And I believed you,' she scoffed. 'I thought everything was straight between us. You said there would be no more secrets or lies. So why did you tell me your family come from Siena when they don't?'

Saying it out loud made the numbness in her chest spread to her throat. It wasn't as if he had just lied about what his favourite colour was. And what made it worse was that only this morning she had poured out her heart to him.

'I don't understand—I don't understand why you wouldn't just tell me the truth.'

There was a longer silence this time, so long that she thought he wasn't going to answer, but then she heard him take a breath. 'And that's exactly why I didn't tell you.'

She felt her entire body tense. His voice sounded taut, as if he was fighting to get the words out, or maybe to hold them back.

'Because you wouldn't understand.'

Her heart was beating hard—so hard she could feel it pounding through her like the drumming in the *piazza*. Only it was beating in panic, not triumph.

'Understand what?'

He didn't say anything, and she reached out and touched his arm. It felt like stone, as if she was touching one of the statues in the garden. All the warmth and vitality, the fierce elation after the Palio, had drained out of him.

'I was born in Naples. But I didn't lie to you.'

She stared at him in confusion. His words made no sense, but she knew the answer to her question was hidden in them. Like those clues in the cryptic crosswords her grandfather had used to love so much.

Her thoughts scampered back to the beginning of the day, when they had both stood gazing up at the Duomo's star-encrusted ceiling. The trip had been his idea, and she'd thought it was for her benefit. Now, though, she knew without fully knowing why that she had been wrong.

'Did something happen in Siena? Something important?' she asked softly.

There was a longer silence.

'My parents brought me here on holiday. It was the first holiday I'd ever had. The first time I'd ever left Naples. The first time I'd been in a cathedral.'

'That's a lot of firsts.'

He nodded. 'It was also the first time I felt safe. Wanted. Loved.'

How could that be? He loved his parents. She was sure of that. In Milan he had talked to both his mother and father frequently, and although he'd spoken in Italian there had been a tenderness in his voice that was unmistakable.

'They held my hands the whole time. No one had ever held my hands before.' He hesitated, a muscle flickering in his jaw, then, 'Except social workers or police officers. My parents barely noticed me. My biological parents, I mean. Not that they were around much. Most of the time they were in prison.'

She felt her legs wobble as the blood in her head rushed downwards.

Prison.

The word ricocheted around the silent kitchen like a bullet.

Taking a breath, she tried to keep her voice steady. 'Your parents were in prison?'

Leaning back against the counter, he nodded again. 'Not just my parents. The whole glorious Cannavaro clan. My brothers. My uncles. My cousins.' His mouth curved upwards into a slanting smile that hurt to look at. 'And me. Although I didn't actually commit any crime. I was born there. In the prison hospital.'

The pain wasn't just in his voice now. He was swathed in it like a shroud. Without thinking, she stepped forward and slid both arms around him, held him close, embracing his pain, absorbing it into her body.

'I'm so sorry, Dante. That's awful.'

His mouth twisted. 'I don't remember it. My aunt looked after me until my mother was released, and then I was basically in and out of care until I was five. Then the courts made an adoption order.'

How could she not have known about any of this? That first time they'd met in that bar she had sensed a vulnerability in him, but that, like everything else, had got lost in the heat of their passion. And then, after everything had fallen apart, she'd just thought she'd misread him from the off.

'Is that when you met Connie and Robert?'

Watching his face soften, she swallowed the tears rising in her throat.

'It took about six months for everything to be finalised, and then another six months for me to accept that it was real.'

'But you did. That day in the Duomo?' she said quietly.

He nodded. 'That was when I realised that they loved me. They'd seen me at my worst, when I was so angry and damaged and fragmented that I couldn't accept love. I just kept pushing them away, but they didn't let go. For me, that moment in the cathedral was when we became a family.'

And that was why he'd said what he had.

'I didn't mean to lie to you, Talitha.'

She felt his arms tighten around her.

'When we moved to the States it was like a new beginning. I had a different name, and nobody knew about my past. Most people didn't even know I was adopted, and that was how I wanted it. I couldn't imagine ever needing to tell anyone.'

'What do you mean?' She looked up at him, and he screwed up his face.

'I was pretty uncool as a kid. You know…skinny and short with braces.' His mouth curved minutely at the corners. 'Even more uncool, I was good at maths. I found it hard to make friends, and I didn't even talk to a girl until I went to college. My parents told me it would be different when I met the right woman, but I never did—until you.'

The right woman.

When I'm with you everything is right.

His words jostled inside her head and she felt a ripple of warmth skim across her skin, a bud of hope as he stared down at her.

'I couldn't believe it when you came over to me in that bar. I actually thought it was some kind of dare or a bet.'

'Is that why you were so quiet?'

He nodded. 'And I was shy.'

She bit her lip. 'Not *that* shy.'

His face stilled. 'I'd never done anything like that before. I'd never wanted to. I thought it would be just a one-night stand for you, and that you'd leave in the morning. Only you stayed.' Reaching out, he caressed her cheek. 'I was completely smitten, and I knew I should tell you about my past, but every time I thought about saying something I'd talk myself out of it. I kept thinking you'd call time, only you didn't, and by then we were getting serious, and I still hadn't told you, and it just got harder and harder to find the right time and the right words.'

Talitha bit down hard on the inside of her lip. She had felt the same way—felt the same fear, the same paralysing sense of inertia.

His eyes locked with hers. 'I know now that you would have understood, but back then I felt nobody could ever understand, because they only knew the latest version of me. When you proposed I made up my mind to tell you. Only then that man grabbed your bag, and it changed everything.'

She looked up at him as he paused. 'What changed?'

His grey eyes flickered past her to the darkness of the house. 'It all happened so fast. When I caught up with him I wasn't thinking straight. I wasn't thinking at all. I wanted to scare him, to hurt him—*really* hurt him—but I didn't. I punched the wall instead.'

Her chest tightened as she remembered his bloodied knuckles and the cut on his lip. 'He hurt you.'

Dante shook his head. 'You don't understand. I could feel it inside me—the anger and the violence and the chaos. And I knew that all of it had been for nothing. I'd changed my name, I'd changed continents, but I was still a Cannavaro. Instead of scaring him, I scared myself.' His voice cracked, and he struggled to speak. 'And I scared you.'

Looking up into his face, she felt as if her heart was going to burst. He looked wretched; she could almost see the shame eating at him. 'You didn't scare me, Dante. I was worried about you.'

He shook his head, his beautiful face contorting. 'I didn't want you to worry about me. I wanted you to be proud of me. Only how could I expect you to be proud of someone who was willing to beat a man to a pulp with his bare hands?'

'But you didn't.'

'I wanted to. And I didn't want to tie you to someone like that. Someone like my father and my brothers. But I knew that if I was with you I wouldn't be strong enough to end it. When my dad called about my mum's operation, it seemed like the perfect solution.'

Her heart plummeted. She had been right: he *had* been going to end it. The hope she had felt seconds earlier shrivelled inside her.

'Except it wasn't. The whole time I was there I couldn't stop thinking about you, and I realised that I couldn't not be with you.' He clenched his teeth. 'But I couldn't keep lying either, and that's when I knew that I had to prove to you that I wasn't like my family. If I was going to share my past, I knew that I had to give you a future worth having. I had an idea for a business… I just needed investment.'

'That's why you went and talked to Nick?' she whispered.

When he nodded, the tears she'd been holding back started to spill down her cheeks.

'Don't cry.' He smoothed her cheeks with trembling hands. 'Please don't cry. I don't ever want to make you cry.'

She couldn't look at him. If only she had been whole… if only she had been able to share her past instead of concealing it.

As if reading her mind, he shook his head. 'It's not your fault, Talitha. We both made mistakes.' Sliding his hands into her hair, he tilted her face up to his, forcing her to look at him. 'Everything happened so fast, and I don't think either of us were really ready for a serious relationship.'

And was he now?

She so badly wanted to ask him, but neither of them was in a fit state to have that particular conversation. In fact, the time for talking was over.

'Let's go to bed,' she said quietly, as soon as she could trust her voice. And, taking his hand, she led him upstairs.

Without speaking, Dante closed the door and pulled her against him, their mouths fusing. His hands slid beneath her dress, moving past the silk, and they fell back onto the bed and made love with their clothes on, the heat of their hunger burning their skin through the fabric.

Dante woke up with a start, his heart pounding. He had been dreaming of the Palio, only in the dream he wasn't the owner but the jockey, and instead of there being only three laps, the race wouldn't end.

'What is it?' Talitha was looking at him anxiously, her beautiful face creased.

He drew her closer and kissed her softly on the lips. 'It

was just a bad dream. I thought I'd lost the Palio again,' he lied.

As her face relaxed, he glanced down at their naked bodies. They had made love again and again, and each time they had taken another piece of clothing off. Neither of them had felt the need to talk. And now that light was filling the room he knew that for him, at least, talking would break the spell.

Last night he had told her everything, the words tumbling out of him like a high tide spilling over a breakwater. And now the water had drained away he felt as though he had been washed clean. He had never felt so calm, so utterly at ease with himself. Not even after the adoption had been finalised.

Everything felt right in the world.

His arm tightened around her as he remembered what he'd said to her after winning the Palio. *'When I'm with you, everything is right.'* He had been still in shock, dazed with victory, but it was true, nonetheless.

He couldn't imagine how life could get any better.

He couldn't imagine life without her.

But he was going to have to: she was leaving today.

He'd always known the day was coming, and in the beginning the end hadn't mattered. All he'd cared about was trapping her, making her come out here because he had known she didn't want to. These last few days he had simply ignored the passing of time. Now, though, perhaps out of spite, time had caught up with him in a rush.

That was why he had kept reaching for her in the growing light, knowing that she would soon be gone. Sleep would have been impossible. Now, though, he was awake, and time was running out.

So ask her to stay.

For a moment he lay listening to her heartbeat. He

could ask her. All it would take was three little words: *Stay with me*.

But stay for what? Sex?

Talitha deserved more than that. But what else could he offer her? They might have shared their pasts, but that didn't mean they had a future together. He had made that mistake before, and hurt both of them in the process, and he wasn't about to hurt her again. So why squander their remaining time together in calculating imaginary scenarios?

'Maybe you need a prize.'

Talitha's voice broke across his thoughts and he looked down at her, his hand moving automatically to touch her. As his fingers traced the curve of her hip he felt her shiver, and he felt his own body tense.

'A prize for what?'

'For winning the Palio. Then you might dream about winning instead.'

He stared down at her, his heart jostling against his ribs. 'But I don't need to dream about winning. Because you're here...with me. You're my prize,' he said softly.

He pulled her against him, his lips finding hers, his hand drifting over her body, feeling her shiver again as his fingers brushed against the hard buds of her nipples.

Talitha moaned softly. She could feel herself melting and, unwilling to lose control so soon, she batted his hand away and dropped her mouth to his chest, sliding down the bed, kissing lower, then lower still, her fingers following her lips to where he was already rock-hard.

The desire to taste him, to hold him in her mouth and feel him grow, was almost overwhelming.

Heart hammering, she began to move her mouth over the smooth, blunt head of his erection. His head fell back, his fingers gripping her hair, and she felt him grow even harder as the blood surged into the wet, straining length of him.

With a groan, he raised her head from his lap, pulling her up the bed, lifting her, and heat spilled over her skin as she guided him into her body.

Talitha shuddered as he pressed his thumb against the taut, pouting nub of her clitoris, then lifted his head to suck fiercely on her nipples until she grew frantic in her movements.

'Yes, like that…' she panted.

She tensed, her back arching, and after rolling her under him Dante thrust into her. The aftershocks of her orgasm tightened around him as his body jerked forward in a series of mindless shuddering spasms.

'What are you looking at?'

Glancing up from her laptop, Talitha felt her heart swoop like a swallow as she looked at the man sitting beside her. Dante was so beautiful, so familiar to her, and as necessary now as the air she breathed. Only also like a swallow she would be returning home soon. Home for her was and had always been Ashburnham—but how would that work if her heart was here with Dante in Siena?

Then tell him how you feel, she told herself, for what had to be the hundredth time since she had woken this morning.

But that was easier said than done.

Last night, in the aftermath of his daunting confession, it hadn't been the right time. And even now she was still searching for the right words to tell him she loved him.

Liar, she accused herself silently.

The words were easy. What was making them stall in her throat was fear. What if Dante didn't feel the same? Her heart skipped a beat as she remembered the blaze in his eyes when his horse had crossed the finishing line.

'When I'm with you, everything is right.'

Everything felt more than right between them.

It felt perfect.

'It's a painting that's just come up for auction in London.' She turned the screen towards him. 'I know we talked about introducing some art to your offices. I thought this might be a good starting point.'

They had talked briefly about the possibility of making art central to the identity of KCX, of using it to connect with the public. But truthfully, it had been little more than a passing remark. What she'd really been doing was giving herself another reason not to go upstairs and pack her bags.

Heart pounding, she watched as he tilted the screen.

'It's a good idea,' he said slowly, handing back the laptop.

'Good.' She swallowed. 'I can set up a telephone bid for you.'

'Or...' reaching across the sofa, he caught her hand and tugged her towards him, his eyes steady on hers '... I could fly back to London with you and we could go to the auction together. And while I'm in England there's nothing to stop us carrying on as we are.'

The world went still.

Talitha stared at Dante, her heart beating slow and hard.

It wasn't a declaration or love—he wasn't even marking a change in their relationship status—but it didn't matter. It was enough that he was offering to come back to England with her, and she was suddenly so filled with happiness and relief that for a moment she couldn't speak.

'Will you stay at the Hanover?' she asked.

'Would that be easier?'

She nodded. 'My grandfather is pretty old-fashioned. And he gets confused.'

'It's okay, *ciccia*. I understand,' he said softly.

Looking into his eyes, she saw that he did, and she was suddenly almost overwhelmed with loving him. She laid her head on his shoulder so that he couldn't see her face.

'Would it be okay if I stayed over?' she asked.

She felt his lips brush against her hair.

'I thought you'd never ask.'

Looking up at him, she pulled his head down and kissed him hungrily, losing herself in the familiar contours of his mouth.

'But I want you to meet my grandfather. Actually, I want him to meet you.' She wanted Edward to meet the man who had saved his home, saved his granddaughter.

'Of course.'

There was a different note in his voice now, one that made her quiver inside, and then he lifted her hand and pressed it to his lips as if sealing the deal.

When Talitha went upstairs to pack, Dante went into his office and pulled open his laptop. Ostensibly he checked his emails every morning, but quite honestly the last few days he had just been going through the motions.

He leaned back in his seat. It wasn't as if he needed to work so hard. He had more money than he could spend, and the compulsion that had driven him for so long, the need to distance himself from the past, no longer seemed to matter now that Talitha knew the truth.

Obviously he wouldn't stop working, but he didn't need to work so hard. Now that Talitha was in his life he didn't want to work so hard…

His eyes froze on the screen, a name leaping out from the words around it as he breathed out unsteadily. Roger Dawson was the ex-marine who managed his security and kept an eye on the Cannavaro clan.

Opening the email, he read the three short sentences once, then reread them. The facts remained the same. His birth father and two of his brothers had been arrested for armed robbery.

There was a lead weight in his chest, pressing down on his lungs so that it was suddenly hard to breathe. He felt the familiar swirling rush of unfiltered emotion. Soon it would be followed by an exhaustion that made ordinary tasks impossible, but before that happened he would call his parents.

They alone understood how this made him feel.

Except this time he didn't even reach for the phone. Instead he got unsteadily to his feet. It was Talitha he wanted... Talitha he needed. And not just for sex, and not just in this moment.

He needed her because he loved her.

How could he not have realised?

He stumbled against the desk, his fingers tightening against the smooth wood not with shock but with acceptance. He loved her. Even when he'd hated her, even when he'd been too scared to let himself love or be loved, he'd loved her.

Heart thumping, he sat down again. And now he had a second chance. A chance to do it right—to love her as she deserved to be loved. His hands trembled against the desk. He felt suddenly close to tears. For so long he had kept to the shadows, but now there was a promise of light, a small but steady spark of hope.

Glancing back at the screen of his computer, he felt his tumbling thoughts stall. There was a second email. This time Roger was even more succinct.

Just to warn you, Il Giorno and Telecampania are running pieces on the Cannavaro family.

He stared at the screen, his blood banging clumsily through his veins like the horses in the *piazza* yesterday. It didn't have to matter. Talitha knew all about his past, and she had neither flinched nor turned away. On the contrary, she had embraced him, taken him into her body. And yet—

His shoulders tensed and he turned his gaze away from the screen, away from the truth he wanted to ignore, the truth he'd done everything in his power to shun, even going so far as to pretend that he and Talitha were different people.

But this wasn't a game of two strangers in a bar.

He slammed the laptop shut.

This was real life, Talitha's life, and she deserved better than this. Better than him.

And now he understood why it had taken him so long to realise that he loved her. It was because deep down he had always known this moment would happen. And that even if he managed to get past it, it would be just a matter of time before it happened again, and at some point this peace, this certainty would all be snatched away from him.

It was no good telling himself that it would change.

This was never going to stop.

There was always going to be another email, another robbery, another trial, and one day soon some reporter would join the dots, and then his past would be out there for the whole world to see and judge.

And if—*when*—it all went public, how would Talitha feel about him then? Here, now, who he was and where he came from felt very distant and contained. But would she really be able to turn away from the headlines? And how would she feel when she saw what it meant to be a Cannavaro? When she found out about their crimes? Could she really love a man who carried that chaos inside him?

More importantly, could he—*should* he—expect her to? She had so much to deal with already. He couldn't

allow her to take him on as well. Not if he loved her—
and he did. And, loving her as he did, he couldn't put
her in harm's way.

'Angelica says the car is ready.'

Talitha was standing in the doorway, her brown eyes
hazy in the sunlight from the window. She smiled shyly
and he had to look away, for fear of betraying the ache
in his chest at the thought of her leaving and of what he
was about to do. What he had to do.

'Slight change of plan,' he said quickly. 'Something's
come up. I've got a couple of conference calls I need to
join in on.'

He watched her reaction. Slight surprise followed by
acceptance.

'Okay, shall I tell the driver to wait?'

Gritting his teeth, he shook his head. 'No, that won't
be necessary. Don't let me hold you up.'

She stared at him, her smile fading now. 'I don't understand. What are you saying?'

'I can't come to London with you. I thought I could,
but I can't.'

'Because of work?' she said slowly.

He nodded. 'I've already taken a lot of time off. Too
much.'

The shock in her eyes almost made him change course,
but he forced his gaze to stay steady.

'I thought you wanted this...us—' She broke off,
frowning, then tried again. 'I thought we were going to
carry on in London. You said there was no reason to stop.'

'I know what I said, but on second thoughts I think
it's more important to have a reason to carry on,' he said
brusquely.

There was a long silence. Then, 'Yes, I suppose it is.'

The hurt in her eyes took his breath away, but he
blanked his mind to her pain. 'In which case, now might

be a good time for you to hand me over to your colleague. I know you had someone in mind.'

'Arielle.' Her voice was small and stunned.

'Good. I'll call Philip, let him know.'

For a moment she just stood there, staring at him, and then she said quietly, 'And that's what you want, is it? You want us to go our separate ways?'

He stared at her in silence, pain splintering through him as if she was twisting his heart in their hands. No, he didn't want that. But what he wanted was irrelevant. He had to do what was right.

'Talitha—'

'Because that's not what I want,' she said hoarsely. 'And I don't think you do either. I think you're scared. And I am too. But I'm more scared of not being with you.' Her fingers caught his. 'Because I love you and I want us to be together.'

Could she ratchet up the pain any tighter? His jaw clenched. It was agony, hearing her offer her love, but she was right. He was scared. Scared of loving her and losing her again or, worse, of pulling her down into the darkness with him.

He pulled his fingers free. 'I'm sorry, Talitha, but I don't love you,' he lied. 'I'm sorry if anything I did led you to think differently, but it's probably best we call it a day now rather than carry on.'

Their eyes met then. For a moment she didn't speak, and then she nodded slowly.

'Yes, it is. You see, I want more. I want more than just carrying on with or without a reason. And I don't think you're capable or willing to give more. Goodbye, Dante,' she said quietly, and then she turned and walked out of his office.

CHAPTER TEN

LEANING INTO THE ROAD, Talitha held up her hand. 'Oh, you have to be kidding—'

She swore as the black cab trundling down Regent Street abruptly signalled left and disappeared down a side street. That was the third taxi in as many minutes, but it was also the final straw, and if there had been a camel standing on the pavement beside it would have sat down by now, moaning in despair.

It had been a terrible day at the end of an appalling week. The plumbing at Ashburnham had finally dried up completely this morning, she had narrowly missed out on a painting, losing to Dubarry's main rivals, Broussard's, and to top it all she had just caught the heel of one of her favourite shoes in a crack in the pavement.

Glancing up at the darkening sky, she gritted her teeth. Now it was going to rain, and she had left her umbrella at work. She watched miserably as a fourth taxi appeared in the distance. It was no good, it didn't have its light on…

Oh, thank you, thank you, she crooned silently as it drew up in front of Gusto, the authentically Hispanic tapas restaurant currently wowing London's diners, and deposited a well-dressed couple on the pavement.

She felt the first fat drops of rain explode against her face, and by the time she reached the shuddering black car, limping as far as her broken heel would allow, she was soaked through.

'Where to, love?' the driver shouted above the rain, which was sheeting down now, streaming off the windscreen as if they were in the middle of a car wash.

She gave him the address and slumped back against the seat, the sound of the rain fading into the background as she stared down at her dress. The pale fabric was clinging to her body and she had a sudden vivid flashback to the moment in the rowing boat when she had kissed Dante.

Her fingers tightened in her lap.

That had been the tipping point, the moment of choice. Except 'choice' implied options, and there had never been any real choice to make. Not on her part anyway.

Not until the end.

Lifting her face, she gazed blankly through the window at the saturated streets, watching the pedestrians scamper from doorway to doorway. They were shielding themselves from the worst of the downpour with umbrellas and folded newspapers and briefcases, and that was what she had done.

She had shielded herself from further hurt.

Would it have made any difference if she had refused to leave?

She was sure not, and yet even now, a week after she had walked out of Dante's villa, and out of his life, a part of her wished she had been brave enough to stay and fight.

But was it brave or just stupid to offer up the most beautiful, fragile, precious piece of yourself to someone who didn't and would never love you? And if she was sure of one thing it was that Dante didn't, and couldn't love her.

The journey home had been appalling. Sitting hunched

in her seat, alone on Dante's jet, she had never felt more worthless or unhappy. With every passing cloud the ache in her chest had deepened and only the last remnants of her pride had stopped her from buckling beneath the sympathetic but unspoken pity of the stewards.

Back in London, she had gone straight to the townhouse, and it had been there that she had finally given in to what she had wanted to do since Dante had made his 'slight change' to their plans, and cried. Great, wrenching sobs—not just because she had loved and lost Dante again, but because there was no more hope.

That was the difference from last time. After Milan, outwardly at least, she had learned to live without him, without his passion, but she hadn't ever really let go of her dream of love.

Her heart twisted as the taxi turned into Ashburnham's long tree-lined drive. She could still taste him in her mouth, feel the urgent push of his body inside hers. And she still loved him. Maybe she always would.

But she had accepted that her love alone wasn't enough to make their relationship work. That blaze in his eyes after the Palio had been triumph, not love, and that was why, this time, it really was goodbye not *ciao*.

The taxi came to a standstill and, leaning forward, she paid the driver.

Outside the rain had stopped, and she let herself in to the house. Glancing into the drawing room, she saw that her grandfather was asleep in his chair by the window and so, tiptoeing back out of the room, she made her way upstairs, some of her misery lifting as she remembered his reaction when she'd got home.

It was true that he'd thought she had just come in from work, but he'd been delighted to see her, and his happiness had gone some way to restoring her equilibrium, as had the knowledge that their home was safe.

She had been dreading work, or more specifically the curiosity of her colleagues about Dubarry's most secretive client, but with a huge auction of German expressionist art only days away everyone had been too busy to do more than smile and congratulate her.

Except Philip, who had been so pleased with her that he was promising a pay rise.

Her shoulders tightened. Perhaps that was why he was holding back on telling her that Arielle would be working with Dante from now on.

Folding her arm across the ache in her chest, she stared at the picture of Cinderella on her wall. It was her favourite scene in the book—the one where the fairy godmother conjured a coach from a pumpkin and turned ragged clothes into a ball gown fit for a princess to dance with a prince.

Maybe that was where she'd gone wrong, she thought sadly, tracing the outline of the dress with her finger. She should have settled for a prince instead of falling in love with a King.

Lifting the oars out of the water, Dante stepped out of the boat and onto the island. Heart pounding, he stared up at the sky, looking at but not really seeing the crescent moon. He had no idea what time it was. No idea how long he had been prowling the estate in the darkness. Nor did he really care.

Except that he should care.

The last few days he had let things slip, but tomorrow he was flying back to the States. He had a week of back-to-back meetings lined up and he needed to be on his game. What he didn't need was to be wandering about here in the dark. He should be in bed asleep.

Sleep! He almost laughed out loud.

He hadn't slept since Talitha left. He went to bed each

night, but all that happened was that he lay there in the darkness as if she were there beside him, her soft, pale body shifting against the sheets, her hand moving with tantalising lightness over the contours of his chest, one finger tracing the line of hair down to his groin—

His jaw clenched. Tonight, he'd had enough. If Talitha wouldn't leave him alone, he would leave her in the bedroom.

But of course she had followed him, just as she did in the daytime. He could be eating his breakfast and catch a glimpse of her in the silver handle of his spoon, or see her face reflected over his shoulder as he pretended to work on his laptop. Just moments ago he had stumbled to a halt as he came across her, standing on one leg, a sketchbook in her hand, her teeth biting into her lower lip.

He had tried everything to evade her. Reading, writing, working out in his gym until he was drenched in sweat and had to lean against the treadmill like some punch-drunk boxer at the end of his career.

When none of that had worked he'd tried just closing his eyes, but that only made everything worse. Then there was no escape. Inside his head she was impossible to resist, and he tormented himself, replaying every movement and gesture she'd made in slow motion.

And if that wasn't agonising enough, to rub salt into the wound all through the week works of art had been arriving, in innocuous-looking royal blue crates with *lato da aprire* stencilled on them in yellow lettering. *Open this side.*

The truth was that it didn't matter how he looked at his life—there was no way out. He was locked in an inferno of his own making.

His eyes fixed on the bare marble plinth in the middle of the temple. His new Diana was yet to arrive, but she wasn't the woman he was missing.

The woman he wanted.

The woman he needed.

After he'd read that email from Roger he had wanted to take Talitha into his arms, but he hadn't. Even after she'd told him that she wanted more. For both their sakes he had pushed her away, telling himself that it was for the best.

Only how could it be for the best when it was Talitha who made him whole?

An ache was building in his chest. He remembered how she had stood before him and offered him her love. Unconditionally and completely. When she'd left she had taken the most vital and precious part of him with her. But it had taken her leaving for him to understand that, and now it was too late.

The oars trembled in his hands.

Then again, London was an hour behind Siena...

Thank goodness it was the weekend tomorrow, Talitha though, dumping her bag on the settle by the door and slipping off her shoes. The summer storms from earlier in the week had given way to a heatwave, and today was officially the hottest day of the year.

Because Philip was such a good boss, he had let everyone leave early, and all the way home she had been promising herself a dip in the lake. But first she would check on her grandfather. Make sure he was wearing his hat.

Her chest squeezed tight. If he was in good form then she might broach the subject that she had been putting off since yesterday.

It was time to make a change. She'd accepted that even before Dante had stormed back into her life, and while their situation might be less perilous than before, they still couldn't afford to keep two houses running. Her plan to sell the townhouse would give them the financial security they both needed and she craved, and so yesterday morning she had spoken to an estate agent and a lawyer.

That left Ashburnham.

She bit her lip. This part was going to be trickier to run past her grandfather, although she knew it made perfect sense. Between the two of them, they only really used about a quarter of the house, so why not hand over the rest to the British Heritage Trust? That way Ashburnham would not just be looked after, it would be filled with visitors again. and her grandfather would still be able to keep living in his home.

If she could just find the right words…

Her footsteps faltered and she frowned as male voices floated towards her through the house.

That was odd. Jill was working today, not Michael. Unless they had changed shifts. Or the plumber had finally decided to turn up. He had managed to sort out almost everything else, but he'd had to order a part for the shower.

She felt a flurry of panic. Would her grandfather remember that? Or even remember the plumber?

She hurried through the French windows onto the terrace—and stopped abruptly, every muscle, every nerve, every fibre of her being stretched to breaking point.

Her grandfather was sitting in his usual chair, an open copy of the *Racing Post* in his lap. On the table next to him a bottle of champagne sat in a bucket of ice, and on the other side of the table was a man wearing jeans and a T-shirt that showcased the hard muscles of his arms and chest.

Her heartbeat accelerated as she stood frozen in the warm afternoon sunlight. He might be dressed casually, and he quite possibly knew how to fix a shower, but he wasn't the plumber.

She had thought about Dante endlessly this past

week, playing out an inconceivable number of conver-sations with him inside her head, but now that he was sitting on her terrace she could only stand and stare. She couldn't understand how he could be here. It didn't make any sense.

This was her world. Her home. Her grandfather.

The same grandfather who was currently sharing a glass of champagne with a stranger.

She let go of the breath she'd been holding.

Happily sharing.

Edward looked flushed with excitement, and younger than he had in years.

Forcing herself to put one leg in front of the other, she walked over to her grandfather.

'Talitha, darling—there you are.'

His voice tugged her gaze towards him and, leaning forward, she kissed his cheek.

'I know it's a little early, but Dante just told me about his win at the Palio and I thought we should celebrate.'

She blinked. *Dante?*

Not Mr King, but Dante.

With an effort, she lifted her face to meet his. Her breath caught in her throat. As usual, the curves of his face looked miraculous, but there were dark smudges under his eyes and he seemed thinner.

'Talitha, darling. Why don't you get another glass and join us?'

Turning swiftly to her grandfather, she shook her head, smiling stiffly. 'It's fine, Grandpa. I don't want one.'

'I can get you a glass.'

Her head whipped round and she glowered at Dante. 'I can get my own glass, thank you.'

'Good girl.' Her grandfather patted her on the arm. 'Why don't you take Dante with you? You can show him the painting of the Pearl.'

Head spinning, she took a breath, trying to stay calm. Her grandfather was sweetly excited, but she just wanted this strange walking-on-eggshells encounter to be over.

'Grandpa, Mr King is a very busy man.' She flicked a glance in Dante's direction. 'I'm sure he has other plans.'

There was a small pause, and then Dante shook his head. 'Not at all. Your grandfather has been telling me all about his horses. I'd be delighted to see the painting.'

Her lips tightened. For a moment she considered up-ending the ice bucket on his head, but then her spine sagged. She couldn't fight both of them.

'Fine. If you'd like to follow me?' She stalked past Dante with her nose in the air.

'Talitha—' He caught up with her by the staircase. 'I'm sorry to turn up unannounced,' he said quietly.

'Not as sorry as I am,' she snapped. 'What are you doing here?'

'I need to talk to you.'

Now he wanted to talk?

She felt her stomach flip over.

'It's not really office hours, Mr King.' Hating how her voice was high and twisted, she turned and stomped up the stairs to the first-floor landing. 'Here. This is the Pearl.' She gestured towards the painting of the grey race-horse. 'Now you've seen him, you can go back down-stairs and tell my grandfather that you're very sorry but you have to leave right away.'

He stared at her steadily. 'You don't think that'll look a little odd? I mean, what could possibly be that urgent?'

He sounded so calm and controlled that she felt al-most sick. She pretended to think. 'Well, they say that if you want someone to believe you when you're lying you should stick as close to the truth as possible, so I guess it would probably be something to do with work. I mean, that's always your number one priority, isn't it, Dante?'

His eyes were fixed on her face. 'I haven't done a stroke of work for weeks. Not since I walked into Dubarry's and saw you standing in front of that painting.'

'And that's my fault, is it?'

'That's not what I'm saying.'

'But you're thinking it,' she said flatly. 'So what is it you want to say?'

Looking up at him, she felt her throat contract. She already knew the answer. His face was taut and there was a rigidity in how he was holding himself. He wanted the last word.

'I'm saying that I don't care about work.' His mouth twisted. 'I don't care about art. I don't care about the Palio. None of it matters. It's you that I care about, Talitha. You that I love.'

She stared at him blankly. Inside her she could feel a thousand tiny flowers of hope blossoming, their petals opening, delicate as butterfly wings. But she must have misheard him.

Say it again, she thought. But she couldn't ask. She wanted to spin out the fantasy just a little longer.

Gazing down into Talitha's pale, wary face, Dante took a breath. He felt as though his whole life had been building to this moment of truth and trust, and he was suddenly terrified that he would mess it up.

'I don't think I ever stopped loving you. That's why I haven't been with another woman since you left Milan. I couldn't. No one ever came close to you.'

Talitha didn't say anything, but he could tell that she was stunned by his confession.

'You haven't been with anyone...?' Her voice was like air.

Taking a step closer, he shook his head. He didn't care

about his ego. Too many times he had let doubt into their relationship and it wasn't going to happen again.

'Why do you think I was so out of control in the boat? Right from the first time we met there was only ever you.'

'You're just talking about sex,' she said flatly.

'I'm not.' He took another step closer. 'I love you, Talitha. I didn't want to. I didn't think I could. But I can't not. Even when you're not with me I'm with you. I eat with you. Walk with you. Sleep with you. I even brush my teeth with you. Every thought I have begins and ends with you. You fill my head. You fill my heart.'

Her face trembled. 'So why did you push me away?'

He ran a hand over his face. 'My whole life I've been scared of my family catching up with me. It's why I've worked so hard. It's even why I wanted an art collection. It felt like I was building a wall. Only then I realised I loved you, and that if I followed my heart then my past would become *your* past, and I couldn't bear the idea of you having to deal with it too.'

Heart hammering in his chest, he stared down into her eyes.

'But then, when I talked to you, I felt better…stronger.' His eyes found hers. 'You made me see that I didn't have to run any more. Or lie or hide.'

Reaching into the pocket of his jeans, he pulled out his phone.

'I should have done this three years ago. I wish I had. But I spoke to my PR department this morning and we worked on this together. It went out on the KCX website at lunchtime.'

Talitha stared at the screen. At the top of the page was a piece about a new arts hub in Naples, the first in a series of specially commissioned spaces to be built in deprived areas that would be funded by KCX. It was followed by a statement from KCX's CEO, Dante King, revealing his very personal reasons for funding the project.

Talitha looked up at him mutely, deprived of the powers of speech again. Not by anger this time, but by love. 'Oh, Dante…'

Letting out a long quiver of breath, she stepped closer, taking his hands in hers.

'Wait.'

She heard him swallow, and he pulled his hands free and reached into his pocket again.

'In Siena you said you wanted more—more than I was capable or willing to give. And I know it's probably too late, but that's why I'm here. I had to tell you that I *am* capable and willing, only I know that's not enough. I know you need more. I can't just tell you. I need to show you how I feel.'

Looking down, she felt her breath catch. The ring lying in his hand was both familiar and different.

'I had it reset. I didn't want to forget how we got here.' He pointed out the three sparkling sapphires. 'But I wanted to add something to mark the journey we've taken.'

His eyes were blazing like they had after the Palio, but this time she knew that she was the reason.

'I love you Talitha.'

'And I love you too.' Tears were streaming down her face. 'When I'm not with you it feels like I'm drowning,' she said shakily.

Leaning forward, he kissed her as he had at the Palio, kissed her until she was floating, not drowning, until finally they broke apart to catch their breath.

'You hold my heart in your hands,' he said softly. 'Please let me hold yours. Please will you be my wife?'

There was a long, pulsing silence. She knew Dante

was staring at her, waiting for her to react, but her brain seemed to have shut down. Or perhaps it was too busy fighting the sudden wild beating of her heart.

'Yes…' she whispered, and as he slid the ring on her finger the love and certainty in his eyes filled her with a happiness that was as pure and warm and unwavering as the sunlight streaming through the window.

* * * * *

COMING SOON!

We really hope you enjoyed reading this book.
If you're looking for more romance, be sure to
head to the shops when new books are
available on

Thursday 31st March

To see which titles are coming soon, please visit

millsandboon.co.uk/nextmonth

MILLS & BOON®

Coming next month

REVEALING HER NINE-MONTH SECRET
Natalie Anderson

She needed him to turn. Would she see those disturbingly green eyes? Would she see a sensual mouth? If he stepped closer would she hear a voice that whispered wicked invitation and wilful temptation? All those months ago she'd been so seduced by him she'd abandoned all caution, all reticence for a single night of silken ecstasy only to then—

A sharp pain lanced, shocking her back to the present. Winded, she pressed her hand to her stomach. How the mind could wreak havoc on the body. The stabbing sensation was a visceral reminder of the desolate emptiness she'd been trying to ignore for so long.

She'd recovered from that heartbreak. She was living her best life here—free and adventurous, bathing in the warm, brilliant waters of the Pacific. Her confusion was because she was tired. But she couldn't resist stepping closer—even as another sharp pain stole her breath.

'That's interesting.' He addressed the man beside him. 'Why are—'

Shock deadened her senses, muting both him and the pain still squeezing her to the point where she couldn't breathe. That *voice*? That low tone that invited such confidence and tempted the listener to share their deepest secrets?

Massimo hadn't just spoken to her. He'd offered the sort of attention that simply stupefied her mind and left her able only to say *yes*. And she had. Like all the women who'd come before her. And doubtless all those after.

Now his brief laugh was deep and infectious. Despite her distance, it was as if he had his head intimately close to hers, his arm around her waist, his lips brushing her highly sensitised skin—

Pain tore through her muscles forcing her to the present again. She gasped as it seared from her insides and radiated out with increasingly harsh intensity. She stared, helpless to the power of it as that dark head turned in her direction. His green-eyed gaze arrowed on her.

Massimo.

'Carrie?' Sereana materialised, blocking him from her view. 'Are you okay?' Her boss looked as alarmed as she sounded.

Carrie crumpled as the cramp intensified. It was as if she'd been grabbed by a ginormous shark and he was trying to tear her in two. 'Maybe I ate something…'

Her vision tunnelled as she tumbled to the ground.

'Carrie?'

Not Sereana.

She opened her eyes and stared straight into his. 'Massimo?'

It couldn't really be him. She was hallucinating, surely? But she felt strong arms close about her. She felt herself lifted and pressed to his broad, hard chest. He was hot and she could hear the thud of his racing heart. Or maybe it was only her own.

If this were just a dream? Fine. She closed her eyes and kept them closed. She would sleep and this awful agony would stop. She really needed it to stop.

'*Carrie!*'

Continue reading
Revealing Her Nine-Month Secret
Natalie Anderson

Available next month
www.millsandboon.co.uk

MILLS & BOON

THE HEART OF ROMANCE

A ROMANCE FOR EVERY READER

MODERN

Prepare to be swept off your feet by sophisticated, sexy and seductive heroes, in some of the world's most glamourous and romantic locations, where power and passion collide.

HISTORICAL

Escape with historical heroes from time gone by. Whether your passion is for wicked Regency Rakes, muscled Vikings or rugged Highlanders, await the romance of the past.

MEDICAL

Set your pulse racing with dedicated, delectable doctors in the high-pressure world of medicine, where emotions run high and passion, comfort love are the best medicine.

True Love

Celebrate true love with tender stories of heartfelt romance, from the rush of falling in love to the joy a new baby can bring, and a focus on the emotional heart of a relationship.

Desire

Indulge in secrets and scandal, intense drama and plenty of sizzling hot action with powerful and passionate heroes who have it all: wealth, status good looks…everything but the right woman.

HEROES

Experience all the excitement of a gripping thriller, with an intense romance at its heart. Resourceful, true-to-life women and strong, fearless face danger and desire - a killer combination!

To see which titles are coming soon, please visit

millsandboon.co.uk/nextmonth

MILLS & BOON
MEDICAL
Pulse-Racing Passion

Set your pulse racing with dedicated, delectable doctors in the high-pressure world of medicine, where emotions run high and passion, comfort and love are the best medicine.